20 UNDER 35

IAIN BANKS
PETER BENSON
H. S. BHABRA
JAMES BUCHAN
PATRICIA FERGUSON
RONALD FRAME
PATRICK GALE
CARLO GÉBLER
JAMES LASDUN
DEBORAH LEVY
ADAM LIVELY
AIDAN MATHEWS
CANDIA McWILLIAM
GEOFF NICHOLSON
TIM PARKS
PHILIP RIDLEY
JOAN SMITH
RUPERT THOMSON
DAISY WAUGH
MATTHEW YORKE

sceptre

20 under 35

Original stories by Britain's best new young writers

Edited by Peter Straus

With an introduction by Graham Swift

Compilation copyright © 1988 by
Hodder and Stoughton Ltd.

For copyright in individual stories
see page 336

Introduction copyright © 1988 by
Graham Swift

Sceptre is an imprint of Hodder and
Stoughton Paperbacks, a division of
Hodder and Stoughton Ltd.

British Library C.I.P.

Straus, Peter
  20 under 35.
  I. Straus, Peter
  823′.01′08[FS]

  ISBN 0-340-48637-6

*The characters and situations in this
book are entirely imaginary and bear
no relation to any real person or
actual happening*

Printed and bound in Great Britain
for Hodder and Stoughton Paper-
backs, a division of Hodder and
Stoughton Ltd., Mill Road, Dunton
Green, Sevenoaks, Kent TN13 2YA
(Editorial Office: 47 Bedford
Square, London WC1B 3DP) by
Richard Clay Ltd., Bungay, Suffolk.
Photoset by Rowland Photo-
typesetting Ltd., Bury St Edmunds,
Suffolk.

CONTENTS

20 under 35

INTRODUCTION

IT IS EASY to be condescending about the short story, to see it as a lesser species compared to that greater and grander creature, the novel. Publishers (happily not the present one) are notoriously wary of it, allowing authors the luxury of a volume of stories only after they have won their spurs with a novel or two, and this has endorsed the view of the short story as an inferior, subordinate form, a stepping-stone towards the larger terrains of fiction.

And yet who can resist the classic magic of a tale well told? The enjoyment of a good story is hardly an esoteric or acquired taste. It is something we discover in childhood.

And there have been writers who, while they may have dabbled with the novel, have clearly found their forte in the story – Maupassant, Chekhov, Mansfield. In our time, the American, Raymond Carver springs to mind as an author for whom brief is undoubtedly best. And brief need not mean scant: the collected stories of Carver, like those of Maupassant, show a prolificity rich as any novelist's. Then again, there are writers who have practised both forms, who are even best known as novelists, yet whose finest work is arguably to be found in their stories: Lawrence and Hemingway, for example.

Clearly, for some the story is a sufficient and ultimate form of expression, while for others it is a forcing and refining discipline which can purify their work and elicit their best. What then is its special power and attraction?

For the young writer (and one of the few perks of authorship is the privilege of being thought of as still young at thirty-five) the short story affords certain obvious, practical advantages. Above all, it can be finished relatively quickly. It offers an accessible sense of achievement and the opportunity of recurring newness. Nothing is more important for the young writer than the fact of having work *completed* – work which can be judged, gloated over, shown to others, submitted for publication and which will lead the way to further experiment. To embark on a novel, on the other hand, is to set out on a singular and perilously isolating journey.

For the author, perhaps the most seductive aspect of the short story is its seeming to offer an unimpeded, frictionless and exhilarating ride to inspiration. One has only (only!) ten or twenty pages to fill. Surely that first deep breath of excitement one takes on beginning will sustain one all the way through? Surely that first flickering flame will not be extinguished but catch further fire as the pages progress?

But how treacherous this seduction can prove, once the real and very rigorous demands of story-writing emerge: the problems of compression and balance, the problems of keeping the texture neither too thin nor too dense, the problems of a burgeoning complexity that needs to be reconciled with economy, the problem of determining *exactly* the point at which to end.

And yet, if these problems are surmounted, the result, for the reader, can be precisely that rushing career of excitement that the writer bravely anticipated; a clean, intense transmission of feeling that the novel cannot match.

Setting aside matters of sheer stamina, of which the novel clearly takes a heavier toll, the short story is in fact both the more testing and the more precarious form, if only because it chooses to work within limits. A novel can establish its own extent, its own boundaries by a process of accretion and exhaustion; it accommodates, absorbs, adapts. In a short story everything is prominent and conspicuous: every move, every shift is like adjusting a house of cards.

These technical differences only underline the different tenor of the two forms and their different rewards for the reader. A novel can fully explore its own world; a short story can only touch, glimpse a world. And yet in either the 'world' must fully convince. How do you make authentic a world you can only glimpse? That is the problem but also the justification of the short story. If the novel is a gradual process by which the strange is made familiar, the story is a process by which the familiar can be made suddenly strange; or, more powerfully, it is a naked, uncompromising encounter with strangeness itself.

When one reflects on these different and opposite processes, it becomes clear that experience itself requires us to be, as it were, both short story writers and novelists. We all have a sense of life as a comforting colonisation, a gradual mapping out of known ground, and yet we are all haunted by those sudden collisions and abrupt exposures which defy our power of acclimatisation. We even *need* such moments. It would be a sad and bad thing if in becoming seasoned pioneers we lost our sense of life as raw encounter.

It is no accident then that so many of the stories in this book are stories of *interruption* – points of estrangement and severance, of sudden shifts in the zones of experience (how many of them involve a traveller in a foreign environment), of brief, tangential encounters with other worlds which are yet authentic because their *strangeness* is authentic. Such material is generic to the short story.

It would be tempting to say that young writers (begging the question again of how old is a young writer) make more adept short story writers precisely because they are likely to be among life's susceptible wanderers rather than life's settlers. But this would be an unfair distinction. Writers depend on their imaginations, not their circumstances. It is a poor writer who cannot be young and old, nomadic and rooted at the same time. The short story and the novel do not mark a fictional divide; they are complementary, one would not wish one without the other. And what they have in common (begging the question of that halfway house, the long short story or novella) is the marvellous compulsion of story-telling itself, the irrepressible urge to narrate – and be narrated to – that lies deep in our human nature and to which the writers in this collection all, in their different ways, bear witness.

Graham Swift
1988

ROAD OF SKULLS

IAIN BANKS

IAIN BANKS

Iain Banks was born in Fife and brought up there and on Clydeside. He read English, along with Philosophy, at Stirling between 1972 and 1975; was variously employed – and travelled – between then and 1980, when he moved to England, first to London, and then to Faversham, Kent. In 1984 he took up writing full time, and in 1988 came home to Edinburgh. He started writing novels at the age of sixteen and his first, *The Wasp Factory*, was published on the day of his thirtieth birthday. Since then he has written *Walking on Glass*, *The Bridge*, *Consider Phlebas*, *Espedair Street* and, most recently *The Player of Games*.

THE RIDE'S A little bumpy on the famous Road of Skulls . . .

'My *God*, what's happening!' Sammil Mc9 cried, waking up. The cart he and his companion had hitched a ride on was shaking violently.

Mc9 put his grubby hands on the plank of rotten wood which formed one of the cart's sides and looked down at the legendary Road, wondering what had caused the cart's previously merely uncomfortable rattling to become a series of bone-jarring crashes. He expected to discover that they had lost a wheel, or that the snooze-prone carter had let the vehicle wander right off the Road into a boulderfield, but he saw neither of these things. He stared, goggle-eyed, at the Road surface for a moment, then collapsed back inside the cart.

'Golly,' he said to himself, 'I didn't know the Empire ever had enemies with heads *that* big. Retribution from beyond the grave, that's what this is.' He looked forward; the cart's senile driver was still asleep, despite the vehicle's frenzied bouncing. Beyond him, the lop-eared old quadruped between the shafts was having some difficulty finding its footing on the oversized skulls forming that part of the Road, which led . . . Mc9 let his eyes follow the thin white line into the distance . . . to the City.

It lay on the horizon of the moor, a shimmering blur. Most of the fabled megalopolis was still below the horizon, but its sharp, glittering towers were unmistakable, even through the blue and shifting haze. Mc9 grinned as he saw it, then watched the silent, struggling horse-thing as it clopped and skidded its way along the Road; it was sweating heavily, and beset by a small cloud of flies buzzing around its ear-flapping head like bothersome electrons around some reluctant nucleus.

The old carter woke up and lashed inaccurately at the nag between the shafts, then nodded back into his slumber. Mc9 looked away and gazed out over the moor.

Usually the moor was a cold and desolate place, wrapped in wind and rain, but today it was blisteringly hot; the air reeked of marsh gases and the heath was sprinkled with tiny bright flowers. Mc9 sank back into the straw again, scratching and squirming as the cart bucked and heaved about him. He tried shifting the bundles of straw and the heaps of dried dung into more comfortable configurations, but failed. He was just thinking that the journey would seem very long, and be uncomfortable indeed if this outrageous juddering went on, when the crashes died away and the cart went back to its more normal rattling and squeaking. 'Thank goodness *they* didn't hold out too long,' Mc9 muttered to himself, and lay down again, closing his eyes.

. . . he was driving a haycart down a leafy lane. Birds were chirping, the wine was cool, money weighed in his pocket . . .

He wasn't quite asleep when his companion – whose name, despite their long association, Mc9 had never bothered to find out – surfaced from beneath the straw and dung beside him and said, 'Retribution?'

'Eh? What?' Mc9 said, startled.

'What retribution?'

'Oh,' Mc9 said, rubbing his face and grimacing as he squinted at the sun, high in the blue-green sky. 'The retribution inflicted upon us as Subjects of the Reign, by the deceased Enemies of the Beloved Empire.'

The small companion, whose spectacular grubbiness was only partially obscured by a covering of debatably less filthy straw, blinked furiously and shook his head. 'No . . . me mean, what "retribution" mean?'

'I just told you,' Mc9 complained. 'Getting back at somebody.'

'Oh,' said the companion, and sat mulling this over while Mc9 drifted off to sleep again.

. . . there were three young milkmaids walking ahead of his haycart; he drew level and they accepted a ride. He reached down to . . .

His companion dug him in the ribs. 'Like when me take too many bedclothes and you kick I out of bed, or me drink your wine and you make I drink three guts of laxative beer, or when you pregnanted that governor's daughter and him set the Strategic Debt Collectors on you, or someplace doesn't pay all its taxes and Its Majesty orders the first born of every family have their Birth Certificates endorsed, or . . .?'

Mc9, who was well used to his companion employing the verbal equivalent of a Reconnaissance By Fire, held up one hand to stem this flood of examples. His companion continued mumbling away despite the hand over his mouth. Finally the mumbling stopped.

'Yes,' Mc9 told him. 'That's right.' He took his hand away.

'Or is it like when . . .?'

'Hey,' Mc9 said brightly. 'How about I tell you a story?'

'Oh, a *story*,' beamed his companion, clutching at Mc9's sleeve in anticipation. 'A story would be . . .' his grimy features contorted like a drying mudflat as he struggled to find a suitable adjective. '. . . Nice.'

'OK. Let go my sleeve and pass me the wine to wet my throat.'

'Oh,' Mc9's companion said, and looked suddenly wary and doubtful. He glanced over the front of the cart, past the snoring driver and the toiling beast pulling them, and saw the City, still just a distant shimmer at the end of the Road's bleached ribbon of bone. 'OK,' he sighed.

He handed the wineskin to Mc9, who guzzled about half of what was left before the squealing, protesting companion succeeded in tearing it from his grasp, spilling most of the remainder over the two of them and squirting a jet of the liquid spattering over the neck of the snoring driver, and on out as far as the head of the horse-like animal (which lapped appreciatively at the drops spilling down its sweat-matted face).

The decrepit driver woke with a start and looked around wildly, rubbing his damp neck, waving his frayed whip and apparently fully expecting to have to repel robbers, cut-throats and villains.

Mc9 and his companion grinned sheepishly at him when he

turned to look down at them. He scowled, dried his neck with a rag, then turned round and relapsed into his slumber.

'Thanks,' Mc9 told his companion. He wiped his face and sucked at one of the fresh wine stains on his shirt.

The companion took a careful, dainty sip of wine, then twisted the stopper firmly back into the gut and placed it behind his neck as he lay back. Mc9 belched, yawned.

'Yes,' his companion said earnestly. 'Tell I a story. Me would love to hear a story. Tell I a story of love and hate and death and tragedy and comedy and horror and joy and sarcasm, tell I about great deeds and tiny deeds and valiant people and hill people and huge giants and dwarfs, tell I about brave women and beautiful men and great sorcerorcerors . . . and about unenchanted swords and strange, archaic powers and horrible, sort of ghastly . . . things that, uhm . . . shouldn't be living, and . . . ahm, funny diseases and general mishaps. Yeah, me like. Tell I. Me want.'

Mc9 was falling asleep again, having had not the slightest intention of telling his companion a story in the first place. The companion prodded him in the back.

'Hey!' He prodded harder. 'Hey! The story! No go to sleep! What about the story?'

'Fornicate the story,' Mc9 said sleepily, not opening his eyes.

'WAA!' The companion said. The carter woke up, turned round and clipped him across the ear. The companion went quiet and sat there, rubbing the side of his head. He prodded Mc9 again and whispered, 'You said you'd tell me a story!'

'Oh, read a book,' mumbled Mc9, snuggling into the straw.

The small companion made a hissing noise and sat back, his lips tight and his little hands clenched under his armpits. He glared at the Road stretching back to the wavering horizon.

After a while, the companion shrugged, reached under the wineskin for his satchel and took out a small, fat black book. He prodded Mc9 once more. 'All we've got is this Bible,' he told him. 'What bit should me read?'

'Just open it at random,' Mc9 mumbled from his sleep.

The companion opened the Bible at Random, Chapter Six, and read:

'Yeah yeah yeah, verily I say unto you. Forget not that there
are two sides to every story: a right side
and a wrong side.'

The companion shook his head and threw the book over the side
of the cart.

The road went ever on. The carter snuffled and snored, the
sweating nag panted and struggled, while Mc9 smiled in his
sleep and moaned a little. His companion passed the time by
squeezing blackheads from his nose, and then replacing them.

. . . they had stopped at the ford through the shady brook,
where the milkmaids were eventually persuaded to come for a
swim, dressed only in their thin, clinging . . .

Actually, the horse-like beast pulling the cart was the famous
poet-scribe Abrusci from the planet Wellitisn'tmarkedon*my*-
chartlieutenant, and she could have told the bored companion
any number of fascinating stories from the times before the
Empire's Pacification and Liberation of her homeworld.

She could also have told them that the City was moving away
from them across the moor as fast as they moved towards it,
trundling across the endless heath on its millions of giant wheels
as the continuous supply of vanquished Enemies of the Empire
provided more trophies to be cemented into place on the famous
Road of Skulls . . .

But that, like they say, is another story.

RAJASTAN, 1987

PETER BENSON

PETER BENSON

Peter Benson was born in Broadstairs in 1956. He was educated in Ramsgate, Canterbury and Exeter, and worked in a variety of jobs before his first novel, *The Levels*, was published.

The Levels won the *Guardian* Fiction Prize, the Author's Club First Novel award, a Betty Trask award, and was short-listed for the Whitbread Prize (first novel) and the David Higham Prize for Fiction.

I WAS LYING on a desert plain. I was fantasising about water. Jugs, streams, drops, canals, pipettes, sinks and glasses. Bones grew around like bushes. The only shade for miles was a ruined wall.

Once a village had stood where I lay. People had worked and played, argued over grazing rights and noisy dogs. Weddings and births had been celebrated, funerals arranged, women haggled over the price of cotton goods and spices. A well had been there, a bucket had been a treasured possession. The people's best clothes had been silk and rich with ornaments.

I was ill. A few days before I'd been staying in the ancient city of Bikaner, protected by its walls. I'd been befriended by a cloth merchant. He owned a shop on a street so narrow the sun never entered any of the rooms.

A pair of clerks worked in a front office, sorting sheaves of invoices and receipts; it was to the sound of flicking paper that Karna and I shared a pipe.

He claimed to be descended from the Dacoits. These people were a breed of outlaw, sworn to rob only the rich, and only in daylight. He laughed when he told me this.

'No daylight in this shop,' he said, 'even in the daytime!' He passed the pipe. The gloom filled with swirls of smoke. 'And,' he coughed, 'if a man's got pockets, he's rich!' He laughed again, coughed again and took the pipe back. He took a deep draught of smoke, held it down and blew out.

I stood up and walked to a pile of silks, rolled and stacked against the wall. The dark couldn't disguise their beauty. I stroked a bolt of bright green.

'Five hundred,' he said.

'What! You are a Dacoit!' I laughed. 'What about that?' I pointed to a roll of Bagru, a cotton covered in blue geometric patterns.

'Ah,' he said. 'A cheaper cloth altogether. Not silk. I can't let you have something so poor.'

'How much?'

'Oh . . .' He stroked his chin and took another puff.

'How much?'

'To you . . . I can offer it at seventy-five.'

'Seventy-five?' I laughed again. I'd seen the same in the bazaar for twenty, so I offered eighteen.

'Eighteen!' Karna stood up. His movement disturbed a curtain of smoke, the clerks shuffled their papers in the front office. 'You are playing a joke,' he said.

'No. I saw the same in the market for twenty. I could have had it for fifteen.'

'The same?' he said.

'Sure.'

He walked to the bolt. 'But not as fine as this?'

'Exactly the same,' I said.

'Well,' he said. 'If you want to buy, maybe I could make you a special price. I can see you are a business man.'

I nodded. I wasn't a business man, but if it was useful to pretend I was I wouldn't disagree. 'What sort of price?'

'Maybe twenty-five . . .'

'But I told you. I could buy the same in the market for fifteen.'

'This is a finer cloth.'

'Is it?'

'I say so.' He went back to his pipe.

'Fifteen,' I said.

He puffed.

One of the office boys poked his head into the room. 'Refreshment?' he asked. Karna nodded and looked at me. 'Yes please,' I said, and the boy disappeared.

He came back ten minutes later. In that time, as a sun we couldn't see set over the desert, and the day cooled, we'd struck a bargain. I'd pay him twenty rupees, he'd give me a yard of the cloth and a lift along the road to Jaipur. I wanted to get back to the city. I expected a letter to be waiting for me at the post office.

Pleased with the deal he'd struck – the cloth was worth six rupees wholesale and I wouldn't inconvenience him by joining him on the road – he cleaned his pipe, refilled and relit. We ate slices of melon the boy brought, and felt better for them.

Better. Not cured, but better.

The worst drought in over a hundred years was ravaging Rajastan. As Karna explained, 'These melons are no good, but they are all I can offer. Last year was bad. The melons were small then, too sour; these,' he spat a pip, 'are the worst they've ever been.'

I apologised.

'Why?' he said. 'It's not your fault. There's been drought for ten years now.'

Ten years. No water. He finished his melon, puffed and took my money.

As a consequence of this drought, Rajastan was suffering seventy-five per cent crop failure. In some areas of the state this figure rose to ninety per cent. The massive brick-lined water courses that stretched hundreds of miles into the desert – once expected to make three million acres of desert bloom with maize, millet, wheat and cotton – were empty. Cows, goats and camels stood in their empty bottoms, women waited with cups, men stared at the sky.

The following morning, before the sun had begun to scorch the road, Karna harnessed his camel to a cart, invited me to sit on piled rolls of cotton and set off on the road to Jaipur. He was to visit a customer in a desert village. 'Good people,' he said, and goaded the camel out of the city, past a group of soldiers.

As the sun rose and the road snaked across arid plains, I said something about the weather.

'You English!' he exclaimed. 'It's all you ever talk about. Why?'

I wasn't sure. 'I don't know.'

'I do,' he said.

'Oh?'

'Oh yes.' He leant forward and clipped the camel. It was a bad-tempered animal and our progress was slow. 'You are a very reserved people. You don't like to tell other people anything about yourselves. You keep that all in, so you need some-thing else to talk about when you have to. The weather's a good choice. Everybody's affected by it, so you talk about it.'

I laughed. My wife was into amateur psychology. Thinking about her made me laugh louder.

'No!' Karna was offended. 'It's true. Take yourself. You haven't told me anything about yourself. If you were Indian I'd know what you worked in, who your parents are, what they did, and your brothers and sisters too. You'd tell me if there was a woman in your life, and why you were travelling alone. But you haven't.' He clipped the camel again. 'You talk about the weather.'

I didn't say anything for a while. I could have, but why I was there was my own business, and painful enough to have in my mind without talking about it.

'I'm sorry,' I said, 'but I . . .'

'No need,' he interrupted. 'You talk about the weather.' He smiled and gave me a swig of water. 'The last before midday,' he said. 'So drink slowly.'

I sat back to watch the scenery pass. We were travelling through the Thar desert. The tenth consecutive year of drought had given it the chance to advance across sixty per cent of the state of Rajastan. It was flat and seemed to stretch into a distance that wasted itself in heat. The heat churned in massive waves that rose and fell towards and away from us, over the rocks and sand and back again, folding around us, it would not let go.

Boulders and rubble-strewn ridges disturbed the uniformity of the place, the occasional thorny bush providing the only shade. A single raven sat by the road, a perfect and bleached goat's skull was there. Karna spat and lit a pipe.

The cart wheels squeaked regularly, the load swayed beneath me, the morning passed slowly. I'd been dozing when Karna's destination appeared: a clutch of huts clinging to the side of a mountain. He reined in the camel and pointing ahead said, 'Jaipur that way. I leave the road here.'

'Could I meet your friends?'

He shook his head. 'My friends would not be yours,' he said. 'You are best going on.'

I didn't argue. He said a bus would be along later. I wondered about that. The road had been quiet. Only other camel-drivers and goatherds were using it. I said I didn't think any bus could survive the ruts, but he held up a hand. 'Believe,' he said, and gave me a slice of melon.

I walked for hours. I kept to the road. The afternoon sun beat down; my hair stuck in strings to my head. Sweat poured off my forehead, down my cheeks to my mouth. I licked some, coughed and sat down.

I thought about the letter I hoped was waiting for me in Jaipur. A letter, a note, a telex . . . a word from Rachel. Some news. I hadn't heard a thing for weeks.

Rachel (my daughter) loathed Steven (her mother's boy-friend). He was someone I'd never suspected. Rachel was my eyes and ears at home and had suspected all along. A fourteen-year-old with the intuition of a seventy-year-old; she had known about Steven for six months before I found the note that read, 'Darling, I'm tired of shandy. I want a case of Jack Daniel's.' Written in my wife's hand and left on the mantelpiece, I wondered why she'd been so careless. Later, I realised she'd left it there on purpose. Rachel told me.

Notice I call my wife 'my wife'. I won't give her the satisfaction of seeing her name in print. She has grabbing hands, big bitch green eyes and uses a strong anti-perspirant.

Being in India was my idea. She thought I was kidding when I replied 'I'm going to Rajastan,' to her 'What are you going to do?'

'Why Rajastan?'

I shrugged. I wasn't sure myself; all I knew was that something about the place attracted me. I imagine everyone has a place like that. First noticed as a child in a black-and-white photograph in an encyclopaedia/ an adventure story/ a half-remembered scene from a half-noticed news report. The place nags for years, chasing you until something happens, the chance comes. You say 'I'm going to . . .'

'Why Rajastan?'

I shrugged. 'I don't know. I've always fancied it, that's all. OK?'

She shrugged. 'Sure. But just remember. You're her father and . . .'

'Yeah!' I shouted. 'And you're her mother, and if he comes between Rachel and I, I'll, I'll . . .' I jabbed a finger.

'You'll what?'

I didn't have to answer my wife.

I was being turned out of my own house. So I packed a rucksack, kicked the empty milk bottles off the front step ('*get him to clear them up!*') and climbed into a waiting taxi. Rachel watched me leave. She waved from an upstairs window. I waved back, the only one that day, and said 'Heathrow,' to the driver.

Heathrow seemed a million miles away from the Thar desert. I ate a slice of the melon Karna had given me, wiped my face with the back of my hand and set off again.

I walked for miles, wondering when a bus would be along, asking the occasional goatherd if he knew. But they stared through me, pointing in the direction I'd just come and nodding, pointing the way I was going and shaking their heads.

'But there's no other road,' I said. 'Does a bus come this way?'

No one knew what I was talking about. My rucksack straps cut into my shoulders but I walked on. Eyes bore into the back of my head, the sun strained itself through itself, became stronger, matched the eyes and followed me. By evening, tired and eating the last of the melon, I lay down in a hollow of sand and spread a blanket over my legs.

I knew I was lost, but I could re-trace my steps in the morning and get back to where Karna had left me. I remembered the huts on the mountainside, the curl of the road through the desert to Bikaner, the bleached rocks and empty water courses. I normally liked a drink before bed, but had nothing, so closed my eyes and fell asleep.

Dreams are bastards. I found myself talking to Steven. He

couldn't believe that I hadn't suspected. 'But we made love in front of you!' he said. 'You were watching telly and we did it on the carpet by the sofa. Didn't you notice?' 'No,' I said. His face changed colour. A flock of geese blew in through the living-room window. They honked, flew around the room without knocking into anything and flew out again. 'I noticed *them*,' I said, when the geese had gone. 'What?' said Steven. 'I didn't see anything.' Rachel carried a tray of drinks into the room. Roses were bleeding in their vases, the sound of laughter came from the kitchen. My wife. She turned on a tap, I looked at the drinks, Rachel's face was obscured by a handkerchief that hung in the air. Steven smiled. I woke up.

I was very thirsty. Ribbons of pink and pale yellow light streamed across the eastern horizon, a crow flew across the scene. I was cold. I pulled the blanket to my mouth and sucked it. There was some moisture there. I rubbed my face, shivered and sat up.

'Good morning,' I said to myself. One of my little habits, one of the things my wife cited as irritating her. She irritated easily. 'Good morning!' I hoped Steven picked his teeth and left the gunk he retrieved on chairs.

'Good morning.' I said it again. I rubbed my arms and stood up, folded the blanket, packed my rucksack and walked back the way I'd come, away from the sun. I wanted to cover as many miles as I could before it got hot. Heat. In England, looking daggers at my wife while rain blew against the kitchen window, I'd thought of nothing but a decent climate, a peaceful life, an empty road. Anything but her . . .

I walked for a few hours. They passed slowly, the road was rough, the rucksack heavier than ever, no bus came towards me. I wondered about Karna. Dacoit blood runs thick against the sons of imperialists. Dacoit blood comes a bright scarlet, flows quickly, clots quickly. But I couldn't believe he would lie to me, or lead me astray. He had nothing to gain by doing that. I hadn't done him any harm. When the sun had risen high enough to flake the desert rocks, I stopped and sat on one. I thought I'd try to rest.

Rest, for me, has never worked. Sleep I can manage, but

when I try to simply rest my mind begins to churn. In the heat, this churning rumbled off in a direction I wasn't used to. Sand suggested things to me, the sound of running water came and disappeared. Distant mountains appeared closer, surrounded me and swirled around and around, twisting on axes I couldn't see. The wind wailed around them, stopped, started; I closed my eyes, opened them and the mountains were distant once more.

They rushed towards me again, flashed their crags and escarpments and whispered. I closed my eyes and lay down.

How long did I lie down? Did the afternoon pass without my noticing it? Usually, I'm careful with time. There's not enough to afford yourself the luxury of wasting it. I've never been a clock-watcher but my wife used to say I was. She thought I was a hundred things I wasn't. 'You're a fool/maggot/nuisance/bonehead.' She didn't have an imagination. I called her 'a bleeding paperclip!' but refused to explain what I meant. She tried to work it out for herself but couldn't get past the word 'bleeding'. Poor Steven, I sometimes thought. She would end up calling him a 'moron'.

The sun was cooling when I stood up and walked on. All the time I was watching the road in front of me, trying to recall the shape of rocks and other features, and hoping someone would come along. No one did. Normally, camel-drivers and goatherds were easy to meet; something was wrong with the day. Maybe it was a holy day.

I hadn't eaten all day. I hadn't had a drink. I followed the road into a valley I didn't recognise. I knew I was really lost then; a string of camel-drivers whipped their animals across the far horizon. I opened my mouth to shout, gasped and fell over. I imagined birds watching from a crag behind me. I turned around – nothing there. I crawled to a wall, propped myself against it and passed out.

(My wife never understood why I couldn't take alcohol. But I have low thresholds in many areas. Boozing is one. Half-a-pint is my limit. Anymore and I pass out. In the Thar desert, my dreams laughed at me. 'What's the matter with you?' they screamed. 'Strike a balance, for God's sake!')

I woke once in the night, again in the morning, later in the afternoon. My body raced all the time; thousands of tiny fingers seemed to be pinching me, flashes of flight worried my eyes and I began to fantasise about water. Jugs, streams, drops, pipettes, sinks and glasses. The few bushes that grew around seemed to be made from bones.

A bird really did squawk behind me. I passed out again, let my head tumble through my body, heard voices, grunting camels and harnesses jangling, and I felt arms around me, lifting me up and carrying me away.

I was treated for sunstroke and dehydration in Jaipur Hospital. Nurses shook their heads at me, the camel-drivers who delivered me into their care couldn't understand how I'd got lost.

I lay in a crowded ward. People milled around, my head milled around, doctors came and checked me. I was fed, and though water was in desperately short supply, I was given more than my fair share.

When I was well enough to sit up, I asked an orderly if someone could go to the post office for me. I explained about expecting a letter.

'A letter?'

'Yes. From my daughter.'

'Your daughter? Then certainly, sir. I go myself, sir. Back in a tick.'

He was back in a tick. 'Yes, sir. A letter for you.'

'Thank you . . .'

'But you, sir, you have to sign for it.' He coughed. 'I'm sorry.'

'Oh.'

'But when you're well, sir, I'll show you to the post office myself. We can go together.'

I had to lie in bed for another week, thinking about that letter. I had no idea what it said, but as long as Rachel was well and coping with Steven . . .

I was discharged from hospital on a sweltering day in late October 1987. The orderly insisted on showing me the way to the post office. 'This way . . . watch the pavement . . . careful, sir . . .' I gave my name at the counter, waited ten minutes, signed a form and was handed the letter.

'Thank you,' I said, and gave the orderly some rupees. He bowed and left me on the street. Hawkers yelled, bicycles streamed by, men with business to see to rode by on gaily shawled camels.

I looked at the letter. It wasn't from Rachel. I recognised my mother's handwriting. I opened it.

Dear James,

Just a quick note to say that Mr Miles was in touch today. He said there's a position for you if you're still interested. He wouldn't expect you to start until the new year. Maybe you should drop him a line.

I saw Rachel last week. She's fine. Father sends his love too. Do take care.

Your loving mother.

My loving mother. I folded the letter, crossed the road and stood in the shade of a canvas awning and thought that was good. All I needed to know. End of story, even if it was false.

The following day, I was walking through the market and saw a poster advertising a cricket match. *England v. Pakistan at the Mansingh Stadium.* I had stumbled upon the World Cup Cricket Competition. My favourite game.

I bought a ticket on the black market from a man with a scar on his forehead. He said, 'You're a lucky man to have this ticket. Many people wanted it.'

'I'm sure,' I said, not minding the cost. I had been gripped by a sudden need to see Englishmen in whites.

'Would you like to buy water too?' He held up a jug. 'Very cheap.'

'No thanks,' I said. Supplies in the city were so depleted that they were only turned on for one hour in the morning and another in the evening, but I had had some earlier and collected a bottleful. 'I have my own.'

'Clever man,' the ticket seller said. 'Very thoughtful.'

I climbed the stands. The ground was buzzing, the sun massive. I was wondering how anyone could grow a decent pitch in a drought-bound desert city when I saw it. So lush it wept; so green it hurt my eyes. I wanted to strip and lie in it. I wobbled and sat down.

I mopped my forehead and looked for an official.

'Hey!'

'Yes, sir?'

I pointed to the grass. Players were walking down the pavilion steps, swinging their arms and rubbing their crotches. 'How come?'

He explained. The stadium had been connected to an underground reservoir. For about a month, twenty-six sprinklers had been watering the ground for ten hours every day.

I asked him what he thought about that. He was cagey. 'I'm not sure. We all want this very much.' He pointed to the field, the players, the crowds, the television cameras beaming pictures to four continents. 'But I'm thinking about so much water when people go without. It's not really cricket.'

'It is,' I said without much thought, 'where I come from.'

A WARDEN FOR ALL SAINTS

H. S. BHABRA

H. S. BHABRA

H. S. Bhabra was born in Bombay, India, in 1955 and has lived in England since the age of one. He was educated at Reigate Grammar School and won an Open Scholarship to Trinity College, Oxford, where he read English. From 1977 to 1983 he pursued a successful career in the City. His first literary novel, *Gestures*, was published in 1986 to wide critical acclaim. It was hailed by Robertson Davies as 'A first novel of unusual sophistication and complexity', and by John Carey as 'An absorbing feat of historical imagination'. Since 1984, H. S. Bhabra has travelled and written full-time. He is currently in Central America.

'Ready, Warden?'

'Damn it . . .'

'You'll have to get used to it.'

'It isn't that. It only took – oh, about six seconds, to get used to being addressed as Warden . . .'

'What is it, then?'

The new Warden of All Saints looked up at the Senior Fellow and asked nervously, 'Have you seen Matthew this morning, Monty?'

James Montagu laughed, then reassured the younger man. 'Don't worry about him, Warden. I've known Matthew since he was an undergraduate, which is rather longer ago than either of us cares to remember. He'll behave.'

They stepped out of the Warden's Lodgings side by side, steel-quartered heels ringing on stone, and set off towards the New Quadrangle where their Fellows were already gathering.

Simon Evans had some reason to be anxious. It had been a bitter election, even by All Saints' savage standards, not least because it had been so unexpected.

According to the Statutes Tom Fitzsimmons, the old Warden, had had twelve years of his term left to serve the morning, half-way through that summer term, he had keeled face down into his Eggs Benedict. The clot in his brain, too deeply embedded to be operated on, had taken a fortnight to break up, a fortnight he had lain silent and immobile in the Radcliffe Infirmary, before the fragments had swept down to his heart, killing him with a single sigh.

It was a fortnight in which the lobbying began, furtive, and soured by what felt like guilt, at almost wishing death on the incumbent.

James Montagu had been the obvious and favoured candidate, but it had taken the various factions within and without the college no more than fifteen minutes to establish that the old sybarite did not seek, and would not serve in, the office. He had also refused to express a preference, easing back to watch the fun begin.

There were, after all, no students and few educational responsibilities to take into account. The college had been created by Henry III as a graduate-only foundation, with some of its fellows resident but many dispersed in the outside world, as a kind of medieval think tank. Its critics claimed that it had slipped steadily further into the past ever since. What even they did not deny, however, was the Warden's status as the unofficial chairman of the Establishment.

The lawyers who made up all too many of the college's non-resident fellows had, as always, run one of their own – Willie Henshaw, Privy Councillor, Queen's Counsel, Knight Bachelor, Chairman of two Royal Commissions, author of a major report to the Governor and Court of the Bank of England, and international corporate lawyer. His candidacy had seemed strong at first, until his supporters began a series of informal lunches with him for the other fellows; lunches which had led them all to agree that Willie was terribly bright, their sort of chap, and the most howling bore.

There had been a late run by Lord Siegenthal, Tory ideologue and recently retired Cabinet Minister, but it had foundered as the fellows recalled that everything he had set his hand to since his election to the college forty years before had ended in ashes and ridicule.

The obvious had finally become apparent: the election was between two internal candidates, Matthew Moore and Simon Evans. They made an unlikely pair. Somehow Matthew, the fifth member of his family to be a fellow, long, thin-lipped and autocratic, the finest Middle Eastern archaeologist of his generation, a man who held the whole modern world in derision, finding democracy and egalitarianism a conspiracy of the common and the cretinous, had been made by a handful of television appearances about his digs in Syria and Iraq one of the most recognisable and obscurely popular academics of his time. In London, taxi-drivers spoke proudly of the contemptuous dismissals they had received from 'that Dr Moore' when they had tried to urge him into conversation. Simon, however, the grandson of a miner and son of a grammar school scholarship pilot killed in a bombing raid over Aachen, fell altogether more clearly into All Saints' traditional image of itself. Affable, indulgent and oddly influential he was widely acknowledged as the doyen of Slavonic Studies in the West and the head of that informal freemasonry of Kremlin-watchers which helped define international policy and mould major negotiations; a man almost unknown to any save his peers.

Matthew had been the early front runner. By the fourth ballot, however, it was Simon who was only two votes short of the two-thirds majority the Statutes required. For a while it looked as though Matthew might refuse to release his supporters, forcing a reference to the College Visitor. Then and then only, James Montagu had unleashed a metaphorical weight as impressive as his actual bulk, refusing to allow the college's fate to be put in the hands of an ignorant bishop. In the end, Simon's election had been almost unanimous, but in the week since the two men had not exchanged so much as a grunt over High Table.

Today, the last day of the academic year, Simon was giving the Warden's traditional party in the New Quadrangle and it was the prospect of it which made him uneasy. He hoped that Matthew Moore would offer some gesture of reconciliation or, at the least, would do nothing to exacerbate the residual tensions of the election. You could never tell with Matthew, though, whatever Monty might say.

Warden's Gaudy, in the immediate aftermath of the University Encaenia, was traditionally a happy occasion, the last time most of the fellows would see each other before October and the new academic year. They were off on their several travels, some to work, some on holiday, some both. Tom Ducassis was off to the Library of Congress; Max von Ehrenburg to the new National

Archive in Vienna; John Wilmshurst was cataloguing a private library in a palazzo in Venice; Susan Shines, one of the few women fellows elected since the Statutes had been amended with the Privy Council's permission, was to be a guest of the Russian Writers' Union at an estate outside Odessa; that even more radical departure from tradition, a scientist, Tara Devereaux was awaited at the neutrino counter being built a mile deep in the Rocky Mountains; Ved Menon was due in Beijing to advise on a new administration for Hong Kong which would take account of the territory's historic procedures, while Jack Ainsley was off to bugger little boys in Morocco and Leo Dart to be buggered by lifeguards in Big Sur. As Simon and Monty crossed the quad, the Warden could not help remembering one of the last things his predecessor had said to him. 'Really, Simon, why can't some of us manifest some sense of responsibility? You'd think a few of us might breed.'

For now, however, he contented himself with a head count of the fellows gathered by the trestles set up in the cloisters, canted over kirs royales and academic malice.

'Looks like a full house,' Simon murmured as they approached the party.

'Not quite,' the Senior Fellow corrected him. 'The Kampucheans opened the border yesterday. Young Wemyss should be in Angkor by now. And Kit Browne's in Lhasa, of course.'

'Of course. Pity. Translating?'

'Indeed. Mantras.'

The warden smiled furtively. 'Don't tell the Chapel Clerks.'

There were cheerful barks of 'Warden!' and a ripple of applause as Monty and Simon joined the party. Simon found himself relaxing into the excitement of his colleagues, remembering at last that many of them were friends.

It went well, the fellows taking congé with their usual mix of snobbery and gossip, all of them, with the possible exception of Matthew Moore, exuberant as soldiers on furlough. Simon let himself be encompassed by their happiness and high humour and found himself, in the end, concurring with the old All Saints' axiom: the Prince of Darkness could not be a gentleman for, if he were, he would have been elected.

At last the hubbub was interrupted by Matthew Moore marching peremptorily to one of the trestles and rapping on it, fist down, with his heavy signet ring. Simon's heart sank.

'Doctors!' Matthew called, 'your attention please . . .' Conversation faded in quizzical coughs and shushing. Matthew raised his long hands, looking, for an instant, like something off the West Front of Chartres, and went on. 'As most of you know, I leave for Babylon this afternoon . . .'

The fellows broke into hooting and baying, Tara and Susan calling in chorus, 'Day-break and a candle-end . . .'

Matthew did something almost unparalleled and smiled, at his own expense. 'I know, I know, but someone has to make sure the French aren't wrecking the site as they rebuild it.'

More cries of, 'The horror! The horror!' and, 'A dirty job but someone has to do it,' and, '*schmerzvoll, unruhig*!'

'You also know that, a week ago, I lost one of the harder-fought elections in the college's recent history . . .' The silence was immediate, hesitant, ambiguous. 'What I want to do before I go away, we go away, for months on end, is to settle something. I think it's about time that we, I, drank a toast to the new Warden and welcomed him properly to his high and arduous office.'

There was more applause, and the relaxation of relief, and the charging and raising of glasses. When it was done, Matthew Moore spoke again. 'In particular, to show I harbour no grudges, I'd like you, Warden, to accept a small gift, from our last dig in Syria.' He produced it from the folds of his gown, a small black figurine, basalt by the look of it, with some form of writing carved in the base.

Simon took it in his hands, weighing it in his palm and saying, 'Matthew, this is terribly kind of you . . .' before adding sheepishly, 'I don't suppose you'd have an export licence to go with it?'

Moore shook his head, to the laughter of the fellows.

'Really, Matthew, I always guessed you archaeologist chaps were nothing but tomb-robbers.'

The Warden and Monty were the only fellows in full residence that Long Vacation, Simon settling himself and his furniture into

the Lodgings and working on a long article on Soviet policy in
Africa, Monty preparing an evaluation of Champollion's work to
be published under the auspices of the Collège de France. Even
so, they saw relatively little of each other, both caught up in
their own concerns, without the term-time rhythms of collegiate
life to bring them together. The Warden, moreover, still found
himself, or at least his body, in occasional demand with a number
of rather fetching London social personalities, while Monty had
years ago decided that food and wine were altogether more
varied, subtle and delicate than sex. A pity, Simon had always
thought, for that tall, big-boned and ponderous figure still attracted its admirers. Pretty, some of them, too.

So, by the time they met for lunch one week in mid-July, it
had been the best part of a fortnight since they had last seen
each other. Nonetheless, Monty found himself struck by the
change in the younger man.

'Are you feeling quite well in yourself, Warden?' he had asked.
'You look a touch peaky.'

'I'm all right, Monty,' Simon had replied, his voice thick with
phlegm. 'Just sleeping rather badly. Change of locale, I suppose.'

A fortnight later the change in the Warden was unmistakable.
He looked years older, patches of grey hair showing through
the auburn, his face gaunt and yellowed, great lines scooping
his cheeks from his nostrils to the corners of his mouth.

'Bad dreams, Monty,' he explained. 'Don't understand it.
Them.'

'What kind of dreams?'

'Nothing that makes much sense. Anxiety, of course, but no
continuous narrative, no real objects. It's a sort of insubstan-
tiality, really. Nothing, in the dreams, seems to have any solidity.
I'll be in a chair, or lying in bed, and suddenly the whole room
will go soft, as though the furniture were flesh, suppurating, and
the walls, the walls were made of hair. As though everything,
everything that shouldn't be, were alive, but dying . . . Sometimes, I'm almost frightened of going to sleep.'

'Have you seen a quack?'

'Yes. Sleeping pills. They don't help. They don't stop the
dreams.'

Monty looked at the Warden with a flat, frank uncertainty before saying, 'I have to go to Paris. Take lunch at Lapérouse off that young pup Fenwick and see Ibn Zaghloul before he goes back to Cairo. And Duparc's invited me on to his place in the Vosges for August. I thought I might finish the writing there. Why don't I leave you the name of my physick in London? You might think of getting in touch with him if this goes on. Good man.'

The Warden accepted with a distracted air. 'Do that, Monty. Yes.'

Returning in early September, Monty found Simon much improved, plainly benefiting from a six-week course of calmative drugs prescribed by his own physician. With the Autumn Solstice, however, came a sudden and undeniable change for the worse. The Warden woke that morning to find his sheets wrapped about him, drenched with sweat, his hair gone almost completely white, and his once enormous capacity for concentration almost completely vanished. It was days before he could bring himself to speak of it to the Senior Fellow. For the first time since the election the old man found himself wondering if he had supported the right candidate.

'They've come back, Monty, worse than before. Behind the living things, the ones which shouldn't be alive, are other living things I never see. I only hear them. And a horrible apprehension. Something's coming. Something's on its way.'

'Have you seen my vet?'

'Couple of days ago. He won't prescribe the drugs again. Too powerful, evidently, but they stopped the dreams. At least I think they did. He seems to think that because they've come back more powerfully the pills may just have suppressed my consciousness of them. He wants me to see some kind of witch-doctor, but I'm not mad, Monty. I'm not.'

As the other fellows returned, there were those who might have disagreed with him. Montagu found himself having the same conversation again and again in variant forms.

'Is there something the matter with the Warden, Monty? It won't do for him to shut himself away. I gather he's returned and commented on neither of the reports by the Bursars. And there's no sign yet of an agenda for the College Meeting. Tom Fitzsimmons would have had that waiting for us. If he isn't up to the job . . .'

Only Matthew Moore, bronzed and contented from his sojourn in the past, in an excess of discretion and decorum, remained silent on the subject of the Warden's weakness, but even the college servants were speaking of Simon's fearfulness and inattention.

Somehow, the Warden willed his way through his first College Meeting, but the effort of it both sapped his fellows' confidence in him and precipitated some kind of collapse. He took to the lodgings and, gravest failing of all, avoided High Table.

Matthew Moore remained a sure foundation of support for him, murmuring, whenever canvassed or confronted by a dissident, 'Give him time. It's early yet. You have to give him till All Saints at least. All will be well, you'll see, once All Saints is upon us.'

In private moments James Montagu found the archaeologist's simpering compassion almost the most unpleasant thing about that period. He expected, and needed, the savage and ironic from Moore, not generosity, not sympathy; not, if he was honest, all those things which made the other fellows say to themselves and each other, 'Good chap, Matthew. Underestimated him. He'd make the devil of a Warden. Next time, perhaps. Perhaps quite soon.'

Even so, he found himself almost agreeing with them when he next called on the Warden. Simon seemed to be shrinking inside the Lodgings. He had closed up room after room, reducing his existence to a smaller and smaller area based around the study, an area which was beginning to manifest the unavoidable evidences of squalor as he, in mounting paranoia, made it harder for anyone, including the servants, to come within its compass.

There was a hunted, feral aspect to him as he sat at his desk wrapped in an old plaid blanket, which Monty found himself repelled by, positioning himself as far away as he could, his back to the fireplace, one elbow propped atop the mantelshelf.

'You have to pull yourself together, Warden. You know this House. It's too clever to be forgiving.'

Simon seemed to ignore him, muttering, 'They're coming for me. Coming. They think I don't hear them, but I hear them. Millions of them, by day and by night. I haven't seen them yet, but I will. Dear God I will. When I see them, when I . . .' He suddenly gripped his head in his hands as though it might explode, rocking back and forth, fat tears rolling unnoticed down his cheeks. 'Help me, Monty. Help.'

'I can't help you, Simon. You need a psychiatrist.'

The Warden shook his head, as though he despaired of ever explaining. 'I'm not going mad, Monty. I know I'm not. I'm dying. I'm being killed.'

'Nonsense!' Montagu snapped. 'I won't allow it. I will not tolerate a Year of Three Wardens. This college is not some flibbertigibbet institution like the Roman Church or the Flavian Empire.'

That sudden flash of collegiate arrogance and anger seemed to reach Simon as nothing had in weeks. 'Then help me,' he asked simply.

'How?'

Simon extended what had become a bony hand, to the mantelshelf. 'That,' he said, 'that brings them. Find out what it means.'

Monty turned to the object at which the Warden pointed. It was the little basalt figurine Matthew had presented. The old man almost laughed. 'Why not ask Matthew?'

'I have. He says the writing is unknown. I don't know if that's true, but I know it brings them. Find out, Monty. Tell me what it says.'

Montagu shook his head in bafflement. 'If it worries you so much, why not get rid of it? Give it back to Matthew. Tell him it was too generous.'

'I can't. You know I can't. It would be an open insult, even if I just lost it. The servants would know. He'd know. Everyone would know. It would swing the whole governing body behind him, but I need to know what it means.'

Montagu picked the small object up. It was heavier than it seemed and its matt surface swallowed light, generating darkness. It was strange and compelling and primitive, the carving on its base apparently some variant of cuneiform. 'Can I keep this?' he asked.

The Warden shook his head. 'It isn't leaving my sight. Copy it.'

An hour later, James Montagu sat in his rooms between the Towers, a pencil rubbing of the figurine's text before him and a telephone receiver in his hand. 'Yes,' he was saying, 'the obsession seems to centre on this wretched figurine, which he won't destroy or return, but it's driving him crazy.'

'Not a term I'd care to use,' the discarnate voice of his doctor told him. 'I'm not a specialist, of course, but it's not so very unusual, an external objectification of anxiety. A variant of the child's blanky, really.'

'What should I do?'

'Well, in a perfect world, he'd seek therapy . . .'

'Won't happen. Too late anyway. We need, the college needs, something a deal swifter than that.'

'Then you could do worse than doing what he asks. Quite often, some reasonable explanation of the object will allow the patient to rationalise his anxieties and deal with them. It's often the quickest way.'

'Damn,' James Montagu said. 'Damn, damn, damn.'

The college was used to Monty's vanishing tricks, but it missed him. Only young Kit Browne, back from Lhasa, knew where the old man was, and he said nothing, for the chain of telegrams from Baghdad, Jerusalem, Cairo, Athens and Rome asking him to wire confirmation of Montagu's status to the appropriate authorities came to him in confidence, a confidence he kept. Still, in those two weeks, James missed the worst of the Warden's illness: the sealing off of most of the Lodgings, the complete withdrawal inside the study, the flight from sleep, the avoidance of callers, the ravings in the night, lights blazing. The fellows missed Montagu's good sense and advice, missed being able to ask him about the worst evidences of the Warden's condition. Kit Browne almost wrote to him about them, but was never certain, as Monty's travels continued, that any mail would reach its destination, so the old man was not to hear just yet of the marks upon the fabric of the Lodgings: the furniture smashed by unknown hands, the slivers of wood clawed out of doors, and those last marks, sly and delicate, made in the night when the Warden seemed at his most insane which alone made Kit hesitate in ascribing all the damage to the man himself – the marks made by animal extremities, by teeth and claws, not on but in the glass of the windows. All the fellows had to succour them through those days was Matthew Moore's suddenly gentle voice reiterating, 'All will be well. Give him till All Saints. After All Saints the Warden will be worthy of us.'

James returned on the morning of All Saints, the day of the Feast, the most important day in the collegiate calendar, to find the whole institution in a state of quiet uproar. Kit Browne explained.

'No one can get an answer from the Warden, Monty. He hasn't been out in days and we have to know if he's coming to the Feast . . .'

'He's coming.'

'The Statutes say there can be no Feast without the Warden present . . .'

'I know very well what the Statutes say. No Warden, no Feast. No Feast and a Warden still living and the matter is to be referred at once to the Visitor to appoint a new Warden. Sort of medieval impeachment clause, to remove an incapacitated Warden. Or, presumably, a hated one, by barricading him in and preventing a Feast. I've always rather thought that must have been what happened in 1522.'

'I almost hope he doesn't make it. Quite a lot of us do. Maybe we should have elected Matthew after all.'

James shook his head. 'You're wrong, and he's coming to the Feast.'

He did, on Montagu's arm, but it was not a festive affair, the fellows scattering before eleven, as at least one of their number had intended, no happiness in their hearts, and precious little hope.

Back in the Lodgings, Montagu faced the warden down. 'You have to go, Simon. You have to. Whatever this matter is between you has to be resolved.'

Evans looked down on the note in Matthew's clear script requesting his company in the New Quadrangle at five minutes before midnight 'to finish a matter between us I think you already understand'.

'I can't, Monty. You have no idea what these past days and nights have been like. They're coming. Whatever they are, they're coming. I should have guessed it would be All Saints Night. You've found out what it says, haven't you?'

The old man looked down at his shoes. 'Not what it says, no,' he murmured. 'But I found out what it means.'

'I can't go.'

'You have to, or you will lose the Wardenship whatever comes. I will be in the cloisters five minutes before you.'

Simon Evans entered the New Quadrangle as summoned, the towers and domes of the city looming above him under a gibbous moon. The hands of the college clock gleamed palely towards twelve. Matthew Moore was waiting for him. He extended no hand in friendship.

'You took what was mine, Simon. You have to pay.'

He threw back his long, aristocratic head, and in the moonlight it seemed as though some unearthly longing shone in his eyes, and then he spoke, in an ancient and barbaric tongue, unheard upon the earth these many thousand years. He spoke, imploring and summoning, long liquid syllables as chilly as the grave.

James Montagu stepped from the darkness of the cloisters, saying, '"Come, Lord, to thy servant. Come, Lord, for thy servant calls thee." Thank you for the enunciation, Matthew. The most I could manage was a kind of translation.'

Moore's loom was a sneer. 'It's too late, Monty. There's nothing you can do.'

As the college clock shivered the first stroke of midnight, they heard, far, far away, something, something at the very edge of sound, approaching. At the third stroke, they felt rather than heard it passing through the college gates and across the small Old Quadrangle. With the fifth stroke, the small hairs of their heads prickled, as the not-sound took form, filling out, becoming manifest as something low and soft and disgusting. At the sixth stroke, it passed the Middle Gate, and they knew it, impossibly, for a rank and corrupted buzzing. And with the seventh stroke, they saw it, entering New Quad.

It was something very like a man, but of greater stature, and black, even against the night. With each clangorous stroke of the bell it came closer and they saw there was something strange about its shape and gait. It seemed almost liquid. It did not so much walk as re-form its limbs in another place, one pace on.

On and on it came, forming and reforming, and before it came a stench of rot and decay like something from the jaws of an ancient hound, its buzzing growing and extending until it seemed greater than any ocean's roar, and at last they saw it and understood.

They saw the explanation of its shape and movement and knew at last that it was not one, but many. They saw that it was composed, entirely, of flies.

With the eleventh stroke it was upon them, reaching out one travesty of an arm. Simon fell to his knees, and it hesitated before him, as though puzzled, and passed, like the shadow of a cloud across a valley floor, extending, and searching, until, with the twelfth stroke, it wavered before Matthew Moore, and the look of reverence in his eyes became one of bafflement, and it seemed to embrace him, enfolding and engulfing him till it was impossible to tell the two figures apart, and there was only a darkness on the grass that seemed to dance in a buzzing howl.

The shape softened, and sagged, sinking, spreading out across the quad, and fell away, like a mist, and it was done, no sign of any visitation, save only the corpses of a myriad flies.

Later, much later, when Simon Evans could speak and stand again, he looked on James Montagu and asked in wonder, 'What happened, James? It came for me . . .'

The old man still trembled. 'Don't think about it, Warden. You have a college to salvage, and a missing person to report. It's enough for now.'

But it was not. 'Why, James? How? You knew, didn't you?'

'I guessed, with a little help.'

'What happened here? What went wrong?'

For the first time in weeks, James Montagu smiled, and took the Warden by the arm to lead him to the Lodgings, and said, '"Come, Lord, to thy servant." I do not suppose, Warden, that the Prince of Darkness is ever to be trusted, but it may be, just may be, that sometimes he keeps, exactly, his word.'

INTENSITY

JAMES BUCHAN

JAMES BUCHAN

James Buchan is New York correspondent for the *Financial Times* of London. His first novel, *A Parish of Rich Women*, was published in 1984 and won the Whitbread, David Higham and *Yorkshire Post* awards. *Davy Chadwick*, a second novel, was published in 1987 to acclaim. The author is married and lives in Greenwich Village.

THIS HAPPENED IN 1982, in Kiev, on the last night of the prime minister's visit. I was in the party to look after the press, because Pat Clark was on paternity leave. The trip had been a failure and we were all getting on one another's nerves.

We were in the Hotel Ukrainiya. It was worse than anything in Moscow. The passages were dark and stank of disinfectant. Inquisitive women in brown overalls stood guard at the lifts and confiscated room-keys. Meal times were brief and, as far as I could see, quite unpredictable. I was working flat out in the prime minister's suite on his farewell speech. Once, I got away to the dining room, but waiters were stacking chairs on tables or locking up.

I had eaten nothing since Moscow, but I could not face the farewell banquet. I wanted to be on my own. All day, I had prodded the Ukrainiya into finding me a seat at the theatre. To my surprise, the concierge produced a ticket for *Yevgeny Onegin*. I looked forward to being alone in the Soviet Union, first in a theatre, then in a restaurant. With twenty minutes to go before the performance, I stood up and put on my coat.

The prime minister looked at me and picked up my draft of the speech. 'But Richard, there's no political content,' he said. 'None whatsoever. It would be a gross error, having put across my point so forcefully in Moscow, to confine myself to . . .'

'Banalities . . .' said Maynard. 'All right for the Germans, I suppose, but not for a UK delegation.' He was sitting with his back to the window. On a blackboard set on an easel beside his chair, someone had written: CONVERSATIONS IN THIS ROOM ARE NOT SECRET. Maynard had his coat off. The prime minister had his coat off. I had seventeen minutes to get to the theatre and no Soviet money.

'Krazno is doing wheat, Prime Minister,' I said. 'My new friend at the Palace of the Republic showed me an English draft of his speech.'

'That, I'm afraid, is the point, Richard. Wheat matters.' Maynard raised his voice as if for the benefit of an eavesdropper. 'We cannot afford to de-couple economic cooperation and security, whatever Anatoly Krazno does or does not do.'

'Yes, that is the point, Richard.' The prime minister looked tired out. I think he had no interest in theatre or, indeed, in anything outside political life. He had refused the morning's sightseeing programme. I felt I was letting him down.

'There's a reference to the force-reduction negotiations on page three of the draft, Prime Minister. And I've provided an alternative toast, if you want to turn the heat up a bit. But I rather thought, as this is the private visit, and we're not in Moscow . . .'

I had twelve minutes.

'Yes, yes,' said Maynard. 'Of course, there is quite a good chance that Krazno will be elected to the Central Committee in October.' He turned and looked out of the window.

'Yes, Richard. We must look to the coming generation of leaders,' said the prime minister.

'I could easily redo the draft, Prime Minister. There's a good, oh, half-hour before the delegation has to leave. And I could work during the fish-eggs.'

'Don't you worry about it, Richard.' The prime minister took his pencil and made a slashing diagonal mark on the top page. Without looking up, he held out a page to Maynard. Maynard rose. They were waiting for me to leave the room. I hesitated a moment, then left.

I tried to put the scene from my mind. I had just ten minutes to pick up some money and get to the theatre: ten minutes for the dark passages, the interminable lift, the floor-lady, the room-keys, the passages, the floor-lady and lift again, and then a car and driver. I had no hope of arriving on time. I would miss the whole first act. If only I had carried Soviet money with me!

Maynard carried no roubles. The prime minister had none. We had not needed money in Moscow. The cars that took us to the Kremlin cost us nothing, not even tips. The laying of wreaths cost nothing. The prime minister's unplanned walk in Red Square cost nothing. The flight to Kiev cost nothing. The Ukrainiya cost nothing. Even the opera ticket came with the compliments of the City of Kiev. Only I needed money, because I was hungry.

The lift opened at last on the thirteenth floor. A lamp burned weakly on the floor-lady's desk, but there was nobody about.

'Madame! Madame!' I whispered. I was beside myself with frustration.

'Yes.'

I turned round. Near the end of the passage, I could see the lower half of a tall woman. She was leaning against the passage wall but her head, which was in darkness, must have almost touched the ceiling. She wore a brown overall.

'Room 1319? It's open.' She spoke English with a self-assured American accent, rather like the readers on Moscow Radio.

'You're an angel,' I said, hurrying past her. I saw her feet were bare.

'No I am not,' I heard her say.

My room was open. The radio was on. It was playing an Italian pop-song. I had nothing confidential in my luggage but the intrusion made me even angrier.

At the other end of the passage, the woman had sat down behind her desk. She looked about thirty. Her hair was dirty and her eyes were half-closed from tiredness or boredom. The brown overall did not help but she gave an impression of dinginess. I returned the key and called the lift. After a while, her presence at my back embarrassed me.

'You speak good English,' I said, for want of anything better to say.

She took such a long time to reply that I looked round. Her eyes were fully closed.

'In tourist hotels, every person understands English,' she said at last.

'What? So you know what we foreigners are doing?' I smiled to show this was a joke.

She opened her eyes. 'I also have travelled to the United Kingdom and North America,' she said.

I felt too chastened to say more. The lift-doors opened and I escaped.

I was in luck. The delegation cars were already lined up in front of the hotel. I took the last in line. The driver seemed to know what he was doing. We rolled past a sports stadium and along a double highway, where the tarmac glistened in the warm dusk. There was little traffic, but the pavements were crowded with people walking slowly, as in a Mediterranean town. We came to a wide boulevard lined with steel-and-glass buildings. It seemed to end at the foot of a tall and elaborate stone apartment block, like the Stalinist skyscrapers we had seen in Moscow. In its shadow was a tiny, old-fashioned building covered in pink plaster. This was the theatre. The crowds on the pavement were thick and there was a lot of elbowing and jostling as I pushed my way through.

I need not have bothered. The orchestra had not arrived and the theatre was still half-empty. The interior had once been splendid. Busty caryatids supported the balconies, which showed the remains of stucco decoration. The seats were covered in pink velvet, though mine was black at the top from hair-oil. The scene curtain was embroidered with wheat-sheaves and the arms and initials of the Ukrainian Soviet Socialist Republic.

My seat was the best in the house. I sat directly behind the conductor's podium. As the house filled up, four seats on each side stayed empty. Behind me were rows of middle-aged people in shirt-sleeves and work-dresses. The people talked through the overture. When the curtain rose, they applauded wildly but went on talking.

It was warm in the theatre. I was relaxing after six days of nerves and exertion. My head became intolerably heavy. I pinched my nose and cheeks. The stage blurred and rearranged itself into familiar and comfortable shapes. I woke in a gale of applause. Two old women were handing a small bouquet to the conductor.

I hurried to the exit, then made my way downstairs, where a queue had formed. At the top was a lobby, with an elaborate clock that showed the wrong time. The queue stretched along and around four walls of the lobby and ended at a refreshment stand near where I stood. Red caviar gleamed on what looked like scones. There was a big urn of tea. I went back down the stairs, looking at signed photographs of singers. I recognised Caruso. I bought a programme and received an astonishing amount of change. The programme was in Russian and Ukrainian. There was no English synopsis.

In the second act, there was a dance and a duel. The audience applauded every aria, duet and ensemble. When the curtain came down, I tried to slip away upstairs but was caught in my exposed position as the conductor turned to take his bow. His face was shining with sweat. By the time I escaped, the queue was at the foot of the stairs.

The third act opened at a ball in St Petersburg. I did not try to concentrate. I thought of food. I thought of everything I had eaten in Russia. I thought of the party given by Novosti for the visiting press at a magnificent house in Moscow. There was sturgeon and red and black caviar, and a sort of ravioli made with minced meat, and pancakes full of dill and sour cream and odd dishes that looked savoury and tasted sweet and vice-versa. We toasted one another in vodka flavoured with lemon or pepper. One vodka tasted of honey. Another smelled of hay. By the end, we were all seated on gilded chairs against the walls, shouting greetings across the devastated table.

As I left the theatre, I hesitated a moment on the pavement. Two young men offered to help me. I brushed them off at first, but then welcomed them, because I did need help. They spoke English. They were students at the university, which was on the morning's tour we had not taken. They commented on this, which embarrassed me. They were in the middle of their exams. When I said I wanted to go to a good restaurant, they looked surprised.

The streets were still crowded. We kept coming on their

classmates, some of them carrying books. The girls were very pretty. They bombarded the two young men and me with questions. I was evidently something of a catch for the boys. I felt a certain discomfort: the prime minister's acting press secretary walking arm-in-arm with young Ukrainian students. I had already forgotten their names.

At last we came to a restaurant above an underground station. A porter blocked our way. His breath stank of drink. I explained I was a tourist and the young men were my guests. I lost my temper. The man simply locked the glass door in my face.

We walked to a park and sat under some chestnut trees. On other benches, soldiers and militiamen sat holding the hands of girls. There was white pollen in the air which the students said came off poplar trees. We talked about the British army in Northern Ireland. I asked about Afghanistan. We all became heated and then calmed down. I thought it was silly to quarrel on such chance acquaintance. I am sure they felt the same. We walked to a vast flood-lit monument, which they said was to the dead of Babiy Yar. I asked them to join me at the hotel for tea. They were turned away at the door. We exchanged addresses but I lost theirs and they did not write.

The hotel restaurant was locked and empty. I rode wearily to the thirteenth floor in the lift.

'Hello,' I said to the floor-girl. 'Is there anything to eat up here, by any chance?'

She was seated at her desk, a packet of Marlboro cigarettes and an ash-tray in front of her. 'You can try the foreign-currency bar on the second floor,' she said. 'It is sometimes open late.' Her eyes were glazed but they suddenly flashed with enthusiasm. 'Do you know the group Panic? From Milan. They're playing. They're famous in West Europe.'

'I don't know about modern music. I was at the opera.'

'I know. *Onegin*. There were tickets for all your group but only one person went. I've never seen it.'

'It was good. Better than London.' I sat on the edge of her desk and looked down at her long legs.

'Why do you say that when it isn't true,' she said, hiding her legs under the desk. 'And you can't sit down. You must go to the first floor. Suite 001. Another tourist. There was a message for you.'

'That's not a tourist. That's our prime minister,' I said, laughing.

'Kohl?'

'No, that's West Germany.' I laughed again, and then thought I was being unkind.

She seemed quite untroubled. 'I learn something new here every day. That's why I like to work here.'

'Will you still be here when I come back. It's nice to talk with Russians.'

'I'm not a Russian. Of course I am here. I must be here. I have your room-key.'

The lift arrived. She picked up a newspaper as I stepped into it.

The prime minister was seated in the same armchair when I came in. Maynard was standing, looking out of the window. The blackboard was still there, with its warning.

'Agriculture,' said the prime minister.

'The point was cleanly made on both sides,' said Maynard, stretching languidly. 'Economic relations will survive, may even be extended, despite unbridgeable differences over security issues.'

'I entirely recast your reference to the independent deterrent, Richard,' the prime minister said.

'Decisively,' said Maynard. 'The emphasis was not lost on the Soviet side.'

I was having difficulty concentrating. The prime minister had a peculiar mannerism of speech: he pronounced 'the' as 've', so that it became 've independent deterrent.' This sounded silly to me. CONVERSATIONS IN THIS ROOM ARE NOT SECRET: the chalk message gave a staginess to the proceedings, as if we were performing to an empty house. Perhaps it was just hunger.

'Do you by any chance have any biscuits?'

'For God's sake, Richard,' said Maynard. He came forward from the window and made a face over the seated prime minister. 'I'm sorry to drag you here so late, but the prime minister has moved the programme forward. The RAF VC-10 will leave at 8 a.m. sharp.'

'Oh,' I said. 'What about the monastery?'

'Really, Richard,' said the prime minister. He picked up a file and unwrapped the pink tape round it.

'You, Richard, will be briefing them on the way back, of course,' Maynard said.

'I thought I would go back to them for a bit before they get too pissed. But there's not much to say. This is the private visit.'

The prime minister was absorbed in his file. Maynard looked at me closely.

'You could go on background, couldn't you? On, say, how the Soviet side reacted to the PM personally?'

I said nothing but looked, I hope, receptive to this idea.

Maynard sighed and then spoke quickly. 'There was that Foreign Ministry man, Rostov I think, who was talking after the press conference. You said he was talking about Sir Winston.'

'He was being sarcastic. He was as furious as the rest about the PM's line on the independent deterrent. It wasn't even meant for my hearing.'

'I suppose you know that for a fact, Richard,' Maynard said. He again raised his voice ostentatiously. 'My feeling was that despite differences, irreconcilable for the moment, over nuclear forces in Europe, the Soviets were deeply impressed by the PM's clear, forthright and principled exposition of the British line.'

'Yes, I'm sure that's so,' I said. 'Do you have anything to drink here?'

'I wouldn't trust the tap-water,' said the prime minister, without looking up from his file.

'I'll rough out a few ideas before bed. Good-night, Ian, Prime Minister.'

'Good-night, Richard,' said Maynard. 'Krazno is coming at seven.'

It was two in the morning. I took the lift to the second floor but the foreign-currency bar, if it had ever been open, was well and truly shut now. Through a wall of frosted and clear panes of glass, I could see artificial palm-trees and a microphone and drum-set. I was thoroughly fed up.

On the thirteenth floor, the girl was still wearing her brown overall, seated at her desk. The paper was fallen to the floor. I could see it was *Izvestiya*. She looked up with a start as I came out of the lift.

'What's Trident?' she asked.

'Our nuclear rocket. That's why we English are here.' What the hell, I thought.

'Why is your negotiating position so inflexible?'

'We say that about your side,' I said. I sat down on the desk and smiled to show that I did not want to dispute about nuclear weapons. I felt a perverse sense of excitement.

'I found some chewing-gum, that's all,' she said. 'Enzo of Panic gave it to me. They came up here after their concert last night.'

I took one piece, and then, because she shook the packet, a second. My jaw ached as I unwrapped each piece. The gum was very sweet.

'What's your name?'

'Helen. It's a Greek name.'

'It's nice. I'm Richard.'

'My grandmother was Greek. My grandfather was Polish.'

'And you're Ukrainian?'

She smiled. 'There are no Ukrainians. They all died in the war. I have a son called Anton. That's Greek, too.'

'Does your husband look after him when you're working?'

She looked at me. I felt I'd been caught in a clumsy ploy. But I did not care.

'My mother looks after Anton. You may be tired. You should go to bed.'

'Helen, why is your English so good?'

'I said I had travelled. Even to England, Gatwick Airport. And New York, John Kennedy Airport. And Toronto, all over the city. I was an athlete. I was a competitor at the three-cornered games: USA, USSR and Canada. High jump.'

She had closed her eyes again.

'How high can you jump, Helen?'

'I used to jump 1.85. Anton is five now.'

'Did you do the best jump in Toronto?'

She opened her eyes. I felt again that I was going too far, that I was bruising her in some way. She said, 'You know, you should have gone to the foreign-currency bar. Panic is very well-known.'

I could not stop. 'Did you win in Toronto, Helen?'

She shook her head impatiently. 'It doesn't matter, you know. My mother asks, everybody asks me, why I work here, shut up all day and night except the days off. I could have gone back to college. My mother was an engineer. My father was a journalist. I was all-Ukraine champion for three and one-half years. I can do anything. But I want to meet tourists, people from other countries.'

'Oh come on, that's silly . . .'

'No, it is not silly,' she said. 'You would not understand. You travel as you wish. You have been all over the world. Moscow, Kiev, they are just cities. I have been just to Toronto, and it is beautiful. I had such friends. We had a feeling, all of us: Cathy, Carmel, Heather, all the girls. We could do anything. We lived with such . . . I can't express it, because English is not my first language. We lived with freedom, with intense-ness . . .'

'Intensity.'

'Intensity. Thank you. And that is all I am going to say. What time do you want the wake-up call?'

'Never.'

She looked confused, so I said, 'Five-thirty. You should sleep a bit as well, Helen. You look tired.'

'It's my job. One tourist is getting up at four o'clock. English. Maynard.'

'I know,' I said.

She offered me the rest of the gum, which I took.

I woke to the sound of a football rattle. It was my telephone ringing. Maynard was at the other end.

'Morning, Richard. I'm afraid Krazno will not be coming to the airport. We leave at once.'

'Oh God,' I said. 'I knew we should have done the sightseeing programme.'

'Don't be absurd, Richard. It's clearly a health matter. The Soviet side says that he is indisposed. There is no point hanging around. We leave in ten minutes.'

Helen had a glass of tea on her desk. In the saucer was a broken piece of sugar. She handed the glass to me. She did not seem to have slept at all.

'Helen, would you like this Soviet money? I don't need it any more. We're leaving.'

'Thank you.' She took the rouble notes and put them in the desk drawer.

'We're leaving early,' I said. 'Your prime minister is registering displeasure.'

She looked uninterested, or simply tired. I tried again.

'Helen, if you tell me your surname, I'll write to you from London.'

'I get postcards from tourists all the time.'

'I could send something for little Anton.'

She glanced at me, and then I knew I had gone too far. 'Thank you. He has everything.'

She stood up. I had forgotten how tall she was. She walked past me in her bare feet and called the lift. She returned to her desk and sat down.

'Don't forget to give me the key,' she said.

'I never had it.'

I got into the second car with Maynard. Motorbikes stood on each side, their engines going. Maynard was reading a telex.

'Did you get some breakfast?' he asked.

'No. I thought the prime minister might need me.'

'No. He's with Zortin who is, quite frankly, the coming man in the Ukrainian party. Interpreters only. I could not explain over the telephone, but Krazno has a history of heart trouble. That's what scuppered his election to the Central Committee in Moscow. The PM is making some points we roughed out after you went to bed.'

'Oh,' I said. We were moving at high speed. Through the

window, sunshine flashed off the gold dome of a church. I wished we had seen the city in the day-time.

Maynard was speaking beside me. 'Look, Richard. I have to be brutally frank. The PM is far from happy at the way the qualities have covered the trip. I have not seen the cuttings myself, but Number 10 was not encouraging.'

'It was a difficult visit.'

'Certainly. If you don't mind, Richard, I'd say you concentrated too much on the security issues and not enough on the trust that the PM has built up with the coming generation of Soviet leaders. Really, the very best performance I have seen from a prime minister. Pat Clark would have picked up on that.'

We were speeding through birch-woods. Militiamen were stationed at intervals along the roadside verges. One emerged from trees, smoothing his uniform, as we passed.

'Well, there's still the in-flight briefing,' I said cheerfully.

'There is, as you say, the in-flight briefing.'

The airport terminal was a long, low building of 1950s' vintage. It looked like something out of Tin-Tin. The press bus was already at the entrance. The journalists were straggling through various control posts. At the back, sweating, was my particular favourite, Alan Bristow of the *Daily Mail*. He was carrying two large plastic bags and searching clumsily through his pockets for something. He was also hampered by a cigarette.

It was not that Bristow was reliable. He was not. I liked him, I suppose, because he made heavy weather of life. If I had been a journalist, I would have been like Bristow: perpetually anxious about what I were writing and jealous of what others were finding out. I tapped him on the back. He jumped.

'Ah Richard,' he said, with relief. I did not mind his using my Christian name. I hated it from the others.

'Do you want me to carry one of your bags through duty-free at Heathrow. It's just one more worry, isn't it?'

'I hate diplomats,' he said. 'Thank you very much.'

He had now found what he was looking for: a currency form. He handed it to a lady in uniform. She waved me through but I waited for Bristow, and we joined the next queue.

'Bit of a blow about Krazno, eh? The last straw, isn't it, Richard?'

'I'm lost, old fellow. What do you mean?'

'Rather a snub, isn't it? Not coming to see the prime minister off.'

'Oh, I see what you mean. I never thought of that. Well, I suppose . . . You do know he's on a dialysis machine. We never expected him to come.'

'Yes,' said Bristow firmly. Like many journalists, he didn't like to admit ignorance. 'Still, the visit hasn't been the greatest success, has it?'

'Depends how you look at it.' I spoke quickly. 'If you seriously expected that in six days a UK prime minister could forge a breakthrough on arms control and secure the peace of Europe for a generation, you have to be a little disappointed. Actually, we're rather chuffed – and not just about the cooperation agreements. Moscow . . . ' I broke off.

Bristow was now trying to find something else, but he turned half-round to face me. 'Go on, Richard, tell me. I'll treat it as off-the-record.'

'Oh all right. It's more sentiment than substance – and that's what matters in diplomacy. Who cares about wheat and student exchanges.' I paused again. 'Did you by any chance meet General Bezukhov?'

'Mmmm.' Bristow did not like to admit not knowing anybody.

'For God's sake, don't use his name or mine, or I'll never speak to you again. He came up to me, after the first round in the Kremlin, and said, quite without prompting, that despite the whole Trident question, he was impressed. We were talking English. He said he was impressed by the prime minister's . . . by the prime minister's . . . '

Bristow disappeared into a booth, and a curtain was drawn behind him. I heard the clatter of things falling to the ground: coins mostly and something heavy, perhaps a cigarette lighter.

'Intenseness,' I said loudly so he could hear. 'That was the word he used. Intensity, really.'

I showed my passport and sidestepped the booth. On the

other side, Bristow had a pen out and he was writing on his cigarette packet.

I felt hot and tired, though it was not yet eight in the morning.

Soon after the Soviet trip, I left Number 10 and went into PR. I kept meaning to go back to Kiev, to see the city. Then Chernobyl happened, and it became impossible.

EDDIE READS THE CARDS

PATRICIA FERGUSON

PATRICIA FERGUSON

Patricia Ferguson took an Arts degree at Leeds University, and trained as a nurse and midwife at a London hospital. Her first novel, *Family Myths and Legends*, won the Somerset Maugham award. Patricia Ferguson is single and lives in London.

'I'LL TELL YOU what I'll do,' said Eddie. He was sitting on the carpet at my feet, drinking champagne from a tooth-glass. 'I'll read the cards for you.'

I was pleased for an instant. Once a woman had read my palm, in a booth on the front at Brighton, and told me I'd make a good florist. I'd upped and bought two pot-plants on the strength of it, but neither had lived for long.

'You buy a pack of cards tonight. Godda be a noo pack, OK?'

'Tonight?' I laughed. 'At this time of night?'

'Seven-eleven. You go past one, don't you?' Eddie shrugged. 'No problem.'

I thought of myself drawing up to the brilliant shop in the darkness, my car's headlights reflecting in the window like an animal's eyes at night. I felt shaky.

'I don't know if I want you to read them,' I said.

'Suits me. Whatever you want, baby' Eddie began to sing, some flattened snatch he'd murmured in my ear when we were dancing downstairs in the bar. 'Whatever you want, baby, tell me and I'll do it, baby, do it baby . . .'

I looked at his wife. She was sitting next to me on the bed.

'OK, he's *really* good!' she cried, widening her eyes for emphasis, 'he's *really* good. That guy over in Fremont . . .'

'That was wild.'

'. . . it all came true, all of it! Everything Eddie said! I asked him to read mine, but he wouldn't,' she finished proudly.

'No, no,' Eddie slowly shook his head. He often made slow gestures. 'Wouldn't read yours, ma'am. Would *not*. Too close. Too close to ya –'

'Yeah, we're too close!' Sally broke in. She often interrupted him. Perhaps the slow manly gestures get to her too, I thought. 'And I mean, suppose he saw us getting a divorce or something – oh, sorry!' She clapped both hands to her mouth and looked at me over them, stricken. 'Ooh, I *am* sorry –'

'That's OK,' I said. Sally was a bouncing sort of girl. Sometimes it was hard to remember that she was grown up, a married woman. But she meant well, of course. They both meant well, surely.

God knows I can't stand either of them, I thought in a sudden painful spasm of honesty, but the weekend's nearly over and they both mean well.

Sally had called me on the previous Thursday, all boisterous compassion, like a jolly young ward sister. Unstoppable. I had tried, feebly, to plead weather. 'Oh, but I couldn't possibly let you come down now, I mean you just can't, there's so much snow, there's drifts, blizzards, it's terrible.'

'No problem!' Sally had bawled back. 'We got a noo truck, a four-wheel drive, hey! Got sicka the ol' gas-guzzler. We figured, money on the line, right? Move with the groove, hey?'

I hadn't the energy to come up with something else to put her off. Besides, I was bothered by some half-remembered idea that, after an initial failure, further excuses never convince, but simply make lies or evasion insultingly obvious.

Sally rattled on. I just held on to the receiver and listened. She was pleased and excited; so there were no English sounds left in her voice at all.

Sally was Stephen's cousin; he was her only blood-relation in this foreign Canadian land, as Sally was fond of pointing out. Their families had been close, and they had grown up together.

Poor Sally, I had thought, on first meeting her; poor Sally, living all her life with the smart of Stephen's effortless superiority. Stephen always won. Play Monopoly, play chess, play A-levels, play careers – Stephen always won.

Except that he'd married me.

'She's still a child somehow,' he'd told me, as we'd journeyed East on our first visit. We had bought a big blue Chevrolet in Edmonton. Stephen drove it lovingly. 'Always young for her age. Used to drive me nuts.'

The highway was so straight for so long that, far ahead, perhaps ten or fifteen miles away, its parallel edges narrowed and converged. I could see more sky than I was used to, it met the flat horizon all around like a tight-fitting lid on a casserole dish, an enclosing, circular immensity. Sealed in, we drove at infinity, chatting.

'So she fled the country . . .'

'Yes. Stepped off the plane and straight into this Eddie-bloke's arms. Course I don't know what he's like, I've never met him, 'cept he's English, too – well, first generation Canadian anyway.'

Sally and Eddie had no address. They lived so far from anywhere that the gravel road beside their house had no name, no number. The house, set back a little from the road at the end of a rutted mud driveway, was also anonymous. One front window was broken, and a sheet of plastic flapped and glittered over it in the mild summer wind. Two rusting, wheel-less cars squatted beside the house like a pair of enormous dozing hens. In front an ancient, green pick-up truck stood in for a porch, and a strange scattering of objects lay along the path among the bushy weeds: a rotovator, its little buttock-shaped seat split open, showing a broad yellow grin of padding; a large formica wardrobe, on its back with its doors shut and its small brass feet in the air; two hula-hoops; a wooden mallet, two rusty spades, and the spiky remains of a dog-basket.

'Jesus,' said Stephen, turning off the ignition.

We climbed out and picked our way through the thistles and the pink Alberta roses, to the side of the house, where Sally already stood, bouncing up and down on her toes with happy excitement and waving a wet wooden spoon. Something dripped from it on to Stephen's shirt as he kissed her.

'– and this is Eddie!'

Tall, fattish; a soft, bespectacled face beneath the regulation cowboy hat-brim.

'This is the part I like!' said Eddie, hugging me. He lifted me from the ground. 'Hey, you lucky guy!' said Eddie to Stephen, setting me down again but squeezing me about the waist with one arm.

'Don't mind him,' cried Sally, briefly English again and all smiles, 'he's awful!'

He most certainly is, I thought crossly, escaping the squeezing arm by stooping to pick up the suitcase Stephen had set down.

'Hey, she's not a women's libber, is she? You give me that!'

He took the suitcase from me. It was very heavy. He swung it.

'Man's job, ma'am.' He reached up and tipped the cowboy hat forward with a gesture I recognised from a hundred Westerns. I watched him as he strode easily – yes, I thought, he's definitely using the Easy Stride – towards the house, past the dozing cars, through the knee-high thistles. Was he guying himself? And if he wasn't, what sort of person was he, and what was a whole week with him going to feel like?

'He's neurotic,' I whispered to Stephen in our damp, cold bedroom four days later. A coyote howled outside in the dreadful prairie dark and homesickness warmed my eyes.

'What, who, Eddie?'

'Yes, don't you think?'

'Ah, get away,' said Stephen mildly. 'He's all right.'

'No, he's not. He's not all right. I mean, this act, this macho act of his – it's so unsubtle! I mean, how can it take even him in, let alone you and me! All that stuff about how tough he is, and the great big guys he's beaten up; and he saw my camera, the first thing he said was, "Now wait a minute, hey wait a minute" – you know how he says that all the time – and, "I can really teach you something about these cameras," and he knew damn all! And teaching you to shoot when you outshot him, he missed every time, I thought I'd die.'

Stephen laughed.

'And always the handyman,' I whispered on. 'All those plans for the acreage, and the house falling down round his ears!' I enjoyed disapproving of Eddie.

'Broken windows,' conceded Stephen. 'That's a bit much, I suppose.'

'It's crazy. And the frames all rotting with damp. It makes me feel uneasy somehow to see all this carelessness, all this disorder.'

'Now who sounds neurotic? He's happy-go-lucky, that's all.'

'With Sally's money.'

'It's none of our business. Just simmer down, will you? We've got three more days here yet.'

'It's easy for you, you're a man. He's so patronising to me, he's such a creep! I hate it when he pays me all those compliments. I bit into an apple today, just an apple! And he says, "Oh Gahd, was that sensual, what a sensual lady!"'

Stephen giggled.

'No, Sally was there. He said it to upset her, to make her jealous.'

'He was joking, that's all.'

'I don't think so. He wasn't joking.'

'Ignore him. It's not long to go.'

I was angry now, with a chill unfocused anger. 'It's all right for *you*,' I said bitterly. There was a silence, and then I heard him sigh. I knew I should be quiet. I won't speak, I thought to myself. I won't.

I said, 'I hate it here. Canada. You *knew* I wanted to stay in England. Or we could've tried America . . .' My voice quavered.

'I'm going to sleep now,' said Stephen. He had turned and lay with his back to me. 'Good-night.'

It had been a difficult week. English understatement. It had been hellish. Eddie told us stories about dreams of his that had been prophetic. He relayed to us many facts he had come across in *Reader's Digest*. He taught Stephen the rudiments of canoeing, while Stephen, who in every respect could paddle his own canoe, listened politely, with polite male indifference.

I did a lot of washing-up, chewed my fingernails, and decided that Eddie was an alcoholic.

'A fairly heavy social drinker,' said Stephen.

'An alcoholic.' I'd read the magazines; he fitted all the criteria.

Eddie liked to make little jokes about his drinking. ('. . . An ol' alcafrolic like me.') He ate very little, but drank breakfast, drank lunch and drank supper. Never seen to touch fruit, vegetables, or good bread, he would sit at the rickety table Sally was one day going to mend and re-finish, forking very hot pickles out of the jar, throwing them all alone into his poor empty stomach.

On subsequent visits ('She is my *cousin*, you know,' Stephen would stolidly remark, his hand over the telephone mouthpiece, while I mimed fierce negatives in response to Sally's latest invitation), I began to feel rather sorry for Eddie's stomach, as if it were a live and separate creature, while Eddie tormented it with big bleeding T-bones and sauces made by mixing several types of ready-bottleds together in a basin: Thousand Island, French dressing, tomato ketchup, all with a good slug of malt vinegar to sharpen things up. During the day he drank beer; at night, rye-and-coke.

'He just eats like a bird,' Sally would proudly lament.

'Ain't got much appetite. Never have. Never eat breakfast.'

I had noticed before that people who never eat breakfast are often proud of the fact, and like to say, in so many words, Oh, I never eat breakfast, as if this were a minor but definite virtue on a par with never forgetting one's mother's birthday or keeping library books out too long.

'Nope, I never eat breakfast,' Eddie would say, patting his beer-gut and very slowly shaking his head.

Did I glare at him, over my plate? Did my undisciplined eyes shout, *Phoney!*

Of course I did, of course they did. I thought I understood Eddie, saw through his illusions, when he could not. And so I despised him, though without much pleasure; he made me feel too anxious on my own account. If I could so easily kick aside poor Eddie's defences, how sturdy were my own particular barricades? Were they as cleverly disguised as I'd thought? Might I be someone else's Eddie? Stephen's, perhaps?

It was no use trying to explain all this to Stephen, whose armour might have been Achilles' own for all the breaches I could make in it.

'Why d'you let him *get* to you so much? Poor sod's just boring that's all. He's not so bad . . .'

Well, he was, Stephen. Eddie suspected that I suspected. If I gave him proof, he might then want revenge. Not that I realised this, of course, when Sally called me that Thursday. Grief had made me stupid.

They'd arrived in town on Friday night. On Saturday morning, at Sally's invitation, I had gone to breakfast at their hotel, the priciest in the city despite the new four-wheel drive and the still unmended windows and the mortgage.

'I feel,' said Eddie over his second Molson Light. 'I feel that you are blaming yourself.' He looked into my watery eyes. 'I feel that you're blaming yourself, and I say, "Hey! wait a minute! Hey wait, these things take two." It's his fault, it's your fault, it's no one's fault. No one's. Hey, it's not your fault.'

I saw real kindness in him then, and self-reproach filled my eyes still further.

'And you know,' said Sally in a low voice, 'do you know, of the two of you, I'd a thought, if anyone got someone noo, it was gonna be you, y'know?'

I was rather pleased at this. I didn't know then that people always say this to comfort abandoned wives. I wiped my eyes.

'We just wanna help you,' said Sally in a whisper.

And you want to try out your new four-wheel drive, I thought – a piece of wickedness that worked better than any Kleenex.

'Hey, you know we love you,' said Eddie.

Well I don't love you, I wanted to snap back smartly. You're here because you can't accept that you dislike me, because disliking me doesn't fit in with one of your dopey self-images, and I want you to go away right now, right now, right now . . .

After breakfast Sally and I went shopping while Eddie settled down to some serious weekend drinking. Sally bought Marks and Spencers underwear, imported English biscuits, a bright new leotard for her aerobic dancing and a pair of glittering diamante earrings. She was starved for shops where she lived. She talked happily all the time. I dragged along beside her feeling as light and chatty as a dinosaur. The shopping mall was stuffy and over-heated. My head ached. I thought of all the times I had been there with Stephen. Stephen had gone. Seen through me, perhaps. I had not seen through her, that Other Woman, who had seemed to be my friend. I thought about arson, of

punching Stephen on the nose, of screaming myself hoarse. I
was afraid. Could unhappiness, mere misery, drive you mad?

'Say hey, wait a minute. Looking beautiful, baby, you are one
beautiful chick you know that?'

Saturday night. We were in the bar of the priciest hotel. A
rock group were playing. They were young, British, outlandish.
Sally scoffed at their clothes. I felt that she and I, washing up
on the tide of our twenties, looked dull and dowdy. I remembered
how I had felt about the tired-looking thirty-ish, when I was
twenty and pretty. Though I'd thought myself bowed down then
with cares.

'Hey wait a minute, baby, let's boogy!'

I felt old and churlish, too old even to be irritated. I said
gently, 'I don't really want to dance. Thank you.'

'C'mon, do you good!'

Sally was raising her eyebrows, nodding me her permission.

'Go on,' she yelled encouragingly over the roar of the syn-
thesizers as if she thought shyness held me back. 'Go on!'

One dance, I thought fretfully. Give the man his pound of
flesh. I stood up and managed a smile.

What am I doing here in Canada, alone all alone!

Eddie took my hand as we made our way to the dance floor.
His hand was very soft, softer than my own, rather a shock.
Almost as soon as we reached the floor the song finished with
a crashing drumroll and the band began a new slow number.

'Smoochy,' said Eddie, and took me in his arms. He pulled
me close. I smelt his after-shave, very sweet. I felt him against
me, all the way down, and I was afraid. It felt like fear, anyway.
Sexual fear. Twenty-eight years old and I was afraid I would
feel a penis stiffened against me. I concentrated. Oh, could I
feel it? I was afraid. I grew cunning; I put my arms round him,
hugged him as if in friendship, a big friendly hug, one teddy-bear
to another, and pulled away.

But he pulled me back and kissed my cheek, softly, his lips
very soft. I felt all the unbearable falseness of our position: here
was a man who did not desire me at all, whose strongest feeling
for me, I knew, was an understandable dislike, and whom I

deeply disliked in return. Yet here he was, nuzzling my cheek with every appearance of sexual affection; because that was how, in Eddie's book, you behaved towards women, particularly towards single women.

He held me very tightly. 'It's all for you,' he whispered in my ear, 'it's all for you.'

I began to fear that the strength of his illusion would so overwhelm him that he would go further, make an overt sign or statement.

I looked round wildly at the dark, crowded bar, at the other couples, up at the ceiling, pretending to be interested in what I saw, pretending to be cool.

'C'mon.'

His breath warmed my ear. How could he not feel my distress? Perhaps he did feel it, misinterpreted it as guilty lust? The indignant reaction of my own mind to this new thought at last freed my paralysed courage.

'No. I want to sit down.'

'Hey wait a minute –'

'No, I . . .' I resorted, coward still, to lies. Suppose I'd got it all wrong, I who, completely in the dark, had gone on inviting the Other Woman to dinner parties? Suppose he'd just been being friendly after all, just a nice chap who'd be all aghast at my demented spinsterish fears? I couldn't risk him pretending to be like that, as he possibly would if I made my revulsion plain. He'd have to make some defence anyway. Best not to provoke him too far.

'. . . it's making me feel worse,' I said. 'That Stephen's not here. Please. I just want to sit down, I'm sorry.'

Back with Sally I recognised that, if I'd been less polite to her over the telephone on Thursday, I would not now have found myself delivering this far more personal insult to her husband. And I had insulted him. Why else would I be trembling with guilt and confusion?

'We go?' said Eddie, knocking back his latest double and abruptly standing.

'What, already?' asked Sally, disappointed, but gathering up her handbag. 'Oh, Eddie –'

Escape! But I had to go back to their hotel room to pick up my coat. And there was the champagne Eddie had ordered, neat in its ice-bucket.

'We have champagne every night when we're in the city!' cried Sally, cheering up at once, and she gave me a glass.

I would have preferred a cup of tea, like an accident victim. I downed my drink with difficulty. I seemed to have given up making choices, though at the same time felt I was being strong, taking my punishment. I had let this dreadful couple come and take me over. It was all my own fault. I drank my fizz like medicine. Let this be a lesson to you, I scolded.

Eddie sat down on the carpet, wearing one of his range of vaguely-aggrieved expressions.

'Not too cool,' he said over his tooth-glass of champagne.

I remembered that he habitually complained about service, as if he expected the Ritz even at Smitty's. I remembered looking hard out of windows while Eddie berated the waitress; and how, in more expensive restaurants, he would always send something back: the snails were burnt, the sole was off, the wine was just terrible.

'Not too cool.'

There. I thought to myself, comforted. He's just the same. I haven't done him any harm. He's all right.

'I'll tell you what I'll do,' said Eddie. 'I'll read the cards for you.'

They came round at about ten the next morning to the basement apartment I'd rented. It was the first one I'd looked at. The landlord and his wife lived in the house above me. More than once I heard them arguing, like ancient deities squabbling in the heavens.

My landlord had nailed the windows of the flat shut to conserve heat, which was provided by a gas central heating system that exploded into life every forty-five minutes or so with a fierce muffled *whump*.

There was a big colour television in my sitting room. I left it on most of the time. I had told no one at work about Stephen because I had found that any gesture of sympathy from anyone

I liked made me burst into tears. So at work, I acted Myself-Before-Losing-Stephen. At home in my basement I lay on the floor while the television talked and laughed and sang: *That's Incredible, MASH, Hill Street Blues, Two's Company*. Whatever was on, I watched it. Sometimes I put my face to the floor and, if the programme was noisy enough, cried loudly into the carpet. Sometimes I curled up and rocked myself to and fro as I cried. Mostly I just watched television.

Sally and Eddie arrived. They looked a little unreal in my dark basement: oversized, somehow. They seemed to fill the place up between them.

'Would you happen, ma'am, to have anything like a beer in this here apartment?'

'In the fridge, help yourself.'

I cooked Sally some breakfast. I had eaten already, I told them. I was lying.

'You buy those cards now?'

'Well, yes I did, actually.' God only knows why, I thought to myself. Lying again. Not quite the truth anyway. I knew too.

'Open?'

'No. Here.' I gave him the pack of cards, still in cellophane. The Seven-eleven had sold two kinds. From superstition I had bought the dearest.

Sally put her plate in the sink, and came back to sit down.

Eddie closed his eyes, the cards between his soft pale hands. 'I ah have to get into this.'

Sally winked at me. I was so surprised that I blushed. I knew why I had bought the cards: I wanted the future revealed. Then I could begin to deal with the present. It was simple. If I knew whether I could get Stephen back or not (I pronounced the 'or not' very quickly and lightly to myself, a mental whisper) I would be released from my present gaol-sentence of grief. At least, I thought I would have some idea of how long my stretch was going to be.

Sally winked at me, and I felt relieved and undermined all at once. If it was nice, the future, I would believe it; if it wasn't what I wanted I would scoff. So I told myself. The central heating made its exclamation: *Whump*.

Eddie began to spread the cards out in an intricate fan shape, some face-down, others face-up. Sometimes he hesitated. He was, I thought, trying to remember the instructions from some paperback he'd skimmed through, beer bottle in one hand, book in the other.

So I jeered, inwardly; and trembled, longing to know the future; and remembered the night before, that I was atoning for something.

There he sat, my undeclared enemy, loading the machine gun I had put into his hands.

'Well, lemme see now. Uh-huh.' Eddie slowly shook his head. 'Well. I'm sorry. I'm real sorry about this.'

'About what?'

'This here.' He pointed at a group of four cards on his left.

Charlatan, I thought, holding my breath.

'I think you two are . . . Well, I'm sorry. A divorce, that's certain. I'm real sorry.'

'Oh.'

'No doubt about it.'

Charlatan, charlatan.

'Shall I go on?'

'Oh. Why not?'

'This here. Family discord. Ten, twelve years ago? That's what I'm seeing. That so? Something about your brother, that's what I feel.'

I was silent, racking my brains to discover whether I had ever told him about the disastrous winter long before when my brother had dropped out of university, and gone to live in a squat, and got himself done for shop-lifting and possession; for the sort of scene that had followed this series of disclosures, family discord seemed hardly the phrase.

'Twelve years ago, something like that, am I right?'

'Yes.' I told you, I must've done. Or Stephen did.

'All over now though.'

I nodded. Perhaps I had told Sally during one of our chatty washings-up.

'Still you want to watch out here.'

'Oh?'

'Yup. This here. This knave. You could have a whole lot of problems with your father. Yeah. He could turn against you. You gotta be careful.'

Sally was puzzled. 'You said that was a love affair before. To the man in Fremont.'

Eddie blinked. 'No . . . no. That was then. It's what the cards say to me now, yeah? This is psychic. This is what it's all about.'

'I've never had any arguments with my father.'

'Well you sure could now. It's a warning, hey? But this. This here's a warning too. This is you here, see?' He made a concerned face. 'You are gonna be *ill* if you carry on this way. I mean, you are really suffering, and it's more than you can stand. You could be ill, yeah, like, *mentally*!'

I folded my arms. Man the barricades! But it was far too late. There seemed to be nothing behind them to defend. The twitch of outrage ceased. I sat and listened.

'Real sickness. See, here you could be travelling. A long way away. A long way. Maybe – I hope you don't mind me saying this – maybe an affair here. With a much older man. Yup, *much* older. Sheesh, I'm real sorry about this. There's not really anything, I mean, it's not my fault, OK? I'm just reading what's here, and there's not much that's nice about it, but you know, I could be wrong . . .'

'Are you all right?' asked Sally.

I shrugged. I felt fine, all things considered; there was nowhere lower to go.

Eddie collected the cards together very carefully.

'I could lay 'em out again, see if we get a better reading?'

'Ah . . . no, thank you.' There. It had been easy. No, thank you.

'Are you sure you're all right? Ed, I feel terrible, we've made things worse.'

'No, no. I'm OK, really.'

'Don't you use those cards for anything, now,' said Eddie. 'That's bad karma. Don't throw them, but don't use them.'

'Right.'

'Zit eleven already? 'Cos we ought to be hitting the road, get back before nightfall . . .'

'Of course.'

I rose. We all stood, making goodbye-noises like normal people.

'I'm real sorry about how it turned out, I feel real bad about it, wish I'd never read the damn things.'

'I wanted you to.'

'Yes,' said Eddie. His eyes held no meaning.

I remembered that I would never have to see either of them again, and this gave me the strength to see them off. I stood in the snow waving at the new four-wheel drive. Eddie was wearing his cowboy hat as he sat behind the wheel.

I watched until they turned the corner. The daylight was yellow with snow ahead. I looked down at the footprints beside my own and at the truck's wheelmarks. Then I went back inside, and put the television on, and lay down in front of it.

After a long time the telephone rang. I got up quickly in case it was Stephen and felt so dizzy that I knocked my shoulder against the door-jamb as I reached the kitchen.

'Hello?'

'Hi, is Peter there?' No voice I knew.

'Ah, wrong number.'

'Sorry.'

I hung up, sat down on the floor beside the telephone and took some deep breaths. The television suddenly irritated me so I got up and turned the set off. I sat down on the sofa.

It was very quiet then. I heard a car swish by outside, and twice the central heating switched itself on again but apart from that it was very quiet. I was wondering what I was feeling.

'I must think,' I said aloud, but no revelation, other than that I was rather hungry, arrived. I got up again and made some toast, and ate it with only a touch of nausea. Then I put my padded snowsuit on and went outside.

It was getting dark. Fresh snow was falling, and I walked up the street listening to the dry familiar creak it made underfoot: just like the sound the new filling makes, I decided, as the dentist rams it down tight. I felt rather cheerful; peaceful, if a bit weak. The fever of my grief seemed to be gone, as if Eddie, setting out to harm me, had instead applied a successful cautery. At any rate he had given me something else to think about.

I thought about him, poor daft boring Eddie. I remembered Sally, confiding over the washing-up, voice low:

'His dad. Right sod. Used to beat him up. And his mother too, he used to beat her up, put her in hospital. I've met him and I don't like him much. Eddie sort of does, know what I mean?'

It was your father, wasn't it, Eddie? Your father always against you, not mine against me. Was all the rest of it yours as well?

I saw him, Eddie in his cowboy hat, icon of my homesickness. Eddie on the great converging snowy highways, genuinely sorry for the pain the cards had caused me. He would need, perhaps, a little more rye-and-coke than usual to send him off to sleep that night. Eddie had no insight into himself, and thus no shame – nothing so small.

For a moment I stood still in the snow, and made myself Eddie, to taste properly the all-pervasive numbing blur of his disappointments, his dis-ease. Poor Eddie; for that great hopeless unnamable wound, apply beer, rye whisky, and the cold scour of vinegar. Only the healthy can afford to use insight.

Which I still can, I decided, hopping from foot to foot in the clean lovely snow. Which I still can. My pains for now are finite; Eddie's are his life. I've been lucky, I thought.

I walked on to the next lamp-post, and stopped to admire its misty blue halo. Perhaps I would go to California, let bloody Stephen stew in his own chilly juice. He wanted the frozen North, let him keep it. I smiled to myself. I would go to California and see the orange trees.

It was about minus ten, and I was beginning to feel cold, despite the snowsuit. So I went home and made myself some scrambled eggs. Then I took out Eddie's cards, and played a few games of Patience with them, before I went to bed. I even made it come out, once. But then, I've always been rather lucky at cards.

TRIO

RONALD FRAME

RONALD FRAME

Ronald Frame was born in 1953 in Glasgow, and educated there and at Oxford. He was joint-winner of the first Betty Trask Prize for fiction; he has also won the Samuel Beckett Prize and PYE's 'Most Promising Writer New To Television' award. His seventh book, a novel called *Penelope's Hat*, will be published in spring, 1989.

SHE LIFTED HER arm and waved. He shaded his eyes, as if he'd only just noticed, and smiled to her across the surface of the swimming pool.

She was wearing her black swimsuit. When she'd shown it to him, he'd said very nice, but he'd thought it a perverse colour for summer. He hadn't known what *she* did, how good it would look against the tan on her legs and arms. It was cut low on top and high at the hips and darkly suggested at the parts that were hidden.

He watched her as she stepped up on to the board. She straightened herself to her full height, and waited till she had her balance. Then she raised her arms and held them out rigid in front of her, hands angled. She calculated, pushed up on to her toes, bent at the knees, bent a second time to give herself full lift, caught the board's momentum, and entered into the dive.

She fell in a graceful, flawless, architectural arc. Her hands and arms broke the surface, cleaved it, and her head and torso and legs dropped into the water in perfect, ordered sequence.

What could better suit the perfectly ordered sequence of their lives?

He continued to look as she stretched out beneath the water. She could hold her breath for longer than he could, and moved like someone possessing another element for herself. Reflections from the surface rippled across her, distorted her, she shattered like an image in flawed glass. Through the colours of sky and cloud and green tiles she changed form from second to second, she changed substance, from meat to sinew to fish to bone to fin, and only back to the human he recognised when the head reappeared, her face.

She shook off the water, smiling, blinking at him where he sat in the glare of the sun. Then she flipped on to her back, somersaulted, and was gone again, with a deceptively simple flick of her feet that would steer her in the direction she meant to take. Again she was stretched, squeezed, elongated, she blurred, she had three heads, then several waists and disappearing legs, then she changed again – she must have been on her side, or twisting round on to her back – and for several seconds she was no person he could identify. The water was speckled with white flares of light, spreading arabesques of violet in the blue green. The bottom of the pool was ribbed like soft turquoise chamois. He thought he could just sit there and be endlessly fascinated by those shifting suggestions of patterns, by his wife's metamorphoses and disappearances.

'Well . . .?' Her voice called to him through the shudder of a splash. 'Are you coming in?' The water frothed.

He shaded his eyes. He smiled, and shook his head. She belonged in the water by herself: he had no claim on it. But she knew that anyway, maybe the question was only to remind him, to goad.

'No?'

She laughed. She balanced like a tilted embryo, with her back curved. Her legs rose in front of her, her knees and toes floated up from beneath. Her hands paddled, her ankles flexed.

She continued to smile, in the full brilliance of sunlight. He knew she wasn't expecting any other answer. He couldn't swim like her, and she would have danced porpoise circles round him.

She disappeared again, she sank through a hole, and only bubbles were left behind, like a snorkel diver's.

She returned to her element; she was escaping him, smooth and slippery and dissolving from the familiar, what he knew and could recognise, or so he imagined, into her other capricious refugee self.

2

It's dark when he leaves her and the streets are shiny wet. Figures hurry for the doors of apartment buildings, to get out of the rain; the cabs all have fares, a broken umbrella lies in a gutter.

He drives along Columbus. She has told him her 'ex' inhabits some of the singles bars, certain nights. How come she knows that? Is it just from hearsay, or does she do her own line in private investigations? He tries not to mention Don now that he's wifeless, unhooked and thrown back into the West Side pond. But it might just clear the air some if he did, and it might rid them of a subject he always feels is there, at a level beneath.

He makes for Lincoln Square, past the cafés. Then turns into Broadway and joins the slow crawl of traffic towards Columbus Circle.

Headlights dazzle through the rain runs on the windshield. The whole of New York is on the move, East to West, West to East. Hands smack irritably at klaxons. Pedestrians bad-mouth back, and maybe with justification, because the night's too lousy for jay-walking; it's just that the green turns to red, Walk to Don't Walk, too soon, or the green doesn't come on quickly enough.

They'd gone to the little counter bar at the front of the Blini: officially – so he'd told Ann – he was meeting a client, a man from Peru. Then he'd driven Teresa back along Amsterdam to drop her off at her apartment. She'd said, 'Come up, just for a while.' At the moment she said it a car drew away from the kerb and he turned the wheel, nursing the grille into the space.

Upstairs she made them both drinks. She asked him how he'd eat when he got back and he said he'd probably fix himself a sandwich, or Ann might offer to do it for him.

'Is that all?'

It sounded like a criticism of Ann, although she very seldom made them. Or maybe he was just becoming too sensitive, imagining barbs where there weren't any.

'No, it's OK,' he told her. 'For some reason, the later it is the less hungry I get.'

'Even so . . .'

She opened the refrigerator door and looked inside.

'Scrambled eggs,' she said. 'I've never made you scrambled eggs . . .'

'No, just a drink, really.'

'David!'

'I'll be fine . . .'

'But you haven't had *my* scrambled eggs. Have you, ever?'

He shook his head. She took a plate from a shelf and peeled off the covering cling-wrap.

'There! My secret ingredient!'

'What is it?'

'Smoked salmon. End-cuts, I hasten to add . . .'

'Really, I should be heading back . . .'

'. . . heading on out there?' Her voice mock-drawled. 'To stockade country?'

'What?'

Her voice reverted. '*When* you've eaten, David. I'm not sending you back with nothing,' she said, and laughed.

She was different tonight, he realised. She was in charge of him. She was caring for him. Caring with a capital C. Somehow he felt less comfortable with her like this, not more so. Eating hadn't properly mattered before. They'd only done it when they happened to be hungry. They *had* eaten here in the kitchen, but usually it was outside, in a restaurant: a drink followed by a main dish. It wasn't any big deal to them what it was; they were only there to have a different spotlight shine on them, to see themselves anew.

Now they had no soft music, no surrounding chatter, no waiters' enquiries, no faces passing the window. The heat was already under the pan, the melting butter sizzled. In Ann's kitchen there was always noise: the children, the small-screen TV, the arcane plumbing that hadn't changed much since the building was a millionaire bootlegger's town-house.

'How did you learn about this?' he asked her, nodding at the smoked salmon, diced beforehand as if she had been anticipating the use they would put it to.

She hesitated momentarily.

'Actually – it was Don who taught me.'

He nodded. Wrong question, wrong answer. He didn't discuss Don with her, as a rule.

With the pan handle in her grip she smiled at him, maybe too brightly.

She turned the pan in readiness, then she reached for the bowl on the counter top.

And that's when it happened, as she stood by the cooker plates still smiling.

On TV, chefs split the egg with a single decisive crack against the rim of the bowl, deftly parted the halves of the shell with their fingers spread like a claw and let the contents slip-slide out, all achieved in two or three seconds and using only one hand.

But that wasn't her way. With the egg held in the palm of her left hand she worked a crack round the waist of the egg with one of the outer tines of the fork, held in her right. She proceeded not slowly but very, very carefully. With a round almost completed, she left a flap, a hinge of shell, and – with sudden and almost subliminal speed – she tucked the fork between the thumb and index finger of her right hand and started to ease apart, gradually, the two hemispheres of shell with the fingers of her left *and* right hands.

He was so used to seeing it happen that he wasn't aware for several seconds that it had. *Ann broke eggs in exactly the same way.* Ann also held the egg in her left hand and tap-tap-tapped around the middle with the tines of the fork until there was only a very little shell, the vital margin, left untouched. She would balance the fork in the clutch of her right hand, narrowest point of the handle locked between thumb and forefinger, and then she would – gradually – draw the halves of the shell apart with the fingers of both hands. The yolk would drop whole and clean into the centre of the bowl and the white would fall after it.

A third egg followed the second. Tap-tap-tap. Tap. Her brow furrowed with concentration. Once Ann's might have done the same, but she had served them up scrambled eggs and omelettes hundreds of times. She fried eggs and poached them and

baked them in ramekins; she made pastry for her family when
visiting; she cooked rich winter puddings, she separated eggs for
meringues and pavlovas; she strained single yolks into advocaat.

At first his time with Teresa had seemed unreal to him – a happy
dream. A cliché time. The green door/a secret garden. The East
Side by comparison was so desperately real and actual, coming
in on him from so many angles when really he was thinking only
of his next escape. He'd tell himself, I could leave this, walk out
for longer, for keeps, and it would continue just so without me.
Ann would have known very well how to cope alone and he could
have left for the other side of the Park, for Columbus and
Amsterdam, for everything that being at home was not.

Six months later, a curious and unexpected shift had taken
place in his sensibilities. Life with Ann had become hazy, elusive
to him in a different way. Instead it was with Teresa that he
sometimes came to feel he was going through the motions.
Being with her it would happen that he'd fall prey to a sense of
purposelessness, a puritan instinct from his family's past perhaps, as if all it was in the end was ego-gratification. Returning
to the routine with Ann and the children was how he re-estab-
lished his 'function' in full. Maybe with Teresa there was now
too much time to think, when he hadn't been able to before, and
it was unfortunate that her apartment orientated east, Park-side,
instead of west, Hudson-wards. Bit by bit being with Teresa
had become the routine while being at home he would find
himself forgetting where certain toys were put away or on which
shelf of the pantry they kept the Wendell's tea for when Ann's
Anglophile great-aunt came calling. At Teresa's he knew exactly
where to locate his toothbrush, his towel, his Braun, the hand-
painted bow-tie for evenings (her present to him), his shoe
stretchers (for when it rained). Also where to look for a change
of underwear. This last had been Teresa's suggestion – a
sensible one, but wasn't it maybe *too* clear-sighted, as if she
was viewing the situation with a detective's eye?

Reality had become a lot less sure with Ann, and (perversely?)
more interesting to him, semi-familiar and semi-mysterious: an
evening alone together now seemed full of changes and surprises

and not unpleasant ones – phonecalls, rings on the doorbell, people dropping in, something they both suddenly remembered out of the past, cooking smells, oven alarms, the children's latest drawings tacked to the cork board on the kitchen wall and inviting his comments.

At the beginning, in Teresa's apartment, they'd danced in the dark, slow dancing, to forties and fifties torch songs. Now the two of them went out, they danced in the anonymity of public places, on small floors, to Whitney Houston when she sang soul ballads. The East Side seemed the stronger, more exotic dimension in his life whenever he went back to that complex ritual of marriage and fatherhood: a bizarre, awesome harmony ultimately prevailed, all the pieces would somehow fall, beautifully and naturally, into place, and the effect was like – like, he'd decided, handling a good piece of furniture or a fine piece of luggage, the maker's confidence is practical and sure but you sense it's generations old, here's the impersonal wisdom and meetness of time and custom. More than once or twice it had occurred to him that Anita Baker in quadrophonic, in the ultra-violet glow, was – dangerously – very nearly beside the point, even with Teresa's knee wedged in intimate, proprietorial contact between his trouser thighs.

On Central Park South he passes the crossing with Fifth. He looks over at the Plaza fountain, blowing in a wind. Beyond it the Pierre's sheer frontage is lit like some colossal mathematical rubic cube.

He turns into Madison. Another four or five blocks on and he sees the signs for the Zoo. He hasn't been back there with the children since the renovation work was finished. Maybe this weekend they'll go. Cages with or without metal bars have always unsettled him, but he guesses, if that's all you've ever been used to . . . He'll take them to the sea-lion pond and they can watch the tricks and overlook the real art of the spectacle, which is as a sleight of mind: forgetting how it's come about that sea-lions got to the very middle of a city in the first place.

He turned off parallel to the Frick, and drove for several blocks. Past Third, with home still not in his sights, a car revved out of a parking space just ahead of him. On the spur of the moment he spun the wheel and moved into the kerb.

He eased his feet off the pedals and turned the key back in the ignition lock.

The sidewalks were quiet and pale under the streetlights. Twice he'd come this far and then he'd driven all the way back again, round the Park. Jealousy had made him do it, stopping across the street from her building and watching for movements in her lit rooms. Jealousy, and restlessness, and loneliness maybe, and guilt, and the craziness of intrigue, and desire worse than any ache, like cramping nausea. His gut and his head had been in collusive tandem, and there hadn't seemed to be any choosing between them. Nobody – not Ann, none of the children – could have helped him then.

Tonight the bare trees caught a west draught from the Park and some last leaves fell. Red creeper on a housefront shivered and made the house look haunted.

He crossed his wrists on the driving-wheel. He looked in the mirror. Under the streetlights his skin was pallid.

Another time he'd been coming back, another night of the Hudson cold and having to plan a new alibi for Ann, when the wind worked loose a length of white plastic sheeting hanging from a building that was being spray-washed. He saw it starting to drop from the scaffolding, then the wind filled it like a sail before it could become entangled on railings and trees. The plastic ensign cracked like pistol-fire and rose into flight, serene and aloof and candidly white against the night sky; it spirited past penthouses and lofts like a cartoon ghost, off across First and York and (maybe) out to Queen's.

The bare trees caught a west draught from the Park and some last leaves fell. Red creeper on a housefront shivered, and the house might have been haunted.

He leaned forward, with his wrists crossed on the steering wheel.

He flicked his cuffs back and looked at his watch.

He lifted his eyes to the mirror. Under the streetlights his skin was pallid. As he had done for the past few weeks he saw through the appearance of this man, through the temporary assurances he offered, to a perplexing, disturbing vacancy. Magritte would have painted the interior of his head as a sky-scape, a view of uncoloured shifting clouds.

East Side, West Side, this was the witching hour, the phantom time, when all those who live between two lives make their ghostly passage in the smart Manhattan night. In the shining they frighten others less than fear seriously for their own sound reason, for the safety of their unhoused souls.

3

Madame Géraud is a regular guest at the Excelsior Hotel. She comes twice every year and has done so ever since her husband died, in 1965.

She is the widow of *the* Géraud. Once three of his paintings went under the hammer when Sotheby's auctioned the contents of the Comtesse de Benouville's duplex on the Avenue Foch, and there have been several other instances over the years of owners or estates selling and galleries buying. But it is common public knowledge by now, which most of the Excelsior's guests must have read in past newspaper stories, that the finest paintings were those left in Madame Géraud's possession after her husband's death. Each year she lets another one go to auction in Paris or Geneva or London, and the price on each occasion rises by at least twenty-five or thirty per cent. More recently, with the large canvases gone, she has been selling a number of the sketch books, but taking care – acting on very practical, sage advice – not to flood the market.

Hubert Géraud is now more than a French Father, he is a major European post-impressionist. This is partly as a consequence of such judicious husbandry and foreplanning. For herself and her own affairs, his widow much prefers forward thinking to the retrospective kind, whenever that is possible. She wouldn't be staying at the Excelsior with such a comparatively easy conscience if she hadn't worked so hard, systematically and unceasingly, to achieve her specific end.

On each visit she takes the same suite, which has been occupied before her by such as King Farouk, Elizabeth Taylor, Jean Jardin, Ernest Hemingway, King Zog of Albania. She believes she is entitled to the best, and quite blithely charges up the 'extras' to the Blue Suite on her account.

At home in Paris it is a different matter. There she leads a considerably more modest, self-denying existence, even though the apartment is an opulent one she moved to in the early 1970s, the middle floor of a mansion overlooking the Parc Monceau. Seventy-nine years of age, she makes do with very little domestic help, she eats frugally, wears comfortable but worn and even torn clothes when there is no one to see her; she lives in a tiny sitting room off the kitchen in winter, and cleans the bath herself rather than leave it to the Armenian maid who 'does' her few hours a week. She is very particular that the responsibility for wiping round the bath with scouring powder should be hers and hers alone.

Of course she remains for posterity the unique 'Madame G.', the one and only, to be seen in all the famous Géraud 'Bathroom' paintings: lying in a tub, crouching in it, walking to or away from, looking at, even cleaning out. Most highly regarded of the series, completed over a dozen years, are the seven or eight later studies where she's supine in the water, with her body covered, her form dissolving into streaks of graded colour, apparently as purely harmonic (according to the expert academics) as the perfect pitch of certain singers.

Frankly, she herself has never quite understood the worth of the 'Bathroom' works, either critical or financial. She married a man who painted flowers in jugs and humble pots and pans from the kitchen, objects she could recognise, but he became a man who represented human matter in (even *she* could judge) a novel, experimental, completely individual way. He told her many times that it was *she* who had – indirectly – brought about the change in him, because he had sought the 'truest' means of painting her, 'capturing your beauty on the canvas'.

She had never been a beauty in the ordinary fashion, or anything more to her own eye than wholesomely pretty. She had been compelled to take that very factual market view of herself when she watched the models her husband used in those earlier days and compared herself with them. Later he turned his attention to *her*, and she was bemused. Later still she became much less comfortable when he didn't seem able to curb his preoccupation with her everyday, common-or-garden activities.

She half-knew at the time what was happening, and was increasingly uneasy about the process: being put down on each stretched canvas as *that* woman, one with features that became less and less distinct, who began by washing clothes and ironing them when he was painting her in the house in Sarlat, who (not so recognisably *her*) progressed to reading books and tidying her hair when they moved to Paris, and who (even less identifiable as herself) ended up looking out the window – all the house's windows – and lying in the bath dissolving into streaks of colour after they made the last move, to St Paul-de-Vence in Provence. She grew to – it wasn't too strong a word – truly hate the *im*-personality of her appearance, the evolving nothingness of her function.

Her intentions for herself had been quite otherwise. She had foreseen that her life must become a development, a reaction to changes in their social circumstances. Over the years his paintings had begun to sell, and she had tried her best to mature naturally into a more sophisticated, more intelligent person. It wasn't her fault that they later became able to afford a maid, then a cook, and she had less to do in the house. To fill her time she read more, she learned languages, she cultivated tropical plants that were notoriously difficult to keep alive – but which she did keep alive. She felt he misrepresented her, as a much simpler person than she knew she was, a reduction of herself merely sitting in the sunshine or reclining in the tub in a light-dappled bathroom, looking like a beached mermaid before she became a messy, elongated streak floating above a black-and-white tiled floor.

More and more she felt she wasn't what she wanted to believe was the true, personal version of herself, but enclosed and trapped on those oblongs of canvas with no hope of release. When people were introduced to her, she was aware that they weren't looking at the person in front of them, they were seeing whoever appeared in the paintings, a woman slowly turning stage by stage to an abstraction, someone losing her individuality as her features blurred and losing her hold on herself, melting out of reality.

Now it was different. The tables were turned.

All sorts of dignitaries with fine credentials arranged to call on her in the Monceau apartment. She had been photographed for magazines and newspapers, not nude as *he* had rendered her but clothed in an expensive little something from the Avenue Montaigne or Rue Faubourg Saint-Honoré. She was described as being many things, the gamut, from 'sweet' to 'stern'. At any rate, in the photographs she had a full complement of character, all that she could put into her face. It was *her*, this was Alice Géraud née Jacquin, and no misunderstanding about it this time.

The experts, so-called, knew better than to come disturbing her *en vacances*. This was her rest-period when she lay fallow, and she would have given intruders short shrift indeed. If she'd let it, her marriage in widowhood could have become a full-time occupation, answering all the questions about their life between 1932 and 1965. 'I had a life "before" and "after"', she wished she could impress upon her interviewers: but she realised their interest in her was only in respect of her having been a famous man's wife. She answered their questions as completely as she thought she could; she was no more evasive than any other wife would have been, conscious that there were private corners, incidents which if they'd been recalled would have shown neither her nor him in a very favourable light.

Their marriage had been as reasonably successful as the general run are: or at any rate, like most wives and husbands, they had taken the highs and lows and shaken down somehow or other and survived not to tell the full tale. They had settled into habit and custom and even a certain kind of banality: a common enough fate for marriages, although when it was written up by journalists and populist scholars she couldn't quite square the affable, rose-tinted published version with what she remembered – a lot of dullness, and heel-kicking, and a good deal of truce-making. But whatever she said was largely translated into what the press or academics wanted to hear, to confirm their own preconceptions or theories. Once she had thought she was at their mercy: now, however, almost twenty-five years after his death, she was impervious to their stupidity or insipidness.

This was her true life, she believed: it became truer the longer you lived it, the more practised you became at dominating the past. This wasn't living on borrowed time, because she had never allowed herself to believe that that was finally 'her' on the canvases and that she'd had to die with her husband. Being her real self now, she was supplying a different perspective, correcting a partially true/partially false impression, re-establishing the status quo.

She didn't lift a finger at the Excelsior. She lived like an empress. The bathroom floor was patrician green marble like the walls, not bourgeois black-and-white tiles. Her bath-times smelt of a lush, extravagant tropical garden. The view from the windows wasn't of a Provençal hillside, sunflowers and cacti and lemon trees, but a prospect of sea and sky: as vast as infinity sometimes, with no horizon showing, like a glimpse of the hereafter – whatever that might be, either the soul's eternal travelling or maybe nothing at all, utter desolate emptiness. A full-stop.

At least it was a glimpse, through the exotically fragrant bath foam, sufficient to remind her that she wasn't ready for her end just yet; that wherever Hubert was – if he was anywhere – he would have to wait a while longer, until all her outstanding accounts were finally settled to her satisfaction.

DRESSING UP IN VOICES

PATRICK GALE

PATRICK GALE

Patrick Gale was born on the Isle of Wight in 1962 and raised in Hampshire. He was educated at Winchester, and New College, Oxford, where he read English. He lives in London and sings with the London Philharmonic Choir.

His novels, published both sides of the Atlantic, include *The Aerodynamics of Pork, Ease, Kansas in August* and *Facing the Tank. Little Bits of Baby* is his novel-in-progress. He has had stories, reviews and articles published in the *Daily Telegraph, Literary Review, London Daily News, Whitbread Stories One, London Evening Standard, Plays and Players, Gay Times, Tatler*, and *L'Echo de Rabastens*. He has also reviewed for *Kaleidoscope*. He has just contributed two chapters on Mozart's piano and mechanical music to a forthcoming *Mozart Compendium* (ed. H. C. Robbins-Landon & B. Millington).

'THE ONLY TIME I ever lost control – I mean truly lost control,' he said, 'was with someone else's wife.'

'Go on,' she said and pushed aside the carcass of the small bird she had just eaten.

'Well he was some kind of financial genius. I met them through Flavia.'

She wrinkled her brow to show that she knew no Flavia.

'You know,' he went on. 'Flavia. The broker who used to lead Edward around like a spaniel.'

'Oh yes,' she lied, keen for him to press on.

'Anyway, the genius, who incidentally was ugly as sin, had to go away to Washington for some secret advisory mission and she turned up on my doorstep and we sort of fell into bed.'

'Gosh,' she said.

'Quite. I mean, she was dead sexy and all that but . . . Actually, now that I think about it she wasn't sexy at all. But that was just it, you see.'

'What?'

'Why I lost control. It was all forbidden. She said she loved him, or at least that she had immense respect for him. There was something else too, because she forbade me to let on to anyone else what was going on.'

'So she turned up on your doorstep more than once?' she asked, for whom his doorstep was as yet no more than a dot lovingly marked on an *A to Z*.

'God, yes. Every day for a month.'

'No more?'

'A month was quite enough. Anyway, he came back. She seemed to be scared of him, terrified that he might find out. She wouldn't talk about it, but now and then there was a close shave – someone meeting her on her way to my place, that sort of thing – and I'd see the panic in her eyes. Smell it almost.'

'Goodness.'

'Of course, it was only the trappings I fell for; the secrecy, the air of the illicit and probably the knowledge that, all being well, I'd never have to take up any responsibility for her. Anyway, I lost control. Utterly. She would ring up at about six to ask if I was free and I would say yes, ridiculously excited, then ring whoever I was meant to be seeing and cancel. Even really good friends.'

'Didn't anyone suspect?'

'Well of course they did, but I blinded them with half-truths. There was a married woman, I said, but no one any of them had ever met. I think, when a month went by and no one had been introduced, I think they just assumed that I was ashamed of her.'

'Or that she was ashamed of you.'

'What?' He looked up from the napkin he had been shredding and saw that she was mocking him. He snorted. Their waiter took away his spotless plate and her bird carcass. He asked him to bring them both a pudding. He asked for it in fast Italian.

'What did you ask for?' she asked, cross because she had wanted zabaglione.

'Oh it's their speciality. It's a kind of ice-cream grenade, encased in white chocolate and dribbled with Benedictine.'

'Oh.'

'Sorry. Did you want something else?'

'No.'

'No, come on. Did you? 'Cos I can grab someone and change the order.'

'Well,' she looked across the candle into his pale green eyes. He wore the apologetic expression she had seen last night. He had been doing something delectable back and forth across her abdomen with his short blond hair and small pointed tongue. She had run a hand across the back of his neck, as much to feel the stubble there as to make some dumb show of gratitude but he had stopped and looked up at her with that apologetic look on his face. A painfully proper child caught out at an impropriety.

'No. Go on,' she had told him then. Now she merely smiled and confessed to a hankering after a warm froth of egg and marsala. He had the waiter at his side with one brief turn of the head.

'You do have zabaglione, don't you?' he asked.

'*Certo, ma è freddo,*' the waiter told him. '*Per i barbari americani.*'

'Oh no,' she burst out. 'Please. Don't bother. The ice-cream thing would be fine.' Cold zabaglione. It was like offering a virgin a bed with dirty sheets. She had wanted the world's most erotic food and they were trying to fob her off with a pornographic approximation. She loathed Benedictine, but now would suffer it quietly.

'But I'm sure they could heat it up for you,' he urged her, visibly embarrassed. 'They use a bain-marie.'

'No, Gus, honestly,' she said and turned to send the waiter away. 'What he ordered will do beautifully,' she told him. The waiter left them with a tinge of a sneer. Gus's ring-hand lay on the table. 'Sorry about that,' she muttered and reached out to touch his fingers with her own. He let his hand lie dead beneath hers then withdrew it to effect a needless adjustment to his hair.

'How about you?' he asked.

'What about me?'

'When did you last lose control?'

'Oh,' she laughed. 'It's sad but I don't believe I ever have.'

'So your books aren't autobiographical? All that rage? All those thwarted lusts?'

'Lord no,' she said, peeling a runnel of softened wax off the candle. 'I mean, of course I have to write about feelings I can sympathise with, but I couldn't begin to live such a violent life. The very idea!' And they both laughed. The very idea of such a sane animal running fabulously amok. How too absurd! How . . . How endearing! She felt herself grow dim before the massed jury of her heroines and continued, 'Besides, I don't think you can put real happenings into fiction. Not without toning them down.'

'Too wild?'

'Sort of. There are too many jagged, messy bits. Heaven

knows, there's nothing more dead than a tidy story, but there needs to be some kind of perspective.'

'Oh look. *Perfetto,*' he pronounced as their white chocolate grenades of ice-cream arrived before them. He attacked his at once with that same decorous greed she had noticed in bed. She sank a spoon into hers and watched the chocolate armour crumble into the alcoholic ooze below. She carved out a spoonful then let it lie.

'I'm not altogether sure that I've ever been in love,' she said. He failed to interrupt so she continued. 'It's not that I'm heartless, or even incapable. I've *thought* I was in love several times.'

'Tell me about it,' he said, eyeing her pudding as his own all but disappeared.

'I suppose you could call my attitude romantic insofar as I believe in the possibility of meeting someone with whom one could pass the rest of one's life and for whom one would be prepared to die.' She realised of a sudden that the man at the adjoining table was listening with keen interest so she paused to take a mouthful of her grenade and give him time to resume his conversation with the youth before him. The ice-cream hurt her throat. Benedictine was as reminiscent of dry-cleaning fluid as the last time she had tasted it. Mutely she offered her plate to Gus.

'Are you sure?' he asked. She nodded. He accepted it and began to eat again.

'And each time I meet someone and they say they love me, I'm flattered and usually for them to have got that far they have to be fairly attractive, so I'm excited as well. And. I don't know. The whole business is so very beguiling. Other people's bedrooms and breakfasts. Going through a day with that mixture of smugness and light-headed exhaustion.'

'Bliss.'

Was he talking about the pudding?

'So I throw myself into it, fingers crossed and hoping that this time it'll be the "real thing". But of course that's stupid because, as I realise each time I bring something to an end, if it *was* the real thing I shouldn't have had to cross my fingers, or hope, or crank up my indulgence. If it was the real thing I'd have lost control. Of course writers and films exaggerate no end but there's no smoke without a fire and I just know that if I don't feel physically sick at separation and giddy every time I hear someone's voice or find one of their odd socks at the bottom of the bed, then I'm faking. Every time, after I've started faking and got myself thoroughly involved, there comes a sickening moment when some demonstration of theirs shows me that they've lost control and I'm still sitting there with fingers crossed and my spare hand still firmly on the joystick.'

The man with the youth tittered. Gus quashed him silent with a sharp look. It was one of the unimportant things that made her sick at their every separation and giddy when she heard his voice. That and the wholly irrational whatever that caused her to invite him repeatedly to her bed while the furies of rationality keened a despairing no.

She had found him at an unmemorable dinner party three years ago with his pretty and seeming vacuous girlfriend, Loulou. Gut-stabbed by lust, she had set out perversely to woo the girl rather than charm the man. Loulou proved far from vacuous, was calculating indeed, and she had been made swiftly a party to her ceaseless round of infidelities. They would ask her to supper and she would dutifully play the role of professional wit and novelist, gabbling away about nothing when she needed to take Gus by the lapels and scream about the betrayals that passed unseen beneath his patrician nose. More recently there had been a falling off in their meetings because the strain had been becoming too much for her. Also she had been busy convincing herself that she loved another man who was yet too ghastly to trundle out for friendly inspection. Then, three weeks ago, a postcard had arrived.

'As you may have gathered from the radio silence, my life has been suffering a sea-change,' Gus wrote. 'Have severed communications with Louise and am anxious not to lose you in the ensuing drawing-up of ranks. Let's have supper. Soon.'

On one heady impulse, she sacked the horrendous man whom no one had met, and invited Gus round for supper and sympathy.

She had planned to take a leaf out of Loulou's book. She had planned to question him mercilessly about his domestic disaster and shattered faith in love then offer a shoulder to cry on and a brave new bed-fellow to help him forget. ('Poor Gus,' – *bang*.) In the event she sat back and watched the unfamiliar spectacle of herself losing control. After feeding him with what she knew to be his favourite dishes, shopped for and prepared with passionless care that afternoon, she started to tell the truth then could not stem the confessional tide.

'I want you,' she had told him, curled in her chair as he sprawled across her sofa. 'I've wanted you ever since I first saw you in Nadia's horrid green kitchen. And I hated Loulou because she had you and I only became her friend so as to find out more about you and get as close to you as I could. I thought she was vacuous and that you deserved better and then she started to . . . Gus, I knew everything. She told me everything and I didn't tell you because I wanted her to be as unfaithful as possible. I thought that the more she slept around, the less likely you'd be to forgive her if ever you found out. Sometimes, knowing what I knew and not telling you was more than I could stand. But I couldn't tell you, you see, because I knew you loved her and that you'd hate whoever opened your eyes. So I couldn't come between you. I had to wait. And now you're probably wondering how best to extricate yourself from this appallingly tawdry little scene.'

But he hadn't left. Not until after breakfast. And he had come back. Again and again.

As he drank a cognac and she a small black coffee, she realised that they had made no plans for the night. Tomorrow was a bank holiday Monday, so there would be no need for him to get up early to be at his office. She had kept tomorrow free on purpose so as to share his day off but he had still said nothing. He talked about how depressing it was to watch one's friends marry off, settle down and revise their address books according to their partner's whims. She listened with half an ear, making sighed or chuckled responses where necessary, but she was thinking about that night, the next day and the following weekend. She wanted him to ask her back to the 'smallish place' in Islington that she had never seen. She wanted to wake up in his bed, feel his back beside her then fall asleep again only to have him rouse her later with coffee and a wet, late rose. (She watched the man and the youth leave. She saw the fleeting brush of his hand across the youth's own.) She wanted to explore Gus's bookshelves and record collection while he shaved. Would it be indescribably sordid, with a dirty frying pan on the stove and a mattress on a dusty floor, or was Gus hiding behind a landlord's furniture and non-committal colours? She drained her cup to the bitter dregs and slid her miniature macaroons across the table to his eager hands.

'Shall we, er?' he asked, when he had finished munching. She hummed assent and smiled until he had to smile back. She watched as he summoned the bill, and she reached for her wallet.

'Here,' she said, crinkling a note at him.

'No,' he waved it away, deftly handing back the bill to the waiter with a piece of plastic inside. 'You bought the tickets so this is on me.'

The tickets had cost far less, but she demurred for only an instant as his salary far outweighed her publisher's most recent advance. Proportionately, her concert tickets had cost her several of his grand meals.

'I'll wait for you outside,' she said and headed for the door.

'Your coat, *signorina*.'

'Of course. How stupid of me.' She had forgotten her coat. She stood awkwardly as the waiter insisted on helping her on with it.

'*Buona notte*,' he said and held open the door with a grin.

'Good-night,' she replied and went out.

The pavement was nearly empty, although it was not long past eleven. She had forgotten how even the West End could become suburban on Sunday nights. Autumn was coming. The sky was cloudless and there was a chill in the air. She watched a woman dancing, drunk, with her reflection in a darkened hairdresser's window, then turned back, nervous, to see if Gus was coming. There he was, swinging into his cream mac with a frown, mildly irritated by a hovering waiter, and she knew that she would have to speak first. As he emerged on to the pavement he did not return her smile but the words were already on her lips. As good as spoken so,

'*Dove adesso?*' she asked.

'What?'

'How shall we get back?'

'Um, look.' He drew her alongside him with an arm across her shoulders. 'We need to have a talk.'

We've talked too much already, she thought, panic clutching her from within. That's our trouble. We've talked everything to death. We should hurry home, hurry to either of our homes and make rapid, violent love without a word being spoken. Then again, slowly, still in silence. Then make ourselves over to sleep. Tomorrow all will be well. Then. For now.

'I'm all ears,' she said, making as if to meet his eye but seeing no further than his coat buttons before cowardice drove her to look straight ahead. They began to walk.

'We've had a lovely time,' he said swiftly. 'A good time. And I'm very fond of you, but . . .'

'But,' she echoed.

Don't say another word, she meant to say. Least of all fond. Fond, with its connotations of passing folly. I'll find a taxi, leave you here and we'll never meet again. Oh Christ, Christ, Christ. This is going to hurt whatever you say and the least you could do is let me go without you making a little speech to make your suffering less. The least you could do would be to shut up and hurt; suffer a part of what I . . . We shall have to meet in hot Christmas sitting rooms and bray delightedly.

They came to a line of scaffolding poles ranged along a length of pavement. She slipped apart from him and walked on the pavement's edge so that the metal came between them. She was looking sternly ahead and felt that he was too. She pictured their two, pinched white faces as an oncomer might see them. Second division terrorists trying to pass plans for an assassination without it being seen that they are known to one another. But the pavement was empty. They waited, obedient, at a crossing although there were no cars coming through the green lights.

'But I don't think we should carry on with the bed bit,' he said. She said nothing. They walked on and she could find nothing to say. 'Do you see,' he asked eventually, as they came into Trafalgar Square and waited at another crossing.

'Yes,' she said. 'It's just that I can't think of anything to say that isn't banal.'

'"What a pity"?'

'Yes. That would do.'

No more words. Leave me. Let me go home. I want so *much* to go home.

'How will you get home?' he asked.

'Walk in the right direction until I find a taxi, I suppose. What about you?'

'Can I walk with you until you find one?'

'If you like.'

Go away. Take your patrician nose and go away. No. No. Stay and get in the taxi with me. Come home. Unsay it all. Gainsay.

'I think the trouble was that I'd got so used to not thinking of you in, well, *that* way. With Loulou around and everything. And you were so . . .'

'What?'

'So horribly clever.'

'That's *no* reason. That's a worthless thing to say.'

'Yes it is.'

'I moved too fast,' she cut in. 'I frightened you off.'

'No. Not that.'

'What, then?'

'I don't think it would have made any difference how fast you moved. I just wasn't ready. Not for you. Not for anyone, anything.'

'I think I could tell,' she said slowly.

Of course she could tell. He had organised the entire weekend so that, while spending every hour together, they spent as many of them as possible out of doors, in public, away from any kind of bed. He had engineered the discussion over dinner. The disgusting, cold discussion. He thought he had prepared the ground so that it would be less of a shock for her. Well he made a lousy job of it.

'I suppose, if the chemistry is wrong, then no amount of good will can help,' she said, feeling cheapened by the words.

'Yup,' he said. 'And believe me,' this with an awkward little tug at her shoulders that made her teeter and graze one of her ankles on a heel, 'there was plenty of good will.'

They walked the length of Whitehall in total silence. Three late buses sailed past them, buses she could have taken to escape him, but she needed to hurt herself. She resolved on taking a taxi or nothing, knowing that taxis on the route she would take were rare. They reached Parliament Square and she clutched at a straw.

'Look, Gus, this is silly. There are loads of cabs going in your direction. Leave me here. I'll be fine.'

'Are you sure?'

'Yup. Easier on my own. I'll be fine. But look, there's some stuff of yours in my flat; that black jersey and some socks and things.'

'Oh God. So there are. What are you doing tomorrow?'

'Nothing much.'

'Let's meet for tea and you can give me them then.'

Success.

'Where?'

'St James's. That funny sixties cafeteria place.'

'OK. Fourish?'

'Make it five.'

'All right. But are you sure?'

'How do you mean?'

'Well,' she paused. 'I could always post them to you.'

'Don't be stupid. I still want to see you, remember.'

'Oh yes.'

Silly me. I forgot.

'Here's a cab,' he said. 'I must run.'

They tried to shake hands but she missed and ended up with a fistful of mackintosh. She waited until she heard his taxi door slam then allowed herself a brief wave as he escaped her up Whitehall.

She walked home along the north bank of the river and over Albert's fairground of a bridge. Buses only passed her when she was between stops and taxis were either busy or going the wrong way and unwilling to turn back. She toyed with the idea of climbing the low railings into the small green space known as the Pimlico Shrubbery for a good weep, or abandoning herself to showier grief on a bench facing Battersea Power Station, but she preferred to walk and punish her elegantly shod feet. If she got home too soon she would not sleep, thanks to the espresso she had drunk and the ideas circling wildly as to how she should approach tea-time tomorrow. A middle-aged black couple were having trouble starting their car at one point and she stopped to help the husband push it. When it started, he offered her a lift home but she said no thank you she was almost there, although she had at least a mile to go. Pushing the car she had broken the heel of one of her shoes. Before letting herself in, she leaned into a neighbour's skip to vomit all she had eaten in the restaurant. This was easily done; there had been gobbets of blood around the small bird's bones and she had only to think of these. Sleep came, thick and dreamless. She woke with blisters on both big toes and fresh resolution in her heart.

She rarely wrote short stories. Her novels were fat, exhaustive expositions of character and possibility that drove critics to wield terms like 'sprawling' or 'magisterial', and she found the smaller form unsatisfactory. The short stories she had written gained most of their poignancy from the fact of their being dismembered first chapters, and could not stand comparison with the more finished work of specialists. She had spoken truly in telling Gus that her novels made no use of autobiography. She left herself alone but, unconsciously, she did use her acquaintances, transmogrified with bits and pieces of each other. Her method resembled a child's picture book whose pages are cunningly split into threes enabling one to join head of stork with body of rhino and mermaid's tail; Janet's temper might join with Edward's charity in Susan's body. Susan's body was one of a kind, but neither she nor Janet nor Edward ever recognised their contributions to the hybrid result. Hardly surprising since even the authoress frequently failed to recognise what she had done. Though using real people, she had never drawn on real events. Real events were too hard to transplant; each had its peculiar logic and trailed sticky strands of cause and consequence that refused to adapt to the simpler systems of fiction. This morning's material was different, however, because she would treat it in isolation with the bare minimum of adaptation. At least that was the idea.

She was in the bath inspecting her blisters when the idea came to her, so she went straight back to bed, her head turbanned in a towel. She always worked in bed in the winter months because she suffered from the cold when immobile. She kept the word-processor on a hospital table that she could swing over the mattress before her as she sat cross-legged and furled in a quilt. The green letters sliding across her glasses, she worked for several hours without answering the telephone or pointed beseeching of the cat, and told the truth. She wrote about how she had met Gus and Loulou, how she had inveigled her way into their lives and eventually into Gus's bed (well, Gus into her bed). She told how they had walked around Clapham looking at hurricane damage, how she had taken him to hear her favourite pianist playing her favourite Brahms *intermezzi* and how he had found her ugly after feeding her on a small bleeding bird and hateful French liqueur. Ugly as sin. She told of her walk home. She changed the facts in only a few points. She had herself accept the lift from the middle-aged black couple, whose lasting devotion she then envied until they took her home for a drink and she saw their child's wheelchair. She turned herself into a scholarly lesbian and she switched Gus and Loulou's genders. Loulou became, with perhaps wanton cruelty, a philandering estate agent called Lucian, while Gus became Rose, an uncertain blonde. Gus had many faults, one of the more endearing of which was his failure to understand why lesbians should exist, much less to sympathise with what they might do. Even if she had herself and 'her' do almost exactly the same things in bed, he would never recognise himself in Rose.

She stopped writing towards three because it was time to feed the cat and dress for tea but also because she could not finish the story until she knew how their own would end. As long as she had been tapping at the computer keyboard, she had kept thoughts of the night before at a bearable distance, but as she brushed her hair and chose her clothes, the hurt returned. She realised that she still had not wept. For all the fluttering in her chest and the returning tightness in her throat, she found herself yet capable of selecting clothes with an unselected look and of lending a mournful pallor to her make-up with a pale powder she had once bought by mistake. His black jersey (surely one that Loulou had given him), a pair of very unwashed socks and a tie that was rather too wide, were in a carrier bag near the front door. She had gathered and folded them last night in a daze between vomiting and brushing teeth.

She arrived at the cafeteria far too early, of course. He was nowhere in sight so she forced herself to walk over to the crowded bridge to kill time. Several nondescript women and an elderly man with a crutch were leaning on the eastern railings staring crazily at the sparrows that clustered over their crumb-filled hands, as if this minor miracle were not something they indulged in every afternoon. A few children shouted amazement and a youth in a Chinese revolutionary cap filmed them on a Japanese camera. She walked on, past the hideous Walt Disney candelabra and crouched a while to watch the aggressive patrolling of a black swan. She should have brought it something to eat. She wondered if she could remember to return with a piece of cake when their tea was over. She held out her empty hands to it, fingers spread.

'Sorry,' she told it, then saw a woman crouched, photographing her from a few yards away. She had on a brilliant white dress that looked far too thin for the day and she wore her armfuls of almost pink red hair in a mane. The woman lowered the camera and smiled, showing her teeth, then stood to show that she was tall and built like Juno. She couldn't smile back so she stared. Then Gus called her name and set her free. She turned and hurried to the squat round cafeteria where he was waiting.

'There was a dreadful queue when I got here so I got us stuff without waiting for you. Do you mind?'

'Of course not.'

'Shall we sit in or out?'

'Oh out, I think. It's cold but the sunshine is so lovely.' She led him to an empty table. There were no free-standing chairs but circles of wood were fixed on arms that splayed out from each central table leg. It felt as if they were sitting at either side of some chaste playground mechanism; a miniature roundabout that, with a few thrusts from their short, childish legs, would set them gently turning, very safely, always equidistant.

'While I remember,' she said and passed him the carrier bag.

'Oh. Thanks,' he said, feigning surprise then peering inside to make sure she had held on to nothing that was his. 'My favourite,' he said, inspecting the outside to see which shop it hailed from. 'How clever of you. You got home OK?'

'Yes. But I walked, like an idiot, and now I've got blisters on my toes.'

'Now look,' he said. 'I know you like fruity teas and they had a huge choice so I brought several bags and some hot water.'

'Goodness.'

'Cherry, mandarin or . . .' he exaggerated the need to peer at the third. 'Yes, or mixed fruit.'

'Cherry sounds lovely.'

'Pop the others in your bag.'

'Are you sure?'

'Yes. Go on.'

'How absurd we both sound; like maiden aunts stealing sugar lumps from Fortnums.'

They laughed, uproariously almost, and she saw that he was wearing the tie she had given him two years ago, at Loulou's Christmas party. He had bought a plateful of cakes and proceeded to sink his teeth into a chocolate one. His nose just cleared the icing. She decided on the vanilla one for the black swan and set it aside on a paper napkin.

'What's that for?' he asked, dabbing crumbs off his chin.

'A black swan. I teased it by crouching down with nothing to give. Made me feel guilty.'

'Wouldn't it rather have bread?'

'Would you?'

'Point taken.'

'Bread or cake; they're neither of them exactly natural fodder for a water bird.' She took a mouthful of a rather nasty, dried-out flapjack and dunked her cherry tea bag up and down. The water did not turn pink but became a disappointing, traditional sort of brown. Suddenly she saw the statuesque camera woman approaching and turned back to Gus.

'What are you up to this evening?' she asked.

'Nothing much. Tabitha's having a drinks party.' She wrinkled her brow to show that she knew no Tabitha. 'You know. *Tabitha*. She helps run the Burden Friday Gallery. Anyway, it's a choice between her or the reprint of *Dolce Vita*. Want to come?'

'I don't know her.'

'To the Fellini.'

'No. I can't.' He looked a question at her and she thought quickly. Why couldn't she go? Wouldn't she love to? Sit close beside him and be bombarded by glamour in a darkened room? She met his pale, bland gaze and thought that on reflection she wouldn't. 'I've got a story to finish.'

'I didn't know you stooped to stories.'

'Actually it's a question of aspiring; they're far harder than novels. And yes, I do sometimes. This one's for a magazine. They pay absurdly well.' She saw that he was not listening to her but was smiling politely up over her shoulder.

'Can I help?' he asked.

She turned round to a warm brown cleavage and what, close-to, proved to be pure white cashmere.

'I *thought* it was you!' The woman's camera – a large, professional thing – dangled from one hand. There was no time to make any kind of face as she bowed and kissed her warmly at the edge of each cheek. The brush of lip whispered in her ear and a scent of ambergris hung, delicious, after she had withdrawn. 'How are you? You look so well.' A long, smooth hand stroked her jaw and shoulder. The stranger laughed, brushing back tumbling hair. 'Sorry. How awful of me!' She turned to shake Gus's hand. 'Joanna Ventura.'

'Angus Packard.'

'I must run. I'm late again, but please,' she turned back and touched the shoulder again. 'Ring me. Please?' As she vanished into the crowd, Gus all but gaped.

'Where have you been keeping her?'

'Oh,' she said. 'Joanna's hardly ever in town so when she is I tend to keep her all to myself.'

'She looks like Anita Ekberg.'

'Who?'

'The one in the fountain in *Dolce Vita.*'

'Oh.'

'I didn't know you knew any Americans apart from squat Jewish publishers.'

Funny. She had not noticed the accent.

She finished the story swiftly, perched on the edge of the bed, her coat unbuttoned but still on. Her women in love held their last meeting over cheap muscadet outside the National Film Theatre. The rendezvous was ostensibly held for Gus/Rose to return an unlikely black silk petticoat. She handed it over to the jilted heroine, wrapped in a used, brown paper envelope, then broke down. She begged her to forget the hasty words of the previous night then went on to make an absurd scene when her generosity was rebuffed. The heroine paused in her return across Westminster Bridge to open the envelope and send the petticoat dancing down to the brown waters beneath then laughed wildly in the face of a man in a suit who stopped to rebuke her for littering the city.

She pressed a button that corrected her spelling then set the machine to print. As the daisywheel rattled away, she felt in her coat pocket for a handkerchief and found a ticket for the next evening's showing of *La Dolce Vita.* There was writing on the back. A woman's hand. She read it, turned the ticket over to check the performance time, then turned back to reread the writing.

'I dare you,' it said and there was a telephone number.

Suddenly the printer went wrong. There was a high-pitched bleep and a grinding sound as a half-typed sheet of paper was chewed up. She threw the ticket aside and, scowling, busied herself with freeing the page and returning the cursor to the beginning of her new text. The challenge was in red ink, however, and she could see it from the corner of her eye.

FOUR PESOS

CARLO GÉBLER

CARLO GÉBLER

Carlo Gébler was born in Dublin in 1954. He is a graduate of the National Film and Television School. He is the writer and director of several films for television and one short film for the cinema. He has published three novels and one travel book, as well as several short stories. He has two children and lives in London.

SHE WAS ALWAYS late so this once she determined to be early. She was at the cafeteria by half-past ten. It was empty. There were grey piles of snow outside which she looked at through the windows. Peter was prompt. He sat down and straightaway looked at the envelope on the table with the bulge in the corner.

'There isn't much to say,' he said.

'No, there isn't much to say,' she said.

She felt a pain inside, somewhere behind her stomach, pressing outwards.

'We've come to the end of the road,' she heard herself saying.

'I'm sorry,' he said, picking up his gloves, 'I never thought this would happen.'

Then he stood up and walked out of the door of Pierre's into the Montreal street and back to his life as a civil engineer on Prince Edward Island.

The envelope, she thought, I've forgotten to give it to him, and she looked down and saw it beside her half-drunk cup of coffee. With the sharp end of her spoon she pressed on the taut part of the envelope that was stretched over the wedding ring inside like a drum-skin and went on until the paper tore. Then she finished her coffee and asked for another. It came and she drank it without thinking of anything and after walked slowly outside. It was cold. The cold hurt her face. She stood and pulled her hat down on to her head.

'Hey!'

The proprietor, dark-skinned, an apron across his middle, was calling from the doorway.

'You forgot this.'

He stretched towards her with the envelope. She took it with her mittened hand and put it in her pocket.

At the office of Laforque & Company (Leather and Suede, Import and Export Specialists), Sherri sympathised.

'Sometimes it doesn't work out,' Sherri said. 'He went away to work. You drifted apart. Don't blame yourself.'

The first Mary knew of the tears running down her face was when she suddenly tasted them on the edge of her mouth. Sherri opened the drawer of her desk and passed over a box of Kleenex.

At the end of the afternoon Mary asked Mr Laforque for a week's holiday and booked seven days of February sun in Cuba.

Two days later she flew to Havana. She transferred to the airport which handled domestic flights and was in Cienfuegos by the afternoon. A gleaming tourist bus met her and half a dozen others and drove them out of the city on the last leg of the journey towards the hotel Pasacaballo twenty miles to the south. There were rolling hills, scrawny cattle nibbling at parched grass, and shacks by the roadside. There was a cassette player in the bus and among the tunes she recognised *Eine Kleine Nachtmusik*. Suddenly, at the top of a hill the blue sea appeared below and her heart lifted. It sank a few minutes later when she saw the hotel – a gaunt, white building standing in emptiness. She felt the thought forming, This is a terrible mistake, and she stopped it by opening her handbag and rummaging for her passport which she knew she was shortly going to need. There was an abandoned taxi on blocks outside the hotel entrance, no wheels, the axle-ends flaking and rusting.

She registered and changed some money. She was only allowed to change ten dollars and got eight pesos back. 'You pay for everything in hard currency,' the clerk told her.

A bellboy with bow legs showed her to the room on the fifth floor. It was long, like a railway carriage, with an olive-coloured ceiling, orange furniture, and a view through the tiny window of a dilapidated swimming pool. She offered the bellboy a tip of a peso but he declined and asked for the empty Coca-Cola can she was holding instead.

He left and she took off all her clothes. She was thirty-three and white; her stomach was flat. She lifted her suitcase on to the bed and opened it. From the crumpled clothes inside there came the faint smell of the flat where she lived, a smell of wood and rubber and the fur inside boots and coffee. With the smell came a sharp twinge of feeling. The hotel was not right. In fact it was awful. She just wanted to lie down and let go. Inside, she felt as if there was a huge volume of liquid so compressed it was hard, and she imagined it puncturing and everything flowing away and afterwards feeling well and healed. She opened the cupboard door; only two hangers, poor and buckled. She hung some of her clothes over the bar and put the rest in the drawers. She began to feel a little better.

She turned on the shower and got under the water. She had forgotten her soap and the hotel's came in small bars smelling of sugar. There was a knock at the outside door. She shouted back, 'I'm in the shower.' Whoever was outside said something and went away. When she had washed, she wrapped a towel around her middle and another around her head. She opened the door. The white papapet wall opposite dazzled her. She looked along the walkway as far as the lifts. Empty. Then she saw the light bulb in the doorway and remembered the bellboy had pointed at the bedside lamp which didn't have one and said something. She carried it in and put the bulb in the socket. She clicked the switch several times. Nothing. She turned and saw the cupboard with her clothes hanging in it, and the dress with the collar and the little white dots just like those on a domino . . . No, she mustn't even think about it.

She closed the doors and picked up the wrapping which the bulb had come in. Written on the side was 'Made in the USSR'. She went back outside and leant on the parapet wall. Below the hotel was a channel half a mile wide which connected Cienfuegos bay to the Caribbean, and on the other side of the channel was a village which came down to the water's edge. It was then she noticed the wall at the side of the village on which was written, presumably so everyone in the hotel could read it as they walked backwards and forwards to their bedrooms, *Bienvenidos a Cuba Socialista*.

*   *   *

It was dark when she left her bedroom. In the lift it was *Eine Kleine Nachtmusik* again, the tail-end, followed by a piece of Bach. She had pressed the wrong button and the lift stopped, not on the ground floor but at the basement, which was below the enormous lobby. She walked out and it reminded her of an underground car park. All was dark except at the centre where there stood a shop with large glass windows. She went inside. It was filled with racks of clothes, fans, televisions and other electrical items, bottles of liquor and cosmetics. The shop was packed with people who were buying large amounts of goods and speaking languages she did not recognise but imagined were Czech, Russian or Hungarian. She bought a packet of Marlboro Lights, paid a dollar and was returned 20 cents change.

After supper in the cavernous dining room she went back to her room. Her handbag lay on the bed. The impulse took her by surprise and before she knew what she was doing, she had taken the photograph out of the side pocket and was looking at it. It was her husband, Peter. She felt a little kick inside and heard laughter from below. She ran to the window and saw people were sitting around the swimming pool.

She put on some lipstick and immediately went downstairs. The pool was large, with tables and chairs arranged around the edge and a bar. There were men standing along the bar with their feet on the brass rail beneath. She sat down. A waiter brought her a beer and took away a dollar.

'*Bon soir,*' she heard and, realising she was being spoken to, looked up and saw a man. He was dark and wore a blue shirt with pleats down the front and pockets at the side.

'*Permittez-moi,*' he said.

'I speak English.'

'I'm sorry. We mostly have French-Canadians. I assumed you spoke French,' he said in a North American accent.

She shook her head.

He introduced himself as Eduardo. He was in charge of customer relations in the hotel. He asked if he could sit down and was already reaching for the chair when she said, 'Yes.'

'How are you enjoying our beautiful country?' he asked.

'I've only just arrived.'

He told her Cienfuegos was a wonderful city. He told her there were many touristic excursions in the province, and he told her what they were. Then he said, 'Would you like another beer?'

She nodded and he called '*Psst, psst*,' to the old waiter. It was an extraordinarily offensive sound which she'd already heard from the other men along the bar. Nonetheless she was surprised to hear him make it because he had been so polite up to that point.

The old waiter brought two *Claros*. The bottles were brown and had no labels. The Cuban beer was light and had a faint tang of yeast to it. There was a jukebox and somebody put on a record. It was a song in Spanish. Two girls started dancing, jumped into the pool with their clothes on, were pulled out by two men and went on dancing. Eduardo smiled and she smiled back.

When Mary went to bed later, she could hear music and dancing was still going on by the pool. Some time in the night she dreamt of a lighthouse with its steps not inside but on the outside; like a helter-skelter slide and she was running frantically up and down.

She was woken in the morning by the sound of knocking on her door. She sat up in bed holding the sheet over her damp, naked body, heard a key turn and a moment later saw a trolley appearing, followed by a black woman in her thirties who was wearing a nylon housecoat. The top of the trolley was piled with sheets and towels and Mary realised it was the chambermaid.

The maid said something in Spanish and put her hand quickly in front of her mouth. She backed out closing the door. Mary looked at the alarm clock beside her bed. It was seven in the morning.

Mary went down to the dining room. She took a table at the far end from where she could look over the water to the village on the other side. Why, she wondered, did her bedroom and the others along the balcony not face this way?

The food was laid out on tables in the middle of the room. There were pieces of grapefruit, orange and watermelon, pieces of cheese and slices of cold meat she didn't recognise. There were little squares of vanilla cake, chocolate cake and piles of

petits fours. Everything looked old and brown, off or stale, so she
took a hard-boiled egg with an abnormally white shell. When she
cracked it open she found the white so white it was almost bluish
and the yoke hard and powdery. She sat back and drank her coffee
– sweet and oily because it had been made with boiled condensed
milk – and looked across at the village. Eduardo had told her it was
called Jagua and boasted a sixteenth-century Spanish fort.

She went back upstairs. She found her bedroom door was
open and heard music coming from inside. She went in and found
the maid who had woken her up that morning had turned on the
radio.

'*Hola,*' the maid greeted Mary. She had the pillow gripped
under her chin and was working the clean pillowcase around the
end.

Mary went into the bathroom, sharpened her kohl pencil and
began to run it around the rims of her eyes.

'*Ay, que lindo.*'

In the mirror she saw the maid had come into the bathroom
behind her. The maid was holding the domino dress which had
been a present from Mary's husband on their first anniversary.

'*Es muy bonito,*' said the maid, holding the dress up in front
of Mary. '*Si, si,*' she continued, looking up and down.

Then the maid caught Mary's eye, and put a hand over her
mouth to stop herself laughing at her own audacity. Mary felt
herself smiling. The maid walked out and Mary heard her putting
back the dress and closing the cupboard door.

Turning back towards the mirror, Mary remembered the
morning of the anniversary. They had so little money, she and
Peter had agreed not to give one another anything. Nonetheless,
she couldn't believe they wouldn't exchange at least token gifts,
so she had bought him a cup and saucer which she gave him
when they woke up. He thanked her fulsomely, but said nothing
about having anything for her. They started breakfast. As she
stood watching the milk heating, she thought, how could he not
have bought me anything? They sat down. They started to eat.
The news was on the radio. He asked her one or two questions
about what she would be doing that day. She answered automati-
cally while thinking, he hasn't got me anything. 'I have to go,'

he said. He went into the bedroom. She heard him brushing his teeth. He really hasn't, she thought, and her eyes felt hot as she sat at the table. He returned to the room with a coat and a bag, holding something under his arm.

He tossed the box to her saying, 'You'd better have this or I'll never hear the end of it.'

Inside was the domino dress and she shouted her thanks out the window after him as he walked away down the street.

With the memory an ache welled up. She started brushing her teeth, walked out on to the balcony, brushing as she went, and looked across at the cranes and the rising blocks of flats beyond Jagua. This was a new town, Eduardo had told her, and was still in the process of being built. It was going to house workers from the new nuclear power station.

Eduardo had mentioned the bus to Cienfuegos. She went down to the lobby to enquire and found him sitting at a table beside the desk. There was a poster advertising the Cuban National Ballet on the wall beside him.

'Very beautiful,' he said, showing his straight, immaculately white teeth.

It crossed Mary's mind he'd been lying. He wasn't in charge of customer relations. He just sold tickets for tours.

'Today I am a servant,' he said, as if reading her mind. Then he shouted, '*Psst*,' across the lobby, and a young man who was walking by came over and agreed to sit in for him.

Eduardo brought her over to the desk. He showed her a map of the area on the wall. He wrote down the times of the buses.

'Have you money?' he asked.

'Only about eight pesos.'

'That's fine. You won't spend that in town.'

She went out to wait for the bus on the brow of a hill. The hot wind carried little pieces of grit and she screwed up her eyes. Men sat in the lower branches of trees while they waited. Nobody leered. After forty minutes the bus came. She stared at the change on the palm of her hand and a man pointed to the ten centavos piece she was going to need to pay the driver. She crowded on with everyone else and a passenger with an aisle seat gave his place up to her. The bus lurched off, the standing passengers swaying together. Mary was uncomfortable and crushed but she was happy. There was no anger from others as there would have been on a bus back home. She looked at the tulle bow tied in a child's hair; and the smoothly shaved underarm of the woman squeezed against her. It was a good idea to have come to Cuba, and she wondered how long before the pain would start to trickle away.

In Cienfuegos, the sun beat down into the still streets of low, Spanish-looking houses. Mary found an ice-cream parlour and went inside. It was a cool room with iron tables and chairs, a counter and a couple of waitresses in white blouses and black skirts. They wore the same uniform at the hotel. Two children walked out past her, carrying their ice-cream away in empty Coca-Cola cans. That explained the bellboy's request.

She sat down at a table and waited. Nothing. She lit a cigarette. Nothing. She tried to catch the eye of the waitresses who were standing, talking. Nothing. She tried to call '*Psst*,' but lacking the courage to do it forcefully, came out with a snake-like '*Ssss*,' instead.

She got up to leave. One of the waitresses approached her.

'*Acquí esta cerrado*,' said the waitress, '*pero allí esta abierto*.' She ran a hand across the middle and Mary understood.

Where she had been sitting was, for some mysterious reason, closed but the other half of the ice-cream parlour was open.

Mary transferred to a new table. The waitress gave her a new menu, listing many different flavours. The waitress returned. Mary pointed at what she thought was coconut.

'*No hay.*'

The waitress waggled a finger flecked with old nail varnish and then pointed. It was either chocolate or vanilla. Mary chose vanilla.

She looked out into the street as she waited. An old Chevrolet from the 1950s went by driven by a man in a battered straw hat. The impression she was forming was that in Cuba there was nothing to buy, unless she counted the shop in the basement of the hotel, where she hadn't seen Cubans anyway, not the night before, or that morning when she'd bought a jar of face cream. The shops in the city all had queues outside and nothing on sale inside. The cars she had seen were all old US cars which rattled along. The houses were all very old with tiled roofs and paint flaking off the walls. It was the opposite of Montreal in every way but she liked it.

A party of tourists came in. About a dozen of them. Mary recognised their language as German. They sat down on the side which was closed. Mary watched as they went through the motions she had gone through of waiting, staring and trying to say '*Psst*'.

The waitress brought Mary her ice-cream, and then went over to the tourists.

'*Acquí esta cerrado pero . . .*'

They moved over and everyone squeezed around a table except for one man who was left standing. The waitress handed out a couple of menus and everyone, bunching together, began to speculate on what the flavours were. The excluded man made a face and went back to the table where everyone had been sitting. Doesn't he understand? Mary wondered. He sat down. She shook her head, trying to catch his attention. He looked out into the street. She got up and went over. 'This part is closed. You have to come to the other side.'

He looked at her. He had a pointed chin and had not shaved for several days. She wondered if he had understood.

'I see,' he said suddenly, surprising her.

'Come and sit at my table,' she said, and he did.

He told her his name was Stefan, he was from Zurich and he was not enjoying his holiday.

'Have you met any thieves?' he asked abruptly.

'No. I've only been here a day.'

'I was robbed in Havana.'

'Oh,' she replied, thinking what an inadequate way to show sympathy.

'I was punched in the breast and they ran off with all my money.'

An old woman sidled up holding her hand out. Stefan shooed her away like an animal but the woman would not budge until one of the waitresses pulled her away.

'Have you tried the black market?'

'No,' she said, and thought, All these things I know nothing about.

'It's much better than the official rate. That's about eighty-five cents to the dollar. On the black market, for every dollar you sell, they give you five pesos in Havana. Four out here. When they want something from a dollar shop, you buy it, they give you the black-market rate for the dollars you've spent.'

'Isn't it illegal?'

'Only when they take your money and run.'

In the morning, Mary was woken by a knocking on her door. She was lying naked on top of the bed. She pulled the sheet over herself and called out, 'Yes, *si*.'

'*Compañera?*' The maid appeared at the end of her bed. She wore a headscarf this morning and had a piece of graphpaper which she showed Mary. There was a childish drawing of a dress on it with a pocket on the left breast. The maid began to speak slowly, pointing at the picture. When she wrote $11.00 and then 44 pesos, Mary realised what was happening. She patted the bed and the maid sat down on the very edge. Mary pointed at the dress and the maid nodded ecstatically.

'What colour?'

The maid looked puzzled for a moment and then started to look around the room.

'*Rojo . . . marrón . . . verde, no importa.*'

'Big or small?' Mary asked, moving her hands.

The maid pointed at Mary. Mary pointed at herself.

'Like me,' she said.

The maid nodded.

'Eleven dollars,' said Mary pointing.

'*Acquí,*' the maid pointed at the other figure, '*es igual a cuarenta y cuarto pesos.*'

Mary took the pen and wrote out her name. The maid did likewise. Her name was Pata. They smiled and shook hands.

After breakfast she went to the Dollar Shop in the basement. As she was searching through clothes on a rack she realised this task was absorbing her to such an extent, she had forgotten the ache. Her self-consciousness brought it back but she decided this was the first sign of recovery.

She bought a medium-sized dress and paid in dollars. Then, for no reason, she walked up to the lobby to catch the lift. Eduardo was waiting by the call button.

'Good morning,' he said, 'are you still liking our beautiful country?'

'Yes.'

The lift door opened. They stepped in.

'Which floor?' he asked.

'Fifth.'

'Me too. Today I check on the maids up there. It's very important to ensure their work is good.'

Hoping he wouldn't notice, she slipped the package under her arm.

'You've been shopping?'

'Yes.'

The lift stopped. They stepped out and started to walk along the walkway past the orange bedroom doors. The sunlight dazzled.

'Beautiful, isn't it?' he said, waving at the view. 'We are building a new town for nuclear power workers over there.'

'You told me.'

Pata was wheeling her trolley along the balcony towards them. Mary looked and thought she saw Pata was moving her head as if saying no, with a faint movement which was almost imperceptible. She took the bag with the dress and put it behind herself.

They drew level.

'Goodbye,' said Eduardo, stopping. 'I have to talk to this maid.' He put his hand out and squeezed Pata's shoulder.

'Goodbye,' Mary said.

'Come down and see me later. We go and see the ballet one night,' Eduardo called.

Mary turned. Eduardo, with his hand under Pata's chin, was making kissing gestures. Pata was trying to move back. Neither had seen her turning so Mary went on.

At her door, Mary heard Pata shrieking. She turned just as Pata was swinging at Eduardo with the flat of her hand. He caught Pata's wrist and started to laugh.

'These girls, so hot,' he called out to Mary.

Mary went into her room.

Half an hour later Mary found Pata in a bedroom at the other end of the walkway. The maid seized the dress and immediately thrust it under a pile of towels. Then Pata took out the graphpaper from her pocket, drew a cake with candles and wrote '15' in the middle. It's a present for a fifteenth birthday, Mary thought.

Pata opened her purse. There were ten crumpled pesos inside. She handed them to Mary and wrote '34' on the paper.

'Thirty-four tomorrow,' said Mary.

'Treinta y cuatro, mañana, si.'

'What about Eduardo?' Mary said. She took the pen and wrote his name down.

Pata made an 'O' with finger and thumb and then jabbed the index finger of her other hand in and out of the hole.

'Es un jefe. Me desea.'

Mary nodded. He wants her, she thought.

She was taking spoons out from between layers of tissue paper. Her husband appeared and only then did Mary realise she was naked.

Pata woke her from this dream the next morning with the money and another drawing. It was of a jacket this time and Pata wanted it for herself. Mary agreed she would buy it at a price of eleven dollars.

After breakfast, Mary went down to the Dollar Shop. She was looking through the jackets hanging on a rack when an argument broke out in Spanish between a young man smoking a cigar who appeared to be drunk and the girl at the cash desk. From what Mary could see, the cashier appeared to be ordering the young man to leave, and he appeared to be refusing to go. Two police came with night-sticks and revolvers slapping against their thighs. They knocked the young man about and made his nose bleed and then dragged him towards the door. Outside, beyond the plate-glass windows, through which nothing was audible but everything was visible, one of the policemen kicked the youth's legs open and began to search him. By now he was crying and his cigar lay smoking on the marble floor.

'Cubans aren't allowed in the Dollar Shops,' said a voice and Mary turned and faced the man in a white peaked hat who had spoken to her. 'In Hungary we wouldn't put up with it.'

'Pity the poor Cuban caught with dollars,' he continued, 'or caught with anything from the store.'

Mary found the jacket and, when she came to pay, her hands were trembling.

They were still shaking when she handed it over.

'*Mañana*,' said Pata and pushed off with her trolley along the walkway.

On Thursday morning, Mary heard a knock on her door.

'*Si.*'

A key turned in the lock and Pata appeared a second later. She dropped a bundle of crumpled notes on the bedside table and flapped her hands, suggesting she was in a terrible rush.

'*Ciao y gracias,*' she said. Pata quickly shook Mary's hand and sped from the room.

Mary counted the notes. They were four pesos short.

She ate her breakfast and returned to her floor. She approached the other maids working along the walkway and repeated Pata's name to each in turn.

'*No sé,*' they all said and shrugged their shoulders.

Mary went to the beach and lay in the sun. At lunchtime she went to the cafeteria by the roadside used by Cubans where she had discovered she could spend her pesos. It was a large room with a counter shaped like a roller coaster and seats which swivelled. It was quite like Montreal and the food was no worse than what she could get in the hotel.

In the afternoon it was so hot, Mary sat under an umbrella of reeds. She opened her book but the sentences made no sense. She looked out to sea. She could feel herself growing melancholy. Two beers at lunchtime had impaired her will to resist. She started remembering the events as they had occurred. One evening, Peter came home and told her about the job.

'I don't think you should come with me,' he said.

'Why?'

'The job's temporary. I'm coming back. Why uproot both of us?'

She didn't agree but acquiesced. He went away. She felt lonely. He felt lonely as well, he said, stuck out in a camp in the north-east of Canada. This made her feel better.

The next stage in the story she always found much harder to grasp. What mattered was not so much the events as the omissions. What he didn't say. The warmth he didn't show. The endearments he failed to acknowledge. Then, one day, his letter came. He'd been thinking. He'd gone away so he could do the thinking and now he'd come to a decision. He didn't think they were right for each other anymore. That was exactly the phrase, and Mary could see it, just as he had written it in the letter in his small, sloping handwriting, as she sat on the Rancho Luna beach: 'I don't think we're right for one another.' He'd insisted there wasn't another woman, and she believed him.

Mary looked at a large man sitting in the shallows, the waves breaking over him, a Nikita Khrushchev hat on his head, and felt what she'd been hoping for escape from that week – the ache starting up somewhere deep inside. It was a hard feeling and along with it came a rawness at the back of the throat that made her want to swallow; a hotness in the eyes as if she was about to cry.

The sea murmured gently. She lit a cigarette.

On Friday morning when she woke up, she felt her skin was sore and slightly tight. She had stayed a little too long in the sun, she thought, the day before.

In the restaurant she drank a cup of the sweet, oily coffee made with condensed milk and afterwards walked down to the jetty. She climbed aboard a water-taxi. The boatman took her ten centavos and threw it into an old cigar box. The other passengers, she realised from their clothes, all worked in the hotel, and she presumed all the hotel workers lived in the village of Jagua.

On the other side the houses came right down to the water. From the hotel, the front had seemed attractive, but when she got close she saw the buildings were crumbling and dirty. There was also an enormous slick of rubbish at the centre of which were the bloated bodies of two dead rats.

She disembarked onto a rickety jetty and wandered up the

hill into the village, passing houses even more dilapidated than those on the front. She slyly glanced into dark rooms, where men sat on old car seats watching flickering black-and-white television sets, and children slept on pieces of sacking on the floor, with flies buzzing around them.

At the top of the village, she crossed by a ramshackle bridge made of rotting railway sleepers into the old fort. The walls were lined with rusting six-pounder guns all marked 'Made in the USA'. The ammunition galleries were filled with the whisper of bats and their black, evil-smelling droppings.

Coming out from the fort, she saw there was a church on the other side of the road. Although it looked small, as she walked towards it she imagined that inside there would be quietness, coolness and the intoxicating smell of wax and incense. Then she opened the door, saw the mould growing up the wall, the bare altar, the brown, dreary pictures of the Stations of the Cross. She turned straight around and left.

Mary walked back down the hill. The sun scorched the back of her head. She looked into a miserable shop where they only had green bananas for sale and hurried down towards the jetty.

An hour later, walking along the walkway towards her bedroom, she was surprised to see Pata, without her trolley, coming towards her.

'Where's my four pesos?' Mary asked when they drew level, holding out her palm so there could be no doubt what she meant.

'*Si, si, mañana, mañana,*' said Pata quickly. The chambermaid had something behind her back and, as she passed, she kept her front to Mary so it couldn't be seen.

'Give,' said Mary. It was hers; she was owed it. And she was going to have it.

Pata was backing down the walkway.

'Now!'

Pata turned and started to run and Mary saw what she'd been hiding behind her back. It was the maid's purse.

'Pata!'

'*Mañana,*' the maid shouted, and disappeared down a service stairs.

In the evening Mary went on a 'touristic excursion' to see the

National Ballet in a theatre in Cienfuegos. Bats flitted from the wings in their hundreds during Act One of Swan Lake. Eduardo accompanied the party and, sitting beside him in the bus on the way back, Mary considered telling him about Pata and the four pesos but decided she would wait.

On Saturday morning, Mary was dressed and waiting in her room at seven o'clock.

After waiting until nearly nine, she went on to the balcony and saw Pata and her trolley outside a bedroom half-a-dozen doors away. When Pata saw Mary she went into the bedroom.

How can she pretend I'm not here? Mary asked herself.

She ran along the walkway.

When she reached the trolley, she found the door beyond it was open, and Pata was inside the room by the bed.

'Four pesos!' Mary shouted.

Pata shrugged, walked down the passage and slammed the door shut right in her face.

Mary took the lift to the lobby and when she stepped out she saw Eduardo at his table. She ran across and told him about Pata. His face grew very dark and he looked angry. It worried Mary who had thought no further than telling what had happened but it was too late now. 'Where is she?' Eduardo demanded and Mary heard herself saying, 'Upstairs.'

They travelled up in the lift together and, when they got to the balcony, they saw Pata wheeling her trolley away from them.

'Is that her?' Eduardo asked.

'Yes.'

'Hey, *chica*,' he called.

Pata stopped. Eduardo went forward, Mary following. He started shouting at her in Spanish. Pata looked at the ground, chewing her lip, but even with her face at that angle Mary could see she was frightened.

'It doesn't matter,' Mary started. 'I don't care about the money. Can we just forget it?'

'Miss Mary,' said Eduardo angrily, 'what this one has done is very illegal. It's wrong, it's bad. She's going to be punished. Now, you go to your room. I'll speak to you later.'

Mary went into her room, closing the door behind her. She could hear Eduardo shouting. After several minutes the shouting stopped. Mary opened her door and looked out.

Down the walkway, Pata was pinned against the wall. Eduardo was kissing her and Pata appeared to be letting him have his way. Mary retreated into her room and closed the door.

After waiting twenty minutes, Mary peeped out again. They were gone but the trolley was where it had been before, lying across the walkway, piled high with sheets and pillow cases. Mary crept up and through the bedroom door heard the unmistakable sound of Eduardo violently making love to Pata.

Mary took the bus to the beach but instead of going to the sea she went straight to the cafeteria. The barman was stacking bottles in the refrigerator. He ignored her.

'*Psst,*' she called and he stood up and immediately served her.

She drank neat rum with lemon juice until every centavo of every peso was spent. Then she swam in the ocean and the cold sobered her up.

She returned to her floor in the hotel and was relieved to see Pata's trolley was gone.

On her last morning Mary was awake well before seven. She went down to the dining room. The waitresses stood in a cluster and watched her sitting alone with her back to the window.

She returned to her floor. The maids had started work. She saw a trolley, half in, half out of a door. With her heart beating she went up, put her head round the lintel and then saw it wasn't Pata, but another woman, rounder, older, and white.

'Pata?' Mary asked. 'Pa-ta?'

The maid leant her broom against the wall, licked her index finger and pointed into the distance.

'*Se acabó para ella.*'

Twice more the maid repeated the phrase and the gesture and Mary thought, She's lost her job.

She turned away and then stopped. Was the woman staring after her with resentment? Mary wondered. She looked back over her shoulder and saw the dumpy woman was looking at her and shaking her head.

In her room Mary folded her clothes without care and stuffed them into her case. The bellboy came at eleven o'clock and she followed him down. Eduardo wasn't at his desk and so she couldn't present the knowing smile she had planned for him.

She got on to the courtesy bus and made her way to the back. She put her handbag on the next seat so no one would come beside her. The other passengers going to the airport got on. They were all in high spirits and two or three were wearing enormous, outsize straw hats with palm trees painted on the sides. She looked out the window at the flaking axle-ends of the abandoned taxi.

The driver came aboard, the same man who had driven her at the start of the week. He drove the bus slowly out of the car park and turned on to the road. On the other side of the water Jagua glided by. She remembered Pata but after a few seconds the thought was eclipsed by a great rush of feeling. In a few hours I will be home, she thought. Mary imagined herself coming out of the lift in the condominium, turning the key, and stepping into her hallway smelling of wood and coffee, and with the two letters on the side-table addressed to Peter, which she had not yet forwarded to him in Prince Edward Island. With a growing sense of dread she started picturing the evening which would follow. She would unpack. She would load the washing machine and turn it on. She would boil a can of soup. And at some point the ache would start; after that her mind would be filled with half-formed thoughts, conversations and memories. They would overwhelm and exhaust her but when she went to bed she would not be able to sleep for a long time and would just lie in the darkness, wet cheeked and in pain. She dreaded her return but at the same time it was curiously consoling and reassuring to know she would be overrun and by what. All she had left of the marriage was the ache but that, at least, was something. Lifting her eyes, she turned her head and looked at Jagua receding into the distance, and felt a hot tear trickling down her cheek and running into her mouth.

The first notes of *Eine Kleine Nachtmusik* started to drift from the speakers.

THE JUMP

JAMES LASDUN

JAMES LASDUN

Born in 1958 James Lasdun read English at Bristol University.
He is the author of a collection of stories *The Silver Age* and a
volume of poetry *A Jump Start*. He has won an Eric Gregory
award for his poetry and the 1986 Dylan Thomas award for *The
Silver Age*. He is currently teaching at New York University.

A FAMILIAR NAME appeared on the screen, above a little American flag. The figure in goggles and ski hat, crouching at the top of the jump slope, could of course be anybody. Nevertheless, Victoria peered forward, wondering whether she might glimpse some recognisable feature among the phosphorescent colours framed in her old television.

The figure launched himself on to the steep slope, driving his poles into the snow with big, gleeful, muscular stabs. His name still hung above him as he plunged towards the lip of the jump, and Victoria had a distinct memory of seeing it in a similar square-angled computer print at the top of a series of papers on Greek literature. Was this the same Carl Pepperall? His face was too masked, his body too crouched, for her to tell. She turned the volume knob, but the commentator must have fallen silent for the build-up to the jump. The figure gathered speed through the rush of static. A different camera showed him in profile slicing across the screen, and for the first time Victoria felt less than amused by the blotting-paper definition of her set. Could it be him? He hurtled down towards the lip, and with a final convulsion of his doubled-up body, took off into the lurid blue sky. But instead of turning into a sleek missile of compacted limbs and skis, he seemed to trip over some invisible rift in the air, and open out into an ungainly assemblage of flailing, wheeling spindles that tumbled through the sky like an enormous daddy-long-legs.

Victoria watched askance as the man crashed to the ground and lay there in a heap, abruptly motionless, the unnatural colours of his ski clothes bleeding into the snow around him.

The commentator started to speak again, but Victoria lunged forward and turned off the television, wishing she had done so before the sports coverage had begun, though glad at least to have been quick enough to protect herself from a knowledge she did not wish to possess.

She took up her work again, and edged herself back into the mood of delicate scorn with which she had been reviewing her old professor's latest offering on Epicharmus (how invigoratingly difficult it was to have a reputation for an unflinching critical eye!). The words flowed easily until, like a sudden *whump*! of oxygen into a smouldering fire, a glimpse of something vast, shadowy, and unnamable opened up in her.

The year before, Victoria had taken a teaching job at the small college of Branderhaven, in Eastern Connecticut. From her classroom she could see across the campus to a buttressed gothic fantasy that had been built to house what the prospectus described as a gym of unrivalled sophistication. It would already be full of students when she arrived to teach her morning class, and however late she left at night, there would still be dozens of young men and women exercising on the mysterious contraptions gleaming in the golden interior light.

'Occasionally they make a sortie,' she had written to her colleagues back in London, 'for a lecture or seminar, but reluctantly, and you feel a little cruel dragging them away, even though it looks like a Bosch hell in there. *Mens Sana* indeed. The faculty are the same. Not for them the salt of bracing inter-disciplinary debate as seasoning to their (epicurean!) lunches; no, any remarks that don't bear directly on the subject of fishing are considered practically scandalous. My contributions are lavish, as you can imagine. Do you remember Chester Platkin, the "corn-fed Oklahoman"? The men are all like him, though the head of Humanities – a Hadley or Bradley – does show minute signs of life. He has offered to escort me around New York. No flowers please.'

A hard, blue light was at work on the city; chiselling and bevelling angles, glazing planes. The cold sky looked packed with cut crystal. The place produced its customary effect on this latest initiate.

'It's like being inside a diamond,' Victoria announced. They passed a luminous violet tanning parlour, a shop selling the flowering parts of tropical plants. 'No, I'll tell you exactly what it's like – it's like a mixture of London, Rome, Madrid and Venus.'

The brilliance of the morning and the affability of her companion had released a surge of effusive spirits in her, and she talked as she had not done since leaving London. Her phrases grew steadily pithier and more daring.

'There's a saurian strain to everything, even the people,' she informed Brad. 'They seem alert to different disturbances, do you know what I mean? As if they get their energies from different food sources. Any second now we're going to see a coiled tongue dart out to catch a fly.'

'Why, what are they eating in London these days?' Brad said, hoisting his amiably gloomy, hound-like jowls into a smile.

Victoria felt herself fuelled by his apparent pleasure. 'That car – it's like a hybrid of a Mercedes and an anaconda. What on earth is it?'

'Just a stretch limo.'

'A stretch limo! Even better!'

They were lunching in the West Village when Victoria, in full cry, experienced a distant pang of a kind she associated vaguely with the first suspicions of material loss – a lost wallet or set of keys. For a while the feeling hung in abeyance, unconnected with any discernible source. But its strength gathered until it made her falter mid-speech. The interruption seemed to startle Brad, and although he had shown no visible signs of inattention, he now smiled guiltily at Victoria, as if he had been caught drifting off. She resumed her flow, but in that fractional pause, her sense that she had been captivating this comfortable, weather-beaten, armchair of a man, had already begun to cloud. When had she lost him? Had her appreciation of his city been too pert for his liking? A few days ago he had seemed like one of those miracles that arrive in your life so matter-of-factly you hardly remember the anguish, the aridity, that preceded them. The smell of his big, damp sheepskin coat had intimated such vastnesses of friendship and repose. Surely she can't have been mistaken. She could feel a shrillness in her voice. She suspected she ought to be quiet, stopped talking for a moment, but Brad said nothing, and the silence pushed them apart like a spreading pool. An ill-looking man went by the window leading a poodle with a bondage stud collar.

'Enter the age of sex by proxy' Victoria said with a little laugh.

Brad smiled, but seemed unamused. Or was she imagining things? She tried again, but all her words came out off-colour, or faintly condescending, and she wished she could shut up. But the more she felt herself grating on Brad, the more she felt it imperative to gain back his attention. As they left the restaurant, she gave a rendering of her dinner with the dean on her first night in Branderhaven, roguishly quoting the catch-phrases that had been bandied about, the *hidden agendas, significant others*: 'Oh, and yes, Brad, *serendipitous moments*, I counted three *serendipiti . . .*' But he wasn't to be tempted into the cosiness of a secret conspiracy, and his non-committal, barely audible response made her feel shallow and treacherous. 'You mustn't think I'm being disloyal, now,' but that only made it worse . . .

All the while, however, she retained a provisional quality in these feelings. She was quite possibly imagining things; one was usually nowhere near as awful as one feared.

In a tunnel of the 14th Street IRT subway, they turned a corner and came face to face with a man defecating. The man stared at them brazenly, furiously, from the ghetto of his hood. As they passed by, Victoria began to say something – not, as it happened, anything to do with the man – but Brad silenced her unceremoniously with an abrupt, upward gesture of the back of his hand.

'I mean,' he said, at once conciliatory, 'I guess that doesn't require any comment.'

Victoria was too crushed to explain that she had actually been about to ask him if he had ever taken a Mediterranean antiquities cruise.

There were tulips on her desk the next morning, white ones with feathery waves bred into the curl. She recognised them vaguely, but couldn't remember where from. There was no note. Brad? It seemed unlikely after the silent, humiliating train journey home last night. But there they were – white, fresh, cleansing the air about them. Perhaps Bradley was one of those men who have to insult you as a way of testing their own feelings. She smiled. She was not averse to the idea of a little combative wooing.

Her performance in class that morning was freer and lighter than usual, leavened by her secret excitement. At one point, several students spontaneously began taking notes – a sight that was always astonishing and gratifying. Even the curly-haired, tracksuited Carl Pepperall, who sat at the back in a permanent foment of suppressed calisthenics, was unusually attentive. He was gazing at her with a look of shy wonder. Had his ears been opened at last to the riches of Greek verse? She asked his opinion of a Sapphic conceit. A panicky look came over him. She smiled, and asked another student. A breath of the tulip fragrance sent a flutter of delicate apprehension through her.

After the class, she made straight for the faculty building. Ita, Brad's bun-guzzling Maltese secretary, gave her a faintly imbecile grin (a crumb on her lower lip), and asked how she'd enjoyed New York. Victoria thought she detected a trace of archness in the woman's voice, though it was hard to tell with the chomping and swallowing going on.

'It was very pleasant, thank you.'

'Bradley sure enjoyed himself.'

'Did he?'

'Sure!' *Shewer*, Ita bellowed it with a shower of crumbs and a rolling of eyes, as if her word had been doubted. She put a glistening finger to one of the trollish warts on her chin, tilted her head, and stared.

Victoria had attempted to make a motherly confidante of this woman, but there was something not quite decently maternal about her; some unresolved grievance or need that came out as quirky sulks or unexplained girlish giggles. She pointed at the door to Brad's office and said, with what was almost a leer, 'He's in there now,' as if Victoria's single thought had been emblazoned on her forehead.

In fact, the woman's peculiar clairvoyance so disarmed Victoria that she found herself opening Brad's door in a state of dreamy suggestibility, without even stopping to think of an excuse. Brad was lounging back with his feet on the desk, and fiddling with a quiver of small, brightly coloured feathers. He glanced up.

'Hi. What can I do for you?'

Victoria faltered. Brad began to wind thread about the feathers while she tried to think of something. His hands were absolutely steady. He did not have the air of a man who had just sent an anonymous gift of fancy tulips.

'I wanted to thank you for a lovely time yesterday.' Victoria improvised at last.

He gave her an empty look.

'Oh, sure.'

She stood helplessly. She felt mortified, but she couldn't bring herself to leave. She watched herself in horror as she stepped forward and touched the little posy of feathers in Brad's hand.

'It's pretty, what is it?' she said.

Then she felt something prick her, and simultaneously heard Brad roar 'fly', or seem to, making the word sound so much more like a command than an answer that she jumped back and fled from the room, smarting.

Ita avoided her eye, busying herself with a sticky finger; a look of sly, sullen amusement on her face.

For a few days Victoria made efforts to find out who her anonymous admirer was. Men who were courteous enough to sit next to her at lunch, or say hello to her in the faculty building, found themselves at the receiving ends of alarmingly piercing looks, that in no time had them retreating into the iciest of professional formalities.

A whisper of quiet panic began to greet her wherever she went. She was too shrewd not to notice the rout – the contortions of evasive behaviour; eyes beseeching rescue, mid-sentence flights for forgotten books, the quick getaways made under cover of a dazzling smile . . .

She realised she had better get a grip on herself. *Anyone would think I came here to get a husband* she wrote to her old colleagues, and she resolved to cut a figure of dignified aloofness in the remaining months of her appointment. She dropped her investigation, and in a mood of combined pique and defiance, withdrew from Branderhaven's small social arena. *If they choose to see me as an academic* gastarbeiter *imported from a nation fallen on hard times, then far be it from me to embarrass them with social obligations. I shall henceforth conduct myself with the meekness of a governess in a Victorian novel . . .*

She applied herself to her classes with added diligence, spending long hours preparing intricate summaries and appraisals, going through the students' papers with an attention vastly out of proportion to anything that had gone into their making. She ate lunch at a table on her own unless she was specifically invited to join the others, which happened rarely, then not at all. And at night she retired early, proudly, with a Sanskrit primer.

The magnolia flowered hard and bright all over the campus. A week later it fell and the ground was covered with drifts of rotting blossom. An early summer brought the class out in silks and pastels. Music came on the breeze from the steps to the gym where the students gathered in the warm, lengthening evenings. Victoria watched them as she worked at her desk. They strolled out of the big glass doors in loose tunics and togas, a little more glowing flesh on show every night. *It's the baths of Caracalla over there*, Victoria wrote, *we'll soon be down to thongs and loincloths . . .*

Bradley receded into the background. There remained something silently contemptuous about his presence whenever it encroached on her horizon, but he was not difficult to avoid. She seldom thought of the white tulips now, remembering them merely as an irritatingly mysterious interruption of her life's natural medium, like a blizzard in a desert. Stoicism and work were to form her continuity. She pledged herself to them with a fierceness that was intended to purge every other inclination from her heart.

One evening she was making notes for a class on Greek metrics, when her concentration – usually excellent – began to stray, and would not be brought to heel. She had long ago discovered the flagellant's secret of control, which is to make things harder when they are hard, rather than easier. She turned from the notes to the more arduous task of memorising another passage of Homer (she had resolved to learn the *Odyssey* by heart before her thirty-fifth birthday). When that didn't work, she pulled a newspaper from her bag, picked a column at random, and began translating it into Greek, an exercise she relished for its sublime purity of purpose.

She had worked herself into a cold blaze of effort searching the ancient language for epithets that would do justice to a modern fashion article (in what terms would they have conceived of da-glo and mohair, of jump suits, boiler suits and distressed leather?) when the door opened, and the bare-footed figure of Carl Pepperall appeared inside the classroom.

He looked at her silently for a moment. He seemed very far away, obscured in a tissue of soft sounds and night scents that had trailed in with him, and then further removed by an after-swirl of dictionary print milling before her eyes like a gnat cloud. She heard him speak – 'Oh, excuse me, ma'am' – and had the odd impression of seeing his lips move out of time with his words. 'I think I left my sneakers in here.' He rummaged for them under a table, stood up, and grinned at her. She hoped he would go now. She was aware of him peering at her, and of herself sitting there without speaking or moving. She must have been straining her eyes. The room looked very dark, and everything in it seemed to pulse. Light dissolved from the boy as if he were a body of light steeped in dark water. There was a long pause.

'Are you alright, ma'am?' she heard him say. The words seemed spoken in a foreign tongue. He was approaching, a look of concern on his face. She had an urge to hide the work she was doing, but her limbs felt too heavy to move. He stood by her, looking down at the desk. Her forehead tingled coldly, as if at the onset of fear.

'You're translating the *Times* into Greek,' he said, 'why are you doing that?'

She could hardly look at him, let alone answer his question. Her head was bowed in shame. After a moment's silence he gave an unexpectedly assured chuckle. 'Why don't you take a break?' he said. 'Come over to the gym.'

She was on a walkway above an echoing, cathedral-like space lit so brilliantly she was at first aware only of a multitudinous gleam of chrome and glass and polished wood. She had been led there in what amounted to a state of suspended volition. Protests and practicalities had crumbled in the face of Carl's polite, confident insistence. (Where had he got that sudden flow of confidence from – her own ebb? Some power source unknown to her?) Her glimpses through the window of the gym had not prepared her for the size of the interior. She remembered her arrival in New York. Here was the same dazzle, the same power of pure scale: a broad central aisle given over to game after game of basketball and tennis; glass-partitioned votive chapels full of weight-lifters, masked fencers, squash players hurling themselves at walls like flies in a jar; a huge, blue pool scribbled over with glyphs of gold light (the ringing air above it somehow darker and more solemn than elsewhere). The locker room, where she changed into a borrowed tracksuit, had a primary, carnal reek. How odd it felt to be back where the body was the measure and arbiter of reality. She had seldom been in this Empire since childhood.

She met Carl by the aerobics machines.

'We'll start with some stretching,' he said, 'if you just copy me.'

She allowed her gaze to settle squarely on his body for the first time. There was an unsightly scar – like a livid rose – at the back of his thigh, but otherwise she had to concede that he looked as a human male was probably intended to look. The few others she had regarded with such license were spiders or manatees in comparison. A smooth plait of muscle was visible under his string vest, which flowed like chain-mail over his shoulders as he plunged forward on alternate knees.

Victoria sounded herself for a reaction. Was she impressed? Amused? (What would the old colleagues think if they could see her with him like this?) Ignited? None of these exactly, though when he turned to smile silently after the receding figure of a girl in a Walkman who had flipped him with her towel, Victoria felt the lapse of attention like a chill from a sudden draught.

'What did you do to your leg?' she heard herself ask in a shrill voice.

He turned his attention back to her. 'Propeller got me. I fell out of a boat in a power race off Virginia Beach.' He grinned. 'I have a lot of them. They're my souvenirs. Here, harpoon dart from the Caribbean, St Croix.' He pulled a sleeve over a sheeny white gouge in his shoulder, then touched his hip. 'Got a steel pin in there from a hang-gliding fall. The wind decided to drop just as I did. That was in Northern Spain, Asturias Mountains. My mom swears she dies every time the phone rings when I'm off on a trip.' He spoke with a gentle pride.

There was something touching about the unembarrassed, intimate disclosures. He seemed to take a guileless pleasure in fixing her attention on his body. Without noticing the point of transition in her own thoughts, she found herself trying to picture him stealing through the icy fog of a March dawn with a bunch of white tulips in his hand. She looked at him afresh. The image shimmered in and out of plausibility. There seemed all at once an irresistible hint of affinity between the flowers, and the boy's fair curls and limbs gleaming in the neon light. Had he been a god visiting a mortal in a dream, Victoria mused, he might have left such flowers as his tokens of remembrance. She smiled, and tried to shrug off the idea; the boy must be at least ten years younger than herself.

'Now we'll try the machines,' he said.

He sat her on a bicycle and explained the principles of aerobics. He was standing beside her, just out of her field of vision, so that he was both looming and abstract. His voice was impassively polite, like an airline steward's. It was difficult to get any purchase on him, or on her relation to him, now that they were outside the simple geometries of the classroom, and now that the spectre of the tulips had been raised again. She didn't know whether to feel flattered or obscurely insulted by the way he was ordering her around. Then too, she recalled now, there was the matter of his papers – those punctual, beautifully word-processed reports on classical literature, that arrived on her desk like lambs to the slaughter, so virginally innocent were they of any content. She was almost certainly going to have to fail him at the end of the semester. It would be a pity if he thought he had done anything to make her vindictive. Awkward too. She began to wonder whether she had been incautious coming here with one of her students. Delicate suggestions of impropriety seemed to be flittering through the air. She didn't know what to do. She didn't even know what she wanted to do. The situation seemed globed in a complex burnish, like that of a vase under several layers of glaze, with a dozen different shades and hues. And at the point where her own feelings might have been expected to guide her, the shades merely deepened to a pitch of absolute mysteriousness.

Without warning, Carl touched her throat. As it turned out, he was only taking her pulse, but it felt like a detonation, and in the few silent seconds in which he let his fingertips rest on her jugular, her blood seemed to perform a drum-roll right beneath them, and in her agitation she pedalled furiously, as if trying to reach a speed that would persuade the fixed machine to move.

'You probably should exercise more,' Carl said, and prescribed ten minutes each of cycling and rowing.

She sat on a ledge in the women's steambath, stupefied by pain and exhaustion. *See you later*, Carl had said. Did that mean later on this evening? She was as perplexed as ever.

At first, on the bicycle, the extreme physical effort had been an adventure, and she had reported on it to Carl in her customary style. 'I feel like a maternity ward for new-born muscles screaming into life,' she had informed him, and 'the more pain you're in, the longer each second on the stopwatch seems to last. There must be a point of convergence between absolute agony and eternity. I suppose that's where hell is.'

But at a certain level of exhaustion, her body had begun to reel her mind in like a kite, until it was wrapped so closely about her limbs it seemed merely a dim radiance from them, barely distinguishable from the sweat and heat. No more thoughts occurred in it; only the notation of strain and lung-burn, and the wish to stop.

'I can't do any more,' she gasped after the first ten minutes.

'Quick,' Carl said, 'it's important to keep your pulse up.' He led her to the rowing machine, and was strapping her feet to the boards, heedless of her protests.

'Now pull.' It seemed she must.

The seat slid back on the horizontal spine as she dragged at the weighted chain, her feet braced against the boards. The chain drove a geared bicycle wheel with flaps fixed all around it, which fanned her as she sweated. Carl stood over her, again a little behind, issuing curt instructions – *a little faster, pull harder now, keep that speed up* . . .

A pattern had emerged: she would reach a peak of agony, slacken, be admonished, protest she had had enough, then feel a downsurge of shadow as Carl leaned forward, an indistinct mass of male form, to touch her throat. And once she had discovered the degree of protest that would bring him, she had half-consciously summoned him, as one does summon again and again the thing that most perplexes. She still wasn't sure what it was his touch induced. It felt like a panicky lurch, as over a forgotten step, or perhaps more like the lurch from a step that isn't there. It was always this way in matters of physical experience; one was more than ever the proverbial Greek in Rome; a creature of refinement thronged by the unpredictable barbarians of appetite. One never quite knew what was going on. A limitless, treacherous obscurity would open up, accompanied by a feeling of helplessness. It was this helplessness that kept her to the task. She was only capable of doing what she was told. She recognised the feeling from three or four other occasions in her adult life – the same unaccountable surrender, the same excruciating pain, the same blind obligation to go through with it.

'OK,' he said at last. 'You can stop now.'

She lay prone, awaiting further instructions. But he was already leaving.

'See you later,' he said with a smile, and was gone.

Now what? A drama of folly seemed to be unfolding in some trembling zone between the real and the imaginary. How would it proceed, she wondered; towards a moonlit confession under the magnolias? A silent entanglement in the locked classroom? She felt quite numb towards the eventualities, as if she too were suspended in that indeterminate zone. The steam appeared to have dissolved her skin. It swirled and bloomed inside her. Blurred pink figures moved softly around the room.

And then a paler one came in and sat down opposite. It was the girl who had flipped her towel at Carl. Her skin was almost as white as the porcelain tiles, which boosted the bits of colour on her. She swept back a damp mass of reddish ringlets, yawned, wrinkled her nose, and gazed into the steam with a look of self-satisfaction.

But before that, her eyes had flickered briefly over Victoria's, and in the instant, the older woman had felt the ripple of banished illusion. One flickering look, and it was gone! She wondered at her capacity for missing the obvious. How could she have imagined Carl would be remotely interested in her when a creature like this was at his disposal? It wasn't as if she had even desired the things she had imagined, unless a weakness for the flattery of being desired is itself considered a desire. If she felt anything now, it was relief at what she had been spared.

How familiar this turn of events felt. Fantasy, disillusion, relief: the cycle seemed peculiarly her own. Even when the fantasy happened by chance to land her in a grapple with one of those spiders or manatees, there would always be a moment when something rock-like reared up with an unarguable veto to any pleasure she might have had from it, and in retrospect this moment would always seem one of deliverance. It had even been so, she realised, with Bradley, after that day in New York. She had been too preoccupied with her double humiliation to notice it at the time, but after it was all over, something in her had breathed an unmistakable sigh of relief.

Meanwhile, as she looked at the girl, she could feel the knotted burden of Carl, and the tulips, and the strain of over-work, unravelling, and it was like a physical sensation of loosening in her body.

Gradually, a mood of benign calm settled on her. She smiled ruefully to herself, thinking of Carl and the girl together – an affinity of toned flesh. She felt an almost protective magnanimity, as if she were an old priestess presiding over their nuptials. Steam made the blood tingle in her capillaries. She wondered vaguely if it was dangerous to stay too long in the room, but she had no desire to leave. She had seldom known anything so luxurious as this steam room; one felt almost afloat in the assuaging cloud. She stared at the girl, glazed in good feeling. It wasn't often that she was able to forget herself in this way. She wondered whether the supposedly warmer, more candid palette of American emotion was at last beginning to colour her own feelings. Waves of tenderness seemed to be pulsing out of her.

The girl caught her eye – a green glint – then looked away. Pink blotches had appeared on her skin. The corners of her dark red lips were drawn up further, and to a finer point than most, as if they had been detailed by an uncommonly expert hand. How nice she would look if she smiled. Victoria could hardly believe how well-disposed she felt towards her; towards everything! It seemed to her inexpressibly wonderful that Carl and this girl should be lovers. She smiled, picturing them together. The steam plumed obligingly into boas, bulged into pillows and glistening cherub-clusters. Again the girl caught her eye, and it was like a splash of sea-green against the portholes of a sinking ship. How delightful to sink like this; into a whirlpool of soft contours, mild brushstrokes of bluish shadow, steam-darkened braids and knots of copper . . . Victoria had always considered any form of body fascination to be infantile. She refused to read certain novels: *boredom not prudishness*, she would tell people; *it's like having a travel book that does nothing but tell you about the workings of the car*. And even now she had a suspicion that she ought not to indulge these feelings. But where was the harm? His hand would descend through the meadow of freckles sloping from each sunburnt shoulder to an aureole ringed, she noticed, with dainty marks that might have been cast from the paw-prints of a thimble-sized lion. She imagined the contact of hand and breast. Another green wave crashed as something exulted in her blood.

'Jesus!' The girl exploded, and jumped up, covering herself with her hands. She spat out another word as she left the room.

Victoria recoiled as it tore into her, bulleting through what seemed like a series of opaque veils through which she was able to glimpse briefly the source of her imagined exultation . . . The glimpse faded as the rips healed, though she was not altogether spared the knowledge, because in the flurry of violation, something brilliant and silken had rippled out of her memory, and to her astonishment she was seeing a vase of those white, feathery tulips in the faculty room at the very beginning of the semester, an overheard voice saying *yes, they're pretty, my neighbour gives them to me, he's a commercial breeder;* the voice female, accented, muffled by sounds of chewing and salivation . . .

It took a few days for the glare of revelation to fade. Something in the mixture of cruelty and craving in Ita's gesture, gave it a certain lingering fascination. At last, though, Victoria was able to consign the image and all it insinuated back to the darkness from which it had risen. All that remained of the episode in the gym was a sense of having been made a fool of, and this, along with the other indignities she had suffered over the semester, confirmed her in her opposition to Branderhaven.

A day of blinding sunshine; the shadow-etched campus emptied for some annual, end-of-semester joust between seniors and alumni; cries drifting over from the sports field behind the gym . . . Victoria was clearing out her desk in the classroom, enjoying a rare moment of tranquillity, when a woman knocked on the open door and strolled in. She took off a pair of sunglasses. She was handsome, big-boned, her blonde hair grained with grey; blue eyes that appeared lit from the back with mauve. She smiled at Victoria, extending a hand. 'Hi. I'm Sophie Pepperall. I think you know my son.'

Most of what followed had a dreamlike, faintly incredible quality, even at the time. The woman had stood before her, pleading for her son, though pleading was not quite the word as she seemed sure of getting what she wanted, as if she were going through the motions of an elaborate ritual, purely out of some vague nostalgia for more courtly times. She was relaxed, almost playful, sunglasses dangling from one hand, the other trespassing lightly and confidently on Victoria's arm. Her gist was that Carl's place at the business school his father had attended was contingent on his not actually failing any of the subjects. A bare minimum pass all round would satisfy them, but they drew the line at failure, 'which is lenient of them,' she said, 'considering nobody actually does fail these days. In fact it's pretty rare not to get something in the higher Bs at least. Bradley Crane told me Carl was the only student he'd ever known be given an actual fail . . .' She looked at Victoria candidly, leaving the pleasant spill of colour from her eyes to express the thing that even her idea of decorum forbade her to say. Carl's face stared out from hers, boyish and vulnerable beneath her beautiful smile.

Victoria remembered telling Mrs Pepperall that her son had failed because in five papers he hadn't recorded a single accurate fact or intelligent opinion. Even so it had taken her several uncomfortable minutes to convince the woman that her decision was a matter of grade averages; a solid, simple mathematical fact, and not negotiable.

She was still recovering from the effort a few minutes later, when Brad strode in without knocking. He was carrying the ledger book with student grades, and he looked more dour than Victoria had ever seen him.

'I'd like you to reconsider this now,' he said, opening the book and shoving his finger at the word *failed* written in Victoria's neat, tiny script.

She tried to keep her voice steady. 'I've just been asked to reconsider it by his mother.'

'Yes, and now I'd like to ask you again.' It seemed he had thrust a pen into her hand, which was poised above the ledger. He stood waiting, his face stiff with anger.

'I'm afraid it's out of the question,' she said, and flinched as if from an expected blow, as Brad leaned over the desk towards her.

'Listen to me, young lady. You were hired to give these kids some background in classical myth. That's not a big deal around here, as you may have noticed. Now I don't interfere when I get reports of you making them produce scholarly papers on Greek metrics and God knows what else, but when it comes to fucking up some perfectly innocent student's career over a deal like this, then I have to tell you you're stepping out of line.'

Was this what her Greeks thought of as *Ananke*: Necessity; the force that draws all things forward to their designated place, do what they might to resist it, so that even one's defiance of its decrees is taken into account?

She sat in the wintry shadows of her flat, facing the darkened screen of the television where the figure had tripped and lurched and spun out of control. For a moment she felt an urge to switch the set on again, not that the programme was likely to be on the same subject any longer. But even suppose it was, she told herself, and suppose the figure was indeed her Carl Pepperall, and suppose, yes, just suppose, something unpleasant had happened to him, what did any of that have to do with her? She assured herself that she had done nothing to be ashamed of, that she had acted out of the same high, unflinching principle as she was now bringing to her old professor's book on Epicharmus. In the end one could only shrug, and dismiss the episode, if there even was an episode, as a grotesque coincidence, of the kind that life occasionally throws up in imitation of those engineered by the lesser tragedians. It would be a mistake to look for any meaning in it. She switched on a light, and returned to her review.

But she was in tumult. She saw the empty space again, the white tulips and the treacherous steam, and the vibrant white blur of mountainside with the body sprawled on it. She saw the mother again, and the son's face buried in her features. A tremor went through her. She felt briefly the cold touch of eternity that had used her own soul as its instrument. How exquisitely it had fingered the keys!

For a moment her resistance had begun to falter. She could feel the various pressures urging her hand to make the necessary movement. She even began to lower the pen. But as it came to within two or three inches of the page, something stalled her. It was more a matter of *can't* than *won't*. The decision seemed to come from some inflexible source of command that sent its veto like a cold wind between pen and page.

She had looked back up at Bradley, and found that her strength had rallied. With a little smile she offered him back the pen.

'You do it,' she challenged him, her head tilted back. 'Go on, why don't you? I won't tell anyone.'

She assumed he would now inform her that this was precisely what she intended to do, and that he didn't give a damn who she told. Let him. She had acted correctly; what they did with the boy's grades was no longer any concern of hers.

But he merely snatched the pen from her hand, and snapped shut the book.

'Very amusing,' he said, and walked out, leaving her with a sense of victory which, even at the time, had felt curiously incomplete.

AN ACT OF LOVE

DEBORAH LEVY

DEBORAH LEVY

Deborah Levy was born in 1959. A playwright and a poet, her most recent work for the theatre was *Heresies* for the Royal Shakespeare Company. An anthology of her short stories will be published by Jonathan Cape in November 1988.

A NURSE IS on a road somewhere off the Western coast of Australia, pushing a Honda 50 which seems to have broken down. She is thinking she can smell the sulphurous odour of the devil at work.

'Oh God . . . Expiate all the sins I have committed today . . .'

She notices some of the wild grass, bleached from the sun, is blighted.

She is stuck on a road full of plague.

'Oh God . . . Expiate all the sins I have committed this day . . . And during all my life . . .'

Despite her vow never to pray again, these words leak from her mouth.

When her father told her it was her destiny to become a nun, he meant her economic destiny. She is the daughter of struggling, sometimes starved agricultural labourers and knows a field full of plague is a field full of grief.

She adjusts the carburettor with a little stick and the Honda starts.

At the age of eleven she delivered, single-handed, the last of her nine brothers. It was at this time she began to have serious doubts about the immaculate conception, and unwisely confided to her father in her country hick drawl that she thought Jesus must have been born with blood and faeces on his face, just like all her brothers were.

He dragged her to the garage where he beat her for twenty minutes with a bundle of canes. When he saw he had drawn blood and it was running down her legs, he told her to kneel down while he beat her shoulders and breasts.

Her mother held her son in one hand and stuffed a lemon in her mouth with the other. Every time she heard the thwack of the canes, lemon juice squirted into her mouth. She hoped, somehow, that suffering the sour juice would help her daughter suffer less.

After she had thanked her father for beating her (this was customary) she ran away forever. Ran in her shorts and plimsols, bruised and bleeding, into the sun. Or so it seemed then. Two days later she was taken in by nuns who ran a small rural hospital. They bathed her cuts, took out the splinters of cane with tweezers, fed her broth and home-baked bread, promised never never to return her to her father. Instead, they trained her at eleven and half to become a nurse. She was known locally as the child healer, and when she paid visits to poorly families left little footprints in the red dust.

The nurse says it was the splinters in her breasts that put an end to her prayers. Even the pressure of putting her hands together hurt too much. But praying was getting difficult anyway. Every time she spoke to God the Father she tasted lemon juice in her mouth and this made her think of her mother and cry. She preferred to talk to her sisters who thought she was a miracle child and prayed for her to be happy.

By the time she was seventeen-years-old she had delivered three hundred and ninety babies. How clever of God, she thought, to have assumed the most heart-warming of all disguises, a baby. The Baby God.

So many mothers. So many babies.

At nineteen-years-old she performed her first abortion.

A woman who had come to her to be birthed seven times, came to her for the eighth time and wept on her shoulder. She said she was tired and poor. And sore. There. To avoid sleeping with her husband for whom she had no love, she sat on the stairs all night pretending to read a book, but he would always come and get her and fuck her and fuck her and fuck her. She didn't want any more babies. Life was bad and sad enough. The nurse coughed, fiddled with her handkerchief, looked the woman in the eye . . .

'Why me?'

'A hunch.'

Ah, she thought, I always knew it was my task on earth to weave heresies of various kinds. It is possible this woman, who smells of ache, this woman with knotted hair, is a saint summoning me to perform what is my calling.

'Give me a week to get sorted out,' she drawled, and went off to study her medical books.

Day and night and every minute she could snatch from her other duties (delivering babies) she drew diagrams, worked out the instruments available to her, worried about what she should use as an anaesthetic, collected sterile pads and towels. Heart beating too hard, she lay awake counting the days, dreaming the act, imagining each moment of it, until the roosters told her it was dawn and crowed and crowed as if this was the last day of the world. The freckled nineteen-year-old who ran into the sun when she was eleven, emptied the contents of the woman's womb into a silver tray.

Half-a-mile down the road she could hear the sisters singing mass, their voices rising and falling just as the belly of the woman rose and fell; she looked like a child in her pink nightdress and this made the nurse weep. She wept for her own mother, for her childhood, and because, as the woman began to wake up, murmuring thanks, sighing, kissing the intelligence in the young nurse's hands, she suddenly got a glimpse of her whole life.

She made some tea and they played a game of chess, very slowly, while the cicadas outside croaked in between stones.

The woman sent her a box of marrows and sweetcorn, fell pregnant two months later, and died in childbirth.

*   *   *

So where is the nurse going to on her Honda? She is buzzing off to perform her five-hundred and seventy-seventh abortion.

Afterwards, she washes her hands and purées pumpkin to make soup. Adds cayenne pepper, nutmeg and sour cream. Then she makes a lemon souflée and while it is in the oven, wanders out into the garden where she tends three types of jasmine.

She is forty-five years old.

Her hair is silver and she ties it back with a green ribbon. The chickens in the yard peck her ankles.

She is standing on a rock above the sea.

Alone. She baits her hook, casts, squints, moves a little from side to side.

As the sea pulls under her, she looks out at the small island ahead and lights herself a small cigar.

CITY OF LIES

ADAM LIVELY

ADAM LIVELY

Adam Lively was born in 1961 in Swansea. He studied history and philosophy at universities in England and America. His first novel, *Blue Fruit*, was published in January 1988. He is an active member of CND and European Nuclear Disarmament.

THE CITY WAS often covered by heavy cloud, the nights as impenetrable as pitch. New day, and the sky would explode. Blueness. Clouds racing up the sky like frightened cats scrambling up a ladder. The seasons were extreme, but stagey and not quite credible. They were like creaking backdrops, absurd mechanics of an ancient theatre. The city itself was beyond weather. Only in the poorer parts, in midwinter, did the buildings expose their bones to the raw.

It was in one of these parts that I first arrived in the city. I took a room in a ramshackle house from whose window I could watch the streets. I sat wrapped in furs and looked down at the crowds struggling through the snow.

The city was so enormous that nobody could ever leave it, even at the moment of death. People arrived all the time, but the city could absorb them without growing. It was infinite. The gypsies, for example, were from somewhere else, but no one could ever say where it was or when they had come. So they were ignored by the citizens. And because they were invisible, many of them became musicians. For the best musicians are heard and not seen.

Gypsy bands roamed the length and breadth of the infinite city, mustering an audience where they could or plunging themselves into apocalyptic street parties. I have never seen the air look so dark as at those parties. Who knows how long I sat in the midst of them, allowing my body to be shaken by the stamping feet, distances folding and unfolding before me as day turned to night and night became day? All things glittered and absorbed me: the routines of hedonism change through repetition. So taken was I by surfaces, like a listener mesmerised by the mere sound of a story's words, that it was many days till I heard the music. All I saw were the responses, the phenomena. Not the thing itself.

Ten musicians stood in a loose group, watching each other and smiling occasionally as they played. Their music was wild, highly pitched, tripping over its own syncopations. It wailed abandon. The rhythms that carried it, that churned through the body of the audience, came from the cracked violin of an old man. He sliced his strings with his bow to a regular beat, the off-beat, while the chorus of pipes and trumpets ululated above him. Since the main beat was only in the old man's head, the music was always pitching forward, inducing mania and edginess. It was as if it were always rolling towards an abyss.

(How can one describe music with words? Words rise stiffly and vertically from the page. Music moves sideways, in ten dimensions. It billows like a sail, or cuts the nostrils with its acridity. It drains from the words that describe it like water down a hole, leaving the words as dry as wind-blown corpses.)

I was so taken by the music that I asked the old man if I could become his pupil. He agreed. We sat together in the cold, by the mournful embers of the street-fire, and he told me his history. He had been a musician for fifty years, since the days when the city had been wealthy and peaceful. Now it was only the poorest that knew what music was. He also told me what music meant to him. 'Music,' he said, 'is pure love. The slightest inflection of it can capture a man forever. After someone has heard music, that person is a better person, because they have created something that is perfect but does not exist. For what is music? Where is it? It's not the violin, for that's merely the thing that makes it. Can you see it? Can you smell it? Yes, you can hear it. But do you hear it all? Does it not draw you along, pointing always beyond itself in your mind, whispering to you that outside it, within it, there is a yet more beautiful secret? We musicians educate, we lead people out of blind faith in what is. That is why we are dangerous. We are the purveyors of what is not, of moments that are destroyed and rebuilt even as we think of them. The people who have heard our music have constructed in their minds things that are not, which gives them power to judge better the things that are. That is why we are utopians, because we deny the priority of what is over what is not, has not been, and could never be. Music opens our minds to the inadequacy of what is.'

I was moved by what my teacher had said. All through the winter I followed him backwards and forwards across the freezing city. I took lessons from him when I could, and talked with him over the smouldering ashes of a hundred fires. He was a quiet man, always listening for that silent, mystical downbeat upon which his livelihood depended. Sometimes he was so quiet as to disappear, and indeed the audiences that heard the band never noticed him. For accompanists are only noticed if they play badly. My teacher had never played badly, and had thus only ever been present in the mind of his audience through his absence.

For months I was gripped by the idea of my teacher and his music. It was only with the spring thaw that I began to change. I fell in love. It happened in one of the city's tiny public parks. The music was keening out into the streets, and I was sitting hugging my knees in the shelter of a broad-leafed, plastic tree. Soft rain was falling. I had long ago abandoned my furs, for one never knew whether another winter would come. She came in out of the rain and sat beside me. We talked for many hours. She had green hair and green, beautifully squinting eyes. At first as we talked, the music was still present in my ears along with the words she was speaking. But gradually the music faded away.

She asked me who I was. I told her how I had arrived in the city, met the old man at a street party and become his pupil. She remarked that she could never love a man whose ambition it was to become invisible. A true man, she said, was one who grasped his own life firmly and held it up for all to see. That was a man. She got up and left.

Since music no longer held any attraction for me, I left the gypsy band. Weeks passed. The motorised planets spun around the neon sun. The lights of the city challenged the blackness of the sky. By night it was as bright on the streets as day. People were grateful to be shielded from darkness, but felt unsure of their bodies. The stories they told in the bars were invented.

The city was so vast that in certain parts different languages were spoken. One day I was entering such an area when I saw an eminent politician hurrying along the street. He was scared of poor people, and always hurried lest he should meet some. It suddenly dawned on me that the girl might love me if I were a politician. Politicians are visible. I followed the man home, and waited outside his house for four days.

Four times the sun crossed the sky, efficiently and on time. Four times the politician left his house and returned home. Here, I thought, was a man who had firmly grasped his own life. On the fourth evening, as he was entering his house, I came forward and introduced myself. At first he was suspicious. I was asking a lot of him, that he should take me on as his disciple and apprentice in politics. But when he realised I was a foreigner, and after I had demonstrated my naivety, he relaxed. He asked me in. I flattered him and promised him things. He agreed. He would take me on, but in return for my services as tutor to his son.

Next day, he took me to the Parliament. One gazed in wonder. It was hard to believe that everything around one was so important. We had not been in the chamber long when a vote was called on the matter under discussion. At a signal, as at the beginning of a race, all the Members leapt forward and grabbed one of two levers before them. The noise was tremendous.

When things had died down, I asked my mentor the reason for this strange procedure. In reply, he furnished me with a history. It seems that for years both citizens and Members had been so strongly against any divergence from the majority that Members were loath to commit their vote without knowing which way the majority was going. For to be perpetually among the losing minority could cost a Member his lucrative career. Hence, it had been in the interests of each Member before casting his vote to wait until a majority of levers had been pulled, and the totals for yes and no racked up on the scoreboard at the front of the chamber. Things had got to the stage where nobody was pulling their levers any more. A vote would be called, and the Members would sit quite still, eyeing their neighbours for signs of movement. For hours the Members would sit in nervous silence, and frequently the session would have to be abandoned with no decision taken.

A number of remedies for this problem had been tried. One, which grew up spontaneously among the Members, was to conduct private polls before a vote to determine which way the majority would go. Individual Members would hire their own private pollster, who would scurry around the other Members before a vote to discover their views on the issue. But this way out of the impasse soon ran into thickets of intrigue and deception, since it was in the interests of Members to mislead their political competitors. Also, the pollsters were a mercenary and unprincipled collection of rascals who could be easily bribed to deceive their employers. Members were spending all their time poring over sheets of statistics, or concocting elaborate schemes to ascertain the trustworthiness of their own pollsters. Such was their bewilderment that they reverted to the safe old practice of sitting firmly on the fence, rather than risk an unpopular move.

Then, by a mutual, silent consent, another remedy had emerged for a while. It was discovered that if just one Member cast his vote, he could set in motion a satisfactory and predictable landslide of votes to that opinion. This game of follow-the-leader soon came to an end, however, as more than one ambitious Member made the initial plunge in order to decide the issue at hand for themselves. As soon as things began to revert to that dangerous state where votes were being cast without sure knowledge of the outcome, the Members once again refrained from committing themselves.

So in the end, a time limit of four seconds had been imposed upon the voting. This interval, it was thought, would be sufficient for the most elderly Member to raise himself from his seat and depress his lever, yet brief enough to forestall calculations as to which way the vote might be going. This was the source of that hasty commotion as the Members leapt up to vote.

I asked my mentor why the Members didn't do away with the elaborate system of levers and mechanical scoreboards, and instead conduct a secret ballot. His reply was that a secret ballot would be contrary to the free and open expression of each man's principles.

The setting of time limits upon voting did not, of course, obviate the need for private pollsters. The Members needed them more than ever, and it was in that capacity that I was apprenticed, to garner the Members' opinions and report them back to my mentor. Before I entered Parliament, I hadn't grasped how precious a commodity is the truth. Too precious to be squandered, it should be guarded and only released judiciously, with economy. I had thought that truth and lie were simple matters. In fact, they are the object of a science. To talk merely of 'lies' is gross philistinism. There are underestimates, terminological inexactitudes, ironies, mental reservations, and a thousand other gradations and qualities. I learn them all.

In return, I taught the politician's sly and surly son. I kept to the established curriculum to begin with. When I tired of that, I told him of things I had seen on my travels. I told him about other worlds, where people walk on their heads, pulled along by their hair, or where the mountains reach up out of the atmosphere into space. The boy didn't believe me. But these truths were more thrilling than the mundane, pragmatic lies I told in Parliament, so I continued to tell them.

Then one night my mentor called me into his study. He said that word had got round the Members of the eccentric tutor he had engaged. It was said that I talked of places outside the city. I protested that what I had said was true, and that these places really did exist, to which my mentor replied that if that were the case it only made my crime more heinous. I was dismissed. I should leave his house at once, before I covered it with disgrace.

Hot summer burned logic from the pavements. The neon sun was turned up brighter. The sluice gates of the city were opened, and the people poured out onto the streets. There were riots and diseases. I bobbed about for weeks on the flow of the crowd until one day I found myself washed up at the stall of the Doctor of Ideas.

The Doctor of Ideas had set himself up in one of the busiest streets in the most crowded part of the city, where the passing crowd could eddy around him. He was a tall, fat man, half-naked and sitting cross-legged on a dais like a guru. To the many who stopped to listen, he said that he ministered to the sick and that his method was to touch not their bodies but their minds. Everything, he explained, has a name, and to each name there corresponds an idea. The sick are only sick because they call themselves sick. The Doctor of Ideas would call them 'healthy' or 'vigorous', and thereby change their ideas and cure their bodies. As he talked, the Doctor of Ideas handed out leaflets, stretching out his long plump arms to the people:

TONIGHT !!!!
At the Old Central Hall
A cleansing of your *Enterprise*
And *Commitment*
BE THERE!
To purge your sickness
With the expert Doctor of Ideas
Entry Toll: 5 Rollads

I went to the old Central Hall that night. I found a large crowd milling about the square, waiting for the doors to open. Sitting on a low wall, I watched the sun as it was switched to orange, then red, and was gradually dimmed. Suddenly, out of the crowd, appeared the girl whom I had met beneath the plastic tree. She sat with me on the wall. We talked. I asked her why she was there.

'I'm finding myself,' she said. 'I'll go anywhere to look.'

She stood up. At that moment, the doors of the hall swung open and the crowd surged forward. I lost her in the crush.

Nothing had prepared me for the magnificence of the interior. The Hall itself was plain but it had been wondrously decked out for the occasion. Traces of incense greeted the nostrils, so that one invested the place immediately with mystery and esoteric promise. In the gallery above the door, at the back of the Hall, musicians played an ethereal dirge on fiddles, trumpets, and deep, resonant drums. Down one of the side aisles, through the passive congregation, the procession had started. In front came two boys swinging silver receptacles that billowed forth fragrant smoke. The smoke rose in delicate wreaths above their heads, and on their chests hung large mirrors. Behind them, swaying slowly from side to side in time to the music, came the Doctor of Ideas. His fat figure was draped to the ankles in a resplendent tunic of pure white cloth, into which had been sewn a thousand tiny mirrors. From time to time, these, and the giant mirrors that hung from the necks of the boys, caught the brilliance of the enormous lanterns that hung from the ceiling, so that all at once the whole scene would be a flash of light and silver splendour. After the Doctor of Ideas came a dozen of his closest disciples, each with his own likeness pinned to his breast. And members of the congregation, gazing at this spectacle, would find themselves looking on their own reflection in one of the giant mirrors that led the procession. Everything seemed amplified.

They processed once around the Hall and came to a halt at the front. The Doctor of Ideas turned to the congregation and said, 'Come forth, all ye who are imagining yourselves sick.'

At which he spread his arms out, there was a rustle and a movement in the congregation, and they began to go forward. One group at a time, they knelt in a long line before him. He passed from one to another, handing them for a few seconds a small mirror and saying these words: 'Take this image and look. Whensoever you feel sick, do this in remembrance of what you may become.'

The supplicants gazed reverently into the mirror, then rose and stumbled back to their seats past the waiting multitude. And when all had feasted on their image, the Doctor of Ideas retreated to the high pulpit. Standing amidst a blaze of purple light, he spoke, smoothing the words with waves of his hand.

'My friends, we are gathered here today to find ourselves, when all about us is crumbling and disease. When a man loses himself in the city, he tries to get back to where he started. That is what we must do, we must return to the vision of the children. The little children see things as they are. They are like transparent eyeballs. They are open. They see everything, and they see that everything is beautiful. Forget your brother, your friend, your master, your servant. They are all just objects in your all-seeing vision. They say, "We are special objects." But why should we listen to them? A man should be alone before what is there, and then he will no longer be alone because the universe will fill him and he will fill the universe.

'And what are your brother, your friend, your master, your servant? They are words. It is *you* who assign words. Words are like hands you reach out to grasp the world and mould it as you will. Or like this purple light that flows into every corner of the Hall and changes what you see. Or like the face that smiles and watches its reflection smile too. Yes, it is that close. If the one moves, if you gently smile, the other does so also. Smile, my friends, and you will be well. Smile!'

At which the people cried with happiness, their ailing bodies racked with sobs, that all would be well.

But I could not help thinking about my old friend, the old musician who had taught me. He had lived his whole life to be invisible. Thinking of him, I suddenly stood up and shouted at the Doctor of Ideas:

'We can't see everything. We can only see the objects because of the spaces between them. It's the spaces that present the objects to us. *They* are the most important thing. But they're invisible!'

A deathly hush fell over the congregation. Only the Doctor of Ideas moved. He slowly turned his head in my direction and let his eyes spear me on a shaft of hatred.

'Get him out of here,' he hissed.

My arms were seized from behind and I was dragged to the back of the Hall. My assailants were two of the attendants from the procession. I remember how my head banged against the images they carried on their chests, as they dragged me – my feet trailing across the floor, kicking the chairs aside in impotent protest – through the congregation. They kicked and punched me a couple of times, then gave me one mighty push, which expelled me from the door and sent me, arms spinning like a windmill, to the bottom of the stairs outside.

The sun was moving away from the city. The city itself was rotating slower and slower. These changes were being effected in such minute increments that no one noticed them, and only in time would they mean anything. For the present, they were merely bureaucratic adjustments. The day only seemed longer because that year, for the first time, it had been decided to continue the summer forever. As the days grew hotter, thousands of people flocked to the large fields near the imagined outskirts of the city. These people were not needed for anything.

High-rise blocks stretched away through the heat haze like the autumn stubble I remembered from another world. I climbed a high tower and looked down at the distant people filing on to the field through a large, metal gate. As they passed through the gate, they each paused for a moment before proceeding to lie in rows on the plastic grass. I asked a woman who was standing beside me what was happening, and she told me that there was a device implanted in the gate that radiated an electro-magnetic pulse. This pulse altered subtly the brain-waves of all who passed through the gate.

Expanding on the purpose of the gate, she explained to me that by nature we experience time not as a succession of linear moments, points on a straight line, but as an ever-shifting pattern of retentions and protensions, of memories and expectations. Just as the beginning of a melody is only revealed in its full meaning by the melody as a whole, so is time created by growth, movement, hope. The excellent achievement of the electronic device in the gate, apparently, was to break this pattern, to sunder the troubling links whereby our past and future haunt us. All who passed through the gate experienced themselves in a floating world of forever present.

They lay passive on the grass, gazing up into the blue sky. I watched, fascinated, as more and more filed through the gate on to the field, adding to the thousands that already lay there in neat rows. Then I seemed to see something way above them in the sky, shimmering in the summer heat. At first I couldn't make out what it was. Then it resolved itself before my eyes. It was a hologram, a field of passive people gazing up into the sky. The people gazed up at it. Recorded and projected instantaneously, it replicated every detail, every tiny movement that occurred on the vast, flat field. And the most important detail that it included was the hologram in the sky, the self-image that the people stared up at, so that above the first, spawned by it, appeared a second, and a third projected by the second, and on and on, like a hall of mirrors, in an endless succession of layers. Yet this appearance of multiplicity across space was an illusion. The image was one, imploding, multiplying itself internally to infinity. It had those attributes the Scholastics used to assign to God: 'One, simple, existing by and through itself, measureless, unbounded, incomprehensible.'

I listened. The field was eerily still, as soundless as death. The tower-blocks, solid in the heat haze of the city, seemed to make silent comment on this tower of illusion. As my eyes swept the thousands of people below me, they paused for a moment on the girl with green hair. She was staring up with rapt expression. Perhaps she had found herself. Through the hot silence, I could hear her surroundings fall away from her, her ears go deaf. Her eyes succumbed to the click of depthless repetition.

I asked the woman who stood next to me what it was they were staring at. She gave a mirthless laugh.

'Pictures of reality,' she said.

I looked back at the field. Time had stood still, lost its elastic rhythms. The space had closed up between what is and what might be. Squeezed out were music, imagination. The field had fallen absolutely silent. I descended the tower, pulling myself down by my hair, and continued on my way.

TRAIN TRACKS

AIDAN MATHEWS

AIDAN MATHEWS

Aidan Mathews was born in 1956 in Dublin. He was educated by the Jesuit Fathers before attending University College, Dublin, Trinity College, Dublin, and Stanford University, California. His published work includes two selections of poetry, *Windfalls* and *Minding Ruth*, and three plays: *The Diamond Body*, which has been produced in Dublin, London, Boston, Avignon and Paris; *The Antigone*, an absurdist re-working of the original text; and *Exit/Entrance*, a surrealist play about a suicide love pact which was produced in Dublin and London. His much-acclaimed collection of short stories *Adventures in a Bathyscope* was published in 1988. He has received a number of prizes, including the *Irish Times* award in 1974, the Patrick Kavanagh award in 1976, the Macauley Fellowship in 1978–79 and an Academy of American Poets award in 1982. He is at present a radio drama producer with RTE, living with his wife and daughter just outside Dublin.

TIMMY LEANS ACROSS the arm-rest of his window seat and tells the airhostess that he's sick. He might have told the cabin steward, the one who brought him the magnetic chess set with the missing bishop ten minutes before, but he didn't; he may be only twelve, twelve and a bit, but he's learned already from his mother and his sister that secrets are best shared with women.

The hostess smiles at him. Her smile is brisk, professional; her eyes are tired. A little fluid is oozing from her left earlobe where the pearl stud ought to be. He wonders whether it's tender, remembers his sister having her ears pierced by the ex-nun on her thirteenth birthday. Did the Germans take the earrings as well as the gold fillings from the men and women they killed in the camps he couldn't pronounce?

'Sick?'

'A bit.'

'In your head or your tummy?'

'In my stomach,' he says.

'Maybe you drank that Coke too fast. Would you feel better if you put your seat back? Or if you got sick? Sick into the bag.'

'No.' He has already stowed the sick-bag and the in-flight magazine and the sugar sachet from the lunch that was served, in the pocket of his school blazer as souvenirs of the flight.

'We'll be in Dusseldorf soon,' she tells him; and she reaches across the other, elderly passenger to rumple his hair with her red fingernails.

Now that she's touched him, he has to confess. He hopes the other passenger won't overhear, but the man seems to be asleep, his mouth open, a dental brace on his bottom teeth as if he were a child again, and a slight smell of hair-oil from his button-down collar.

'I can't go,' Timmy tells the airhostess. 'I've tried to go ever since I woke up at home this morning. I tried at the airport, in the departures lounge, and I've tried twice since the plane took off, but I had to stop because I was afraid that there'd be other people waiting outside. And it gets more sore all the time.'

She laughs; it's meant kindly.

'That's only constipation,' she tells him. 'It'll pass. And now you know how women feel when they're having babies.'

She begins to move away as the elderly passenger comes to.

'I could report her,' he says to Timmy. 'I could report her for saying things like that.'

Timmy doesn't answer. Instead, he stares out the window, tilting his glasses slightly on the bridge of his nose to bring the countryside beneath him into sharper definition. What do women feel when they're having babies, and why is it wrong to say so? His stomach tightens again, the pressure to pass a motion makes him gasp.

'Are you all right?'

'Yes. Thank you.'

The elderly passenger in the next seat holds a Ventolin inhaler to his mouth, and sucks sharply on it. After ten or fifteen seconds, he exhales again slowly, as if he were blowing invisible smoke rings. He glances at Timmy.

'The good life,' he says.

'Were you in the army during the war?'

'Yes, I was.'

Timmy's delighted. He puts the bottoms of two pawn pieces together, and their magnets meet precisely.

'In the commandos?'

'In catering.' The boy's face falls. 'Don't despise it. An army marches on its stomach.'

But Timmy looks away at the window. Far below him, he can see a river that must be the Rhine, a thin tapeworm the colour of concrete; and near it a road, perhaps an autobahn, a relic of the Reich. But where are the train tracks? Surely there must be train tracks between Dusseldorf and the city of Krefeld where the

Sterms have their home. After all, there are train tracks everywhere in this strange, sinister land; and the train tracks lead from
the cities through the country to the concentration camps, and
everybody knew that they did, knew at the time, and said nothing.

The boy thinks of the depots, of the huddled deportees. He
thinks of the chemists, the teachers, the mezzo sopranos,
squeezed into stifling cattle-trucks, sealed carriages; men with
beards who had lectured in anatomy, artists and actresses
whose dressing rooms were lavish with insect-eating plants from
Argentina; people who could talk in three languages, yet who
had to pull their dresses up or their trousers down and squat
over straw while the train roared towards the watchtowers.

'Would you like to see the cockpit?'

The hostess beams at him. She seems revived. Or is she
coming back because of what the elderly man said? Could she
lose her job because of him?

'No, thank you.'

'Don't you want to be a pilot when you grow up?'

He looks at her, at the weeping earlobe, a wisp of brown hair
black at the roots.

'No,' he says. 'I want to be a Jew.'

She frowns, the elderly passenger turns to stare at him; and
the plane begins its descent.

His classmates troop through the shallow chlorine pools back
into the men's dressing-room. They peel off their swimming
togs, and wring them out over the basins, excitedly chattering
in this vast wooden space with its lockers like baskets. One of
them whistles the theme song from the *Monkees*; another
pushes a hairclip up his nostril to scrape out a scab.

'I'm dying for a drink. Water, water.'

One of the boys, pretending to be thirsty, lets his tongue loll.
A taller child volunteers the tiny pink nipple on his chest, and
the thirsty one nibbles greedily at it.

'There you go, my child. Suck away.'

Timmy twists his regulation gym shorts, twists and tightens
them until the last little strings of water drip down on to the
floor. He'll have to wear them again on the bus journey back to

the school, because he forgot his togs today, for the third time in a single term. As a penalty, he has to write out the Our Father twelve times, once for each year of his life.

'Into the showers! Into the showers! Quickly, quickly!'

It's Mr Madden, standing in the doorframe, shouting. He's carrying the large Tayto crisps carton where he puts the boys' glasses and watches for safe-keeping while they're in the pool. Timmy hurries into the shower, jostling, being jostled in turn, the hips and buttocks of the other boys grazing against him. He lifts his face to the hard hail of the water.

'Do it now, Hardiman. Come on. Do it now.'

One voice, two, then many, all of them. Timmy joins in, though he doesn't quite know what it is that Hardiman must do. The boy beside him lifts his wrist. There's a phone number written on it, a five-letter phone number; it looks like a camp tattoo, it looks like –

'You all have to pay me sixpence. All of you.'

They nod solemnly; they're hushed now. Hardiman folds his arms across his chest, and stares at his penis. One of the boys stops the shower; the others surround Hardiman to shield him from the door. Outside they can hear the shrieks of the prep class, dog-paddling on their yellow floats, and a distant whistle. Timmy wishes he had his glasses. Things are blurred without them. He has to squeeze the edges of his eyelids with his fingers in order to make anything out.

'You look a bit Chinese that way,' says the boy beside him.

'Do I?'

'A bit. Listen, Tim, when you go to Germany next week, will you bring me back some Hitler stamps?'

'Any moment now,' says Hardiman; and, sure enough, his penis begins to grow: slowly at first, then more swiftly, it stiffens, straightens, and stands up. The boys stare at it in silence, at its beauty, its lack of embarrassment.

'And I didn't even have to stroke it,' says Hardiman. 'Most people have to stroke it. But I can make it big just by thinking.'

'Thinking what?' says Timmy. 'What do you think?'

'Never you mind,' Hardiman says.

*   *   *

They've left the airport, arrived at the station, boarded the train and found a compartment, before Timmy has an opportunity to examine Frau Sterm closely. Modest and mild, she doesn't much mind such inspection. Instead, she smiles benignly out the window, watching the long, low barges on the river.

'The Rhine,' she tells him. 'The Rhine.' And she laughs, laughs because this strawberry-blond boy is looking at her so seriously, as if she were an icthyosaurus or some other creepie-crawlie in the Natural History Museum where she brings her own son, Claus, on rainy Saturdays. She laughs, and lifts her hands to her forehead to flick back her fringe. The two boys will hit it off, she thinks: they're different, and difference, despite what universities may say, is the fountainhead of friendship. That was the aim and outcome of these programmes, a pairing of peers, of boys whose fathers had fought as enemies but whose sons, she thinks, whose sons will build rabbit hutches together.

Timmy's intrigued by the hair under her arms. He's never seen it before. Neither his mother nor his sister have anything like it. He hasn't even come across it in the *National Geographic* or in his father's large, forbidden volume called *Diseases of the Breast*. Is it restricted to Germans or to German-speaking countries? Or is it found in Italy and France as well? Frau Sterm doesn't seem shy or secretive. After all, she's wearing a sleeveless dress. Besides, Europeans are different. In Spain, his sister wouldn't be allowed out without an escort; in Greece, she'd have to wear a black frock if her husband went and died. The world is peculiar.

'Are you afraid?'

She grins at him, showing her teeth. She has many gold fillings. If she were a Jew when she was little, they would have torn the gold out of her mouth with mechanics' tools. But she can't be Jewish, and not because the Jews are dead now, but because she's married to a man who served in the Wehrmacht, to a man who got frostbite in Russia. So perhaps the gold is from a Jew, perhaps it's migrated from one mouth to another; perhaps it was used to the sound of Lithuanian, to the taste of kosher sweetbread, and now it hears German greetings, and chews sausage.

'No,' he says. 'I'm not afraid.' And then, because he can't bear her to look at him without speaking, he decides to tell her about the presents.

'I have duty-free bottles for you,' he says. He can't remember what they are; his parents chose them. 'I have a model airplane for Claus. I have a Heinkel, a Heinkel bomber. There are a hundred and fifty bits. Do you know Heinkels?'

'Yes,' she tells him. 'Yes, I know Heinkels.' She becomes silent again.

Timmy's got to go to the toilet. It's the same problem, the need to shit something strong and solid that seems stuck inside him, the inability to shift it. He leaves the compartment, squeezes past a woman holding a hat-stand like a stag's antler in the passageway. He excuses himself as the two of them manoeuvre, excuses himself and wonders whether she'll think he's English, and, if so, whether she'll hate him, remembering perhaps a charred torso under masonry.

'Thank you,' he says.

'You're welcome.'

In the toilet, he's alone. The seat is plastic, not wooden like at home. And the lever for flushing is attached to the cistern behind; it doesn't hang from a chain. Timmy lowers his trousers, studies his underpants to ensure that they're not stained, but they are, slightly. How is he going to clean them without Frau Sterm finding out; and if she does, what can he tell her? His mother's warned him twice, three times that a boy is judged by the state of his shirt-collar and the condition of his underpants. He sits and strains, sits and strains. He feels behind him with his fingers, between his cheeks, to where the tip of the shit is wedged, but he can't pass it. The pain is too much.

The toilet is dry. Timmy can see down through it, though there's a loop in the exit pipe. Sleeper after sleeper after sleeper, thin strips of gravel and grass, a whirling monochrome, a rush of field-grey greyness. They would have seen the same, the ballerinas and the butchers, their eyes pressed to the chinks in the shoddy wooden goods trains.

The boy tears the identification tag from the lapel of his blazer, the one with his name and flight number on it, the one the airhostess with the red fingernails had written. He holds it over the bowl for a moment, feels it flap in the uprush of the breeze, and then he lets it go.

'*Voila*,' says Mr McDonagh; and he whisks the sheet away. '*Voila!* That's German, I think, or maybe it's French.'

Timmy fumbles with his glasses, blows the short hairs from the lenses, and puts the glasses on. Mr McDonagh has followed his father's instructions to the letter. His hair is more closely cropped than it's ever been before. He looks denuded, ridiculous. His cheeks flush pinker.

'I was only obeying my orders,' Mr McDonagh says.

The customer in the next chair chuckles.

'Jesus,' he says. 'You look like something that walked out of the camps. When is it you're off anyway?'

'In three days.'

'Bring us back some reading material,' says the other man. 'Will you do that?'

'A bit of culture,' Mr McDonagh tells Timmy. 'The Rhine maidens out of Wagner.'

'*Die Grossen Frauen*, more like. Do you know what I'm getting at?'

Timmy shakes his head.

'Leave him be,' says Mr McDonagh, blowing quietly on Timmy's bent neck. 'The child's a holy innocent.'

Timmy peers up at Mr McDonagh's reflection in the mirror.

'The boy I'm going to,' he explains. 'His father was in the German army. He was in Russia. He got wounded there. It was the same year mum and dad got married. So while he was sheltering behind some tank during snowstorms, my parents were on honeymoon down in Parknasilla, except that the hotel was full of priests. Isn't that strange?'

'Not really,' says Mr McDonagh. 'Priests had a lot of money twenty years ago.'

'Do you remember the invasion of Russia, Mr McDonagh?'

'Do I remember the day I got engaged? Of course I do. I was in the army myself at the time.'

'Where? Whereabouts?'

'I was stationed in Limerick. I was in the Irish army.'

'Who did you want to win?'

'The Allies, of course. I wanted the Allies to win. But . . .'

'But what?'

Mr McDonagh cleans his glasses with the end of his navy-blue tie.

'I wanted the Allies to get a bloody good thrashing first. After what the British done to us.'

The boy looks down at his lap, around at the floor. Thick tufts of his own hair litter the lino. It was strange to think that your own bits and pieces, toenails, fingernails, follicles of skin, strands of hair, an assortment of your own bodily parts, could be sorted out and swept away, like dog-dirt or a broken salt-cellar. And it was still stranger to imagine the small, sodden mounds of human hair that the barbers of Belsen and Buchenwald had shaved from schoolchildren, from tots whose first teeth were still intact, from teenagers who cycled bikes without holding the handlebars.

'What about the Jews, Mr McDonagh? Did you know about the Jews?'

'Ah, the Jews,' he says, shaking the sheet he has taken from Timmy. 'The Jews. A very versatile people. Sure, every second actor is a Jew; and they're all over Hollywood. What happened to the Jews was such a pity.'

The other customer clears his throat. A soft ball of phlegm sits on his under-lip.

'There's some lovely Jewish women as well,' he says. 'Not so *grossen* now, but every bit as *frauen*. Now why the fuck wasn't I born in Munich?'

Frau Sterm shows Timmy round the house. She shows him the kitchen, the living room, the study where Herr Sterm works on his legal cases, the narrow ground-floor bedroom for any visitors. He doesn't notice much at first, because the whole house has a strange smell he can't identify. Aerosol sprays are new to him; back home, the maid cleans the bookshelves and the table-tops and the brass canopy over the fireplace with sponge and spittle, the elbow-grease of ages. Here it's different, a bright, brittle world.

'You like it?'

Frau Sterm lets the bed down by pressing a catch. It emerges from the wall and folds slowly to the floor. Timmy's never seen one like it before, or the double-glazed windows that overlook the front lawn, a lawn without a fence or a stone wall to protect it, a lawn that slopes unselfconsciously to the public pavement.

'Yes,' he says. 'It's very nice.'

She stretches out her hand to him.

'Come. I have more to show.'

The boy follows her back into the kitchen. There's a low whine, like the noise of a mosquito, from the overhead light. The skeleton of a fish sits on the draining board. Across at the window there's a bowl piled with grapes and pale bananas, but when he looks more closely he finds they're made of glass. And beside him on the polished counter he can see a weighing scales with the brand name Krupps, loose flour in a circle round its stand. He has seen that name somewhere before; he can almost retrieve it, but not quite.

'I have a letter for you,' she tells him. 'A letter from your family. It was here two days.'

Timmy takes it, tears it open. It contains one sheet of paper, paper so thin it's almost transparent. The writing is his sister's.

Dear Timmy,

It is now about nine o'clock, and I am going to bed. You are already asleep upstairs, and Mummy is choosing your trousers for the journey. It is strange to think that when you read this, you will be in the land of Hansel and Gretel. That is why I am writing.

I will go to the shop each Wednesday, and collect your comics, so that when you come home again in ten weeks' time, you will not have missed anything. Isn't that typical of
     Your Adorable Sister.

Frau Sterm is folding laundry at the other end of the kitchen. Timmy thinks that it's kind of her to have turned her back while he was reading his letter; it's the first thing she's done that has made him less panicked and petrified. If only the smells were not so different, if only there were one smell which reminded him of the hot-press or the scullery at home. He wants to sit down straightaway and write to his sister, telling her that he travelled on a jet plane without any propellers, that he saw strange magazines at the kiosks in the airport, magazines with sneering women sticking out their bottoms; that he lost his German phrase book somewhere between Dublin and Dusseldorf, and he can't remember how to say that he's having a lovely time; that there's a weighing scales in the kitchen, made by Krupps, and weren't they the same factory that built the crematoria; and that he's tried, and tried, and tried, but he still can't go big ways.

Frau Sterm pounds the kitchen window very precisely with a twisted kitchen towel, and a bluebottle staggers for a moment around the juices of its stomach before dropping to the ledge. But the blow has activated the sensors on the ultra-modern burglar alarm system. The bell wails through the house like an old-style air-raid alarm. Timmy cannot hear her at first when Frau Sterm tries to explain, and anyhow she hasn't the words.

'I understand,' he says.

His father tucks him in, brushes a few shavings of wood from a pencil off the side of the bedspread. Timmy puts his sketchpad down. They kiss. His father switches off the light.

'I can always talk more easily in the darkness. Why do you think that is? I often wonder.'

Timmy doesn't say. He works himself more comfortably into the sheets. And waits.

'About this trip. You mustn't be frightened. People are kind the world over. You'll see. That bloody Italian you have for Latin's been filling your head with all sorts of nonsense, just because his brother got a bayonet in the bottom somewhere in Sicily. And the comics you read are no better – Boche this, Boche that, Boche the other. Officers with monocles, infantry like wart hogs. The Germans are no better and no worse than anyone else. Do you believe me?'

'Yes.'

'Most of the music I play is German. Don't you like Mozart and Mahler? Don't you like Beethoven?'

'Yes.'

'So you see. Herr Sterm's a lovely man. If he seems a bit
. . . remote, well, that's the way Germans are. Until you get
to know them, of course. Then it's party-time. You remember
playing mushroom billiards with Herr Sterm last year, over in
Connemara, and how he let you win all the time. Now I never
let you win, not if I can help it.'

His father moves towards the door, a dark sculpture in the
soft light from the landing.

'Remember this. To begin with, the Germans didn't invent
anti-semitism; they inherited it. And who did they inherit it
from? I'll tell you. They inherited it from the different Christian
churches. That's who. You couldn't say these things ten years
ago, or people would think you were an out-and-out communist.
But now with the Vatican Council going on, folk are finding out
that a mouth is for more than sucking spaghetti.'

'Yes.'

'If anyone annoys you, just tell them this: in the middle of
1944, the Allies precision-bombed a munitions factory outside
Auschwitz. Precision-bombed it. Pulverised the whole complex.
But they didn't bomb the train tracks leading to the camp.
They knew perfectly well that the camp was there; they knew
perfectly well what was happening inside it. Flame throwers
turned on pregnant women; newborn babies kicked like footballs.
But they didn't bomb the train tracks. And now after twenty
years, they talk about preserving the otter.'

The door swings open.

'I had a patient this morning. On the table. He was different.'
'Why?'

'He died. He died on me. I had to . . . rip open his ribcage. I
had to hold his heart in my hand, and pump it with my fingers
until it started to beat again. I worked his heart with my own
hand, something I use to pick my nose with.'

He stretches out his hand.

'Want to touch it?'
'No.'

His father grins.

*   *   *

Timmy stands up, holding his shorts with one hand at his knees, and turns to stare into the toilet-bowl. He has finally managed to empty his bowels. It has never taken longer to do so, never been so distressing before. His bottom aches. He wipes it gently, inspects the paper before he discards it. It only partly covers the massive turd lying in the shallow bowl. The sheer size of it fascinates the boy. How can there be room for such a thing inside one's stomach?

But he mustn't delay. He's been inside the bathroom for almost fifteen minutes. Frau Sterm may come knocking. He presses the plunger firmly, and blue water gushes down from the rim of the bowl. It swirls in a frothy fashion round the turd, spitting and bubbling; but then, slowly and silently, it ebbs away, it drains and disappears, it leaves the brown, bloated mass where it is. Timmy tugs the lever desperately. Nothing happens. The cistern is empty. It may take minutes to fill again. He hoists up his shorts, buttons the fly, washes his hands, runs them through the stubble on his scalp. Where is Frau Sterm? How long has he been now? How long? The room may be smelly. He opens the window, scatters toilet water on the cork floor. How long?

The cistern has filled again. It must have, because the noise of gurgling has stopped. Timmy forces the lever, more slowly this time, and again the blue water cascades in. He waits, he watches it settle. The waters clear.

The turd has not budged.

The boy runs out of the bathroom. There's a door to the left-hand side, but he hasn't been shown the rooms upstairs. Perhaps it's where the Sterms sleep; perhaps Frau Sterm is in there now. He stops, starts towards it again, reaches it, peers round the door. It's a child's room, a boy's room, Claus's room. There are Disney transfers on the walls, a beachball in the corner, a thin Toledo sword; and on the floor immediately in front of him, there's a model train-set, stacked train tracks, little level-crossings, carriages, tenders, engines, miniature porters and stokers.

The boy listens. He can hear nothing. He leans forward, snatches a long length of train track, and rushes back to the bathroom. He locks the door, listens again. Then he drives the train track fiercely into the huge shit, working it this way and that, stabbing and slashing at it until the motion begins gradually to disintegrate. But he doesn't stop. He pounds and pummels, pounds and pummels again. At last, at long last, he's satisfied; he adds another mighty jab for good measure, and flushes. Piece by piece, fragment by fragment, the turd is swallowed up, swept down.

Timmy begins to cry; but he can't allow himself, not yet, not now. There's still the train track, the train track. How long has he been here now? He fumbles with the tap, turns it full on, holds the track beneath its blast of water, picks at the particles of shit with his fingernails; but it's no use. The thing is sodden, it stinks, he can't clean it. He stands for seconds, staring at the toy piece; then he rushes out of the bathroom, down the stairs to the ground floor, and stops, straining for a footfall, the least sound. Where is Frau Sterm?

When he reaches the garden, he hurls the track with all his strength into the air and over the low wooden stockade behind the rhododendrons and the raspberry bushes. It lands among rosebeds in the neighbouring garden. Timmy has thrown it with such force that the muscle under his armpit hurts him. Now he can let himself cry.

'I won't hurt you.'

Timmy is standing in his pyjamas in front of his mother. It's late, the last night before he leaves for Germany. His bag is packed.

'I put a scapular inside the suitcase,' his mother says as she takes his penis out of his pyjamas. 'Do you know what a scapular is?'

'No.'

His mother pulls his foreskin up and down, up and down. She tries to be very gentle.

'A scapular will protect you,' she says. 'My mother gave me a scapular when I went on my honeymoon with daddy.'

'Did it protect you?'

She laughs.

'What protection did I need?'

Timmy decides to tell her.

'I had a dream last night. A dream about you. I was sitting in a deckchair somewhere, and a whole herd of cows walked up to me. Their udders were dragging on the ground. They wanted to be milked.'

'And did you milk them?'

'Yes. I milked them with my bare hands, on to the grass. There was no end of milk.'

'And where did I come in?'

'You didn't. But I felt the way I always feel when I'm with you.'

His mother kisses the tip of his nose. She slips his penis back into his pyjamas.

'I want you to ask Frau Sterm to do that for you. Will you do that? It's very important. You'll understand when you're bigger.'

'Will you write to me?'

'Of course I'll write to you. Of course I will. And you must write back. But don't just write to me. Write to your daddy. Write to him at his hospital. He'd love that.'

'All right.'

The mother looks at her son, the son at his mother.

'Germany's not that bad. You remember how I told you I was there with Granny, just before the war.'

'You were getting better.'

'I was getting better. I was recovering. I'd been ill.'

'With pleurisy.'

'With pleurisy. That's right. And lots of people had it. It was rampant.'

'What's rampant?'

'Everywhere. All over. An epidemic. Many people died from it.'

'But you got better.'

'I got better. I got better in Germany. Or at least I finished getting better there. And I met some lovely people.'

'Who?'

'I met a woman. A girl, I mean. She owned her own café, a coffee-house. You could order the most beautiful cakes. And a cellist played there in the afternoons. She was a sweet person, but she wore too much make-up. She looked a little like a cake herself.'

'Did you ever meet a man you liked?'

'Yes, I did. He was very like daddy, except smaller.'

'Was he a Nazi?'

'He was in the army. But his real ambition in life was to become a bee-keeper.'

'Did he?'

His mother gets up off her knees, and brushes the wrinkles on her kneecaps.

'I don't know. Perhaps he died. Perhaps he died in the war. His name was Nikki.'

Timmy burrows down in the bed. He shifts his weight to one side, leaving enough room on the other, as he has always done and will always continue to do, for Bernard, his guardian angel.

Claus and Timmy have hit it off. Frau Sterm is certain of it. There may be a little diffidence on either side, but that sort of shyness is only to be expected. Dublin is not quite Dusseldorf, nor Krefeld Killarney. Frau Sterm rather likes the alliterative parallelism. She'll try it on her husband later.

Out in the garden, the two boys are smiling, circling each other. Claus opens his English phrase book, picks sentences at random, reads them.

'This is not the room I asked for at reception.'

Timmy laughs, more loudly than he need to.

'Is the museum open on Sundays as well?'

'*Jawohl*,' says Timmy, and salutes in the old style favoured by fascists. Claus looks at him closely. His face frowns. Timmy's unsettled, uneasy. He brings his arm down.

'I had a phrase book too,' he tells him. 'Only I lost it. I don't know where. On the plane perhaps, or in the airport. But I'll get another. Then we can talk all the time. Can't we?'

Claus hasn't understood. He starts leafing through the Berlitz guidebook again. Thumbing the sections, looking up and over at his new acquaintance every so often. Eventually he finds what he's searching for.

'Can we reserve accommodation on this train?'

Timmy thinks of the train track under the rosebed, of the train-set scattered on the bright carpet upstairs. Is it remotely possible that Frau Sterm would collect the pieces into their box, counting them as she went along? Or that Claus would remember the exact number, the precise tally? Certainly the missing strip would never be found, but what if the whole Sterm family were to realise that, since the arrival of the stranger in their midst, things had been thieved? The word itself they might forgo, they might speak instead of disappearance, but thieving would be what they meant. He would be sent straight home, he might meet the same hostess on the Dublin flight. She might have to serve him breakfast, but she wouldn't look into his eyes. Instead she would look away.

'Is there a couchette available on this train?'

No one could have seen him do what he had done. The window in the bathroom was frosted, the door had been locked or at least he had tried to lock it. Frau Sterm had been nowhere to be found. The neighbouring house with the rose-bed didn't overlook the garden. In fact, now that he saw it for the second time, he realised it was a bungalow. He could breathe easy.

'Or even standing room?'

Claus smiles at him. He's been saving the one bad English word he knows, learned from a mischievous scatterbrain in his *Mittelschule*.

'Shit,' he says.

Before Timmy can answer him, Claus bounds across the garden, and bends down at a forsythia tree. Moments later, he's back with a tortoise in his hands. Timmy steps forward a foot or two, and makes to touch the shell; but Claus throws the unfortunate creature high into the air, then catches it again. Timmy can't believe what he's seen, so Claus repeats the trick, then chucks the tortoise deftly to his new-found friend and pen-pal. Timmy returns it; it's tossed back. The tortoise has edged out of his shell. The boys can see its face and feet emerge. They go on throwing it, back and forth, one to the other, as if it were a rugby ball. But soon the inevitable happens. Claus fumbles a catch, drops the tortoise on the concrete walk, steps back, and stares in horror. Neither boy is sure whether the tortoise is still alive or, if alive, whether it's harmed. Neither speaks. A slight breeze darkens the lawn; sunflowers bob in their beds.

'Claus.'

But Claus doesn't answer. He walks the two steps to the

tortoise, and nudges it with the toe of his sandal, nudges it in under the cover of a bush. No one will see it there. He'll come out later, after dinner, to examine it again. Timmy wonders if a tortoise has a spine. Perhaps a chip or even a hairline fracture in the shell won't matter.

'Shit,' says Claus again. 'Very shit.'

Father Eddy lines up his shot, and putts the ball briskly into the hole. Timmy claps.

'When I was a lad,' Father Eddy says as he moves to the next Latin numeral on the clockwork golf course at the bottom of Timmy's garden, 'Luther was another word for Lucifer. He was the Devil himself, every bit as bad as Hitler, and worse.'

'Really?'

'I kid you not. He divided Christendom against itself. He made war on the Church. You couldn't reason with him. And terrible things happened. Famine, assassinations, sacrilege. So, of course, when I was in the seminary, everybody looked on Luther as an utter blackguard. A bandit.'

The priest putts again, more cautiously this time.

'But now, with the Council and everything that Pope John tried to show us, we know different. We can see with the eyes of charity, the eyes of compassion. We can see that Luther wasn't all bad. He was just bonkers. Stark, raving mad.'

The ball wobbles on the edge of the hole, but it doesn't go in. Father Eddy's vexed.

'Even so, if the Sterms do ask you along to one of their services, say no. Say you're only allowed to attend the Catholic church. And if there isn't one in the area, don't fret. The obligation doesn't bind you when you're abroad. I was in Greece one time, a couple of years before I was ordained, and I went a month without mass. I was a spiritual skin-and-bones case by the time I got home.'

Timmy toes the golfball in, then takes it out again, and hands it back to Father Eddy. The priest crouches over his putter, practising.

'If anybody asks you, tell them you're Irish but that you learned English at school.'

'Yes.'

'Mind you, when you're away out of the country, your real nationality is Catholicism. The Faith. Think of the Irish monks who went out to convert Germany. Columbanus, Cillian. Holy men, whole men, men with a mission. You're following in their footsteps. You see what I'm saying?'

'Yes.'

Father Eddy looks around him at the twelve Latin numerals embedded in the lawn.

'Which is that?' he asks, pointing with his putter to the large metal 'V' under the plumtree.

'Five,' Timmy says.

'And that?'

'Nine. I know them up to a hundred. A hundred is C.'

'Good man yourself.'

It's getting late. Only the upper windows of the glasshouse catch the sunlight. The priest and the boy walk back towards the house.

'Isn't it a strange thing all the same,' Father Eddy says. 'Those Latin numerals were used by Julius Caesar. Augustus used them. Housewives in Pompeii were counting them on their fingers the day Vesuvius burst. And that's not today, nor the day before it either. That's a long time ago.'

'How many popes ago?'

'Many, many, many. And yet, two thousand years later, you can come upon them laid out in a circle at the end of a private garden. Do you know who made that possible?'

'No.'

'Well, you should know. It was the Church. The Church preserved Latin, the language of the very soldiers who crucified Our Lord. That's called an irony.'

'What's that?'

'A wound that gives pleasure.'

The priest stoops to pick a bird's feather from the lawn.

'You could talk to Claus in the Latin you have,' he tells Timmy. 'I imagine he learns it in his school. You know the verb "to love" backwards. And that's enough to start with. It's enough for anyone. Or it should be. You're not nervous? There's no reason to be nervous. Sure, the two of you will be thick as thieves before the plane's refuelled.'

Behind them, out of the cypress trees, magpies circle the clockwork golf course, land, and begin to pick at the glinting metal letters.

Herr Sterm leans back from the dining table, and tilts his chin towards the ceiling. Almost from the moment that he entered the house, his nose has been bleeding. Already the front of his shirt is stained, the green tie that he wore to honour Timmy is flecked with red. Yet Frau Sterm continues to tell the boy that this is no unusual occurrence. It happens all the time, it's a sign of health, not illness. It passes after a while, as all things pass. And she ladles more vegetables on to Timmy's plate, and sets the plate before him.

The food is unintelligible. There are strange anonymous entities Timmy's never seen before. Shape, size, flavour and taste, are all new. He rummages with his knife and fork, sorts and separates the mess, but he can't bring himself to swallow the stuff. He can see fragments of his own reflection on the broad blade of the knife; his lower lip with the scrap of dead skin, his teeth in a white wobble, his eyebrows, eyelashes, eyes. His eyes stare back at him, confessing, concealing.

'Would you like to see a film tomorrow?'

He looks up at Frau Sterm. She seems distant, diminished.

'Yes. Thank you.'

'Would you like to see *The Sound of Music*?'

'Yes.'

Herr Sterm settles his chair back on its four legs again. He holds a large handkerchief to his nose as he speaks in a muffled way to his wife. He speaks first in German, then in English.

'*The Sound of Music* is not a good film. It is anti-German. The music is pretty, but the message, the message is propaganda. But there are other films. There are others; and these we will see.'

They eat in silence. Timmy forces a few mouthfuls of the green and purple rubbish into his mouth. Claus is in another world, playing soccer with the peas on his plate. Perhaps he's thinking about the tortoise; perhaps he's frightened. Herr Sterm begins to bleed again, over the napkin and the napkin ring. He swears in an undertone. His wife shushes him. Silence again for a spell . . . and then the bell rings.

The hall doorbell, its two tones, a little phrase.

The whole table tenses. Mother and father glance at each other. The husband rises, goes out. Frau Sterm peers out the window at the louvre doors into the kitchen.

'I think it is a neighbour,' she says.

And Timmy knows, knows in the pit of his stomach; deep in the boy's belly, there is certain knowledge. Why did the elderly passenger complain about the airhostess? Why had he said he wanted to be a Jew? What made him refuse to visit the cockpit? And how did Hardiman make his penis stand up straight? What was he thinking of when he did that? What was in his mind?

The door swings open. Herr Sterm walks back in. He says nothing. He's holding the train track. Why had he thrown his identification label into the toilet on the train? There must have been a reason. His father is always telling him there is a reason for everything. If so, why were the women sneering on the magazine covers? Herr Sterm begins to beat Claus around the shoulders and neck with the dirty train track. His wife screams. But Claus, Claus doesn't cry, doesn't cry out. He doesn't even try to cover his head. What did Mr McDonagh feel about Jews? What did he really feel? What did '*grossen frauen*' mean? Why was it funny?

Frau Sterm punches her husband in the side. She pleads with him; he doesn't answer. His nose has begun to bleed again. It drips on to Claus's T-shirt, runs down the back. The boy sobs and shudders. Herr Sterm raises the train track one last time, a soiled stretch, still filthy from the toilet and the garden; raises it, looks at it, lowers it. He runs his hand through his hair.

'I bought this . . . machinery for Claus yesterday. It is a new present. For him, but also for you. To play together.'

Why had he not touched his father's hand? And why had the Allied bombers not bombed the train tracks leading to Auschwitz? Why? And when would he know the answers? All the answers to everything, everything that made him feel scared and strange and examined. He looks at Herr Sterm, at Frau Sterm, at Claus. He feels sick in his stomach, sick and sore. The lenses of his glasses have begun to mist from the heat of his sweat. They start to slip forward down the bridge of his nose until the half of his field of vision is a blur, the other half is sharper than italics.

He says nothing. He says nothing at all.

ON THE SHINGLE

CANDIA McWILLIAM

CANDIA McWILLIAM

Candia McWilliam was born in Edinburgh and read English at Girton College, Cambridge. She is married and lives in Oxford. Her first novel, *A Case of Knives*, was published in 1988.

OUR MOTHERS HAD decided that the Chocolate House in Princes Street would be our part of the afternoon, after they had finished in Jenners and Forsyths. We were to meet them at four and woe betide us if we were late back from the baths at Portobello. Anne's mother had said why did we not just away off to the baths at Glenogle but my mother was English and said there was a wave-making machine at Portobello; by this she meant that it was cleaner and did not have the yellow tinge of Glenogle, also that the higher entrance charge kept out what she surely did not describe to herself as working-class people.

On the top of our bus, Anne – with whom I was in love since she was ten and I was nine and she had a dog – and I told lies to each other.

'My Dad's thinking of getting a house out of the middle of Kirkcaldy, I'll have to go to boarding school (this was our dream) and then what'll Mandy (this was Anne's dog) do? Will you not just think of that?'

'My Daddy plays a dab game of ice hockey,' I replied. 'You should see him, though it's no good for his heart since he was a hero in the war.' My father was a quiet man, a doctor. I doubt he knew if ice hockey was a food or a complaint, or if it was at all. His war had been heroic, in an unmartial way; he spent two years in bed with tuberculosis, and had learnt to smock.

'Dad's thinking of getting a purple Consul.' This could be true. Anne's dad was a big man with a lino factory and her brothers were down for Glenalmond. Scottish snobbery is sweet on the tongue, its private signals words which lift the blood with pride of race – Gordonstoun, Oxenfoord, Skye, Buccleugh, and traps to keep strangers out, Auchinleck, Ruthven.

The bus went past the big power station and there were the baths, low, white, harled. They were stepped and across their square gable, in wide-spaced blue letters, thin, elegant, casting their shadow back on to the distemper in the sun, was written 'Portobello Swimming Baths'. Each letter was exaggeratedly tall and thin, half as long again as it need be. The railings of the baths also had this disproportion, and bore long iron ellipses at their tips. The tiles were raspberry red to trim, or white, edged with leaf green, on walls and floor. There was a tremendous smell of chlorine and over the entrance was a notice to tell us that the next waves would be at half-past the hour of two and that spectators would be welcome in the viewing gallery, price 2d. We each paid sixpence and went in through the turnstile which was taller than Anne, though she was older. She was so fair her hair went grey when it was wet. I was so fat that it was a great show of love to let her see me in my bathing suit. Usually, I'd only let my mother, and then in the viewing gallery, what with her bikini and her accent.

The point at Portobello was to get two goes of the waves, to get rescued and to see a grown up (not a man) with as few clothes as possible. We would get the two-thirty and the three o'clock waves which should just leave time for the other two tasks which must of course not be mentioned, certainly not to our mothers, nor, until afterwards, to each other, this to guard against disappointment.

We changed in separate cubicles into our black suits. Anne's hair was short but the baths stipulated the wearing of caps for those with long hair, even men. To be seen in cap at the baths became a paradoxical index of rebellion in Edinburgh for those years. I squeezed my two pigtails into the sore rubber helmet. We wore rubber bracelets at the wrist, to hold the key of the lockers where we had put our clothes. To reach the baths, which were open to the air, we had to walk between the rows of zinc lockers, past the attendants doing wet knitting in white overalls, and through a foot bath, tiled in white rectangles with stiff palmate shapes in dark green on the odd one. The bleach-stinking water was delicious to the feet. The big thing at this point was not to giggle at the notice which said 'NO

SPITTING, NO JUMPING, NO RUNNING, NO PUSHING, NO SHOUTING, NO PETTING'. The trick was to say something dead funny just before you read the last bit, so you had to laugh anyway. Simultaneously, we said the name of a girl two forms above (who had what we called boozums) and we were off, hyperventilating with giggles. We giggled like drunks. It made us wild.

Out in the sun by the baths, we stood at the shallow end; at a foot's interval all down the baths, the height was recorded in green figures on the white tiles in feet and inches. The shallow end was 2'6", the deep end 10'. Four lifeguards stood, one at each corner, in white trousers and singlets; on their feet were white rubber shoes. The pool lay, a flat pale blue rectangle, banks of seats on three sides. At the shallow end was the viewers' gallery. It was in the tall clock tower of the baths, and beneath it was the mighty pump which made the artificial waves, yet spectators could have tea and pancakes and not feel a thing, looking out through glass at their intrepid friends or children breasting the regulated waves each half hour. Portobello is by the sea, but we were never tempted by its untimed grey breakers.

Anne could, of course, swim. I floated very nicely, my mother said. We went up to the place 5'6" was marked, as tall as me and a lot taller than Anne, and we clung to the edge waiting for the two-thirty waves.

There they came, rolling, smooth, every seventh one bigger, so high you could see through it.

Was it every seventh one? There was a magic number, but I forget it now and surely the rhythms of those warm false waves cannot be those of the lunar paradigm awaited by surfers in the real seas? Our waves were warm with the extra heat from the power station; now it might be called recreational pollution-cycling. Between waves, we toiled up towards the shallow end, always combed out and back a little deeper by each inevitable buffet as it came, hitting us in the chin and lifting us so we stood like soldiers held in the apex of each wave, before sliding down its lee-side and readying ourselves to breast the next. By the time the five minutes of waves were done, our eyes were red

and our fingers white and crinkly at the tip. We were also hoarse
with screaming, and ready just to splash in the shallow end for
a while, biding our time. We sat on the red Dumfries sandstone
steps, rough on our bottoms, and watched the youths and girls
(Anne said 'girrul') whose play was as formal and pointed as a
dance. We did not *look* at the youths; this would be too rude.
But we did watch the chests of the girls with the attention of
doctors. The big boys would splash at the girls with their feet,
or dive near them and rush up through the water to stand breast
to breast in the warm blue which might rock them into touching,
skin washed innocent of heat and hair by the water. The
girls made much play of ignoring the boys and when the boys
looked away the girls redrew their eyes with particularly osten-
tatious displays of indifference. One girl moved her head and
clapped her hands more than the rest. Even in the rubber cap
her face was pretty; on her right hip was a tiny embroidered
diver. When she shrieked, she took her hand away from her
mouth as though holding a cigarette. She was not chicken-wired
with pink veins on her legs like Anne, nor was she freckled like
me. She was pale nut colour all over, not the nuts my mother
had with her drink, but the sugar brown of tablet. Her breasts
moved after she stopped, and she wore tiny rings in her ears.
In Edinburgh, it's the Poles and the Scots-Italians who do that.

'You're right stupid, that you are,' called one of the boys to
her, in a yearning voice. 'You canna even do a duck dive. Get
on, have a wee go. I'll help yas.' His voice was about seventeen.

'Och leave her, Ian, I'll give you a race,' said another boy,
with an older voice and a ringleader's way to him.

The girl looked up, and lifted both hands to her rubber head,
touching it lightly as though it were curls. All in the same
moment, she pushed her hands flat to her head and steered her
elbows simultaneously out and over her head, never moving her
eyes and lifting her front, so two solid hemispheres rose between
the scoops of her collarbones and the navy cotton of her bathing
costume. She stared until the boys had gone, knowing they would
be back, and went to clutch and giggle with her plain girlfriend
by the side (4'6", just right for spying out the lads without
getting bombed by the bullies). Anne and I were going to

discover radium, or something of the kind, so we'd not much time for boys, but I did see a glimpse of how that girl could burn in the water, incandescent even in her rubber hat.

For some weeks Anne and I had been doing research in our laboratory; my mother naturally got it wrong and called it the nursery. There we stirred shoplifted fizzy sweets into water and sealed the solution in test tubes; we each had a Letts' chemistry set, though the copper sulphate had run out long ago. We had dissected a shrew and felt a breakthrough was not far away; the teacher who was as near as we had come to Madame Curie was Miss Lindsay. She was firm but fair and wore a blue coat for chemistry, a green one for biology, and thrilling twin sets for assembly. She had quite a front and was said to have had a fiancé who was lost in the Western Isles, so now she was dedicated to science. I did quite good imitations of Miss Lindsay saying, 'If the surface of the Earth was six inches deep in sand, the number of grains would not yet equal the number of molecules of matter constituting a milk bottle.' Atoms came in the next form up. Was that, I wonder now, so only the girls who were ready for it would learn of the divisibility even of the atom?

'Don't look now,' said Anne, nudging me, and rolling her eyes up. Starting from the shiny tiles, I saw two pairs of feet, one hairy, one smooth. Looking further up, I saw the flat modesty apron of an older lady's bathing costume, pulled over wide hips. I was above looking at the parallel part of her companion, so up I looked. Miss Lindsay! She was arm in arm with a man, a man about as old as my father, well, old, anyhow. She was staring into his face and some red hair was coming out of her hat.

'How rude,' said Anne and I'd to agree. We stared as hard as we could and felt horribly let down. They slipped into the water at 6', separating to do so. It was three o'clock and time for the new waves, our last of this afternoon. We weren't that thrilled any more. So, Miss Lindsay was not dedicated to science. We watched her and the man. This man would never be lost in the Western Isles, he was too noisy and hairy for that. His head burst out of the top of each wave like a dog's, hers beside it, pink and laughing. We were glad that we would never be

interested in men, being committed to a life of seeking something
very important, separating it from its baser element, like
Madame Curie with the pitch-blende. We bobbed and floated,
but I, for one, was above all this now.

There was a furious yell, and all four lifeguards rushed to the
deep end, white clothed and muscly on morticians' feet. 'Here,
yous, that'll do, ye can git oot if there's ony mair o' that, d'ye
hear me the noo?'

Miss Lindsay and the man were very red in the face. He
patted her and said, 'There, there.' She ducked her face into
his neck as though she were a child waiting to be carried to bed,
and gave him a great smile, her face shining. She looked more
naked than the girl in the earrings had done. She did not look a
bit rude.

I'd lost my taste for getting rescued by now.

'When these waves are over, shall we get the bus?' said Anne.

'Uh huh,' I said, a noise my mother said was as Scots as 'Em'
for 'Um'.

When we'd had the compulsory shower and I'd wrung out my
pigtails, we rolled our costumes in our towels like Swiss rolls
and went off to wait at the bus stop by the shingle. There was
a drunk old woman crying on the sea wall; she had a Shetland
collie at her side, all nerves and petticoats. Mandy was a Sheltie,
so Anne stroked the dog, though our mothers frequently told
us not to touch strange dogs.

'Oh look at the two of yes, a lifetime to go, two wee girruls
and a' they years tae love.' She smelt. Her hair was in a red and
yellow Paisley scarf in the bitter wind. The white sunshine
showed her blue cheeks and the scum on her teeth. 'Pain and
grief and the vale of tears and it's no go the merry-go-round and
ma gude man dead in his chair with his pipe in his teeth and the
teeth sae clampit they' tae cut it oot Oh Christ and whaur's
the sense two wee girruls tell me that and I'll gie yes the bus
ride aye and the moon and stars an' a.'

Anne was all right, because she could look very hard at the
dog. She gentled its allsort nose in her hand and looked out to
the grey sea with its real waves. Her hair was drying back to
white. The wind smelt of salt and the bleach from the baths, the

old woman of pee and dirt and drink. My mother said the crones in the Canongate drank a mixture of Meths and Brasso, called Blue Billy; she herself drank Cinzano Bianco, 'And devil take the hindmost,' she'd say.

I was fair to giggle or cry and I knew the old woman, (or was she old?), was going to touch me; it was a race against time, would the bus never come?

It rocked around the corner, maroon and white, 'Nemo me impune lacessit' on the side, just as the old woman's hand came for my arm. 'Grace, he'd say, Grace, we've just time, here, now, here, against the wall, quick get yer skirts up.'

Later, though we'd had only milk while our mothers had frothy pink chocolate and cinnamon toast with their feet crunching among the bags under the table in the Chocolate House, I was sick, and I saw that stinking woman tied with string waddle down to the grey sea, her dog beside her flirting its petticoats, nosing in the shingle at the edge of the cold real waves.

WHAT WE DID ON OUR HOLIDAYS

GEOFF NICHOLSON

GEOFF NICHOLSON

The author began his career as a writer of plays and television comedy. He won the 1985 *Custom Car* magazine short story competition; the prize was a customised Ford Escort. His first novel, *Street Sleeper*, was shortlisted for the *Yorkshire Post* Best First Work award. His second novel is called *The Knot Garden*.

IT ALL STARTED as I was enjoying a bottled lager in the saloon bar of the Devonshire Arms. I was celebrating (though celebrating probably isn't the right word) my forty-fifth birthday with one or two chaps from work when I experienced what can only be described as an intense bout of middle-aged angst. The lager turned to ashes in my mouth, and searing doubts and uncertainties crowded in on me like so many gawpers at a road accident.

I wasn't great company for the rest of the evening. I kept asking myself some tricky questions. Who was I? Where was I going? Who were my fellow-travellers? Did I know myself? Did I know my own wife? My children? Did they know me? Did they want to? Was there perhaps more to life than being a pillar of the bought-ledger office for a major chain of furniture retailers?

I couldn't come up with any answers then. In fact the more questions I asked the less I knew. The time had come to take stock. I looked unflinchingly at myself in the etched mirror on the wall of the Devonshire Arms, and I'm not afraid to say that I didn't much like what I saw.

Days passed. My brain was in turmoil. I'll sound like a silly so-and-so if I say I was gripped by the urge to make my life more meaningful and profound, but that's exactly the urge I *was* gripped by.

I wanted to get off this rat race of a roundabout for a while, to take time to think things through, to tarry a while, to look and listen, to sniff the roses, to get to know myself and my loved ones that little bit better. What I needed, I realised, was a holiday.

*　　*　　*

One way or another this is probably the last year we'll take a holiday *en famille*. Next summer my boy Max will be away at the Poly studying earth sciences, and my lovely daughter Sally says she wants to go on a French exchange, preferably to Lourdes. Even my trim and attractive wife Kathleen has suggested that next year we take separate 'singles' holidays, so one way or another the pattern of family life is bound to change; and that's how I managed to get the family to do it my way this one last time. I shall be keeping a free-form journal of the experience.

Caravanning has always been my idea of the perfect holiday-making mode. I didn't want to take any chances on this final epochal holiday so I picked a place that we know and love: the Tralee Carapark and Holiday Centre. It is a well-designed, attractively appointed, carefully screened, compact site. It offers direct access to beach and main road. There are extensive showering and toilet facilities, a mobile shop, a laundrette, a children's playground and a Calor Gas supply. I'm delighted to say it's free from TV lounges, burger bars, games rooms, cinemas, licensed bars, communal barbecue areas and artificial grass ski slopes. Motorcycles are not allowed.

All right, I admit that the term 'holiday centre' may be a slight exaggeration, but as I told Max and Sally when they tried to talk me into a trekking holiday in Morocco, I know what we like.

Well, we've arrived!!

The drive here, I need hardly say, was a nightmare. If I'd only had myself and my own driving to worry about it wouldn't have been so bad. Unfortunately, I had every other cretinous road-user to worry about as well.

To cut a long story short, I ran into the back of some damn fool who braked, completely without warning, to avoid knocking down some old crone with a Zimmer frame who'd wandered into the middle of a zebra crossing. The driver of the other car leapt out of his seat, furious, and looking as though he was about to do me violence. However, he took a good look at the back of his car, which appeared entirely unblemished, looked at my car, which was blemished good and proper, and let out a peal of scarcely controlled laughter before heading on his way.

My boy Max cheered me up no end by saying that if the driver had laid so much as a finger on me, he (Max) would have beaten him to an unpleasant pulp. I thanked Max. It's funny how a crisis can bring a family together.

There's a sign on the inside of our caravan door that reads, 'Please leave this caravan in the state you would wish to find it'. It appears that the previous occupants would like to find a caravan full of bits of stale food, unwanted body hair, used tea bags, cheesy milk-bottles, scum and grease in the sink, soiled sticking plasters in the bed, and a foul smell coming from the chemical toilet.

'Never mind,' I said brightly. 'We can have this place spick-and-span in no time if we all pitch in.'

However, the rest of the family didn't pitch in so it took me a very considerable amount of time. It was a dirty job but somebody had to do it, and I knew there wasn't much chance of that somebody being Max, Sally, or Kathleen.

After Kathleen's tasty evening meal I managed to talk the family into playing a game of pontoon. The run of the cards was pleasantly low-key and easy on the nerves, but our nerves were set rudely ajangle when, quite out of the blue, a house brick was tossed through our caravan window. There was a note attached to the brick which read, 'Go back where you belong. Death to the Evil Empire.' It was unsigned.

I was shocked, but determined not to let a little thing like that spoil our holiday.

'Probably just kids,' I said. 'Probably just misplaced high spirits.'

We returned to our game of pontoon, but my concentration had been broken and my heart wasn't in it. Brick throwing wasn't an everyday occurrence in the Tralee Carapark and Holiday Centre that *I* used to know and love. I immediately lost the bank and before very long I'd been completely cleaned out of matches.

*   *   *

This morning I thought I'd do the neighbourly thing by introducing myself to the folk in the adjacent caravan.

They seem nice enough young people. They're foreign but not offensively so. Their name is Garcia; Axel and Iris. Hubby was a little unshaven, he was smoking a cheroot, looked a little the worse for drink, and insisted on calling me 'gringo'. The whole caravan reeked of garlic, and an Astrid Gilberto record was being played at quite unnecessary volume. Nevertheless, I am a tolerant chap, I take as I find, and I'm sure we can be fast friends of the Garcias.

Set off on my morning constitutional and fell in step with an old gent also on holiday at the Tralee. We talked about winter sports, war, compulsory sterilisation and the younger generation.

'Hanging's too good for them,' he said. 'What they need is a spell in the army.'

I pride myself on being able to see the other chap's point of view so I agreed with him.

'And then,' he continued, 'they should be flogged and made to perform disgusting sex acts and have electrodes attached to their gonads and boiling oil poured up their bottoms.'

'Not sure I can go all the way with you on that one,' I said.

'You'll go all the way,' he said, 'or I'll pull your sodding lungs out.'

So I agreed with him. I didn't come on holiday to play the hypocrite, on the other hand I didn't come to have my lungs pulled out. Ah well, it takes all sorts.

Came across my boy Max at the edge of the caravan site. He'd shot a rabbit with some lethal-looking catapult device, and now he was skinning it. He seemed to be making a pretty good job of it too.

'Hey Max,' I said, 'do you know where you're going to? Do you like the things that life is showing you?'

'Not a lot,' he replied.

'Like father like son,' I said. 'Like me you probably think there ought to be something more.'

'Too right.'

'And the problem is knowing what that something more should be.'

'Not really. What I want is savagery, a feeling of being in touch with my animal self.'

'Not sure that I really know what you're on about there, Max.'

'I'm talking about atavism, the stripping away of the veneer of civilisation, the memory of blood and bone.'

Max was being unusually forthcoming for Max but I was blowed if I could catch his drift. 'We'll talk more about this later,' I said. But I wasn't at all sure that we would.

It appears there must be an airfield nearby. This afternoon we were treated to quite a display of stunt flying by an old Sopwith Camel. It flew directly above the Tralee, scaring a few dogs, children and old dears, and at one point the pilot smashed a wing tip into a tree. For his finale he disappeared over the horizon in a pall of black smoke, followed by an explosion. No doubt the explosion was some kind of sound effect but it was certainly very lifelike.

I expect it was all some kind of advertising trailer for an air circus. I wonder where I can buy tickets.

Found my trim and attractive wife Kathleen reading a book today. Thinking I might stimulate a bit of literary discussion I asked what she was reading. The book was called *Canine Orgasm*, and a quick riffle through its pages left me in no doubt about its lubricious content.

'This is sheer pornography,' I said.

'No it isn't,' Kathleen contradicted. 'It's erotica.'

'Oh, pardon me,' I said huffily. 'Perhaps you'd care to enlighten me about the subtle difference.'

'Yes,' she said. 'Both pornography and erotica seek to excite the reader, but pornography is masturbatory while erotica is celebratory.'

'You've said a mouthful there,' I remarked.

'I want to celebrate,' she said.

*   *   *

As a family we've always found nudity to be normal and healthy without making a big thing of it. Imagine my surprise on finding my lovely daughter Sally prostrate on the ground, legs together (I'm pleased to say), arms outstretched on the grass beside her, naked but for a pair of burgundy slingbacks and a rosary. I felt I had to say something. I suggested that her appearance might cause offence to the Garcias, but that didn't seem to get through.

'Just what exactly do you think you're up to?' I demanded in the end.

'I'm making my body a temple for Christ,' she said.

I couldn't think of a reply to that so I held my peace. Ah well, no doubt she'll grow out of it.

A holiday isn't a holiday for me without a game of beach cricket. Last year I scored a brisk half-century before getting out to a bad shot in a late run chase. I was determined that the same thing wouldn't happen this year. When my turn came to bat I walked to the wicket loose-limbed and relaxed. I took middle and leg, and played a pretty defensive straight bat for an over or two. I felt in good form. I was seeing the ball early and I started to go for my shots. I drove Kathleen back over her head. I clipped Sally briskly off my legs for a boundary. The sound of willow on tennis ball was rich and resonant.

My score had moved rapidly on to seventeen when my boy Max took the cherry. I've always tried to instil into Max the virtues of line and length but he can still be very wayward. He came in to bowl off a short run and unleashed a vicious beamer; and as the 'ball' came at my head I couldn't help noticing that this was not the soft, yellow tennis ball we'd been using until then, but rather a biggish piece of granite that he'd picked up from the beach. I was rattled. I raised my bat, more as protection for my head than in any attempt to play a shot. The granite hit the shoulder of the bat and I inadvertently dollied a catch to Sally who was running in from square leg.

I might have stood my ground. I might have said that a beamer should have been declared a no-ball and therefore I could not have been out. I might also have offered the opinion that pitching a lump of rock at your father's head isn't exactly cricket.

But I said nothing. I walked from the crease all quiet decorum and sportsmanship. Nobody likes a batsman who can't take his dismissal with dignity.

What a storm! The day had been warm, not to say balmy, but as night fell a devilish wind got up, rain lashed the site and lightning tore the heavens asunder. The caravan rocked on its base while rain beat down on the roof like machine-gun fire. It was all extremely un-English.

Kathleen and I are great ones for holiday souvenirs. We enjoy ashtrays, letter-racks, that sort of thing; even a nicely made T-shirt. However, I was a bit surprised when my trim and attractive wife suggested that this year, by way of a change, we get ourselves intimately tattooed.

'Pardon?' I said, thinking I had no great desire to have 'Skegness is so Bracing' emblazoned across my chest.

'I'd like an orchid on my buttock,' she said. 'And you can have a bumble bee on yours.'

I couldn't see the sport in that and I made my feelings plain.

'If you must have a souvenir,' I said, 'what's wrong with a trivet?'

'I don't want a trivet tattooed on my buttock, thanks very much,' Kathleen replied tartly.

Sometimes I think that woman deliberately tries to misunderstand me.

Decided to make the effort and went over to chat with the Garcias, but I've been forced to conclude that they're not really my sort of people.

The sun was barely over the yard-arm but Axel, or Mr Garcia as I prefer to call him, was swigging liquor straight from the bottle. Something called mescal. He offered it to me and in the interests of neighbourliness I very nearly accepted. Lucky for me I inspected the bottle to find there was a dead worm in it.

I told them they should take it back to the shop and demand a full refund. They laughed at me in that rather mocking way that foreigners have. I said I had a pressing engagement and made a hasty retreat.

Was mugged this morning. Hardly what you'd expect in the Tralee Carapark and Holiday Centre. I was returning from the shower and toilet block when I was set upon by a couple of lads in jogging suits. One grabbed me from behind while the other went through my pockets. There wasn't much money, but enough for a couple of teenage muggers I'd have thought. However, not content with money they then beat me up a bit.

As I lay on the ground I shouted defiantly, 'I suppose you enjoy beating up quiet, unassuming forty-five-year-olds who can't defend themselves.'

'No,' they said as one. 'We just enjoy beating up you.'

This evening Max suggested we play a truth game. I'd never heard of such a thing. I'd have preferred Cluedo or Monopoly personally but even so I was prepared to give it a whirl.

Max explained the rules. What happens is this: each player has to reveal some dark secret about himself that he's kept from the other players until now. That's all there is to it. I couldn't see the sport in it myself, and I certainly can't see it ever replacing Cluedo.

But we gave it a go. I set the ball rolling by confessing that when I sold the old Ford Escort to that nice Mrs Henderson I'd said it had a new gearbox. That was a lie. The gearbox was only reconditioned. I must say I've always felt a bit guilty about that, and I admit I felt better for getting it off my chest. Perhaps there was something in this truth game after all.

Max, of course, wasn't very impressed by my revelation. He said we were looking for something a bit more fundamental. I challenged him to do better and immediately wished I hadn't.

Max said, 'The truth is, I want to kill you, dad, and then sleep with mum.'

I laughed nervously but I knew things had gone beyond a joke. I looked to Kathleen for a bit of wifely support but to my horror she'd decided to enter into the spirit of the thing.

'You know, it's always been my fantasy,' she said, 'to be

rogered by two well-endowed dwarfs at the same time, one from each end.'

'Mother!' I said involuntarily. She hates it when I call her mother.

Who knows how things might have turned out if it hadn't been for my lovely daughter Sally, who then entered the fray?

'There is only one truth, and that is the Lord's,' she said, which put a most welcome damper on things.

It'll be a long time before you catch *me* playing truth games again.

Life's funny, isn't it? There was Kathleen yesterday revealing her dwarf fantasy, and today two male dwarfs have moved into a nearby caravan.

I went and did the neighbourly thing. It appears they work in the entertainment field but are resting for the moment. They were civil enough but not exactly warm and friendly. Still, if they want to keep themselves to themselves that's their business. Considering Kathleen's fantasy it may be no bad thing.

We certainly are having some weather on this holiday. I woke to find the Tralee shrouded in an impenetrable fog. Nevertheless I went for my morning constitutional. The old eyes can play you false in the fog, yet I swear I saw the old gent with the radical views on youth, dressed in paramilitary uniform, dragging a youthful, headless corpse along the perimeter of the site.

Perhaps it was just a trick of the light.

'Well,' said my trim and attractive wife Kathleen, 'if you don't want to be tattooed, how about a bit of erotic piercing?'

'Pardon?' I said.

'A ring through the nipples, a bolt through the glans, that sort of thing.'

'I still don't see what's wrong with a trivet,' I said.

'You'd look bloody silly with a trivet through your wedding tackle.'

I hadn't come on holiday to hear language like that.

'You've been watching too much television, mother,' I said. That put her in her place.

Well, the headless corpse seems not to have been a trick of the light. I was returning from the shower block today when I passed a deserted caravan that had its door open. I couldn't help noticing that the door handle had something unpleasant on it, and there was what looked very much like human entrails all over the doorstep. I peered inside and saw that someone had smeared the numbers 666 on the wall in blood, and there was a severed head lying by the stove.

It was all pretty rum. I suppose I should have reported the incident to the site manager but frankly I didn't want to get involved. If you ask me, this world would be a much better place if a few more people kept their noses out of other people's business.

Treated to another aerial display. Two Messerschmitts flew in low out of the sun. Their engines were quite unnecessarily loud and as they approached we heard what sounded like anti-aircraft fire. The planes hedge-hopped the Tralee Carapark and Holiday Centre, strafing it as they went. I must say I was a bit surprised to find them using real bullets, but no doubt these air circus people are absolute sticklers for realism.

The sound of what can only be described as animals being tortured emanating from the Garcias' caravan, kept me awake till the early hours this morning. I popped round to reason with them but it did little good. A red-eyed Mr Garcia opened the door to me. He was underdressed and stank of strange foreign food and drink. I could see into the caravan where Mrs Garcia was clearly visible, performing an illegal experiment on a small goat.

'Beat it,' Garcia said to me. 'I wouldn't want to hurt my knuckles beating some sense into you.'

'That's just the sort of silly, macho violence we could do without,' I rejoined.

But Mr Garcia didn't think we could do without it. He hit me a few times in the eye, and even as I write I can feel a real shiner developing.

Of course, more than anything, I feel sorry for the goat.

I must say that my hopes of getting to know my boy Max have taken a bit of a hammering this holiday. This is largely because I never see him. Every day he takes a packed lunch and goes off on a nature ramble. He returns in the evening, covered in mud, his clothes torn, often carrying a small dead animal or two. I decided the time was ripe for a fatherly word.

'Max,' I enquired as he sat down to dinner, 'would it be asking too much for you to arrive home in the evenings looking a bit more presentable?'

'Yes,' he said. At least that's what I thought he said. His mouth was full and he sprayed food around the caravan as he spoke, so it wasn't very easy to catch his drift.

'Thing is, dad,' I believe he said, 'I'm rejecting civilisation.'

He picked up his plate, licked it clean, then tossed the plate over his shoulder. He'd finished. If rejecting civilisation means the death of good table manners then it seems a sorry show to me.

'I'm tired of this sham,' he said. 'I'm going native.'

'In Lincolnshire?' I asked, but it was too late to argue with him. He was already disappearing out of the door on all fours.

News from home. A message was phoned through to the site office asking me to ring my neighbour George, urgently. I did so and George informed me that my house had been broken into. Apparently the burglars had been disturbed in the act and had run away empty-handed.

'Hardly surprising, George,' I said. 'We lead a simple life. They probably couldn't find anything worth taking.'

George said that was his impression too. Therefore the villains had smeared the walls with margarine and defecated on to the fitted carpets. I was all for returning home but George assured me he was in control. He'll tackle the walls himself and get professionals in to clean the carpets. What would we do without neighbours, eh?

I decided not to mention any of this to Kathleen. She'd only worry.

Woke up in the middle of the night to find my boy Max standing over the bed. He had a bone through his nose, had funny patterns painted over his torso and was holding a sharpened stake that was pointing in the general direction of my heart. He was also chanting in a rather tuneless way.

'What's the game, Max?' I asked.

'I'm here to reclaim what's mine. The king must die!'

I informed Max that he isn't too old to get a thick ear. That seemed to do the trick. I trust we've seen the last of *that* sort of nonsense.

Got a bit of a shock on returning from my constitutional to find my trim and attractive wife Kathleen making the beast with two (or in this case I suppose three) backs with the two dwarfs who work in the entertainment field. They certainly weren't resting now. I didn't want to come the heavy husband but I thought something needed to be said.

'Put some clothes on,' I suggested.

'Can't it wait a minute?' Kathleen asked breathlessly. 'We've very nearly finished.'

I can't deny that woman anything. Afterwards Kathleen claimed she'd just wanted to know whether it's true what they say about dwarfs. Apparently it is.

I've forgiven Kathleen because, as she so rightly says, if you can't let yourself go once a year on your holidays, then what are holidays for?

More airborne fun and games; this time from B52s, American helicopters and what looked like crop-sprayers. The crop-sprayers seemed a little out of place. All they did was douse the nearby trees with some kind of liquid fertiliser.

This afternoon I noticed that autumn seems to be coming very early this year. Either that or it wasn't liquid fertiliser that was being sprayed over the trees.

*   *   *

More news from home. Another message to call George urgently. I did so and he informed me that there's been an accident with some of the industrial solvents that were being used to clean the faeces off our fitted carpets. It seems there's been a bit of a fire and the house has been gutted. I was all for returning home but George assured me there wouldn't be much point.

I've decided not to mention any of this to Kathleen. I wouldn't want to worry her. I'd also prefer her not to know that I didn't bother to renew the insurance policy last month since the likelihood of our house ever being burgled or gutted seemed so incredibly remote.

Woken by the sounds of motorcycles entering the Tralee Carapark and Holiday Centre. The riders were a rough and unwashed lot. They had leather jackets and they really didn't look the type we wanted here. Normally the site manager would be very strict about the 'no motorcycle' rule but he wasn't there at that time of day. Someone had to send them on their way before they got too settled in. I seemed to be the man on the spot.

I slipped into my dressing-gown and went out to offer some friendly advice. However, I'd barely opened my mouth before they'd stuffed an oily rag into it, beaten me with a chain, and tied me to a nearby leafless tree. They pulled open my dressing-gown and began stubbing out cigarettes on my bare chest. It stung like blazes.

It's hard to say how things would have developed if my lovely daughter Sally hadn't come running out to help her old dad. I must say I don't think she was looking her best. She was wearing an old sack that had ash marks all over it. Nevertheless she had a definite aura about her.

The bikers left me alone now. They surrounded Sally and I feared things might get ugly. But no. She said, 'Peace be with you,' and immediately they fell to their knees. She touched each of them in turn and blessed them. They seemed to like that.

When I last saw Sally she was on the pillion of a Norton Commando leading the pack of bikers from the Tralee Carapark.

My gag had worn loose and I shouted after her, 'Where do you think you're going Sally?' She turned and said, 'I must be about my father's business.'

I can't say I ever thought that a group of hell's angels would have a lot of use for a bought ledger, but what did *I* know?

One way or another the allotted holiday fortnight is drawing to a close. I feel pretty bitter-sweet about it all. These weeks haven't been the most restful I've ever spent, but by golly they've been a change. Then I started thinking . . .

I'd been planning to have a week at home before going back to work but in view of the house being gutted it seems a little pointless. I had a word with the site manager who said they'd had a late cancellation and the caravan was free for another week. What a stroke of luck!

Kathleen readily agreed, on condition that she can carry on seeing her dwarfs. I said all right. I can't deny that woman anything.

When I last saw Max I tried to tell him the news, but all I got from him were a series of animal grunts before he disappeared into the distance, moving with all the speed and grace of an uncaged panther.

My lovely daughter Sally hasn't been in touch since she disappeared with the motorcycle gang but I'm sure that in a case like this no news is good news.

Kids: they're a joy, but they can be a worry too, can't they?

It suddenly occurred to me that we haven't sent any postcards. I've just spent the evening dropping a quick line to all our family and friends. I can never come up with anything very original to say on these damn things, so I just wrote the usual: 'wish you were here'.

KEEPING DISTANCE

TIM PARKS

TIM PARKS

Born in 1954, Tim Parks was brought up in Blackpool and London. He is married with two children and presently lives in Italy where he works as a translator and teacher. He has published three novels: *Tongues of Flame* (winner of the Somerset Maugham and Betty Trask awards), *Loving Roger* (winner of the John Llewellyn Rhys Memorial Prize) and *Home Thoughts*. His fourth novel *Family Planning* will be published in spring 1989.

THEY WERE BOTH studying to be doctors, so they had that in common. And then the ages were right, right that is for his preconception of how ages in a couple should be, a difference of three years in his favour, and while she would always have objected in any discussion of the issue to the notion that in the ideal couple the girl should be younger, she nevertheless enjoyed the idea of having an older man, or rather boy, he was only twenty-four, to slip under her thumb.

The same could have been said of their respective heights.

Then the place was right too, Selva di Val Gardena, he skiing with friends, spending his father's money, she working temporarily in a distant relative's hotel – every day bright and clear, the crisp exhilarating thrust of the Dolomites silenced by snow, the chattering of winter holiday-makers barely denting the mystery. You felt different here, cleaner and more passionate.

He was recovering from having been left by his first love – a girlfriend of five years' standing, Paola had walked out on him in August and married another man in November. She, on the contrary, had never had a real love, only encounters.

And then there was the excitement of each other's foreign-ness. He was Italian, she German. Why is it that a foreign lover is always considered a greater prize, a greater adventure? Giuseppe and Hilda made love some hours after having come across each other in a discoteque attached to a pizzeria.

She took all the initiative, for he was still sulking, and having had no other girls but that fatal first love was shy with women, despite his one-of-the-boys, heavy-drinking, loud-laughing man-ner with his friends. Quite simply she took him to her bed, and in doing so fell in love with him. For his part he was most impressed, with her physical prowess, with the suddenness of her devotion. He was a man who loved to be loved. Unfortunately her face was not especially attractive: the nose was too big and wide, the lips too thin, the skin unhealthy somehow. Only the bright blue eyes saved the situation, the bright honest smile displaying well-kept teeth, plus, when it came to introducing her to his friends, her slim but well-endowed and very modern body.

Giuseppe on the other hand was unbelievably handsome. In every department. She loved him and loved him. For the first time in her life she was swooning.

They spoke to each other in halting English. Which separated . them from their friends. They giggled over misunderstandings. When they spoke about medical matters though, they found they had a large vocabulary in common and, being her senior, he had the pleasure of explaining things she didn't know about, at great length. In fact he was rather a bore at times, but she lapped it up: there was his face to look at, the fine intelligent forehead and Roman nose, there were his incredibly broad square shoulders. They both felt pleased to be improving their English, although there was no one to correct them when they made mistakes.

In the mountains everybody wore jeans or ski pants, thick woollen sweaters, quilted jackets. But when, having finished at the hotel, she travelled down to Verona for a week before returning for the next university term, it came as something of a disappointment for Giuseppe. He was an elegant dresser. In a very Italian way he followed fashions. In his imitation Armani sweater and generously cut autumn-coloured wool trousers he walked with an idle strut perfectly adapted for the *passeggiata*. In bright winter weather in Via Mazzini he cut a figure. But Hilda wore the same jeans, boots, sweaters and quilted jacket she had worn in Val Gardena, and her gait had a hurried a-to-b purpose about it which didn't do much for the huge attribute that was her body.

Just when he was beginning to get seriously annoyed with this, and annoyed with the way that, despite her lavish bed-time love and eager if inexpert cooking, she would argue quite belligerently against the notion that women should be sex objects and that money spent on attractive clothes was well spent, just when he was getting seriously irritated (with the fuss she made over finding an old *Playboy*, for example), it was time for her to go home. They were both sad. It had been such a passionate affair and love had been made such an impressive and unprecedented number of times. They both promised letters, phonecalls, visits. She told him very frankly she loved him. He mumbled something in his halting English into her hair, which privately he thought she would have done well to have washed more often. Perhaps permed.

She lived in Munich, five hours in the train from Verona, 400 kilometres, 60,000 lire, 88 marks. It was not an impossible distance, but expensive for young people living on student incomes, or, in his case, no real income at all. Between degree and specialisation she had six years to go. He was nearing the end of his degree, but then there was his military service to get through and the prospect of no jobs in Italian hospitals. It all made the relationship such a safe one, unlike his long affair with Paola. And at Easter Giuseppe thought of himself as travelling up to Germany for a much needed holiday and a week's solid sex.

Hilda greeted him in Italian. The progress she had made in just four months was astonishing, and likewise astonishing was the love she lavished on him. Nor did her lack of dress sense seem so important in Munich, where everybody dashed about under umbrellas between supermarket and bus stop without any regard for style. She held his arm tight and talked about the coming summer. He felt the slim suppleness of her lively body against him.

On Easter day she took him to her family home to the north of the city where he was welcomed with open arms by mother, father and brother. A young doctor and so handsome. Their kindness was doubly welcome, since Giuseppe's own parents lived and worked abroad and it was some time since he had had the chance to experience the warm bath of parental care, parental cooking. Tuned in to modern mores, the Meiers allowed Giuseppe and Hilda to share a room for the night as if already married. This gave a curious touch of respectability, permanence, general acknowledgment to something Giuseppe had so far only thought of as an affair. When he ran out of money, as he regularly would, Hilda lent him five hundred of the marks she had saved from her holiday job, though she did say a few words about not spending so much on clothes. He said if only an Italian medical degree were acceptable in Germany, he would be able to come up permanently in a year or so, after his military service, and do his specialisation in a German hospital. She said, 'That's wonderful,' as if somehow this plan might be feasible.

He did his military service in Naples and every time he had a few days' leave they met in Verona, 700 kilometres north for him, 400 kilometres south for her. There was a train from Rome which left him on a cold deserted platform at 2 a.m. where he stretched out on a bench under his combat jacket till she got in at 3.30 and they took a taxi back to his room together. It was very romantic kissing in the back of that taxi. The railway people should put a plaque up for them at the station, he said, or name one of the trains after them, the amount of money they'd spent. And it was very erotic making love just a couple of days every couple of months. Each occasion became a rediscovery, a first time almost. She said she loved him so much. She said if only the Italian universities would accept the exams she'd already done in Germany, she could come down here to finish her degree while he did his specialisation.

'That's true,' he said.

'My Italian's good enough now,' she said.

'I know,' he said. 'It is.'

'Except I can't throw away my degree at this point, can I?'

And he agreed she couldn't.

They had no time to form a circle of friends in common. Which made her indifferent skin and worse dress sense easier to take. There was no one for him to lose face with. In fact he felt a great deal of affection for her. At times he thought of himself as being in love. Certainly the word was being used often enough. And at the barracks, where he was assistant to the military doctor, he spoke frequently of his German girlfriend and said she had the best pointed tits anybody could imagine.

On returning to Verona he took up residence in his room again and began his specialisation in urology. Which occupied a good sixty hours a week. He watched older people dying of cancers, young people shocked by their first serious illness. He was kind, efficient, but unmoved, in short, well suited to the job. He had no official salary or scholarship, such was the way in Italy, but after a few months they let him do the occasional night duty for a modest sum, and then there were his father's erratic cheques from Algeria. He got by and, spreading his borrowing among everybody he knew, even managed to keep a battered 127 on the road. But he was hungry for money now, for new clothes, a decent flat, a real car. What had he studied seven years for, if not for money? And when Hilda came down, or he went up there, it was so embarrassing to have to scrounge. He kept a close record of his debt to her, which, after two years now, was something over two million lire.

Hilda chided but always gave. Her evening waitressing financed two summer weeks in Yugoslavia. Two very happy weeks; the sun brought healthy colour to her face and in her bikini one could forget the dowdiness of her clothes. Roasting on the beach she thought it would be a good idea if they could both get jobs in the South Tyrol, the German-speaking part of Italy. Except that Giuseppe's German had made no progress whatsoever. And her degree still wouldn't be recognised he pointed out. Satisfied that this course of action was well and truly out of the question, they went back to the camp-site and made love quite passionately on sleeping bags in their tent using contraceptives she had paid for. In the balmy dark later they discussed the most recent advances in cancer research and a theory Giuseppe was developing about prostate problems. Who knew what progress medical science mightn't make during their lifetime? They were both more than satisfied with their chosen profession.

Back in Germany, Hilda completed her degree the following year with excellent results. Offered a paid post to specialise in Frankfurt, she agonised for a month or two, but in the end felt she would be a fool not to accept and went north. The four hundred kilometres became seven hundred.

She rented a room in a nice suburb and put her few belongings in it. She wasn't avid for special comforts or clothes as Giuseppe

was. Being a Green Party supporter, she was quite content to
use the bus rather than buy a car, though she could have afforded
one now. Naturally gregarious, if a little bossy, she was very
soon part of a new circle of friends, but took no lovers. She
wore a ring on her third finger and referred to it as an engagement
ring. The only decorations in her room were photographs of
Giuseppe, who inevitably came up for long weekends those
months when she didn't go down.

This went on for seven years. But it was curious how much
of the freshness and simplicity of their first encounters they
managed to retain, curious how young they still were. Distance
seemed to have frozen time, so that if there was no progress
(whatever that might mean), still there was very little loss
either. He or she would arrive. Coffee would be made and then
love. The mood was one of holiday, a well-deserved break.
Saturday and Sunday they would eat in restaurants, walk in
parks. There were cinemas, discoteques. The weekends, as
ever, gave them no time to gather acquaintances about them.
No social fabric underpinned their partnership. He hadn't seen
her parents since that Easter almost a decade ago. She had
never seen his. So they sat, sipping granita on sultry Verona
nights in the central square, or walking arm in arm under an
umbrella to stare in Frankfurt's shop windows running with
October rain. Both salaried doctors now, their staple conversation was their patients, hospital organisation, Germany versus
Italy, modern medicine. They never tired of it. They could talk
way into the small hours, discussing difficult diagnoses. Of
course her pasty skin and lack of dress sense still bothered
Giuseppe occasionally, but then he was only with her for the
weekend, of which a good fifty per cent was spent indoors, and
a great deal of that in bed. She still chided him for his wasteful
ways with money, but then their resources weren't in common,
his loans had been paid back, and no mention had been made of
saving jointly for a house since the geographical location of such
a house was unimaginable. What they both still enjoyed very
much was their lovemaking, a feeling of physical tenderness
they had for each other. And if either masturbated or ever had
the occasional adventure during the four or five weeks

that separated one visit from the next, this was never talked about.

Until, at thirty-one, Hilda decided, or perhaps it would be more accurate to say discovered, she wanted a child. It was a disquieting discovery, the more so because entirely unexpected. She had thought of herself as a girl in love with her lover Giuseppe, that was one vision; she had thought of herself as a responsible career woman taking her rightful place in society at the hospital, that was another; but she had not thought of herself as a mother. The first two visions were remarkably easy to sustain. She divided her life into work (feminine assertion in what had once been a male preserve), and holiday (Giuseppe, restaurants, bars, summer beaches). There was no conflict here; on the contrary, all was perfect complement. But it was difficult to imagine integrating these two visions, or perhaps it would mean sacrificing them, in that third and new vision, a life that would accommodate motherhood. And yet she did want a child. It had to do somehow with a new consciousness of her life as a whole, as a human creature, of its finiteness, its inevitable span, its trajectory you might say. And this wasn't just a negative discovery, a sense of time running out, although that came into it; it was also a positive feeling of coming to fruition, of being in her prime. This, she sensed dimly – in a way that had nothing to do with politics, profession or love – this should be a moment, *the* moment, of plenitude. Now. And she wanted a child. Otherwise, and she had never really seen this before, her existence would simply go on being forever what it already was, without any shift of gear or change of rhythm or further depth or richness, without somehow being properly harnessed up to life.

Although never bringing the issue to full consciousness, for her professional mind had so much to be busy with, Hilda was aware of two choices. There was, for example, a slightly older doctor in paediatrics, shy, retiring, a little watery, but very intelligent, who had made it clear in one way or another over the last three years or so that he would like to form a relationship with her, if only he could pluck up the courage, if only she were available. A little effort, she knew, a little encouragement, and she could marry him within the year. Or some other local man. Why not? Three months' maternity leave at some point and back to work. A crêche was available for the children of hospital staff.

Or there was Giuseppe. And complete incompatibility with her professional German life.

Again without actually weighing up the pros and cons, she was aware, over a period of some months, of a decision-making process going on. Until, at short notice, just as that winter was turning into spring, Giuseppe cancelled a weekend visit in order to attend, he said, a conference in Naples, on uro-dynamics. Her acute feeling of letdown, her inkling of jealousy (why had he left it to the last moment to tell her? how was she to know there really was a conference in Naples?), her sense of desolation, cutting alone into the cake she had baked for him, brought her to a sudden decision: or so it seemed, for now she was sorting through possible ways to broach the subject, now she was definitely fearing how he would respond, as if quite suddenly he was her only hope. It would have to be him.

As it turned out only the following weekend, Giuseppe surprised and actually rather unnerved her with his ready consent, his willingness to make plans, immediately. She wondered if he wasn't being a little naive. For as it was she who would have to bear the child, so it would have to be she who left her job, who went down to live with him, became dependent on him. Did responsibility sit so lightly on his shoulders? Did he really know what he was letting himself in for? And if he was so ready to agree to the idea now, why hadn't he suggested it before himself? It wasn't a notion that required such a great deal of imagination to dream up, marrying your girlfriend of ten years' standing.

It was a curious weekend this, in that it just wouldn't live up to its apparent momentousness as the turning point of their lives. Perhaps because, with all those years of relaxing holiday breaks behind them, of cinema, restaurant, lovemaking, of fascinating case histories recounted in bed, they had never learnt the knack of declaring themselves, or even arguing. How much did they really know about each other, about living together? Sunday afternoon, after yes had been said, had a flat, dull, unreal feel to it.

In answer to her question, he explained, but unconvincingly, that he'd never felt he had the right to encourage her to leave such a good job, nor, obviously, could he ever have dreamed of leaving his and so becoming dependent on her. But now that she was actually offering to make the sacrifice, to come down and be with him, of course he was delighted. He didn't want to go on living on his own forever. It was tiresome sometimes. And then he fancied himself as a father. It was time life took a turn. Lying beside him, she was profoundly dissatisfied with this, as if somehow he'd let her down, though when you thought about it, what he'd said was perfectly reasonable. And although they had decided now, or said they had, that if a child was to be born it had better be born as soon as possible, nevertheless they used their contraceptives as usual that night, as if it might be unthinkable after all these years, or even obscene, that his naked flesh should at last penetrate hers. They used their contraceptives, all was as it always had been, apparently, yet even so, and they both sensed it, there was something deliberate, something cautious and rather self-conscious about their lovemaking tonight. The embrace had lost its old holiday feel of sheer pleasure and weekend relief between tenderly consenting adults. Their minds were elsewhere.

He found a bigger flat to rent. More decisively, she gave up her job, her world, and travelled south. After some difficulty satisfying the authorities' hunger for documents, they were married in the registry office set up romantically, if rather ominously, in the ancient *palazzo* that was believed to have housed Juliet's tomb.

After all those years of care with contraceptives, the queues in night-duty chemists, the occasional painful renunciation, it now transpired that getting pregnant was by no means automatic. As doctors of course they should have known this. Indeed for doctors they were somewhat naive. Unless perhaps a strong groundswell of naivety is a positive quality in those who daily have to exercise an imprecise profession in the face of calamity. Either way, nothing happened. Lovemaking took on a distasteful, inhibiting significance, but produced no fruit. Installed on the sixth floor of an apartment block within sight of the hospital,

Hilda struggled to fill her unemployed time, cleaning, studying, improving her Italian, giving German lessons and doing the odd translation. She was a resourceful girl. But inevitably there were mornings, afternoons, evenings when time hung heavy. The more so because Giuseppe didn't always return promptly at the end of his periods of duty. For years he had been going regularly to a gym, God knows what would happen to his body if he stopped now. And then there was the paper he was writing in collaboration with someone in the pharmacy on total parenteral nutrition for post-operative kidney patients. Hours had to be spent sifting through data together, assessing case histories. For the first time in her life, Hilda caught herself staring blankly out of windows.

And more effort was required with the time they did spend together too. There was no weekend sense of occasion now. Nor did he, from one morning to the following evening, gather much in the way of news. Routine set in. When he wasn't watching television, Giuseppe liked to go out with old friends, meet in a bar, eat in a trattoria, parade up and down Via Mazzini. But gregarious and sociable as Hilda was, she found such excursions tedious. His friends were frivolous, over-dressed, the women over made-up, the men interested in football if they were interested in anything at all. Back in Frankfurt the staples of her social conversation had been politics, arms reduction, the environment; she had been a serious talker; now she smiled weakly as Giuseppe retailed the endless dirty jokes he picked up on the ward, guffawing loudly as one punchline followed another. And it occurred to her that she had never really heard her handsome lover talking at any length to anybody but herself, never had the opportunity to observe him in a group; where, she now discovered, he acted rather like one of those big complacent dogs who are forever expecting a pat on the head from everybody and frequently launch into fits of barking out of sheer excitement with their own thoroughbred, beautiful, well-brushed selves.

For his part, Giuseppe was privately wondering how it had come about that he had married somebody who was so much not his ideal of what a woman should be. So unfeminine, with such poor dress sense, and never a trace of make-up on her face. Had it been just the excitement of her foreignness, of all that travelling to and fro, the train juddering to a halt at various borders (he missed it now), of saying to people, 'my German girlfriend,' and adding in certain company, 'with the best pointed tits in the world' (though what was the use if she insisted on hiding them in these baggy old sweaters)? It was not that they had stopped caring for each other, not that all tenderness had already gone, just that these two people found themselves soon bored, soon disappointed.

And when they got home, lovemaking was not as voluptuous and eager as it had been on all those weekends always so carefully arranged so as not to coincide with her menstruations. Indeed, perhaps love would not have been made at all, were it not for this child she had set her heart on having, this child whose arrival had become a matter of faith now; otherwise the move south, the marriage, the sacrifice of her job, her life, would all have been an unfortunate and expensive mistake.

But Hilda was not an unintelligent girl, and life now was giving her plenty of time to think. So she came to appreciate over the passing months that all this had probably been fairly predictable, perhaps in fact she had herself foreseen it, or at least had a pretty good inkling; it was just that she had stifled her doubts with that overwhelming determination to have a child. Yet was such determination wise? Wasn't this urgency to become a mother something she should have fought against perhaps, some mental unbalance brought about by changing hormone patterns? Should she have defended the carefree state of mind that was her younger self, the chemical equilibrium she had been so happy with? And shouldn't she have resisted that peculiar sense of fate that had invaded her, that intuition of what life was for, or rather of the subjection of her own life to the great natural cycle?

When winter set in and his paper was written and sent off, Giuseppe watched a great deal more television; adventure films and sports were his favourites it turned out. A lot of their time together passed without words, not in the silence of resolution and serenity, but against the background of a nagging tension, of something unresolved, unsettled between them, which they were becoming less rather than more capable of talking about. So that Hilda had more or less decided to call the whole thing a day before it became a lifetime, had already telephoned the hospital administration in Frankfurt about the possibility of getting her job back, when at last she skipped her period.

What great and genuine excitement! What hours spent lying in the dark in almost mystical communion with her body. What sheepish grins and thoughtfulness from Giuseppe, getting home more promptly, bringing flowers, fruit, as if she had suddenly become an invalid. When in fact she had never felt better in her life. And so elated, looking at baby clothes, calculating dates, choosing names. What festivity!

For about two weeks. Until routine began to set in again. It was, after all, the best part of nine months till the child would be born. And to set in rather worse than before. Why was this? Why, after a fortnight's intense excitement, did life suddenly seem so depressing, so unutterably dull? Why this sudden and dramatic deflation? Was it just winter beginning to make itself felt, the first fogs creeping across the Bassa Padana into the southern suburbs of the city, so that, nose pressed against the damp window pane, Hilda could barely make out the glow of lamps in the street below? Was it to do with the seething hormonal redeployment she had now unleashed on herself, her moods an insignificant by-product of this inexorable creative process that was so much bigger, she knew that, than either herself or Giuseppe? Or was it, more simply, her awareness that with pregnancy, far more than with marriage, a trap had sprung and closed; the phonecall to Frankfurt, the departure note she had already prepared in her mind, these must be things of the past; her life was here now, in this two-bedroom flat on the sixth floor, watching the fog, looking for sensible ways to fill time, battling with a sense of waste. How many years would they live here? How many hours would she spend by this window? Why, now this baby was on the way, was she experiencing such a tremendous sense of desolation? As if she had lost far more in leaving her job, her language, her homeland, than a baby could ever replace. Had lost herself perhaps.

Always businesslike in the past, equable, sensible in her work, playful in her play, well-balanced, admirably capable in every department, Hilda now began to lose her self-control. And, more particularly, she began to lose the attitude of reasonable amenability she had always imagined to be an indivisible part of herself. Why should she get in the shopping and cook for him? Why should she trail into town to eat crusty pizza and listen to him retailing jokes she had heard a thousand times. She refused. She went to the cinema on her own, sat at home and read novels, took even less care with her appearance than she had before. She had no idea why she was acting as she was, was only aware that there was an element of self-destruction involved, which at once made her feel helpless and yet afforded a grim sense of satisfaction.

Giuseppe was lost. Basically carefree himself, he simply couldn't understand what he saw as wilful unpleasantness. And in someone who had always been so friendly, so devoted. He was nonplussed. He didn't possess great powers of intuition, perhaps because it was so very long since he had lived in such close proximity to anyone else. Most of all he didn't appreciate how much his affection for Hilda had depended on her devotion to him. Naturally inclined to be generous, so long as it didn't cost him too much, he oscillated between kind attempts to cheer her up, treats, anecdotes, and angry slammings of the door when she only became more prickly than before. After all, he was tired when he got home, he deserved a little respect, deserved to be able to put his feet up in front of the TV if he wanted. She sneered at him in a German he didn't understand. He stared at her, unwashed hair lank around pale cheeks. And he saw now that she had always thought of him as less intelligent than herself. She despised him, despised his habits, despised his friends. And forgetting, as one does, the ten years of happy weekends, the lightness, the affection, the tenderness, he began to feel resentful. He began to feel he had been used. Simply to fulfil her female craving for motherhood. Because nobody else would have her. Wisely so. Except that he, like a fool, had allowed himself to be drawn in without even thinking about it. Why hadn't he thought about it?

His life before Hilda came to live with him, which he had
frequently found rather dull and dissatisfying at the time, eagerly
looking forward to their weekends together, now appeared to
him in all the glory of its happy blend of achievement and
potential. He'd had his hard-earned job at the hospital, he'd had
his weekends with her for emotional and sexual fulfilment, he'd
had his friends, his gym, his volleyball, and perhaps most of all
he'd had the sense that anything could happen, that he could do
anything, embark on any project, sleep with any woman, because
his future was not a settled thing, but something he had perfect
freedom to decide on day by day. And in contrast now, he
thought, he might never sleep with any other woman again. This
was it, permanence, the end of youth. He was to be a father.
He was to be locked forever into this single embrace with this
rather dowdy woman. And though in the ten preceding years
Giuseppe had only rarely and very casually ended up in other
women's arms, this new awareness of limitation suddenly
seemed deeply disturbing and important. He would go through
life hurrying home, trying to keep her happy (an apparently
impossible task), missing dinners with friends, missing weekend
conferences, losing out in short in every department. It had all
been a terrible mistake. And just to show that he was not the
kind of man to succumb to such servitude, he allowed himself
to be seduced one evening by one of the girls in the lab; she
was notorious. And it felt good, quite frankly, to be using
contraceptives again.

Not that efforts weren't made to recapture that weekend ease
and simplicity that had led Giuseppe and Hilda to believe they
were so well suited to each other. For these two people were
both well-intentioned. They did not want things to go wrong.
So perhaps in the evening he would begin to tell her about some
curious case on the ward, a child with a kidney tumour, a
pensioner whose prostate had returned to normal for no
reason they could imagine. Hilda would give her opinion. But
without the old sense of enthusiasm, the sense of partici-
pating as an equal. The truth being that hospital talk only
heightened her feeling of regret, while for his part he was only
half-aware that she had lost some of her charisma for him when

she had stopped working. Somehow she was less important now. So that the conversations failed to engross as they once had.

Then, the following day, ashamed that she was taking out on him what in the end had been the natural and obvious result of her own decision, Hilda might prepare a treat for his homecoming: a strudel, a plumcake with rum. After dinner she would present it, his eyes would light up and he would gobble it down on the sofa, watching television, looking up at her from time to time and smiling. It wasn't the kind of easy light-hearted communion they had experienced in the past, there was something thin and rather pathetic about it, his quick smiles between concentrating on the inevitable game of something or other on the television. But it was better than nothing. And vaguely she wondered how it would be when she was cooking for a young child too, when there would be breathless demands for second helpings. Would she feel fulfilled then? Would it all have been worthwhile? Perhaps it was just a question of waiting, of not demanding satisfaction here and now. Perhaps with time, she would find some useful part-time job in a private clinic or something, or doing research, one didn't need state authorisation to do research. Giuseppe was such a beautiful man and basically kind. And perhaps anyone would be irritating once you started living with them. So probably it was just a case of hanging on and believing in it all. She stooped to kiss his neck, bent forward over her strudel, and smelt a strange perfume. Surprised, she sniffed again. There was also an unmistakable red mark just inside the collar, the kind of thing one wouldn't imagine girls did any more.

So two days later, when he said he was on night duty, substituting for a sick colleague, Hilda phoned the hospital, something she had never done before, since she knew how irritating it could be for everybody concerned if the doctor was constantly being dragged to the phone.

She asked for no explanations. She wasn't interested. It was extaordinary how suddenly, how firmly her mind was made up, how efficiently she packed, how quickly she penned her little note. With steady ruthlessness and immense clarity she went towards a future she was still in time to turn into a copy of the past.

Some months later, seeing as he was scheduled to attend a renal disorder conference in Bonn, Giuseppe wrote to Hilda via her parents in Munich to try to arrange a meeting to discuss details of divorce. They eventually met in the foyer of a small provincial hospital some thirty kilometres outside Regensburg. It was raining heavily and being a Saturday afternoon in Germany most of the shops and bars were closed. The hospital was scruffy and depressing, so they went back to her flat in his new Alfa 90. She made him tea and offered some of the heavy black fruitcake she always kept for herself for breakfast. He began to tell her about some of the new ways of treating renal failure that had been presented at the conference, and she asked if he could let her have a copy of the conference proceedings when they were available. Her own hospital, for she'd been unable to get back her place in Frankfurt, was hopelessly provincial and out of it. She would be down in Puglia, she said, in September, with another woman, from radiology. They had booked two weeks in a Club Med, for lack of anything better to do. And of course she didn't want to forget all her Italian. Anyway, perhaps on returning she would stop by in Verona for a couple of days to sign the requisite papers and swear what in Italy inevitably had to be sworn. Giuseppe said yes, that was fine, but to phone him a couple of days beforehand just in case. Neither of them for one moment, not in the most allusive of asides, mentioned the abortion.

And then in September they made love again. She was so suntanned, so glowing, so horny to be quite frank, and he so relaxed, laid back, self-satisfied with his various papers published and projects coming to fruition, with his clothes, his car, his expensive furnishings, that there was nothing easier than for them to make love with the same lightness, the same purely physical but tender pleasure of the years before. Even if, the following morning, they went just the same to sign the divorce papers on the grounds of complete incompatibility.

So, little by little, perhaps shamefacedly at first, but progressively less so, the weekend visits began again, the oases of holiday and eroticism in the midst of responsible, even commendable working lives. It was so much easier than taking local lovers with all their demands, their insistence on consequences. The distance, the travel, the hours in car or train (though Giuseppe travelled first class now) seemed to purify them for each other and for the brief weekend that would follow. There were no friends involved, no distractions, they asked nothing more of each other than two days' medical conversation and as much sex as a married couple would manage in a month. Only when they parted sometimes did Hilda reflect what a sad comment it was that with all the advances in medical science it had proved impossible for two healthy young people to have a baby.

LEVIATHAN

PHILIP RIDLEY

PHILIP RIDLEY

Philip Ridley was born in the East End of London where he still lives and works. He studied painting at St Martin's School of Art and graduated in 1984. Since then he has had many successful one-person shows of his paintings and has published one short story, *Embracing Verdi*, in the collection *Oranges and Lemons* (Third House Books).

His first novel, *In the Eyes of Mr Fury*, will be published by Penguin Books in 1989.

I WAS FOURTEEN when I saw my mother cry for the first time. She was sitting at the kitchen table and, as I put my school books in front of her, she clutched at my blazer and burst into tears. I cried with her.

Afterwards, she wiped her eyes on a tea-towel and told me to wash my face. She made a great fuss of peeling some potatoes, complaining of the time, how it flew, how dad would be home in an hour and there was nothing in the oven. When the vegetables were simmering nicely she looked at me and, seeing I was still upset, held me in her arms. She smelt of salt and greens, like some sea creature.

'Sometimes lonliness is like an ocean,' she whispered. 'A vast nothing inside. That's what it's like for me, Felix. You're too young to understand.'

Later that night, as I lay in bed, mum and dad spoke in their room. I strained my ears to hear their conversation. Mum was crying again. Dad tried to comfort her. His voice sounded low and rumbling, subterranean almost.

In the morning they looked awful, eyes red and swollen, and – as soon as dad left for work – mum started to cry again. I held her hand and said I wouldn't leave until she told me what was wrong. She reassured me it was nothing, nothing to do with me anyway, just her loneliness. I asked her if she was dying. It seemed the only explanation. She smiled and kissed me.

'Drowning, Felix,' she said with a grin. 'Not dying.'

I went to school grudgingly. All day I was haunted by the sound of her crying. I couldn't concentrate on anything.

After school, to my surprise, dad was waiting for me in the car. I sat in the front seat beside him and he pulled away from

the kerb without saying a word. I knew something was wrong.
As we pulled up at some traffic lights he glanced at me.

'Your mum and dad are having a few differences, old son,' he
said. 'You're old enough to know what I mean. It's nothing to do
with you. She still loves you. We both love you. It's just . . . just
me. At least she says it is.' He took a deep breath. 'She's in love
with someone else, Felix. She's been seeing him for months.
She's got to make a decision. That's all. Decide what she wants.'

When the lights changed to green we turned left. He wasn't
taking me home. A kind of panic filled me. I asked where we
were going.

'To the station, old son,' he said. 'I want you to spend a few
days with your Aunt Florin. It's all been arranged.'

'Does mum know?' I asked.

'Of course she knows!' he shouted. 'What do you think I'm
doing? Kidnapping my own son?'

He hardly ever raised his voice. We had always been so gentle
with each other, nervous almost. The violence of his response
scared me. Dad stopped the car and put his arm round me.

'Sorry, old son,' he murmured. 'Don't know why I'm taking
it out on you. It's just that . . . it's just that I thought everything
was calm and peaceful, not a wave, not a ripple. Then, all of a
sudden . . . I'm in the centre of a . . . a whirlpool. Been there
for years and never knew it. Do you understand?'

'Yes,' I said. Although I didn't.

He started the car and we drove on in silence.

Because of the traffic it took longer than expected to reach
the station. It was a mad rush to catch the train once we got
there. Dad held my hand through the open window as the train
pulled away. For a while he ran alongside. I could tell he wanted
to say something, but the words wouldn't come and, as he
gasped for breath, a kind of terror filled his eyes.

'Tell mum to stay,' I called.

He let go of my hand and waved.

I stared, watched as he became smaller and smaller, a black
dot against the grey platform.

The journey took three hours and I slept through most of it.
The sound of the train became the roar of surf, a strange,

hypnotic sound, a womb-like vibrating that beguiled me to dreaming.

I was a large fish in a crystal clear ocean. Around me swam smaller fish, multicoloured and gleaming, like a million tiny jewels in the cerulean water. This was my home, my universe, I felt no threat or danger, no sense of loss. Sharks and dolphins swam by, whales spiralled in birth, coral breathed and bubbled, the entire ocean revolved in orbit about me, and I was its comfort. As I swam from shipwreck to shipwreck, smaller fish – pike and salmon – sheltered in the safety of my fins. I was god of the water, gigantic, invincible, marvellous.

The sound of the train stopping woke me.

I looked through the window and saw Aunt Florin. She had put on even more weight since I'd last seen her. Dressed in black, she looked as vast and inflexible as a boulder. Her eyes flickered from window to window until she saw me. She smiled, waved, and skipped over to my carriage, surprisingly agile for her size.

'Come on, Felix, sweetheart,' she said, hustling me from the train and slamming the door behind me. 'My, you've grown. More a frog than a tadpole now. You're as tall as Shilling, I swear. Let's get into the car. We've still got a good hour's drive.'

As we drove along I opened the window and felt the fresh, salty wind sting my face. My aunt lived near the coast. She was my father's sister. Her real name was Florence but everyone called her Florin. Because of the nickname, she christened her only son, my cousin, Shilling. He was three years older than me and wanted to be an astronomer.

'Now don't you worry about a thing,' said my aunt. 'You just have a good time. A week off school can't be all bad. Shilling's got a new telescope. You can see all the craters of the moon through it. And, sometimes, when you aim it at the sea, pilot whales. It scares me.'

I could see the ocean by now, a flat, vast greyness bleeding into the sky. It was like being on the edge of the world and staring into nothing.

'You mustn't blame your mother,' said Aunt Florin, softly. 'Sometimes . . . sometimes we feel safe and happy for years. But it's not real. We're happy because we don't know anything else. Then . . . then something happens. We have to risk a shipwreck or two, you see.'

It was dark by the time we got to my aunt's cottage.

As I got out of the car the air made me gasp. The sky was sparkling with a million stars, cold and beautiful. In the distance, through the darkness, I could hear the surf.

Aunt Florin led me into the cottage.

Uncle Sean was preparing dinner in the kitchen. A tall, thin man, he looked like a stretched version of his wife. He gave me a hug and told me to sit down. I was given all my favourite foods; chicken, garlic bread, pineapple and cream. They treated me gently, sympathetically, as if I were ill or grieving. It wasn't until the meal was over that I asked where Shilling was.

'He's down at the cliffs,' explained my uncle. 'He's taken his telescope down there. Says he can see the stars better. Are you interested in the planets, Felix?'

'Not sure,' I said. 'Don't think so.'

We had some tea and biscuits.

Afterwards, I started yawning.

'Time for bed, I think,' said Aunt Florin.

She showed me where I was going to sleep. A camp bed had been set up in Shilling's room.

'Thought it would do you good,' she explained. 'Both of you. You must have things to talk about. Heaven knows, he doesn't say a word to us.' She kissed me. 'Go to sleep, Felix Frost.'

I undressed and crawled beneath the sheets. They were cold and smooth. It felt so different from my own bed that, despite my weariness, it took me ages to get to sleep.

I dreamed I was a magnificent sea creature, large and grey, barnacled and scarred by time, skin like a map of heavens, protecting fish beneath my wonderful fins.

Slowly, I rose to the surface of my ocean and spat a fountain of water through my body. For a while I breathed air, my tiny eyes tracking the shooting stars. Above me the heavens revolved and sparkled as large and devastating as any ocean. I felt poised between two worlds. Then, in the distance, I saw a dark mass. Land. With one flick of my majestic tail I swam towards it.

A voice woke me.

'Are you asleep?'

My eyes flickered open.

'No,' I said.

Shilling sat on the edge of the mattress. He was stripped to the waist and wiping his short, black hair with a towel. The moonlight shone through the window and shimmered over his sleek, damp body. He smelt of surf and night; a rich, vast odour that filled me with wonder.

'I hear your mum and dad are splitting up,' he said, standing.

He was much taller than I remembered him. As he turned, I stared at the muscular expanse of his back, his shoulder blades, the caterpillar of his spine. It was like looking into another universe or ocean.

'Don't worry about it,' he continued, removing his trousers. 'Parents always argue. Mine don't stop. It never bothers me. You know the only thing I'm interested in?' he asked, standing in front of me.

'What?' I asked.

He told me to get out of bed, then led me over to the telescope in front of the window. Carefully, he looked through it and brought it into focus. 'There!' he exclaimed. 'Come and see!'

I looked through the eye-piece. There, so close I felt I might touch it, was the milky surface of the moon. Craters sparkled silver and blue. I stared in wonder at the luminous terrain.

'It has nothing to do with us,' whispered Shilling in my ear. 'Another place. Nothing can upset me in this world – not while that world exists. You see, there are always other places.'

I looked at Shilling.

'I think my mum's going to leave me,' I said. It was important he knew.

'So?' he said.

I struggled to find a reply.

'Look,' he said, getting into bed. 'I'm not bothered. Whatever happens you'll get over it. Don't bore me with your problems.' problems.'

I got into bed, stared at him. I wanted to talk to him so much. His coldness only increased that feeling.

'Listen . . .' I began.

But he was already asleep.

The next day I went to the cliffs with Shilling. He showed me an upturned rowing boat that he used as a shelter. Sometimes he spent nights in the boat so he could watch the skies and listen to the sea. Shilling said that as he got older he needed people less and less. I said that I needed them more and more.

'Why?' he asked.

'I don't know,' I said.

'Have you got any friends?'

'No.'

'Nor have I,' he said. 'Best that way.'

We crawled through a hole and into the upturned boat.

It was like being in a cave. Shilling lit a candle. There was a sleeping-bag, books, cans of food and a map of the stars. He explained the various constellations to me.

I moved closer to him, felt his breath against my cheek. Instinctively, I reached out to touch his hand. He flinched as if my fingers were white hot. To conceal his embarrassment he named the moons of Jupiter.

That evening, as we ate dinner, I asked Shilling if we could spend the night in the boat. My aunt rattled some plates and advised against it. It got so cold, she said, and I would soon get bored. I assured her that I wouldn't, that I was fascinated by the moon. She was about to deny my request again when the phone rang. She answered it, mumbled something, then said it was for me.

Is it dad? I mouthed.

She shook her head. 'It's your mother,' she whispered.

She handed me the phone.

'Hello, mum,' I said.

'Listen, Felix,' she said. I could tell she had been crying. 'Listen to me, darling. It's all so big, you see. It's vast. I can't stay. Do you understand? It's just so big. Words can't say it. It's endless, Felix. It just goes on and on. I can't tell you. Goodbye.' She put the phone down.

I stood there for a while listening to the buzzing on the line.

Something had changed, something vital, but I didn't know

what. My whole life had been thrown out of orbit and I didn't know why.

I put the phone down and went back to the table.

'Well, well, well,' said Aunt Florin, cheerfully. 'It's getting warmer by the minute. Go and get your things. Shilling can take you to the boat tonight.'

We took a flask of coffee, sandwiches, biscuits, blankets and some extra candles. Shilling was distant with me as we made our way to the cliffs.

It was almost dark when we got there. The first thing we did once we had crawled into the boat was light the candle and have a hot drink. Despite the chill in the air and the damp I didn't feel cold. All the things I wanted to tell Shilling – a million unsaid words – were keeping me warm.

After our coffee we sat outside the boat.

It was dark now and the sky sparkled above us. Shilling lay back and smiled. He handed me the telescope and I tried to find some of the constellations he had named. After a while, I gave back the telescope.

I stared at him for a while.

'Don't you want friends?' I asked.

'No,' he answered. 'I'm too busy to have friends.' He pointed at the stars. 'They are my friends.'

'Are they enough?'

'Enough for me.'

He stood up, brushed grass from his clothes, then crawled into the boat.

I followed him.

I watched him as he sat by the candle and cleaned his telescope, carefully dusting each lens.

'Shilling . . .' I began.

'Yes?' he asked. 'What's wrong now?'

I told him nothing was wrong, that I was merely tired. Shilling told me to go to sleep.

I lay down and closed my eyes. But sleep wouldn't come. All I could think of was Shilling. His indifference made me feel lost and abandoned.

I listened to him leave the boat to watch the stars again. Later

he returned and blew out the candle. I felt him curl up beside
me and shiver as the damp blankets touched his face.

'People beat me up at school,' I said.

'Why?' asked Shilling.

'They don't like me.'

'Why not?'

'I'm not sure. I think it's because I don't join in. Play games
with them.'

'Nor do I,' he said.

'Do they beat you up?' I asked.

'No,' he replied.

'Why not?'

'I'm a good fighter.'

'Do you have many fights?' I asked.

'Yes,' he replied, softly.

'Will you teach me how to fight?' I asked.

'I don't think so.'

'Shall we . . . shall we be friends?' I asked.

I heard him stop breathing. For a few minutes we lay like
that, waiting, hardly daring to move. Then I heard him mumble
something.

'What?' I asked.

But another sound answered my question.

All at once it was everywhere. A sound so vast and lonely I
felt the earth spin beneath me. Suddenly, nothing was safe, all
became desolate.

'What's that?' I whispered.

'Come on!' cried Shilling. 'Whales!'

We left the safety of the boat. The haunted lament grew
louder. It was as if the very sea was crying.

'Whales!' said Shilling. 'I've heard them before. God! Listen
to them!' He fell to the grass. 'So sad. It's like . . . like the sky
is bleeding.' He glanced at me. 'Now *that's* what loneliness
sounds like, Felix.'

'Yes,' I said.

Shilling looked out to sea as if the whales were calling his
name. His eyes filled with wonder and dismay.

'Yes,' he whispered.

The sound echoed round us.

'I'm going to run away from home,' said Shilling, softly. 'I'm going to run away and never come back.'

'When?' I asked.

'Soon,' he said.

The haunting whalesong continued, beautiful high-pitched cries that were everywhere coming out of nowhere.

Shilling looked at me and smiled.

'You all right?' I asked.

'I don't know,' he said.

I put my arm round him.

'Don't worry,' I said.

'No,' he said.

I rocked him gently. He rested his head on my shoulder. It was like comforting something wild and lethal. I had never felt so in control, so strong.

'Everything's fine,' I said. 'Don't worry. Really. Don't worry.'

We talked for the rest of the night.

I re-created myself, built myself anew.

In the morning we went back to the house and Aunt Florin made us some breakfast. About midday there was a phone call from my dad. That afternoon I was sent home.

Mum had gone by the time I returned. She had taken all her clothes and personal things. Dad smiled and looked very cheerful and told me everything would be alright. He asked how I had got on with Shilling and I said, 'Fine.'

That night, as we ate dinner, my dad's joyful facade broke down and I saw him cry for the first time. He apologized and rushed to his room.

Slowly, I cleared away the plates, washed up, them went to bed. From the next room came the muffled sound of my father's sobbing. It was a sound that beguiled me to dreaming.

I was a whale. I rose to the surface of my ocean and swam towards an island where two boys sat on a cliff. I sang them my song of joy and hope, my song of the sea and the stars. It was a song as old as the universe and I sang it to end loneliness.

HONEY MOON

JOAN SMITH

JOAN SMITH

Joan Smith read Latin at Reading University and is a former *Sunday Times* journalist, where she was a member of the Insight team. She has been a freelance journalist and author since 1984; her work has appeared in the *New Statesman*, the *Guardian*, the *Independent*, the *London Evening Standard*, and *Marxism Today*. She has been a regular critic for BBC Radio's *Kaleidoscope* and *Woman's Hour*. She lives in North Oxfordshire.

Her first novel, published in 1987, was a feminist detective story, *A Masculine Ending* (Faber and Faber). Her second, *Why Aren't They Screaming?* is being published in 1988. She is also the author of *Clouds of Deceit* (Faber 1985) – an account of Britain's nuclear weapons tests.

'GOT A MAP? Sure you won't get lost?'

Harriet raised her eyes to the ceiling, a self-conscious smile lighting up her features. 'I have to go out on my own sometimes, Simon.'

Simon got off the bed, crossed the room and kissed her, affectionately at first and then with clear sexual intent. 'Must you? This *is* our honeymoon.'

'I know.' Harriet blushed and playfully pushed him away. 'But we've been here three days and I haven't seen a thing! What am I going to put on my postcards? It's different for you, you've been here before. How can I go back and tell people I didn't see a single picture? I haven't even done touristy things like climbing the – what d'you call it?'

'The bell-tower? All right, all right, *la Torre del Mangia*.'

'I wish I knew Italian. If I'd known I was going to meet you and get married and come to Sienna, I'd have . . .'

'What would you have done?' Simon grasped her hands and held them behind her back.

Harriet laughed and looked away. 'I'd . . . have signed up for evening classes and dazzled you with my perfect Italian!'

'I bet you wouldn't.'

She wriggled out of his arms, and lifted her shoulder-bag and camera off the table next to the window. 'You're just trying to distract me. Sure you won't come?' A wistful note had entered her voice.

Simon threw himself down on the bed and clasped his hands behind his blond head. 'You bet. I haven't got your stamina, Ms Moon. A nice quiet siesta is what I need. *Ciao!*'

Harriet hesitated by the door, drinking in his features as he composed himself for sleep. Then she opened it and stepped out into the corridor.

A couple of hours later, Harriet arrived at the large square in the centre of Sienna, the *Piazza del* – no, she couldn't remember what Simon had called it. Her head was full of images, though her feet ached: a Lorenzetti painting from the art gallery, a black Sibyl worked into the paving that made up the cathedral floor. If only she'd brought her sketch-pad . . . regretfully, she remembered how Simon had whipped it out of her suitcase the night before their wedding. 'No *work*!' he'd said in a shocked tone. 'This is the first proper holiday you've had in years. I'm not going to let you so much as lift a pencil.'

Her protest that she couldn't stop to order, that her mind didn't work like that, had been overruled. Now she wished she'd been more assertive. But then – Simon was her husband. She looked longingly at the busy cafés that fringed the square; surely she wouldn't need Italian just to order a cool drink? She approached one, took a seat, and was relieved to find that the waiter seemed to understand that she wanted a glass of lemonade.

Her husband. She couldn't get used to the word, was unable to make sense of it in relation to herself, Harriet Moon. Perhaps it would have been easier if she'd changed her name, though of course Simon was quite right; she'd established her reputation as a painter several years ago, and it would confuse matters if she suddenly popped up as Mrs Simon Burrows. The waiter returned, dumping a minute black coffee and a glass of water on her table.

'Er – *signor* . . .' Harriet began, but he'd already disappeared into the dark recesses of the café behind her. So he hadn't understood English after all, and her pantomime of a glass had made him think she wanted water. Harriet sighed, and decided to make do. At least the water was cold, and she didn't actively dislike coffee. The drinks revived her, and she looked across to the famous bell-tower, wondering if she could cope with the long climb to the top. Simon had told her it offered an unparalleled view of the Medieval city, though he'd also said he couldn't face all those stairs again, even for her. She wondered, briefly, who he'd been with on those previous visits to Italy. The thought made her uncomfortable, and she took out her purse and looked for the right change. If only she hadn't mixed up her English and Italian money . . . At last she found the right coins, put her purse away, and set off across the square.

The bell-tower was part of the town hall. Harriet went through a pair of open wooden doors and found herself in a vaulted courtyard. To her left the battered stone torso of a bearded man stood on a plinth; not of much interest, she decided. Beyond and round the corner to her left she spotted the entrance to the tower; a notice announced that it closed at five-fifteen and a glance at her watch showed her it was ten to five. She went inside, couldn't see anywhere to pay the 2,000 *lire* entrance fee, and started up a winding stone staircase with brick walls. Her legs were just starting to ache when she emerged in a room where a woman was waiting to sell tickets. Harriet handed over her money and bought a couple of postcards, all without having to betray her ignorance of Italian, and resumed her climb.

Almost immediately she came out into the open air, not at the top of the tower but on a platform halfway up. She looked down at the square, and saw that its unusual fan-shaped brick floor was revealed in all its symmetry from this vantage point. She saw how the bricks sloped gently uphill in the direction of the medieval buildings on the far side; she spotted the café where she'd been sitting a few minutes earlier; she admired the marble fountain which seemed to attract pigeons and holiday-makers in equal number.

A middle-aged American couple, both wearing shorts, squeezed past her; as she leaned forwards over the railing, Harriet experienced a momentary sensation of giddiness. As soon as she'd recovered, and before she had time for second thoughts, she followed them through the doorway to the next flight of stairs. This one was much narrower, positively claustrophobic, and she was very glad to reach the top.

She was on a platform surrounded by a thick stone parapet; at regular intervals it was lower to allow people to look over.

The platform was surprisingly windy, and Harriet hesitated before moving forward to see the view. When she did she gave a gasp of pleasure; across the city, on a hill, the striped marble cathedral floated majestically above a sea of densely-packed brown roofs. Her joy did not last – a glance down brought home the height of the tower, and she immediately felt a return of the giddiness she'd suffered earlier. She hastily stepped back, taking a deep breath, and a gust of wind caught her full skirt and whipped it up over her face. Harriet struggled to control it, her camera slipping from her shoulder and swinging with a clunk into the wall behind her. *I wish I'd never come*, she thought, wrestling with the camera strap which now seemed to be inextricably tangled with that of her shoulder-bag. As soon as she'd got it all sorted out she headed for the stairs, standing back as a noisy and fearless Italian family rushed past her to peer over the parapet.

She went down as quickly as she dared, suddenly oppressed by the weight of stone above her. With a sigh of relief she stepped out on to the halfway platform, pausing to get her breath. Her eyes moved, against her will, down to the square, and all at once her heart stood still: a tall blond man in a yellow shirt was walking briskly across it accompanied by a dark woman in a figure-hugging suit. Simon! she thought, it's Simon! But . . . she'd left him at the hotel, with no plans to go out, so how could he be striding through the city with an unknown woman? What on earth was he doing? She started down the steps into the ticket-hall, only to find a dozen English schoolchildren milling about while their teacher insisted in loud, clear English that it was *not* too late to take his party aloft.

Harriet forced her way through the crowd and hurled herself down the second flight of steps. She ran into the courtyard, swerved to the right and out into the square. There she came to an abrupt halt, peering ahead in the hope of seeing Simon. It was hopeless; he was gone, and so was the woman with him. There was no sign of his yellow shirt, which had stood out so clearly from the bell-tower.

Harriet breathed out heavily and her shoulders sagged. She couldn't have been mistaken, she couldn't. Simon had striking looks, they were what had attracted her to him in the first place, and she would know that yellow shirt anywhere. Then a doubt began to creep in. Simon didn't know anyone in Sienna, at least he hadn't mentioned that he did, and there must be thousands of yellow shirts in the world. Wasn't she jumping to rather large conclusions on very slim evidence? The sensible thing, what any wife would do in this situation, was to go back to the hotel and ask him about it. Perhaps he'd woken up and decided to go for a stroll, and had bumped into an old acquaintance from London – the woman didn't have to be Italian just because she had dark hair. Tuscany was full of English holidaymakers.

Harriet began to trudge across the square, absently hauling her bag and camera straps back up her arm to her shoulder. What an idiot she was, she told herself, what was she doing flying into a panic like that? Simon was her husband; surely she trusted him enough to ask a simple question. She walked up a wide flight of steps leading away from the square and paused at the top. Which way had she come? Uncertainly she turned left, walking slowly uphill past shops and a tall *palazzo*. After a while it dawned on her that the route, though familiar, did not seem to be leading to the hotel; she stopped, consulted her map, and discovered she was walking in entirely the wrong direction. She turned, tired and grumpy, and retraced her steps. By the time she reached the hotel, twenty minutes later, she was thoroughly miserable.

Harriet asked for the key to Room 312, and was relieved to be told that it wasn't there. So Simon was in . . . maybe she *had* made a mistake. She took the lift, hurried along the corridor, and knocked sharply on the door. There was no reply and she tried again. Nothing. She turned the handle, found it locked, and was about to knock a third time when the door swung open. Simon stood before her, stretching and rubbing his eyes. His yellow shirt was crumpled, as though he'd been sleeping in it.

'Hello, darling! Back already? What's the time? Gosh. I've been asleep for hours! Have a good time?' He put an arm round her shoulders and drew her into the room.

'You didn't – you've been here all afternoon?' Harriet was uneasy, more certain than ever of what she'd seen now Simon was standing here in the flesh. And yet – he was behaving as though he'd been asleep since she left.

'Went out like a light,' she heard him say as he drew her towards the bed. 'Sit down and tell me what you've been doing. The conscientious little tourist, I hope?' He was nuzzling her neck, pushing her back on the bed. 'Mmmm, it's good to have you back.'

Against her will, her body was beginning to respond. She struggled to sit up, but he pressed her gently down.

'Simon . . .'

'Later. Tell me later.' His hand was already sliding inside her blouse.

Later, as they lay on the bed, Simon smoking one of the three cigarettes he allowed himself each day, he returned to the subject of her afternoon. 'So what did you see?' he asked. 'The cathedral?'

'Yes.' Harriet rolled on to her side and propped her head up on one hand.

'Wonderful floor, isn't it?'

'Yes. Yes, it is. And I had a look at the art gallery.'

'Ah, the *Pinacoteca*. Never got round to that myself. You've married a philistine, darling. Hey, are you all right? I was only joking! I adore *your* paintings, you know that. Just because I work in the City doesn't mean . . .'

'That's what you always say – "I work in the City". You've never told me exactly what it is you do.'

'Darling, don't look at me like that. So . . . so suspicious. I'm quite happy to tell you. It's just that you said money didn't interest you. And that's my job, money. I don't want to bore you. You can have all the details, if you like – pension funds, overseas investment, all that sort of thing.'

'No, you're quite right.' She admitted defeat. She really wasn't very interested in Simon's job in the City. 'Actually, I'd like a drink. Could you ring room service for me? I'm rather hot and . . . well, I got a bit dizzy at the top of the bell-tower.' She forced a smile because of the suddenly anxious look on his face.

Simon put out his cigarette and lifted the phone. Harriet

looked away, wondering what had got into her. She'd mistakenly believed she'd seen her husband walking through Sienna with an unknown woman, and from that flimsy starting-point she'd begun to weave all sorts of silly fantasies.

'I'll be all right, honestly,' she said, realising that Simon was watching her. Of course he wasn't hiding anything from her. 'Oh . . . er . . . lemonade, please. With ice.' She listened as he ordered her drink and a small whisky for himself. 'What shall we do this evening?' she asked brightly as he put the phone down.

Next morning Harriet was lying in bed, a sheet drawn up over her breasts, while Simon was in the shower. It was late. They'd slept in after going to a concert the previous evening. She stretched luxuriously under the sheet, enjoying with only a mild sensation of embarrassment the heightened awareness of her body that always followed sex with Simon. She smiled, hearing occasional snatches of song above the noise of the shower. Then the phone rang. Harriet paused, hoping Simon would emerge and answer it. When he didn't, she reached for it reluctantly.

'Hello?' If it was a member of the hotel staff, presumably they'd speak English. 'Hello?'

Someone exhaled at the other end, then the phone went down with a click. Harriet stared at the receiver, then dialled the switchboard. Yes, the man told her in heavily accented English, he'd just put a call through to Room 312. The caller had been a woman, Italian.

'Are you sure?' Harriet demanded. 'She definitely wanted this room? Did she ask for anyone by name?'

The man couldn't remember. If the *signora* didn't object, he had work to do . . .

Harriet put the phone down.

'What was that?' Simon emerged from the bathroom, a towel tucked round his waist.

'The phone rang and . . . there was nobody there. Simon, you don't know anyone in Sienna, do you?'

'Good God, no,' he said, turning away. 'Must have got the wrong room.' He seemed to have lost interest.

'But Simon, I rang the switchboard. He said . . . the man said it was definitely this room.'

'Don't be silly, darling, who do we know in Sienna? Unless you've got a secret lover . . . Sorry, just a joke. Shower's all yours.'

Harriet got up, a sick feeling in her stomach. A secret lover, was that who the woman was?

'Simon!'

'Yes, darling?' He turned from the wardrobe where he was taking a pair of light blue trousers off a hanger. He was smiling guilelessly at her; she couldn't get the words out.

'Nothing, I . . . I just wondered whether you were serious about hiring a car?' Anything to divert his attention.

'Certainly was. There are so many places I want to show you. San Gimignano, Montepulciano, Florence even. Let's go and sort it out before breakfast. Lunch, I should say. You'd better be quick with that shower.'

That afternoon they set off in their newly-hired car, a small Fiat. Simon had decided it was too late in the day for a major excursion; instead, he took Harriet for a drive through Chianti country. The views of vine-coloured hills and dusty streets should have been enchanting, but Harriet was unable to quell a nagging worry about the phone call. It didn't take long for her silence to register with Simon, who became immediately solicitous, wanting to know if she was too hot or car-sick. His questions about her health, and whether she'd overdone it the previous day, began to irritate; for the first time since they met two months before, Harriet longed for a few hours on her own. In the end, she persuaded Simon to drive her back to the hotel, insisting all she needed was an hour's rest out of the sun.

As they crossed the reception area, the woman behind the counter called out Simon's name: '*Signor* Burrows!'

They looked round, startled, and Simon said, 'Wait there.'

He went to the desk, where the receptionist seemed to be holding something out. Her view was blocked by Simon's back, but Harriet was sure the woman passed something to him. He turned, thrusting one hand into a trouser pocket and holding up their room-key in the other.

'Forgot this!' he said, showing her the key. As he ushered her into the lift, Harriet twisted round to look at his right hand; he *had* put something in his pocket, she was sure of it. Simon's hand emerged, empty, but of course that proved nothing – the most likely thing was a note, and that was probably screwed up in a ball by now. They got out of the lift and he strode along the corridor before her, fumbling with the key as he unlocked their room.

'Must have a pee.' He headed for the bathroom, closing the door behind him.

The urge to fling it open and catch him reading the note was almost irresistible, but then doubt came flooding back again as she heard the lavatory flush. What if she was wrong? What if he had just forgotten to pick up their key? The bathroom door opened.

'Hey, I thought you were going to lie down? That's better. Anything I can get you? A glass of water, or some tea?'

'No thank you.' All she wanted was to be left alone and think. To her surprise, her wish was granted.

'Mind if I wander off for half an hour? Thought I'd get a few postcards and things.'

So there had been a note. She'd never heard such a trans-parent excuse. And now he was sneaking out to – to what? Make a phone call? Keep a rendezvous? He must think her a complete fool.

'Fine,' she said weakly, her mouth dry.

'Darling, are you all right? You've gone very white. What is it, a headache? Are you sure you don't want an aspirin or something?'

'No, really, I just need a rest.' She put her hand to her head so he wouldn't be able to see her eyes. A plan was forming. Why didn't he go?

'If you're sure . . . oh, er, one thing. Do you think you'll be up to going out tonight?'

'Tonight?' She hadn't thought that far ahead. 'I don't see why not. Off you go.' Anything to get him out of the room.

'OK. *Ciao*, darling.'

Harriet waited until she calculated he'd reached the ground

floor. Then she leapt off the bed, grabbed her purse from her bag, and left the room. She ran lightly down the corridor to the lift, waiting impatiently until it came, then went down to the ground floor.

'Excuse me, my husband forgot something. Did you see which way he went?'

Her instinct was right; Simon was a very attractive man and the woman behind the desk had watched through the window as he'd turned left out of the hotel. Thanking her, Harriet went out and walked quickly but furtively in the direction of the city square. It didn't take her long to spot Simon ahead of her, and now she came to the difficult bit: keeping close enough not to lose him without herself being seen. They continued along the tall, narrow streets in this fashion for several minutes, then Simon came to a halt and looked up at a building on his left. He appeared to think for a moment, then disappeared through a doorway.

Harriet waited a moment in case he came straight out again, then crept along the street, her heart in her mouth. The doorway was just after a shop whose window displayed dozens of luscious cakes, but for once she had no eyes for them. She peered nervously into shadow, making out that Simon had gone into an apartment block; its list of occupants, affixed to the wall, was dauntingly long and offered no clue to his destination. She stepped back into the street, wondering what to do. Behind her, she heard a shop opening up. She turned and saw that it was a bookshop. Darting inside, she stationed herself next to a display of guidebooks which gave a clear view of the flats opposite. Sure enough, after three or four minutes Simon appeared, pausing in the street and turning to talk to someone. He was laughing, his jacket thrown casually over one shoulder, and he seemed pleased with whatever transaction he had just completed.

'*Ciao*,' she heard him say, then he set off the way he had come. The person he had addressed stepped forward to watch him depart, and Harriet recognised the chic dark woman of the previous afternoon. The suit had been changed for a black dress with heavy jewellery, but Harriet thought she'd know her anywhere. Her breathing became rapid and her head swam.

'*Signora?*' The old man who ran the bookshop was at her elbow, alarmed by her appearance. Harriet stared into his kind face and had an urge to blurt out the whole story: how she'd fallen in love with a complete stranger she'd met at a party, married him without a second thought, and now found herself alone in a foreign country while he deceived her with another woman. The blood was singing in her ears, and she thought she was going to faint; she wasn't thinking straight, there must be more to it than that! Simon wouldn't have brought her all this way just to pick up with an old flame.

The old man was speaking to her in Italian; Harriet realised she couldn't explain in English, never mind a foreign language. She backed out of the shop muttering 'I'm sorry, I'm sorry,' and set off in the direction of the hotel. A few doors down she saw a bar, and rushed inside to sit down for a moment. With difficulty, and a great deal of pointing, she ordered a brandy and took it to an empty table. Then she sat, cradling it in her hands, her mind reeling as she examined the possibilities.

At twenty-seven she was a relatively wealthy woman, there was no getting away from that. Her paintings, delicate and disturbing watercolours which seemed at once to reflect and to re-interpret reality, had been a cult success. Even so, she had led what her Aunt Claudie, reacting with astonishment to the news of her impending marriage, had described as a sheltered life. Harriet felt awkward with strangers, and had long ago grown used to the fact that her appearance – her snub nose and severely-cut brown hair – seemed to put men off. Meeting Simon, at a party she had been coerced into attending by the owner of the gallery which exhibited her pictures, had been a dream come true. Except that now, alone with him in a country where no one seemed to speak English, it had suddenly hit her that his passion for her was too good to be true. Why should this confident, handsome man have singled her out? Harriet was far from worldly, but there was one thing she knew: by signing a piece of paper at the register office on Monday morning she had invalidated her will, in which her possessions were divided equally between Claudie and various charities, and made Simon her heir.

That dark, carelessly elegant woman she'd just seen, was she Simon's accomplice in a plot to – no, she couldn't even think the word – *do away with* his wealthy wife? Not just his accomplice, his *lover* – Harriet felt she couldn't bear it. The thought of his blond head bent over that dark . . . her stomach twisted, and she forced her mind on to another track. What was their game, why *had* she been brought here? This was Italy, after all, home of the Mafia – no, now her imagination really was running away with her. Even Harriet knew that the Mafia didn't operate in this part of Italy, it belonged down south. A kidnapping, then. Wasn't Italy also notorious for kidnapping? A fake kidnapping, of course, with Simon all ready to play the part of the distraught husband? Yes, that was why he'd been so attentive to her, so publicly affectionate; she could imagine the hotel staff swearing that *Signor* Burrows had been absolutely devoted to his poor wife. There was a foul taste in her mouth, and she drank the brandy off in one gulp. Then a new thought occurred to her: what would Simon think if he got back to the hotel and found her gone? She mustn't give herself away, she needed time to think about what to do. She felt in her purse, flung some coins on to the table, and hurried out into the street.

When she arrived back at the hotel, the receptionist informed her that *Signor* Burrows had not come back yet. Harriet went up to their room, sat down and tried to think. She had to get away, but how? The flight home wasn't for another ten days, so she'd have to try and book another one without Simon finding out. But where was she to get the money? For the first time in her life, she regretted not possessing a credit card. Then a thought occurred to her: wouldn't there be some sort of British consul in Florence? He would be able to help. That's what she must do – get herself to Florence and throw herself on the mercy of the British authorities. The only problem that remained was getting there; the hire car wasn't insured for her to drive, so it would have to be the train. She remembered passing the railway station earlier that afternoon. But not tonight. She didn't know how long the journey would take, and she didn't fancy doing it alone at night. So . . . she only had to get through this evening, then she'd make an excuse to go out and take a taxi to the station. Then the door opened.

'Hello, darling, how're you feeling?' Simon walked in and dropped a bundle of postcards on to the table. 'Any better? Your colour's coming back.'

Harriet silently congratulated herself on drinking the brandy. Alcohol always made her flushed. Simon sat down on the bed beside her and kissed her lightly.

'That's a relief. I've got something rather special lined up for tonight – a surprise. I was afraid you might not be up to it.'

'A surprise?' Harriet stiffened. What was this?

'Well, I can hardly tell you what it is, can I? Then it wouldn't be surprise! Just trust me. I'm sure you'll like it.' His arm went round her and he hugged her to him. It took all Harriet's strength not to pull away. So that was what Simon's clandestine meetings had been about. He was planning something for that very evening. She had not expected it to come so soon.

'Oh dear, I'm not sure I'm really up to going out. I feel sort of . . . weak.'

'Oh darling.' Simon's face was full of concern. 'Look, I'll cancel it, it can wait. Your health's more important . . . there's no point in dragging you out if you're not going to enjoy yourself. Leave it to me.' He was already getting up.

'No!' Harriet panicked. She had not expected him to give in so easily. Perhaps it had all been a bluff, and he really *wanted* her to stay in for the evening? Wouldn't she be safer in a public place? She turned to him with a forced smile on her face. 'No, please don't put it off. You've made me curious now. What time do I have to be ready?'

They left the hotel on foot at eight o'clock. It was getting dark, but there were still plenty of people around. Harriet kept away from side streets and dark corners, shying away whenever she felt Simon's touch on her arm. He had noticed, she was sure, but there was nothing she could do about that. She didn't want those lying hands anywhere near her.

Eventually Simon stopped outside a small, dark restaurant, one they hadn't been to before. A waiter led them to the table

Simon had booked towards the back, and they sat down facing each other, as usual. Harriet was suddenly close to tears: this was the last time, the very last time, she and Simon would eat together like this. To distract herself, she made a quick survey of her surroundings; half the tables were full, and two or three waiters were scurrying backwards and forwards. At least nothing was likely to happen here. But what about afterwards, on the way back to the hotel? The streets would be emptier then, had Simon and his olive-skinned accomplice planned a bag snatch that was really an excuse for . . .

'Harriet? You were miles away. I was suggesting the sole.'

Simon knew about food, she had always been happy to let him order for her. But not tonight.

'No, I'll have, er, that,' she said, stabbing her finger into the menu at random.

It was a strained meal. After toying with her pasta, Harriet discovered too late that she'd ordered shell-fish as her main course, something she hated, and she was far too worried about the walk back to the hotel to make polite conversation. She noticed that a middle-aged Italian woman on the other side of the restaurant couldn't keep her eyes off Simon; what a fool she'd been to think a man like him could be genuinely interested in her!

A waiter removed her almost full plate, and she waited for him to return with the menu. Then she noticed that Simon was behaving oddly, peering over her left shoulder towards the kitchen as though he was waiting for something to happen. All her fears rushed back, and she half-turned in her seat, jumping to her feet when she saw the same dark Italian woman poke her head furtively round the door.

'*Signor!*' She knocked her chair over with a crash in her desperation to reach the elderly couple on the next table. '*Signor!*' she gabbled, not even waiting to find out whether he understood English. 'You must help me! The consul, get me the British consul! That man, my husband, he's trying to kill me . . . and her, she's in it with him!'

'Harriet!' Simon's astonished voice cut through the hush that had fallen on the room, but she ignored it. Whirling round, she pointed towards the kitchen, determined that his accomplice should not have an opportunity to escape.

Then, as the woman came into full view for the first time, Harriet's finger dropped and she took a step backwards, colliding with a table. 'But . . . what's that?' she faltered, taking in the fact that the woman was bearing something before her on a plate. 'I . . . I don't understand.'

'*You* don't understand,' Simon gasped, advancing towards her. 'What on earth's got into you? Have you taken leave of your senses?' A hush had fallen on the restaurant, and everyone seemed to be waiting for her to speak.

'I . . . I thought . . . What's that?' She moved her hand disbelievingly in the direction of the Italian woman, who was now standing just inside the room with a puzzled look on her face.

'A cake,' Simon said coldly, 'it's a cake. And the woman holding it is *Signora* Lelli. Her family are the best pastrycooks in Sienna, according to the man I asked at the hotel. I tracked her down yesterday afternoon, while you were out. We got married in such a hurry, there wasn't time for a reception or anything, so I decided to lay something on here. Signora Lelli's speciality – it's made with honey, almonds, that sort of thing. A *honeymoon* cake. I thought it would be a surprise. But not half as much as you've surprised me.'

Harriet's horrified gaze travelled from Simon's face to *Signora* Lelli and the huge, sickly confection she was still holding. A wave of nausea passed through her, and she stumbled across the room into the street.

NO GIRL

RUPERT THOMSON

RUPERT THOMSON

Rupert Thomson was born in Eastbourne, England in 1955. He was educated at Christ's Hospital and Cambridge University. After graduating in 1976, he travelled throughout the USA, Mexico and Canada, and taught English in Athens. When he returned to London he spent four years working as a copywriter for various advertising agencies. He retired in 1982. Since then he has built a road in Italy, checked coats in a nightclub in West Berlin, and sold books on 42nd Street in New York. He has also lived in Tokyo and Sydney. *Dreams of Leaving*, his highly acclaimed debut novel, was published in 1987.

THE STORM HAD broken an hour before, after a day of still, poised heat: first lightning, then thunder, and now this rain, slamming into the side of the bus, making Alan flinch back from the window. Two men sat across the aisle, gourds in their laps. Their faces flickered on and off, on and off, a loose connection somewhere, until, during the brief intervals of darkness, they showed up green and purple, disembodied, voodoo masks. The driver took his eyes off the road to shout something back down the bus, but thunder rolled over his words. Alan wouldn't have understood anyway. He couldn't speak Spanish.

It was after two in the morning when the bus finally pulled up in front of a concrete shack. The rain had stopped. Alan saw a slanting sheet-metal roof and stacks of pale blue oil-drums. A Coca-Cola sign dangled on a single nail, that famous red turned brown by heat, age, nights like tonight.

He stood at the driver's shoulder. 'Is this Oaxaca?'

The driver ran both his hands through his hair and stretched, his body giving off the smell of cooking fat. Alan's eyes wandered upwards to the postcards of madonnas taped to the inside of the windshield. One posed in front of silver clouds; another was draped in sequinned robes; a third smiled down at him from beneath a gold-leaf halo. They weren't listening either. None of his prayers would get through. He sighed and climbed down out of the bus. Perhaps there was somebody in the shack who could help him.

He paused inside the doorway. A green room, one naked bulb swinging on a black flex. All the shadows rocking. A feeling like seasickness. A man lay slumped on a wooden counter, his head resting in the crook of his elbow, a black leather cap angled down over his eyes. As Alan walked towards him, the man pulled the cap clear of his face. His eyes were swollen, bloodshot, and the sweat from his armpits had spread across the front of his shirt in two dark misshapen circles. Any time now, Alan thought, they would meet in the middle.

'What do you want?'

'A hotel.'

The man stared at him, then shook his head in a slow, brutal way, and pointed at the doorway. Alan was too exhausted to feel anger. Despair came instead, gathering in his throat, misting his vision. There was nothing he could say to this man. He turned and went out the way he had come in.

Now what? he wondered.

He was standing in a small unlit square. To the left and right, two dirt roads led away into total darkness. They had the bleakness of roads that end up in junkyards and car parks, or run alongside railway lines for a while only to fade into an infinity of tall grasses. He chose the road in front of him. It was probably just the streetlamps, the comfort of light.

Once, as he walked, he heard a noise behind him. He turned to see a dog following in his tracks. It had lost a lot of hair, this dog, and its ribcage showed through its skin like a shell. Alan spoke to it, the one or two Spanish words he knew, but he didn't touch it. He didn't want to get anything.

His arms were aching now from carrying his suitcase, and he could feel sweat forming like a layer of clothing between his shirt and his skin. He was beginning to think he would just sit down on the kerb and wait for dawn when he saw a lit window up ahead. A man stood in the window, his back turned. He wore a white vest smeared with oil and loose blue overalls that had faded round the buttocks. He was frying some tortillas. He was large for a Mexican, sixteen or seventeen stone, but there was a deftness about the way he moved round the kitchen that lightened Alan's heart. Those tortillas smell good, he wanted to say. He said nothing. Somehow, though, he had more energy now. The road felt better under his feet, and the white neon sign he saw five minutes later seemed like a part of this. Hotel America, it said.

He pushed through the front door and found himself in a tiled corridor. The sound of his footsteps suddenly embarrassed him. Something to do with being inside, the silence, how late it was. He rounded a corner and almost cried out. Facing him and asleep was a man in a wheelchair. The man only had one arm. Mosquitoes floated past his open mouth, legs dangling.

Alan watched him for a moment, then approached and touched him on the shoulder. The man's eyelids slid upwards. He studied Alan with a curious, vague patience, his eyes dropping to Alan's suitcase, then lifting to his face again.

'I need a room,' Alan said.

The man moved his head from side to side, as if sleep was water and he could shake it off. He began to manoeuvre himself across the hall, using his arm first on one wheel, then on the other, steering a zigzag course to the far wall where the keys hung. He handed Alan number three.

Once inside the room Alan undressed and dropped on to the bed. There was a noise in his head like railway lines when a train's coming. Just the night, he thought. A mosquito drilled the air beside his ear. And that light patch in the darkness, was that really a hole in the wall?

Yes, a big hole, crumbling at the edges, and blue all too soon with the sky of another morning. And piled on the floor, bricks and plaster, chunks of concrete. Alan closed his eyes again.

Oaxaca.

A kind of panic surged through him, throwing up new debris: fears, worries, memories. The heat from this ran over his skin, making him sweat. He pushed the sheet away from his body, treading it down like water with his feet. He plunged his face into the pillow, not wanting to be awake.

He remembered a room, a much cooler room, in San Francisco.

He saw polished floorboards reaching lengthways into the light, a pattern of arrowheads embedded in the grain of the wood. He saw white walls and plants in brass urns. He saw the sheer silver surfaces of a stereo.

Lewis's apartment.

He had met Lewis at a cocktail party. He was standing alone

in a corner, a glass of wine in his hand, when Lewis came over
and said, 'You must be the English guy, right?'

Alan laughed. 'Right,' he said. He hadn't been in San Francisco
long, but he was catching on fast. 'How did you know?'

'Well,' Lewis said, 'I guess I'm just naturally perceptive.' He
held his deadpan expression, then allowed his face to relax into
a smile.

Later his eyes turned earnest and one hand rested on Alan's
shoulder as he explained, 'There are different rules in this city.'
His other hand toyed with his blond moustache. 'Like if some
guy asks you to go swimming with him, it's probably not a good
idea. Unless,' and his hand dropped away from his moustache
to reveal a grin, 'unless,' he said, 'you want to get out of your
depth.'

Alan grinned back as if he understood.

Lewis talked for most of the evening. The story of his life.
He had left Pennsylvania when he was just turned nineteen.
Jumped a Greyhound heading west and stayed awake all of one
night and all the next day, smoking Vantage cigarettes and
singing Eagles' songs and smiling at the waitresses in their
orange nylon uniforms and their green eyeshadow. Then an old
black guy in a trilby, breath sweet with Wild Irish Rose, shook
him out of a deep sleep saying, 'This is San Francisco.'

'It was seven in the morning,' Lewis said, 'and my neck was
so stiff, it hurt to look up at all the tall buildings.'

Now he was making good bucks as an assistant manager of a
downtown department store and he had a duplex in Haight-
Ashbury and if Alan wanted to stay that was cool.

Alan had spent the last week in a hostel out in Daly City. He
was paying nine dollars a night, which was more than he could
afford – it meant he had to live on Roman Meal bread and peanut
butter and cartons of Vitamin D milk – so he took Lewis up on
the offer.

Lewis left for work at eight every morning. Alan slept late.
When he walked into the kitchen, usually at around ten, he
would always find a pitcher of freshly-squeezed orange juice
waiting for him on the breakfast bar. 'You got to look after your
body,' Lewis had said once, his eyes moving away from Alan's

face, moving down. Sometimes Lewis came home with flowers that Alan had never seen before and brown paper bags swollen with groceries and they would eat dinner together on the white table by the window and watch the light fade over the city. These were uncomplicated days. Nothing was asked of Alan but his presence.

Then it was a Saturday morning and Alan was sitting up on the sofa-bed, a quilt wrapped round the lower half of his body. The window was open, and cool sunny air drifted into the room. Lewis was in the kitchen toasting some English muffins. Through the doorway came a gargling sound that Alan recognised by now as the coffee percolator. A car started up in the street below.

'Lewis?' he called out. 'I have to leave here soon.'

Lewis stepped into the room. White lines ran down the legs of his jeans where he had ironed them. He was smiling. 'Did you say something, Alan?'

'I was just saying that I should really leave here soon.'

Lewis stared at him. His smile had shrunk to nothing. 'Sure,' he said. 'If that's what you want.'

'Well, I can't stay in San Francisco for five months, can I?' Alan said, looking away from Lewis's face.

'Why not?' Lewis's voice was neutral, but there was a new hardness in it somewhere, as if he had earned the right to an answer.

'There are other things I want to see.'

'Why do you want to see other things?'

Alan fingered the quilt, frowning down at the patterns. 'I suppose I'd feel I was missing something if I stayed here,' he said finally, looking up again.

Lewis walked to the window. He leaned against the wall, stared down into the street. After a while he turned and folded his arms across his chest. His face was hard to see. 'Don't you think,' he said slowly, 'that you might be missing something if you don't stay?'

Alan rolled over on his back again and opened his eyes. The cracks on the pink walls meandered, linked, divided – rivers or roads on the map of a country he didn't know. Sticky tentacles of dust reached down from the vent above his head. There was no air.

San Francisco, he thought.

That evening he strolled towards the main square. It felt like a different town: boys with adult faces and crewcuts were selling nuts in twists of paper; teenage girls paraded up and down, arms linked, cheeks sucked in; old men watched from the blotchy walls of bars, their foreheads creased by a lifetime of hats. Dusk came down so fast, you could almost see the sky change. It made you want to walk with your head tilted back. He thought of Lewis and his tall buildings, and smiled.

Then, all of a sudden, people were stopping, pointing at him, laughing. He lowered his head, pretended not to notice. It wasn't until he had passed them that he realised it wasn't him they were laughing at. He swung round. Further down the street everyone was ducking and whirling and hopping, slapping their arms and necks and thighs, beating the air around their heads. Alan, too, began to laugh. He glanced at the family standing beside him. The man nudged him in the ribs and slid some Spanish through his broken teeth. Alan heard the word for mosquitoes. So that was what it was. But now a young couple were racing up the street towards them shouting, 'They're coming, they're coming,' and suddenly everyone was turning and jostling one another and running in the opposite direction. Alan was caught up, swept away, along with a waiter, two chuckling women in black, and a thin man who was holding a violin high in the air as if the crowd was a river and he was frightened his instrument might get wet. Moments later they were absorbed into the calmer waters of the main square, Alan landing up against a low stone balustrade.

A bandstand stood in the centre of the square, its pointed roof lost in the meshing foliage above. Several musicians sat about, chatting, tuning up. Some kind of concert, it seemed, was scheduled for the evening. Alan climbed up on to the balustrade, content simply to watch, wait for developments.

It wasn't long before the conductor arrived. One glance at those short, self-important legs, those coils of gold braid at the

shoulder and cuff, and Alan had a name for him – the General.
The General stepped on to his rostrum and opened his score.
His eyes lifted and passed across the upturned faces of his
musicians. He raised his arms, like a child's imitation of a ghost,
held them stiffly there for several seconds, then let them fall.
The cymbals exploded, and the band launched into a military
march.

Somebody tapped Alan on the shoulder. Turning round, he
saw a boy sitting next to him. The boy was about fourteen. He
wore his dark red shirt outside his jeans. He said something to
Alan in Spanish then, seeing Alan didn't understand, he clenched
his fist and flicked his thumb across his curled forefinger. Alan
smiled, nodded, struck a match. The boy stuck a Baronet in one
corner of his mouth and leaned into the flame. He glanced up at
Alan as he pulled away. Alan noticed the shading on his upper
lip and thought, Yes, about fourteen. The boy drew on the
cigarette and, pushing his lips forward, blew the smoke out
straight away. He couldn't have been smoking long.

'Not good music,' he said. 'Bad music.'

Alan smiled. 'It's OK.' But the boy was right. The music was
so bad it was funny. All the musicians seemed to be playing at
different speeds. Especially the man on the trumpet. He finished
each march at least two or three bars behind everyone else. He
played like an echo.

'From America?'

'No,' Alan said, 'I'm English. From England.'

The boy nodded, studied the end of his cigarette. He seemed
thoughtful, dull-witted, and this made Alan patient with him.
The boy was only trying to be friendly and besides, it felt like
ages since Alan had spoken to anyone.

'You are here alone?' The boy flicked his cigarette into the
gutter; this at least he had mastered.

'Yes,' Alan said. 'I like travelling alone.' The boy nodded, but
Alan wasn't sure if he had understood. 'It's better alone,' he
added. 'You meet more people.'

He turned his attention back to the band. The trumpet was
still lagging, he noticed, but the trumpet-player gave no sign
that he was aware of this. There was a vanity, almost a swagger,

about the way he fingered the valves while he was resting, about the way he moistened and stretched his lips as he lifted the instrument once again. Perhaps it was only the look of the thing that mattered. Smiling to himself, Alan turned back to the boy and examined his face in profile. It still had the fullness of adolescence, but he could see a brutality below the surface, in the cheek and jaw, that would emerge before long. The charm was already vanishing; the face beneath, the adult face, was blunt, stubborn, primitive. Something suddenly occurred to the boy. He swung round, caught Alan staring at him.

'You have girl?' he asked.

Alan laughed quickly. This wasn't a question he'd been expecting, and the boy's curiosity amused him. Then a disturbing thought struck him. What if the boy was a pimp? 'No,' he said. 'Not at the moment, anyway.'

The boy drew his eyebrows together, shook his head. He became aggressive when there was something he couldn't understand.

'No,' Alan said, distinctly now. 'I have no girl.'

The boy smiled. He seemed satisfied. 'No girl,' he repeated. He asked Alan for a cigarette. Alan gave him one and lit it for him. Again that inquisitive glance up through the flame, only this time Alan found it unnerving.

The band had stopped playing. Alan looked at his watch. It was still early, not even ten, but he felt tired. He hadn't slept much the night before, and the conversation was beginning to bore him. All he wanted to do was go back to his hotel and lie down.

'You have hotel?' the boy asked.

For the first time Alan saw animal cunning in the boy's face. These questions of his, they were like pieces of sky in a jigsaw, countless identical pieces of blue that he now lacked the patience, the energy, to fit together.

'Yes,' he said. 'I have a hotel.' He had changed hotels that morning. It had taken less than half an hour, daylight simplifying everything.

'Where is hotel?' the boy was asking.

'Near here. Just round the corner. About two blocks away.'

Alan talked faster now, no longer caring whether or not the boy understood.

'I like look in hotel.'

Alan stared at the boy. 'Why?'

'I never look in hotel.' The boy avoided Alan's eyes, fiddled with the buttons on his shirt.

Alan sighed. 'OK.'

They pushed their way through the crowds. Alan was angry with himself. Why had he agreed to show the boy his hotel? He should've been firmer, said no. Still, it would all be over soon, and he'd be able to sleep.

He turned into the hotel and crossed the indoor courtyard, with the boy walking off to one side and a little behind him. The manager was on the phone. His flat eyes followed Alan and the boy as they climbed the stairs.

Alan unlocked his door and walked inside. 'This is my room,' he said. He sat down on one of the hard chairs.

The boy eased on to the bed and looked round, but it was a small room, more like a lift than a room, so his eyes soon returned to Alan's face again. Alan shifted on his chair. There was nothing to offer the boy, not even a glass of water. 'It's hot,' he said finally, just for something to say.

'Yes,' the boy said, sitting up, 'hot,' and, smiling, he unbuttoned his shirt and let it fall to the floor. He lay back on the bed, naked from the waist up, watching Alan. Now Alan understood.

'No,' he said, 'I'm not interested in that.'

'No understand.' The boy was still smiling, one hand behind his head, the other wandering across his chest.

'No,' Alan said. 'I *don't want*.'

A new expression appeared on the boy's face, something like sadness, or sadness badly acted. He sat up on the bed and, reaching into his back pocket, took out a knife.

Still staring at Alan, he drew the knife across the palm of his hand. The blade travelled smoothly, leaving a fine red line that grew as Alan watched. It must be sharp, he thought, to cut like that. He seemed far away to himself, as if the knife had opened up a gap between what he was seeing and what he was thinking. He looked into the boy's face again and saw no trace of pain, only a kind of control that hadn't been there a moment before. And now the boy's hand was moving closer, the knife flashing, flat on his palm. The boy said something in Spanish, his voice husky, insistent. Alan shook his head, shrugged. He wanted to say that he didn't understand, but he did. The boy was offering him the knife, and he had to take it.

Then he had taken it, and it was lying on his left hand. The blade was four inches long and sprinkled with rust near the hilt, but bright and finely-honed along the cutting edge. He placed the tip of the blade at the base of his forefinger, and pressed down and across. He felt a coldness, nothing more.

He handed the knife back. The boy slid it into the back of his jeans. He leaned forwards and took Alan's hand, the one that was bleeding. He fitted his own bloody hand over Alan's and squeezed them together, twisting them in opposite directions. Then he stood up. He bent down, picked his shirt up off the floor and put it on. Without looking at Alan again, he walked to the door, opened it and went out, closing it softly behind him.

Alan waited until the boy's footsteps faded, then he crossed the room and lay down on the bed. There was one small window set high up in the wall. A piece of night sky sealed off by chicken wire. Through the window he heard the distant clash of cymbals. The band was starting up again in the main square.

HOW DOES YOUR GARDEN GROW?

DAISY WAUGH

DAISY WAUGH

Daisy Waugh was born in 1967. Her first novel, *What is the matter with Mary-Jane*, was published in 1988. She is a journalist and lives in London.

MARY WASN'T WEARING a skirt today, but then she quite often didn't. The freedom her skirtless body gave to Mary's legs was a constant (though complicated) reminder of her joy. The skirt was too small for her and at nights, when she wore it to keep out the cold, she used a safety pin fastened halfway down the zip to keep it on. The pin had broken while she was sleeping last night and she had been awoken with a start of pain; its point was sticking sharply into her behind.

At some time between six and seven that morning the ground on which Mary was resting became too hard for her to continue lying on any longer. It was winter time, not yet light outside. She sat up, rubbed her eyes, wrapped her coat more closely around her and struggled upwards to her feet. Mary shivered. It was a cold morning. She looked down at her skirt. No, not today, she wouldn't wear the skirt today. She stepped out of it and felt the lighter for having done so.

Mary looked around her contentedly. She'd been staying here for almost three weeks now and nobody had yet told her to move on. Perhaps she might even be left to last out the winter here. She was standing in the boarded-up basement of an uninhabited house on the Westbourne Park Road. The flat had no electricity, no furniture, no water. The flat demanded no thought.

Three weeks ago there had been a particularly cold night. Mary, at a loose and frozen end, had found an iron rod lying amongst the rubble in the basement's tiny area. She'd spent almost two hours loosening the planks across the window with it. Now, every morning and every night, as she was coming from the flat or going to it, Mary replaced the loosened planks of her basement exactly. Mary prided herself on discretion. Like that, nobody would be the wiser.

Mary looked down at her bare, disproportionately chubby legs. Legs, she thought, nice, fat legs. But her legs were cold. Somewhere around, she remembered, there was a pair of tights. She found them in the corner of her sleeping room, neatly tucked into her pair of shoes. She lifted them out and held them for a while. They were green, though you couldn't see so in the light; beautiful green with a couple of holes. She didn't mind the holes, the green would make up for any number of them.

Beside the shoes was a pile of coins. The largest – a ten-pence piece – was at the bottom. There were three of those, one exactly on top of the other, then came the two, then the five and finally the ones. Mary had thirty-nine pence today.

It seemed a shame to disrupt the pleasantly arranged stack, but she put the coins into her pocket, rolled on the tangled tights, squeezed her feet into the well-worn shoes and made towards the window boards.

Today she was happy. She knew what she had to do. Today she was going to buy a cream bun from the bakery in Covent Garden. The woman who worked there was a friend. She always looked pleased when Mary came into the shop. Mary hoped that she would be there today.

Ten years ago Mary had a lot more to her name than thirty-nine pence and a pair of ripped green tights. In fact she had £545 in a deposit account at the Midland Bank in Hanover Square and £173 in her current account at the very same place. She worked as a personal assistant for a demanding and highly-strung boss just off Oxford Street, for which she was paid £6,000 a year. And for whom she was expected to be punctual, neat, together, one hundred per cent reliable and one hundred per cent calm. It was a difficult job. Mary found that her boss's moods rubbed off on her. And so, as month followed month, she grew as tense and as highly-strung as he. Then she grew worse. Then far worse.

Mary used to cry on her way to work almost every morning. She always left an hour to get to work from her flat in Hammersmith. Her boyfriend, who lived in the same flat, told her it was absurd. She needed half an hour to get there at the very most. But Mary wouldn't listen. When he told her she should slow down, take things a little easier, she would either cry or lose her temper. He didn't understand.

Mary cried if the bus was late. She cried if the tube happened to stop in the tunnel. By the time she arrived in the office (half an hour early) she was a nervous wreck. On the very rare occasions that she got to work after her boss nothing was said. He would say good morning to her quite politely, but would pointedly not look at his watch. Mary was sure. She would feel there was hell in the air for the rest of the day if not week. Mary had never naturally been punctual, neat, together, reliable or calm. The job was a great strain, and the strain of her work carried itself easily to interrupt the running of her personal life.

A year later Mary thought she'd found the cure to her tearfulness. She now took taxis to and from her place of work. They cost at least half of her annual salary and Mary only found other aspects of her life to sob about. But she was still clinging on to her job – and her boyfriend – just; by the skin of her teeth.

Mary had spent the £545 on a holiday in Tunisia for Paul (her boyfriend) and herself several months ago. Paul was unemployed at the time and had been unable to pay for himself. Her current account wasn't so healthy as it had been a year ago either. Mostly because of Mary's new-found inability to cope without taxis. She was by now several hundred pounds in the red and couldn't see how, in the near future, she would ever be able to put herself back in credit.

Mary used to lie awake worrying about it. She knew that she had nothing to sell. And Paul, who had recently found himself a well-paid job in computers, refused to help her out unless she agreed to stop using cabs. Mary knew that of all things, the cabs would be the last to go. One morning, Mary woke up to find a letter pinned to the pillow beside her. But there was no Paul. She opened the letter and read.

Dear Mary,

We have had some great times together. But I think, in the end, that we both want different things from life. I will be staying away for the next few days. When I come back I shall expect you to have gone.

I am sorry to have to tell you like this – but you are impossible to speak to nowadays.

Goodbye and good luck,

Paul.

It took a while for Mary to understand what the letter was telling her. She read it three times (still lying in bed) then folded it back into its original quarters and replaced it in the envelope.

She lay back and stared at the ceiling. Her mind was a blank. Four minutes later she sat up with a start. And now she was going to be late for work. As she waited for her bath to run, she tore the message and its wrapper into shreds. Tiny little shreds that she scattered, unconsciously, as she paced about the flat.

She didn't cry. This man, with whom she'd been living for almost three years now, with whom she'd been sleeping since her O-level year at school, had just walked out on her. Who was he anyway? Paul. Just another Paul. A Paul in computers this time. So what? She snorted, she'd never thought of it like that – and the noise embarrassed her. She was going to be late for work.

She lay in the bath and her thoughts were no longer moving. Her mind chimed *Just Another Paul* with monotonous rhythm. It meant nothing to her. Her brain was simply acting like her heart, her lungs. They were all ticking over nicely. Mary was unconscious of them all.

Just another Paul; a Paul in Computers this Time – she stepped out of her bath. *Just another Paul Pa-au-au-l* – she made up her face. She was going to be late for work. *In computers this time* – she put on her shirt, her shoes, her coat. Oh God, she was late, she was very very late. Why couldn't she hurry? What about Paul? Paul who? She closed the flat door behind her and forgot to turn the lock. She'd left her keys on the bedside table, but it didn't matter at all.

She walked towards the tube and felt the cold against her legs, but not consciously – not really. She stood at the platform and waited for a train. She was bored by the rhythm of her thoughts. She had forgotten to take a taxi.

A tube arrived behind her; on the other side of the platform. It was heading for High Street, Kensington. She turned around, stepped on to it, pushed the closest contender aside and took a seat.

Paul's left, she thought. My money's run out. I don't have anywhere to live. I'm on the wrong train and I don't have a skirt on this morning. She stayed in her place. She couldn't think what else to do.

She walked through her office door at eleven o'clock that morning.

'Where have you *been*?' whispered a secretary at the next-door desk. 'He's *spitting* with rage.'

Mary shrugged her shoulders. 'Good morning,' she said. And she took off her coat.

'Mary,' persisted the secretary. 'Where have you been? You're going to have to think of something you know or . . . *Mary!* You haven't got anything *on!*'

Mary looked down at her legs. Yes I do, silly woman, she thought, I have my tights on. 'I know,' she said.

The secretary was excited by the diversion. She rose from her desk and walked towards her. 'What's happened? Mary, you look terrible – cover yourself up for goodness sake, he'll be in here any min . . .'

He opened the connecting door, clicked it shut and allowed his hand to rest on the knob behind him. He looked at Mary. He was purple with rage. His eyes followed the shape of Mary's body from the nape of her neck to halfway down her shin. Slowly. Mary stood there. She could not pretend to herself that the sight he had before him was a comforting one. Mary's body had never been among her finest features. The secretary whimpered.

'Would you be so kind as to cover yourself up and then step into my office,' he said. His voice was deceptively calm and the secretary whimpered again.

'Certainly,' Mary said, and followed him, still skirtless, into the room next door.

Seven minutes later she was back at her desk with a thick wad of fivers in her hand. Mary picked up her bag, her coat.

'Mary, are you all right? What happened? What did he say?'

As if she didn't know. Mary didn't bother to clear out her desk. She didn't bother to say goodbye. She took a taxi to Covent Garden and spent the rest of the day in a favourite café behind the Market Place.

After the pubs had closed Mary took a taxi home. She was drunk; she couldn't find her keys. She spent that night on the landing outside her front door. In the morning she picked herself up and wandered off. She never did go back. She's been wandering ever since.

'A hundred pounds in 1988 doesn't even get you a nice skirt,' Mary heard a girl in a nice coat say to her friend as she made her way towards the bus. Mary overtook them. 'Poor woman,' she heard the other one say. 'We don't know how lucky we are, do we?'

'This part of London is full of weirdos.' Mary stepped on to the bus. She walked up the stairs and took a seat. Mary smiled. She liked to travel on buses. She hoped that the bus would take her past a park. She liked especially to be on a bus that took her past a park.

But then the conductor arrived and interrupted her peace. 'Where for, lovey?' he said. She looked up at him and smiled. 'C'mon, lovey,' he said again. 'Let's see your ticket.'

'Hello, darling.'

He clicked his tongue. It wasn't worth the trouble. Leave her be, she'd get off in her own good time. He moved on further down the aisle.

In Kensington High Street the bus was caught up in a traffic jam. The traffic was barely moving at all. A man beside Mary started to fidget. He looked at his watch and then back to his paper. He looked at his watch again, then out of the window then back at his watch again. Mary smiled at him but he didn't seem to notice. She nudged him and smiled again. The man ignored her. He picked up his case and moved towards the top of the stairs. 'Quicker to walk,' he said, but nobody listened.

Mary watched his head as it disappeared down the stairs. She felt sorry for her neighbour, even though he'd been so rude. She spread herself out a little more on the seat. Soon they would be driving past the park, she was looking forward to the park, she was quite excited by it. But then –

'All right, lovey,' it was the conductor again. 'Off you get.' Mary looked up at him. He seemed a little discomforted. He shrugged, 'There's bin complaints.' Mary stood up. 'Sorry, luv,' he said. She didn't understand why he was apologising. It didn't matter. It didn't matter at all.

Back down on the street Mary stood still and wondered what to do. A momentum had been snatched from her and for a while she felt bereft. A woman with a babble of troublesome children shuffled past her and pushed her from the pavement to the road. Mary stood there. She felt the tears welling up in her eyes and she didn't try to stop them.

She stumbled on a bit towards the park and soon forgot her disappointments. She would go to the park. It would feel good to walk in the park. She watched a dog pee against the wheel of one of the cars stuck in the traffic jam. The driver didn't seem to notice. He was combing his hair in the mirror above his head. The dog's owner was pulling frantically at the dog's lead. But the dog was still peeing and now the driver was putting away his comb. Mary watched and felt some sympathy for all three. She wondered what would happen next, but then she was distracted by the shop.

It was a big fashion shop at the end of the road. Mary had been in there before. Lots of colours and loud music and people. She turned in and stopped at the first display. It was a lovely shop.

She fingered all the clothes on all the racks and they felt warm. Mary was glad that she had wanted to come into the shop. It was cold outside.

A beautiful girl sat in a chair in the corner. She was smoking a cigarette and talking to a short-haired man in black. They ignored her. Mary was happy. They were leaving her in peace. But then she saw the blue and golden jacket with the fur-lined sleeves and she wanted to share the discovery. The girl would want to see the jacket; it was such a beautiful jacket.

Mary tried to unhook the jacket from the rack. She had intended to carry it to the girl. But the jacket was chained to the shop. Her smile vanished. She tugged at the jacket but it wouldn't come.

The couple in the corner stopped their conversation and looked up at her for the first time. The woman was mumbling to herself. 'Oh Christ,' the girl sighed. She stubbed out her cigarette and moved towards the problem. 'Can I help you?'

The man in black tittered from behind. 'I mean, this woman needs *help*,' he said.

But Mary only heard them. She tugged at the jacket again. Too frantically this time; the sound of ripped material could easily be felt above the noise of the background music. Mary was horrified. Her hands dropped immediately to her sides. She turned towards the girl and began to cry.

'Jesus Christ,' said the girl. 'Just look what she's gone and done.' The man was no longer smiling. He moved forward to inspect the damage.

'You can mend it can't you?' Mary asked him.

He turned to the girl. 'Get the silly cow out of here before she touches anything else.' And Mary was escorted back out on to the street.

Mary thought about the jacket. It had been such a beautiful jacket. It was silly of them to chain it to the shop. They should have known that she wasn't going to steal it. Mary wondered if the person who eventually bought the jacket would mind so much about the rip. She thought that they probably would and felt a little bad about it.

The woman and her dog were nowhere to be seen. She wondered what had happened. She wondered what it would be like to be a dog for a while and decided she was happy that she was a human.

Something shifted in Mary's stomach and it reminded her that she was hungry. It reminded her of the cream bun and the bakery in Covent Garden. She forgot about the park. She was cold.

Just then a taxi moved towards her with its yellow light on. She loved the light. A feeling from her past flashed through her; how easy it would be to stop the cab. She remembered for a moment the feeling of relief that had used to flood through her once she'd told the driver her destination and relaxed back into the seat, all responsibility lifted from her shoulders until it was time to pay. The cab moved on along with Mary's memories. She thought again about the bun. The woman in the bakery would want to see her. The woman would be worried about her; she often said she was.

So Mary gathered her rambling mind and took it to a bus that would carry her to Covent Garden. She stepped on to the bus and moved towards the stairs but the conductor stopped her. 'Sorry, love, no more upstairs,' he said. And as he spoke the park to the left spun past and behind her.

At Long Acre Mary stepped off the bus of her own accord. Nobody had troubled her for the fare. But she had grown tired of the journey. She wanted to walk for a while.

From the end of the road Mary could see the shop and her mouth began to water. She smiled and quickened her step. She swallowed. The memory of what she was about to eat was so fresh she could taste it already. Her eyes only saw the shop, but it was her entire body that imagined the bun.

'Hello, darling,' said the woman behind the counter. 'You look happy today.'

Mary nodded. She couldn't find the bun.

'You're unlucky,' the woman followed Mary's gaze. 'We just sold out of your favourites.' She saw the disappointment in Mary's face and felt a little sorry. 'Why don't you try a different one for a change?'

But Mary didn't listen. She was still searching for the bun.

Apart from the two of them the shop was empty. There was a moment's silence.

'Hang on a moment,' said the woman. 'We've just had some more stock in . . . I'll go and have a look.'

Mary didn't raise her eyes from the counter. She was still looking for the bun.

'There we are, just as I thought,' the woman bustled back into the shop. 'We've got a whole crate of the things next door.'

The woman wrapped one of the buns in rice paper and rang up the price on the till. Mary fumbled for her change. She took the bun, and as she opened her mouth to say thank you a small bubble of saliva popped on one corner and dribbled down her chin.

'That's all right – enjoy it.' The woman followed the spit as it reached her jawbone and hoped that Mary would leave now. It wasn't that she disliked Mary, just that she might be frightening the customers away.

Mary didn't eat the bun immediately. She put it in her pocket. She knew it was bad manners to eat when she wasn't sitting down.

On the tube she sat herself down right opposite me. She had been unable to wait until then and had started to eat back on the platform.

There was cream on her cheeks and all over her hands. It was four o'clock; I had just come away from a heavy lunch with my editor. The sight of the cream and her uncovered legs didn't please me. She settled herself down and continued to chew on the mouthful she had taken as she stepped through the opening doors. I watched her. She spread herself out on the seat and I saw her fat, mottled thighs. They didn't please me. I scowled at her and I noticed her face. She must have been as old as I am, perhaps a little older; the innocence there gave her an ageless, almost child-like quality.

She licked her fingers. Her coat had fallen open and the spread of her green-covered thighs was a horrible sight. I looked down at my own, tightly covered legs, and felt pleased. Thin legs, elegantly covered.

My editor had taken me to lunch at Joe Allen's. He had offered me a rise. He was pleased with the work I was doing but I was late for the next appointment. I was pleased with the money; I supposed I ought to have been pleased with the work.

Mary took another bite. More cream spilled over on to her cheeks. She was smiling. I'd never seen such happiness on an adult face. Child's face. She had a problem, she wasn't all there.

She licked the cream away from around her mouth. She stretched her tongue and licked more away from her chin and cheeks. I thought about my appointment. The tube slowed gradually to a halt in the middle of a tunnel and I started to sweat. I was late enough already. I looked at my watch. It didn't help. She started to hum. Her neighbours, both of whom were pretending not to notice she was there, leant a little further apart.

I looked at her again. It was the joy in her face that fascinated me. Her face was unlined. It was glowing; there was a beauty in it somewhere, behind the cream.

At some stage, the tube ground forward again, though I don't recall how or when. It came to my stop and I felt the sweat trickle down past my ribcage. I watched her take another mouthful, and the doors opened, and they closed, and the train moved on.

Oh God I was late. I was very very late. Why couldn't I hurry? She finished the bun and started on her fingers. Where were we? Where was I supposed to be? She rummaged around in her coat pocket and drew out the crumpled rice paper. I thought about my appointment. She licked it clean and scrumpled up the remains.

The tube was slowing down for another station. She stood up beside the doors and waited for them to be opened. I thought about my appointment. I thought about my job and my overdraft and my boyfriend. I thought about my clothes and my figure and the spot beneath my eyebrow.

The doors opened. She stepped out. And I followed her.

THE GAP

MATTHEW YORKE

MATTHEW YORKE

Matthew Yorke was born in London in 1958. His first novel, *The March Fence*, was published in 1988. He is currently working on his second novel.

'DON'T BE A cunt,' Edwin scowled. 'There's fook all in 'ere
. . . fook all.'

'I say we stop 'ere for a few more weeks.'

'Don't be a cunt,' Edwin repeated. 'I feel a right dummy
workin' for this money . . . an' in this poxy place.'

'Well, what do we do, then?' Brunton asked.

'We fook off, don't we. We find summat else.'

There was a silence between the two men, and together they
surveyed the shop floor.

This shop – which specialised in the manufacture of burglar
bars, railings and fire escapes – was typical of one of the
many small engineering works to be found throughout London.
Measuring sixty feet by forty, it was equipped with only the
bare essentials of the trade: a guillotine, a brake press, a drilling
machine, several welders and as many steel-topped benches. It
was typical, too, for the rank smell of scorched steel that hung
in opaque curtains throughout the interior, and for the sea of
iron grindings that lay in ridges upon the rough, concrete floor.

Edwin grimaced. 'It were your idea an' all,' he went on, and
he spat.

'I know it were. I thought there'd be money down 'ere, that's
all.'

'Well, yer were wrong, weren't yer? There's nought, and I
say we piss off.'

'What do we do then?'

'We find another job, that's what.'

'But that's what I'm sayin' . . . it's best to find summat else
before we chuck it in 'ere.'

'We can't find work from 'ere . . . There in't time.'

'We can look in paper.'

'Like fook we can . . . Come on,' Edwin said louder, taking Brunton's arm, 'we'll see foreman now.'

Brunton followed. This he did reluctantly, for he could see that they could both be out of a job. But as the two had travelled from Yorkshire only a few weeks before, he did not relish the prospect of a split with his friend. He did not want to be alone in London, a city more alien and forbidding than he had anticipated. Besides, he was fond of Edwin. Even so, as the two stepped into the foreman's office at the far end of the shop, he could predict how their interview would go.

'Graham, we're not stoppin' 'ere for this money,' Edwin began.

'What's that?' the foreman asked, looking up from a drawing.

'I said we're not stoppin' 'ere for this money. When yer give uz job yer said that our rate'd be goin' up after first month. Well, I bin on to yer 'bout it once, and yer done nought for uz.'

'But I have,' the foreman returned. 'I told you, I saw John about it last week.'

'An' what did 'e say?'

'He said he can't put your rate up till he's seen what you're capable of.'

'That's not good enough,' Edwin said at once with a tight upper lip. 'We've bin knockin' up 'em railin's just the same as rest of 'em in 'ere, an' we're gettin' ten quid odd under meat.'

'Well,' the foreman frowned, 'I can't say that I've had any complaints about your work, but John says you're slower than the others.'

'Yer know that in't true . . . An' that in't all . . . There's no bonus in 'ere . . . no overtime . . . there's fook all. I'm tellin' yer, Graham, either we get proper money or we piss off.'

'Well, I can see John about it again if you like . . . but if you go, you'll be the losers.'

'What do yer mean?'

The foreman rose and closed the door to his office before continuing. 'When I did my apprenticeship – and I did it not far from where you two boys come from – I was in a foundry shop, right?'

Edwin did not answer, he simply stared at the other with a dull look of indifference.

'And there was a depression on, right? Well, every morning from seven o'clock onwards there was a queue of men down the street, outside the works. And in that queue were some of the most skilled millers, turners and polishers in the North of England. At a quarter to eight the foreman of the machine shop would go outside and show each man a drawing – a drawing of some flanges, bosses, what have you. He would get each man to quote a price for the work. The man who gave the cheapest price would be allowed in to do the job.'

'But that's got nought to do wi' uz,' Edwin objected.

'That's what I'm sayin'. Things aren't so very different today. There's a long dole queue, right, and there's a lot of skilled men. Think about it, you two, because if you're not prepared to do the job for the money, then there's going to be some who are.'

There was a short silence.

'We're not stoppin' 'ere for this money,' Edwin said again.

'Right, I'll go and see John now. But I wouldn't set your sights too high. Stay here a minute.'

'Fookin' 'ell,' Brunton cursed as the foreman made off through the shop. 'We're goin' to be out of a job.'

'Call this a job,' the other returned. 'We'll be well out of it.'

'What the fook are we gonna do?'

'We'll find summat else . . .'

'But 'e may be right. Supposin' there's nought?'

'There'll be summat.'

But Brunton was not so sure. The prospect of being out of work in London filled him with an immeasurable dread. And yet, at the same time, he could not contemplate the possibility of returning to the North.

'Any road,' Edwin went on, 'it were you who were sayin' there was all this work and all this money down 'ere. We'd 'ave bin better off stoppin' where we were.'

'I say it's better makin' railin's and such than bein' . . .'

'Is it fook. Makin' burglar bars for all 'em ponces? I feel like a right dummy down 'ere . . . workin' in this Mickey Mouse shop.' Edwin waved his hand dismissively over the interior of the factory. There the men were quietly going about their business. He was about to continue when the foreman returned to his office.

'I've seen John. He says there's no chance of your money going up.'

'We're off, then.'

'Think about it, boys.'

'We're off,' Edwin repeated, harsher.

'And you, too, Brunton?'

'Yuhh,' Brunton nodded.

There was a pause.

'Well, I think you're making a mistake,' the foreman pronounced. 'Still, if you're sure, I'll get John to make your money up now. You may as well pack up.'

The two men left the glass office, and began to gather their tools.

Within five minutes they were back in the foreman's office, donkey jackets over their overalls, toolboxes by their sides. Within ten minutes they had been given their pay packets and were walking up Wandsworth Bridge Road.

'Fookin' day's 'ell,' Edwin cursed, glancing through his pay slip. ''Alf a days 'oliday money . . . four pound odd deducted for bein' late . . . What a poxy place.'

'What we gonna do now?'

'Stop yer whinin', will yer? Summat'll turn up.'

There was a silence, and the two men walked on beneath an Embankment light, a light that bleached the paving stones of their colour.

Save for the money in their pay packets, they had nothing. To Edwin, whose eye could trace more clearly the defines between right and wrong, this turn of events seemed nothing out of the ordinary, for though he viewed the future with varying degrees of frustration and resignation, he knew that in the end he would manage. After all, he would argue, they had both been made redundant from their jobs at Hawkins, in Leeds, and if they did not draw the dole in the North, they could draw it in London.

To Brunton, however, their position seemed near hopeless.

The month of being out of work had driven him to distraction. And, though he had never been satisfied with the work at Hawkins, he had learnt that having his mind occupied during the day was infinitely preferable to being sat, penniless, on the estate he had come to know so well as a child.

'I don't fancy goin' back to lodgin' 'ouses now,' he said at last. 'Any road, if landlady sees we're out of job, we'll be out of rooms.'

'We'll stop 'ere for a bit,' Edwin murmured, pointing to the green at the head of Wandsworth Bridge Road. 'There's one of 'em poxy job centres in North End Road, in't there?'

'Yuh . . .'

The two men walked on, disconsolate.

'A double room booked in the name of Berry,' Mr Berry said with a note of triumph as he might at the end of a long, tiring journey.

'Yes, Mr Berry, we have a room reserved for you on the third floor. Room number 361.'

'Darling,' Mrs Berry breathed in her husband's ear, 'don't you think we could be a little higher up?'

'What?'

'Well, now we're in a sky scraper . . . don't you think it might be rather fun to be a little higher up?'

'Yes, of course. I'll just ask. Do you have a room further up the building?' Mr Berry asked the receptionist.

'I beg your pardon, sir?'

'My wife would like to be on a higher floor. Do you have anything on the sixth floor, for instance?'

'Let me just see . . .'

'I think it would be so much more fun to be higher up,' Venetia Berry repeated. 'Think of the view . . .'

'I know. I know,' Mr Berry agreed with lengthened eyes, as if he were peering into the middle distance.

'We have rooms available on all the floors, sir. Which would you like?'

'Well, darling,' said Mr Berry, turning, 'which would you like?'

'The top.'

'The top?'

'Yes, why not?'

'Do you have a room at the top, then?' Mr Berry asked, turning once more.

'Yes, sir.'

'We'll probably spend most of the weekend in the lifts,' he joked. 'But it'll be worth it if the weather holds, eh?'

'I beg your pardon, sir?'

'No worry. Now, fill this in, do I? Good.'

Venetia Berry glanced over the interior of the foyer. There was a good deal of chrome, glass and brass. Furthest from the receptionist's desk was the entrance to the casino, and she smiled, relishing the prospect of a flutter for she was invariably lucky at the roulette table.

'There we are,' Mr Berry finished. 'Up to the dizzy heights now, eh? Can't open the window up there, I hope . . .'

'I beg your pardon, sir?'

'Not to worry. Now, which way?'

'We'll have someone take you up to your room right away.'

'Good.'

The Berrys followed the hall porter. They did not speak in the lift until the automatic doors drew open, revealing a long, bare corridor.

'I say, we really are some way up,' Mr Berry stated, glancing nervously through the window at the head of the passage.

'Well, at least we'll get some fresh air,' his wife commented.

'Oh now, really, darling. Air is air and it probably gets piped in miles down from here.'

'Well, I think it's lovely,' Mrs Berry went on, striding into their room. 'And just look at that view.'

Mr Berry tipped the porter and joined his wife at the window. There they stood speechless, for below lay the sprawling metropolis – an anthill of activity. First their eyes were drawn to the maze of streets that lay like so many tunnels within a warren, and though, in a proportion of these, columns of cars stood stationary, it was plain that each actor on this giant stage had a purpose and a task to perform. And though the Berrys may have been standing many hundreds of feet above, still they could hear the toneless drum of traffic and feel the vibrations that radiated from this tireless and yet reassuring industry.

'Look at the park, darling,' Mrs Berry whispered.

Together they looked. There the trees were turning for winter and stood a hundred shades of beige. Overhead, banks of cumulus cloud moved across the horizon, like so many sheep tracing a path along the contour of an invisible fell. But it was the mid-October light that enabled the eye to penetrate areas that might otherwise have been inaccessible. Everything seemed so crystal clear.

'He who takes the highest room sees furthest, eh?' Mr Berry joked.

'What?'

'Old Chinese proverb.'

Mrs Berry did not answer, instead she moved towards the bathroom. 'I think we should unpack,' she murmured.

'Plenty of time, darling,' her husband countered, but awkwardly as if he were scheming. 'Plenty of time if you're with Eddie Berry,' he went on, advancing whilst his wife's back was turned and taking a breast in each hand.

'Oh, now, Edward . . . stop it . . .'

Mr Berry did not answer; he continued to massage his wife's breasts, and then to knead her midriff.

'Edward, we haven't got time.'

'Rubbish, darling,' the other said more confidently, turning his wife and shunting her through the bathroom door. 'Plenty of time if you're with Eddie Berry,' he repeated.

Mrs Berry did not answer. Instead she gazed at the ceiling with a look of resignation, for already her skirt was tight about her thighs and, rouched, her jersey revealed a pale, marble skin. 'But someone will see us,' she objected at last, though she knew this to be impossible.

'Rubbish,' her husband muttered, 'rubbish.'

Venetia Berry considered how much time she would have to prepare for dinner, and then, hearing her husband's breathing quicken, lifted her backside off the divan, enabling the other to slide off her drawers. She stared through the window. Gulls wheeled at the same level as their room. They were like vultures, she thought, and yet she remembered how, in childhood, she had been led to believe they were lost sailors' souls. Also she wondered why her husband was so sexually active of late.

Mr Berry, for his part, buried his head in the pillow beside his wife's hair. He had been to stay with a farmer friend a fortnight before and, whilst the others were breakfasting, he had watched a Friesian bull serve a Hereford heifer. He recalled the manner in which that brutish beast had mounted the heifer, and the bull's total disregard for the pain those nail-like hooves must have brought to her waxy hide. He recalled the relentless battery that had ensued and how, at the moment of climax, the bull's back feet had almost left the ground. With this image in his mind's eye it was not long before Mr Berry was done.

His wife disengaged herself and moved silently back into the bathroom.

Mr Berry made for the mini-fridge. 'I think I may have a drink,' he said.

'Fookin' 'ell,' Brunton cursed with whisky breath, pointing at a model in the window of Harvey Nichols, 'I'd like to give 'er one.'

'Oh, leave it out,' Edwin sneered. 'It's only a fookin' dummy.'

'Looks like the real thing, though, dunnit?'

'If yer talkin' about dummies, it does.'

'An' fookin' 'ell, look at that,' Brunton went on, pointing now at a sequin dress that spangled in the street lamps. 'That's gorra be some fookin' dress, eh? Think of rippin' that off. Fookin' 'ell,' he exclaimed, much louder. 'It cost twelve 'undred quid.'

'Bloody right, it does,' Edwin muttered, staring at the price tag with mouth agape. 'Twelve 'undred quid for that . . .'

'An' them,' Brunton shouted, placing his toolbox on the pavement, 'eight 'undred quid for a pair of shoes. It can't be right, can it?'

'Them's croc.'

'Croc?'

'Crocodile, yer dozy bugger.'

'Fookin' 'ell.'

'Come on, lookin' at this lot's makin' me sick,' Edwin grimaced. 'Let's go for a drink.'

The two welders made their way down Lowndes Square and turned left into Kinnerton Street.

'We'll go in 'ere,' Edwin said, indicating the Turk's Head.

The two young men pushed through the door.

'It's your round,' Edwin said, sitting. Brunton handed the other his toolbox and walked up to the bar. He bought two pints of bitter, and returned to where his friend was seated.

'Fookin' 'ell,' he whispered, 'two pound eighteen for two pints of ale. What a fookin' place.'

'Well, it were your idea to come down 'ere.'

'There's gorra be some money somewhere.'

'There's no fookin' money.'

'Well, who's buyin' all 'em dresses and shoes and stuff?'

'Fook knows. Foreigners, most likely.'

'Let's fook off abroad, then.'

'Don't be a cunt,' Edwin scorned. 'Yer a dozey bugger, in't yer?' he added, but affectionately.

'Well, I'm not stoppin' in Leeds where there's no fookin' jobs. And I'm not stoppin' down 'ere where a pint of beer costs over a quid and where yer can't even earn a decent wage if yer try. I'm not 'avin' it,' Brunton finished, quite angry.

'Well, there's no one stoppin' yer. Just piss off to Orstrylia, then.'

'Will yer come with us?'

'Will I fook.'

'Why not?'

''Cos this is where I was born. This is my fookin' country en all, yer know,' Edwin retorted, also quite angry. 'Why the fook should I piss off? I'm not a villain.'

There was a silence but this last exchange had attracted the attention of those around about, who now looked on with expressions of disdain. Edwin scowled and was about to continue when the landlord walked up to their table. 'I'm sorry,' he began, 'but we don't have workmen in here.'

'What? Yer what?'

'We don't allow workmen on the premises. I'm sorry, but if

you can read you will have seen a notice on the door saying as
much.'

'I'm not a workman,' Brunton replied.

'Well, you're wearing overalls and you're carrying toolboxes.
If you're not workmen, what are you?'

There was a short silence.

'I'm sorry, but you'll have to leave.'

'I'm not leavin'. I bought a pint of ale, didn't I?'

'I'm sorry. You'll have to leave. I'm perfectly within my rights
– there's a sign.'

'I'm not fookin' leavin'.'

'Come on,' Edwin hissed. 'It's not worth the bother.'

'I'll spill this poxy pint over the floor first,' Brunton said, anger
reddening his neck.

'You do that and I'll have you nicked,' the landlord cut in, sharp.

'Come on,' Edwin repeated, already standing. 'We'll not mess
with these ponces.'

Finally Brunton stood and the two young men left the pub.

'Fookin' 'ell, I should 'ave flattened 'im.'

'Where would that 'ave got yer?' Edwin scorned, 'yer daft
bugger.'

'I should 'ave belted 'im.'

It was cold as evening was turning to night. And though in
part that chill dampened their anger and resentment, at the
same time it sealed it within.

The two men walked through Wilton Place in silence and
turned left into Knightsbridge. Not many minutes later they
paused in front of The Sheraton. Brunton stared at the casino
and the two men dressed in beige suits. Edwin looked uncomfortable, as if he were wrestling with a conflict.

'Come on,' he said at last, taking Brunton's arm and guiding
him towards the entrance of the hotel.

'What? Where yer goin'?'

'Just belt up and follow me.'

'Yer what?'

'I said, just belt up.'

Edwin stopped some ten feet before the swing doors, and
chose his time with care. When he saw the doormen were

otherwise engaged and relatively few busied the threshold, he pulled Brunton once again. They walked straight up to reception.

'We're the 'eatin' engineers from 'ead office,' he said to the girl behind the desk.

'I beg your pardon?'

'I said, we're the 'eatin' engineers from 'ead office. Yer got a problem in yer ducts.'

The receptionist did not answer at first, rather blinked. 'Oh, yes,' she stuttered at last. 'Well, I'll just see the manager. But you can't wait here . . . in the foyer . . . Can you come around the back a bit?'

Edwin pushed Brunton forwards.

'I'll just find the manager,' the receptionist said somewhat uncertainly, and she pushed through a door behind the desk. But the manager was nowhere to be found and, such was the conviction in Edwin's manner, she was easily thrown.

'It's an emergency, luv,' Edwin added as she returned.

'I beg your pardon?'

'System's blowin' cold air, in't it?'

'Oh,' she frowned. 'Do you know where the problem is?' she asked.

'Top floor. 'Ead office give uz details.'

There was a short silence.

'Shall we just make our way up there?' Edwin asked.

'Well, yes . . . I should check, but you'd better.'

With a cunning restraint, Edwin led Brunton towards the lifts.

'But you can't go up in those,' he heard the receptionist cry. But this was too late, for already the lift doors had begun to close silently behind them.

'Fookin' 'ell,' Brunton swore. 'What the fook are we doin' in 'ere? We'll both end up in prison.'

'Don't get excited. Just belt up.'

'But what the fook are we doin'?'

'We're goin' up to top floor and we're goin' to 'ave a mosey around, in't we?'

'What for, for fook's sake?'

'We got nought else better to do, 'ave we?'

'Bloody 'ell, yer'll 'ave us both . . .' But Brunton stopped as the lift doors began to ease open. Both lifted their toolboxes from the floor and walked out into the passage. They stopped. There was an uncanny silence.

'Fookin' 'ell,' Brunton started again; but again he stopped as a door opened some way down the corridor where a couple were preparing to leave.

'Come on,' Edwin whispered, pulling Brunton in the direction of those guests.

The welders walked passed the Berrys. There was a strong smell of perfume and, as the two guests stepped into the lift, Edwin began to laugh. 'Wharra fookin' stench.'

'Come on,' Brunton hissed, 'let's gerrout of 'ere.'

'Naa. We're goin' to 'ave a mosey around.'

Just then the chambermaid rounded the corner ahead and approached with a trolley of linen.

''Allo, luv,' Edwin smiled. 'We're the 'eatin' engineers from 'ead office. Are yer expectin' uz?'

'No.'

'Well, there's an emergency in ducts. Rooms 904 and 905,' he added, glancing down to those numbers before him.

'What?'

'There's an emergency in ducts. Whole system's blowin' cold air.'

'Really?'

''Ead office just sent uz around now. Manager downstairs told uz to come up.'

'Did he?'

'Dead right, 'e did. Sounds like there's bird in there,' Edwin went on, seeing the height they were at through the plate-glass window over the chambermaid's shoulder.

'What do you want me to do? I'm just going off,' the girl returned.

'Well, if yer let uz into these rooms, then we can get on with work. Just gorra take plates off and clear blockage. It were time we were off, an' all,' he sighed. 'Gettin' sent out on jobs all time of night; makes yer wanna cry, dunnit?'

The chambermaid unlocked both doors with a master key. 'It seems quite warm to me,' she shrugged.

Brunton snapped on the lights of room 905 and the two men made straight for the window. There, watched by the chambermaid, they put down their toolboxes and, bent in an attitude of scrutiny, began to inspect the radiator plates beneath the window.

'We'll whip this plate off,' Edwin murmured.

'Allen key, is it, or Phillips?' Brunton asked.

'Give uz the Allen keys,' the other whispered. Then, a little louder but without turning, he said to the chambermaid, 'Oh don't yer worry about uz, luv. We got our instructions. Yer best get off or yer'll be 'ere all night.'

'Well, OK then,' she muttered at length. 'I'd better be going.'

'Righto . . . fair enough . . . tarra.'

The two men allowed a few minutes to elapse. Then Brunton swore.

'Fookin' 'ell, what yer playin' at?'

'Come on, we're only 'avin' a bit of fun.'

'A bit of fun? But this is breakin' law, in't it?'

'Come on, we're not doin' nobody no 'arm. This is empty room, in't it?'

'But it's trespassin'.'

'Trespassin' in an empty room? Relax.'

'But 'ere we are on top floor. We'll never be able to run for it if someone comes through door. We're that far up.'

'Bloody right, we are,' Edwin agreed.

They stood by the window. Below, the traffic, headlamps and tail-lights only, swept up and down Park Lane. To the west of this confusion of red and yellow lay the park concealed beneath a blanket of semi-darkness, and, with narrowed eyes, the two men sought out the ghostly forms of trees that stood caught in a halogen glow. Both stood speechless for several, long minutes and a din of traffic rang in their ears. To Brunton the movements of the cars were beautiful as they swung silent through the night, but to Edwin these same colours were not unlike the sparks in a metal shop.

'Busy, in't it?' Brunton said at last.

'It makes me feel sick,' Edwin replied.

'Come on,' Brunton insisted, 'let's fook off before someone comes in and we end up in slammer.'

'Relax. No one's goin' to come in. Now we're 'ere, we're goin' to 'ave a mosey in other room. I wonder if that bird left the door open. She were a right little belter, weren't she?'

Still Brunton swore, and yet still he followed. Having checked that the passage was quiet, they tiptoed down the corridor to room 904. The door was open.

'What a stench,' Edwin whispered, his hand sweeping the wall to find the light switch.

'Come on, let's go.'

Edwin found the switch and, moments later, the room lay bathed in light. 'It must 'ave bin that bird we passed in corridor,' he went on as they moved over the threshold. 'She don't 'alf 'ave a strong perfume.'

'An' look at that,' Brunton exclaimed, at once engrossed in the personal effects of the Berrys. 'Look at that. It's just like the one in shop window, in't it?' he finished, picking up a sequin dress.

'Get yer mits off that,' Edwin reprimanded him. 'Don't touch nought.'

'Don't touch nought?' the other repeated with a laugh and, at the same time, he slipped into the bathroom. 'Fookin' 'ell,' he shouted from within. 'Look at this.'

Edwin joined Brunton in the bathroom and, with expressions of amazement, expressions akin to anger, they surveyed its interior. To the left was a bath, its head a tangle of gold taps and shower attachments, and all around this white porcelain there was a mosaic of glazed tiles. Above, a shower curtain hung suspended from a brass rail. This curtain was painted gold and green and resembled a bamboo thicket.

'Oh, come on, Edwin,' Brunton said for the last time, 'let's gerrout of 'ere.'

'Naa. We're 'ere now. Them two's gone for their dinner, dressed up like turkeys. I gorra surprise for you.'

'What's that, then?'

'Come wi' uz.'

Brunton followed Edwin back into the bedroom.

'What do yer think is in there, then?' he teased, pointing at the mini-fridge.

'How the fook should I know? What is it, any road?'

'What would yer say if I told yer it were full of drink?'

'I'd say fook off.'

'Well 'ave a look then.'

Brunton moved forward and opened the fridge. 'Bloody 'ell,' he gasped.

'Well, it is nice to see you both,' Sir George Maitland said, handing his guests a sherry apiece. 'The whole of London is buzzing with news of the Dewhurst Ball,' he went on with a look at Venetia Berry. 'Forty thousand is the last figure on the flowers . . . To tell the truth, I'm rather dreading it.'

'Good heavens. Forty thousand,' Mr Berry repeated, wide-eyed. 'Anyway,' he went on, 'I think it is very good of you to have us both to dinner – what with the Ball tomorrow and everything.'

'Nonsense, nonsense,' Sir George retorted. 'It couldn't be easier. Now, come on, let's sit down. I want to hear your news. How is everything in Hampshire?'

'Absolutely stunning,' Venetia Berry said at once. 'It's all looking wonderful and begging a visit.'

'How kind.'

'Yes, Venetia's right,' Mr Berry confirmed. 'The trees are turning for winter . . . a pale sky beyond . . . the hay's in and all's well with the world.'

'I thought you made hay in spring, Edward,' Sir George objected.

'You do, old man, but metaphorically speaking . . .'

The three laughed.

'Trout season closed though, I suppose,' Sir George sighed.

'Still got the grayling,' Mr Berry returned.

'The grayling?'

'Princess of the chalk streams,' Mr Berry explained. 'Can't go wrong with a grayling,' he went on. 'I don't know what all the fuss is about. And quite a tasty fish, isn't it, darling?'

'Yes, dear, a bit like turbot,' his wife joked.

'Really? I never knew a grayling tasted that good,' nodded their host. 'You should have brought a brace up with you because I've no idea what Mrs Flight has got in store for us this evening.'

'Whatever it is, it's sure to be delicious,' Venetia Berry murmured.

'Well it might be,' Sir George conceded with another nod, 'now that I've done a bit of devil work with the cooker. Mrs Flight, you see, Venetia, has this tendency to over-cook meat. So one day, on her day off, I simply got a chap to come in and tamper with the cooker. So now when she thinks she's cooking something on gas mark eight, actually it's on gas mark six. It's made all the difference in the world.'

'Except when you're having pork,' Mrs Berry smiled.

'As a matter of fact, I've got a suspicion that that's just what we're having.'

'Oh well, I'm sure . . .'

Again the three laughed.

'So, how's life treating you, George?' Mr Berry asked.

'Couldn't be better. Never thought I'd hear myself saying that, but it's so good it smells bad.'

'Really, what has happened?'

'Well, nothing; that's the point.'

The three laughed.

'No, the point is,' Sir George went on, addressing Mrs Berry for she had not been married long to his old schoolfriend, 'I had a tremendous stroke of luck. I managed to cash in on the vast demand for nineteenth-century paintings in the sixties. I was made for life . . . so when I say that nothing has happened that's really rather good news.'

'Now, come on, that isn't the whole story,' Mr Berry interjected. 'You were jolly shrewd. There weren't many dealers of your age that didn't get their fingers burnt.'

'Well, I was lucky and got out at the right time.'

'And there have been many men who have made a fortune and been unable to hang on to it. You deserve every minute of this early retirement, you lazy old so-and-so,' Mr Berry finished with loud laughter.

'Well, yes, I suppose that good fortune has given me some freedom of sorts – freedom that, I suppose, I abuse. However, I enjoy myself – and that's the name of the game.'

'It sounds like you've been very clever,' Mrs Berry said, glancing about the sitting room. This was furnished in a manner she disliked; the room was cluttered with small objects and tables, and the host of oil paintings that were hung throughout lay like irregular and blackened windows on the walls.

'But now we're on the subject of business,' Sir George said with a tone of seriousness, 'you must be having quite a time with all these mountains.'

'Mountains?' Edward Berry questioned.

'In the EEC.'

'Oh, the butter and beef mountains, you mean?'

'Yes.'

'Well, George, farming is like a lottery. But it's the sort of lottery that's more just than some,' Mr Berry elaborated, searching for an analogy. 'I suppose it's a bit like the swings and roundabouts – everyone gets their chance sooner or later.'

'What do you mean?'

'Well, when say pigs are in, lamb is out. When the dairy farmers are having a bad time of it, the cereal-growers are making money hand over fist.'

'But can't they . . . sort of steady this imbalance down?' asked Sir George.

'Things aren't like that in Europe, old man,' Mr Berry explained. 'There are many, many factors but I suspect the bottom line of it is that human nature demands a sort of lottery basis for every type of business. Everyone wants to feel that they might be out of house and home . . . Keeps the adrenalin going.'

'Oh, Edward, what tripe,' Mrs Berry retorted.

'Yes, I agree,' Sir George nodded. 'I think that's going rather far.'

'Well, perhaps,' Mr Berry conceded, lifting his glass.

'But how does it affect you, that's what I want to know?' their host asked.

'Well, we're in rather a fortunate position. To use this new phrase in vogue, we have "de-stressed" the farm.'

'De-stressed the farm?' Sir George repeated with loud laughter. 'You've *de-stressed* the farm?'

'Yes, we've de-stressed it,' Mr Berry said again, perplexed, and then he, too, began to laugh.

'The point is, about these mountains,' Venetia Berry said as the laughter began to subside, 'is that it's criminal that we, in Europe, should have vast surpluses of food when others in Third World countries are starving.'

There was a silence.

'That's quite true,' Sir George pronounced at length. 'There's something very wrong with our priorities.'

'It's a dashed difficult subject,' Mr Berry frowned.

There was another silence.

'And Venetia, you're on the Bench?' Sir George commented.

'Yes I am, for my sins,' she replied.

'Well, that is commendable. Here we are both, retired art dealers and de-stressed farmers, and there you are, actually contributing,' he finished. But, aware that this sounded a little patronising, he went on quickly. 'And how are you finding it?' he asked.

'Well, quite rewarding.'

'And what sort of offences are most common?'

'Well, being a rural area it's all pretty commonplace. You know, drunk and disorderly, parking offences, petty theft – all that sort of thing.'

'And crime's on the up or down?'

'Getting worse, I'm afraid. That's the lamentable part of the story.'

'Venetia's theory is that it's all to do with parenting,' Mr Berry put in.

'Parenting?'

'I feel the problem lies with parents,' Mrs Berry said with a reproving glance at her husband. 'Parents should set a good example and discipline their children properly.'

'Yes, I see what you mean.'

'But I believe the problem is nothing like what you've got in the inner cities,' she added, steering the conversation away since she saw that her husband was in an exuberant mood.

'Ah yes, the festering inner cities,' Sir George sighed. 'I must say those architects have got something to answer for.'

'I don't think we can lay all the blame on their doorstep,' Mrs Berry stated. 'It's not entirely their fault.'

'Well, I think it's a pretty good starting point,' Sir George guffawed. 'I mean, how anyone could have imagined humans could live in those skyscrapers beats me. A man's house is his castle, after all . . . Ahh, Mrs Flight,' he went on louder in response to a hollow call from the passage. 'Dinner's ready, is it? Good.'

'May I?' Venetia Berry asked, rising.

'Of course, of course – first door on the left.'

There was a brief silence.

'Well, I think you've done very well,' Sir George commented at last.

'I know. I have. After Eva died I never thought I'd be happy again. Venetia's given me a new lease of life.'

'She's brought you out of the woodwork.'

'She has,' Mr Berry laughed. 'Life can be so beastly, and yet it can have its good sides. I'd forgotten what it was like to be happy,' he finished, quite serious.

'Well, we all have our needs. Some have different ones than others, but if you can get half of them met, you're laughing.'

'True, true.'

'And yet she's quite fiery, she's got spark,' Sir George went on wistfully.

'Yes, but she's one of us, don't you worry.'

Both men stood as Venetia Berry returned to the sitting room.

'I say, Edward, I think you've become quite a dandy,' Sir George exclaimed, indicating his guest's trousers and shoes.

'Oh well,' Mr Berry explained, 'that's Venetia's doing.'

'I've only ever seen this boy in a pair of old flannels,' Sir George went on with a prolonged glance at Mrs Berry.

'Yes, I had to do something about his wardrobe.'

'And a good thing too!'

'A decent change of clothes does give one a bit of a fillip,' Mr Berry nodded. 'Puts a bit of bounce into one's step.'

'It's a reflection of your inner psychic condition, old man,' Sir George joked, ushering his guests through into a small, dark dining room.

'Right, let's piss off,' Brunton said, taking another miniature from the fridge.

Edwin did not answer.

'I said, let's piss off.'

'Don't be a cunt. What's buggin' yer?'

'I just wanna get out of 'ere before these come back.'

'They're not comin' back.'

''Ow do yer know?'

''Cos I use my eyes, dun' I?'

'What do yer mean?'

'Look at this,' Edwin said, rising and beckoning the other to follow. 'This is what them in 'ere are doin',' he went on, handing Brunton two cards.

Brunton read the first out aloud. '"Henry and Lavinia Dewhurst request the pleasure of your company at a party to celebrate the twenty-first birthday of their daughter, Samantha." What's that then?'

'It's a party, in't it?'

'But it's for Saturday, yer dummy,' Brunton said with pride. And then with fear, 'Come on, let's fook off before they get back.'

'Read the other one.'

'Yer what?'

'Read the other card.'

'"I do hope you can come to dinner on the Friday before the Dewhurst Ball." What's a fookin' ball?'

'It's this party, yer dozy bugger.'

'Well?'

'Well, it means they're at dinner, dun't it? They won't be back for hours.'

'But we don't wanna 'ang about in 'ere. What's the good of it?'

'It's better than 'angin' about on streets. Any road, there might be summat on television,' Edwin smiled. He moved over to the veneered cabinet and casually switched on the television. 'Bloody 'ell,' he went on at once. 'It's the boxin'. I've bin meanin' to see this for days.'

'Oh, come on, Edwin.'

'Just shut up and sit down, can't yer? 'Elp yerself to another drink an' sit down.'

'Come on, Edwin.'

'Suit yourself, then, piss off. But I'm stoppin' 'ere, me,' Edwin murmured. 'I'm not goin' to miss this. Bloody 'ell,' he went on, pointing at a girl on the screen who was parading the ring with a placard that indicated the bout number. 'What a blindin' bird.'

'She in't bad, is she?' Brunton agreed.

'Yer said it, lad.'

The bout started and, like cat and mouse, the opponents shuffled about the canvas. Sometimes it seemed these fighters resembled repelling magnets as they moved in symmetry and in identical steps around one another. At others they moved into combat and, in those exchanges, it appeared skill had no place, rather it was speed and a gift bestowed at the hour of birth that enabled one to counter the parries of the other.

Both welders sat on the edges of their seats and, once more, it was Brunton who first forgot their position and became most involved. He began to duck his head as if those blows were directed at him, and with each punch he made a noise that mimicked the sound of leather glancing from flesh.

'Kill 'im. Kill 'im!' he shouted at one point.

'Keep yer voice down.'

'Fookin' kill 'im.'

'Belt up.'

'What a bleedin' pouff. He 'ad 'im against ropes, didn't 'e? If I'd 'ave bin there, I'd 'ave 'ad 'im there and then,' Brunton finished, his upper lip quite white.

'Yer wouldn't. Yer'd be on floor inside first round.'

The fight progressed. It was not a good one and soon both welders became insensible to the punches of either fighter. As the contest finished, Edwin scowled. He rose and switched off the television.

The two sat through a long silence.

'It's not right, is't?' Edwin said at length. 'These in 'ere got money an' we got nought. I've worked every day I could, yer know, since I left school, I 'ave. An' yet there's some that's born to money, some that can go wherever they please, do what the fook they want. It can't be right.'

'I never said it were.'

'Yer clock on at eight o'clock and yer work a forty-hour week an' what do yer get for it? Fook all.' Edwin spat and both men watched the phlegm settle on the pile carpet. 'It's not right, an' I'm not 'avin' it.'

'What yer goin' to do about it, then?' Brunton asked with a smile.

'I'm not 'avin' it,' Edwin repeated. He rose and kicked over the wastepaper basket. Then he threw himself on to Mrs Berry's bed but cracked his head on a hard object that was concealed beneath the pillow. 'Fookin' 'ell, what's this?' he muttered, withdrawing a velvet-covered box from beneath the thick goose down. With grey, stubby fingers, he set about the brass catch, and then gently opened the lid which revealed a knot of jewels within. Both men narrowed their eyes as if the light that was refracted through these gems bore hard and sharp into their vision.

'Bloody 'ell,' Brunton breathed.

'There's no money in eggs,' Mr Berry began, taking his glass. 'Anyone could have told Duncan that. But no, he was determined to make a go of it. Goodness knows how much he invested in the project . . . four brand new units . . . five thousand battery hens . . . and all along he knew that the profit margin was so slim that the only money he was going to make out of it was from selling the chicken manure.'

'The chicken manure?' Sir George repeated.

'The droppings. Anyway, it all went quite well to begin with. Until, that is, the neighbouring farmers cottoned on to the fact that it was they who were meant to be buying all this manure. Then, of course, they clubbed together. It ended up with Duncan having to pay them to take the stuff away. He was ruined . . .'

'Oh no,' Sir George groaned in feigned sincerity. 'How awful.'

'But if it was going to happen to anyone, it would happen to Duncan, wouldn't it?' Edward Berry finished with loud laughter.

'How awful,' Sir George repeated. 'But was this manure really meant to be worth anything?' he asked.

'Well, a bit, I suppose. But he wasn't holding his cards close enough to his chest, was he? Once the locals saw his game, that was it – end of story.'

The two men laughed long and hard.

'Isn't that typical?' Sir George went on at last. 'Nothing like kicking a man when he's down. What do you think, Venetia?'

'Well, I must say I feel very sorry for Duncan. The battery was his pride and joy.'

'Aren't we humans ghastly?' Sir George mused. 'We're nothing more than predators.' And if Mr Berry had been watching, he would have seen their host give an unforgiveable look in his wife's direction.

'Well, that's human nature for you,' Edward Berry nodded with a sigh. 'And I think, in this day and age, it's a pretty naïve man who doesn't expect the worst from putting his trust in another chap.'

'It's lamentable,' Sir George said, glancing at Mrs Berry. 'But if anyone here knows about human nature, it should be you, Venetia, what with being on the Bench.'

'Venetia's got a much more optimistic view,' Mr Berry butted in. 'She thinks it's a spiritual problem.'

'A spiritual problem?'

'Well, insofar as it's a question of attitudes, it is a spiritual problem,' Mrs Berry volunteered.

'Really?'

'Well, yes . . . when you see what I see, the hatred the younger generation have for one another, the mindless vandalism, the gratuitous violence,' she went on, feeling the alcohol warm her to this cause, 'you know that there must be something wrong . . .'

'Yes, but what is it?'

'Well, in short, people forget that, whether they like it or not, we're all here on this planet together, and the sooner we accept that fact and learn to live with our fellow man the better.'

'Love thy neighbour and all that?'

'Yes. It's people's attitudes that are wrong.'

'I'm sure you're right,' Sir George agreed with raised eyebrows.

'And,' Mrs Berry concluded, 'if only man could be encouraged to think more of his fellow man rather than himself, the world would be a better place.'

'I've spent most of my life thinking about myself,' Mr Berry stormed in, '. . . quite an exhilarating subject.'

There was more laughter from the men, but Venetia Berry looked quite stern.

'No, the point is,' Edward Berry said at last, 'that Venetia and I part company here. She thinks if you encourage a man to be good he'll be good. I think we're all rascals . . . you know, give a man an inch and he'll take a mile.'

'Well, I must say, I'm rather inclined to agree with you, Edward,' his host nodded. 'I've got a pretty dim view of human nature. But I think that Venetia's got a very good point. There is a lot of violence, even here in Knightsbridge, and it is about time people stopped just thinking about themselves and tried to have a little consideration for others.'

'Well, it's all very well saying that,' Edward Berry frowned, 'but you've only to look at the animal world to see that it goes against the grain.'

'We're not animals, Edward,' Mrs Berry countered.

'In what ways aren't we animals, darling?'

'An animal is an animal and it doesn't know it's an animal; a human is a human but it knows it's a human.'

'Well?'

'So we have a conscience.'

'I've got a conscience, certainly I've got a conscience, but that doesn't mean I've got to spend my whole time thinking about other people's headaches. It's all very well this spiritual stuff, but what does it mean? That I've got to help Duncan out of his mess? Buy some of his chicken manure?' Mr Berry laughed so hard he beat the mahogany table top with the flat of his hand.

'I'll 'ave that,' Brunton said, reaching forward and taking a diamond brooch.

'Yer won't, yer know.'

'What?' Brunton looked at the other with an expression of astonishment.

'We'll leave this lot where it is . . . we're not thieves.'

'Not thieves, yer said it. I'm not a thief, but I'll 'ave these,' Brunton said again, his eyes upon the jewellery that lay on the thick pile of the carpet.

'This lot stays where it is,' Edwin reiterated.

'Come on, yer dummy. We're out of a job, in't we? We got fook all. We come in 'ere, it were yer idea, yer know, and we come on this lot. It's a gift from gods. We'll be right mugs . . .'

'It stays 'ere,' Edwin muttered, returning the jewellery to its velvet-lined case.

'Well, fook me, I've never 'eard the likes of this. Cop a load of this, then. We got nought, right? 'Ere we are in London with nought.' Again Brunton's upper lip began to quiver. 'We need money, right? An' 'ere it is starin' us in the face, an' yer say we leave it.'

'I've never done no thievin' an' I'm not startin' now . . .'

'We're lookin' a gift 'orse in ' mouth, Edwin.'

'I don't care if it were Crown Jewels, we're not touchin' 'em.'

'Someone's doin' a lot of talkin' 'round 'ere, in't they?' Brunton said finally, his head held well back forcing folds of skin to bulge about his throat. ''Ow about if I told yer I were takin' what were due to me?'

'Yer can suit yerself . . . but if I see yer takin' ought, then I'll 'ave nought to do with yer.'

There was a brief silence and the two men stared at one another. Again Brunton backed down out of fear of losing his friend, and yet, as he saw Edwin returning the jewel-case beneath the pillow, his eyes shone with longing.

'Fookin' 'ell,' he murmured.

'Come on, let's go,' Edwin ordered, moving to the other side of the room.

'Oh, yer want to go now, do yer? That's a bit sudden, like, in't it?'

'Let's go.'

'Why are yer in such a rush?'

'We've finished in 'ere. Let's get goin'.'

As Edwin snapped shut the catches on his toolbox, Brunton grimaced. He was in two minds and, seeing a ring beneath the folds of the bedcover which his friend had failed to notice when returning the other jewels, he stooped to pick it up. He slipped it into his pocket.

'Come on, 'urry up.'

'Wait a minute, will yer?'

The two welders stood by the door in readiness to leave. Edwin turned the light off. 'We'll go down the fire exit this time, all right?'

'Suits me.'

'He's quite a card, isn't he?' Mr Berry said to his wife as the lift doors closed behind them. 'He's quite a chap.'

'Yes,' Venetia Berry murmured.

'Damn good friend. The kind you can rely on. Right from our first day at school together . . .'

'Yes,' Mrs Berry murmured again, and she moved a little away from her husband whose breath was playing on her face. Mr Berry took no heed of this; indeed he placed one hand on his wife's waist.

'Oh now, Edward.'

Mr Berry removed his hand from his wife's waist, placed it on his own stomach and leant against the side of the lift cage. 'You know, this lift is making me feel quite queasy,' he complained. 'It's one hell of a way up.'

As the lift doors pulled silently open, Venetia Berry slipped through and walked ahead of her husband down the corridor.

'You can't get away from Eddie Berry,' Mr Berry shouted. 'It's useless trying.'

Mrs Berry did not answer, rather stood in anticipation beside the door to room 904. For an instant she thought she smelt the odour of iron but as this strain of scent was displaced by that on her husband's drink-laden breath, she thought no more of it. 'Come on, Edward, do hurry up,' she said instead.

'Plenty of time if you're with . . .'

But as the door to their hotel room swung open both stopped dead. Neither spoke for several, long seconds; they simply surveyed the interior of their room.

'We've been burgled,' Mrs Berry ejaculated.

'Oh, my God,' Mr Berry mouthed.

'We've been burgled,' Venetia Berry repeated, moving some paces within. 'I don't believe it.' Then, when she saw her bedclothes lay ruffled and deranged, she cried, 'My jewels – oh, my jewels!'

'Your jewels?'

'I left them under my pillow.'

Both moved to the head of the bed, and Mr Berry watched as his wife began to scrabble at the catch on her jewel-case.

'Damn silly place to have left them,' he pronounced. 'What was wrong with the safe?'

'We were only out for the evening,' his wife muttered. 'I thought that just for a few hours . . . and in this hotel . . .' But, having discovered the loss of her sapphire ring, she stopped dead. 'They've taken the only thing that I cared about,' she cried at last. 'They've got my cluster.'

'Your cluster?'

'My grandmother's ring . . . the sapphire cluster . . . it's gone.'

'Oh no, Venetia.'

'It's gone. It's too bad . . .'

'Are you sure?'

'Yes.'

'But are you sure you didn't leave it in the country?'

'Of course I'm sure. I was going to wear it tomorrow night.'

'I'll ring for the manager,' Mr Berry said with force.

'And look, they've been everywhere, the filthy devils,' she went on, pointing to the armchair beside the television which bore the marks of oil on its covering, and where, below, empty miniatures lay awry over the thick pile. 'God, you can't even go out for dinner these days.'

'Now, darling, we may find it yet,' Mr Berry consoled his wife as he replaced the telephone receiver. 'It may be on the floor.'

'It's not on the floor. Of course it's not. It's gone. And in The Sheraton as well,' Mrs Berry went on, incredulous, 'in The Sheraton.'

'It's monstrous,' Edward Berry agreed, looking up from underneath the bed. 'We'll get some change out of this manager, I can tell you.'

'What good can he do? What good can anyone do? The ring has gone; that's all there is to it,' Mrs Berry finished, tearful.

There was a brief silence.

'It's a good job the brooch hasn't gone,' said Mr Berry with a frown, peering into the jewel box. 'Come to that it's a good job the whole lot hasn't gone. Without knowing it, they've probably taken the thing of least value.'

'The value is incidental, Edward,' Mrs Berry returned quite coldly. 'The ring was a family heirloom. It had sentimental value.'

Edwin and Brunton walked from Knightsbridge to Chelsea Bridge without speaking. But at the sight of water slipping beneath a bridge, specked by the Embankment lights that were reflected on its swollen surface, they both began to laugh.

'Do yer want a drink?' Brunton asked, hoarse. 'I've got 'alf that fridge in me pocket.'

'Yeah, I'll 'ave a Martini. No, I won't, I'll 'ave a vodka.'

'I in't got no fookin' orange, though. Yer'll 'ave to 'ave 'er straight.'

'Give it to uz straight. I'll 'ave 'er straight.'

Brunton handed Edwin a miniature and together, pressed against the pig iron, they peered into the Thames below.

There was a silence.

'Yer know those jobs we went for in Hackney?' Edwin said at length.

'Yeah . . .'

'Well, we'll go back there tomorrow. They might 'ave summat for uz by now.'

Brunton nodded.

'I want to make summat proper,' Edwin went on, as if addressing himself. 'I don't want to make burglar bars and railin's an' such . . . not for these ponces. It's a waste of time.'

'Yeah.'

'Come on, we'll get back to lodgin's an' get up there early tomorrow.'

Brunton followed and, as he did, his fingers closed around the cluster ring that lay in the bottom of his pocket. At first he felt reassured by its touch, but then he frowned. He knew that the ring would be difficult to sell and he knew he could never admit to Edwin that he had taken it. It was a secret between them. As his thumb travelled over the face of the gems he felt their chill.

A draught of river air filled Brunton's nostrils and he frowned again. He fell behind a pace or two and, when he knew Edwin would be unable to see what he was doing, withdrew the ring from his pocket and tossed it over the side of the bridge, where it fell, without a sound, into the depths below.

ACKNOWLEDGEMENTS